"I have no choice."

"Because of this. *Tahlmorra*. I have no choice." Finn put out his hand and made the familiar gesture. "You may call it fate, or destiny, or whatever Ellasian word you have for such things . . . We believe each child is born with a *tahlmorra* that must be heeded when the gods make it known. The prophecy of the Firstborn says one day a man of all blood shall unite, in peace, four warring realms and two magic races. Carillon is a part of that prophecy." He shook his head, solemn in the firelight. "Had I a choice, I would put off such binding service, but I am Cheysuli, and such things are not done."

THE SONG OF HOMANA

Book Two
of the Chronicles
of the Cheysuli

Jennifer Roberson

DAW BOOKS, INC.

DONALD A. WOLLHEIM, PUBLISHER

375 Hudson Street, New York, NY 10014

DAW Book Collectors No. 635.

First Printing, July 1985

6   7   8   9

PRINTED IN THE U.S.A.

To Marion Zimmer Bradley,
for daydreams and realities

and

Betsy Wollheim,
for making mine better

the Tuhle Ocean

Valgaard

Atvia

Andemir

Rondule

Kilore

Homana

Mujhara

Erinn

Lestra

the Idrian Ocean

Solinde

Hondarth

©danforth 1984

the Crystal Isle

PART I

ONE

I peered through the storm, trying to see Finn. He rode ahead on a small Steppes pony much like my own, though brown instead of dun, little more than an indistinct lump of darkness in the blowing snow. The wind beat against my face; Finn would not hear me unless I shouted against it. I pulled the muffling wraps of wool away from my face, grimacing as the bitter wind blew ice crystals into my beard, and shouted my question to him.

"Do you see anything?"

The indistinct lump became more distinct as Finn turned back in the saddle. Like me, he wore leather and wool and furs, hooded and wrapped, hardly a man underneath all the layers. But then Finn was not what most men would name a man at all, being Cheysuli.

He pulled wrappings from his face. Unlike me, he wore no beard in an attempt at anonymity; the Cheysuli cannot grow them. Something in the blood, Finn had said once, kept them from it. But what he did not have on his face was made up for on his head; Finn's hair, of late infrequently cut, was thick and black. It blew in the wind, baring a sun-bronzed predator's face.

"I have sent Storr ahead to seek shelter," he called back to me. "Is there such a place in all this snow, he will find it."

Instantly my eyes went to the side of the narrow forest track. There, parallelling the hoofprints of our horses—

though glimpsed only briefly in the blowing snow and wind—were the pawprints of a wolf. Large prints, well-spaced, little more than holes until the wind and snow filled them in. But it marked the path of Finn's *lir* nonetheless; it marked Finn a man apart, for what manner of man rides with a wolf at his side? Better yet, it marked *me*, for what manner of man rides with a shapechanger at his side?

Finn did not go on at once. He waited, saying nothing more. His face was still bared to the wind. As I rode up I saw how he slitted his eyes, the pupils swollen black against the blinding whiteness. But the irises were a clear, eerie yellow. Not amber or gold or honey. *Yellow*.

Beast-eyes, men called them. I had reason to know why.

I shivered, then cursed, trying to strip my beard of ice. Of late we had spent our time in the warmth of eastern lands; it felt odd to be nearly home again, and suffering because of the winter. I had forgotten what it was to go so encumbered by furs and wool and leather.

And yet I had forgotten nothing. Especially who I was.

Finn, seeing my shiver, grinned, baring his teeth in a silent laugh. "Weary of it already? And will you spend your time shivering and bemoaning the storms when you walk the halls and corridors of Homana-Mujhar again?"

"We are not even to Homana yet," I reminded him, disliking his easy assurance, "let alone my uncle's palace."

"*Your* palace." For a moment he studied me solemnly, reminding me of someone else: his brother. "Do you doubt yourself? *Still?* I thought you had resolved all that when you decided it was time for us to turn our backs on exile."

"I did." I scraped at my beard with gloved fingers, stripping it again of the cold crystals. "Five years is long enough for *any* man to spend in exile; it is too long for a prince. It is time we took my throne back from that Solindish usurper."

Finn shrugged. "You will. The prophecy of the First-born is quite definite. You will win back the Lion Throne from Bellam and his Ihlini sorcerer, and take your place as Mujhar." He put out his gloved right hand and made an eloquent gesture: fingers spread, palm turned upward. *Tahlmorra*. The Cheysuli philosophy that each man's fate rested in the hands of the gods.

Well, so be it. So long as the gods made me a king in place of Bellam.

The arrow sliced through the storm and struck deeply into the ribs of Finn's horse. The animal screamed and bolted sideways in a twisting lunge. Deep snowdrifts fouled the gelding's legs and belly almost immediately and he went down, floundering. Blood ran out of his nostrils; it spilled from the wound and splashed against the snow, staining it brilliant crimson.

I unsheathed my sword instantly, jerking it free of the scabbard on my saddle. I spun my horse, cursing, and saw Finn's outthrust arm as he leaped free of his failing mount. "Three of them . . . *now!*"

The first man reached me. We engaged. He carried a sword as I did, swinging it like a scythe as he sought to cut off my head. I heard the familiar sounds: the keening of the blade as it slashed through the air, the laboring of his mount, the hissing of breath between his teeth as he grunted with the effort. I heard also my own grinding teeth as I swung my heavy broadsword. I felt the satisfactory jar of blade against body, though his winter furs muffled most of the impact. Still, it was enough to double him in the saddle and weaken his counterthrust. My own blade went in through leathers and into flesh, slowed by the leathers, then quickened by the flesh. A thrust with my shoulder behind it, and the man was dead.

I jerked the sword free instantly and spun my horse yet again, cursing his small size and wishing for a Homanan warhorse as he faltered. He had been chosen for anonymity's sake, not for his war-sense. And now I must pay for it.

I looked for Finn. I saw instead the wolf. I saw also the dead man, gape-mouthed and bleeding in the snow; the third and final man was still ahorse, staring blankly at the wolf. It was no wonder. He had witnessed the shapechange, which was enough to make a grown man cry out in fear; I did not only because I had seen it so many times. And yet I feared it still.

The wolf was large and ruddy. It leaped even as the attacker cried out and tried to flee. Swept out of the saddle and thrown down against the snow, the man lay sprawled, crying out, arms thrust upward to protect his throat. But the teeth were already there.

"Finn!" I slapped my horse's rump with the flat of my bloodied blade, forcing him through the deep drifts. "Finn," I said more quietly, "it is somewhat difficult to question a dead man."

The wolf, standing over the quivering form, turned his head to stare directly at me. The unwavering gaze was unnerving, for it was a man's eyes set into the ruddy, snow-dusted head. A man's eyes that stared out of the wolf's head.

Then came the blurring of the wolf-shape. It coalesced into a void, a nothingness that hurt the eyes and head and made my belly lurch upward against my ribs. Only the eyes remained the same, fixed on me: bestial and yellow and strange. The eyes of a madman, or the eyes of a Cheysuli warrior.

I felt the prickling down my spine even as I sought to suppress it. The blurring came back as the void dissipated, but this time the faint outline was that of a man. No more the wolf but a two-legged, dark-skinned man. Not human; never that. Something else. Something *more*.

I shifted forward in the saddle, urging my horse closer. The little gelding was chary of it, smelling death on Finn's mount as well as on the first two men, but he went closer at last. I reined him in beside the prisoner who lay on his back in deep snow, staring wide-eyed up at the man who had been a wolf.

"You," I said, and saw the eyes twitch and shift over to me. He wanted to rise; I could see it. He was frightened and helpless as he lay sprawled in the snow, and I meant him to acknowledge it. "Speak," I told him, "who is your master?"

He said nothing. Finn took a single step toward him, saying nothing at all. The man began to speak.

I suppressed my twitch of surprise. Homanan, not Ellasian. I had not heard the tongue for five years, except from Finn's mouth; even now we kept ourselves to

Caledonese and Ellasian almost always. And yet, here in Ellas, we heard Homanan again.

He did not look at Finn. He looked at me. I saw the fear, and then I saw the shame and anger. "What choice did I have?" he asked from his back in the snow. "I have a wife and daughter and no way to support them. No way to clothe them, feed them, keep them warm in winter. My croft is gone because I could not pay the rents. My money was spent in the war. My son was lost with Prince Fergus. Do I let my wife and daughter starve because I cannot provide? Do I lose my daughter to the depravity of Bellam's court?" He glared at me from malignant brown eyes. As he spoke the anger grew and the shame faded. All that was left was hostility and desperation. "I had no choice! It was good *gold* that was offered—"

The knife twisted in my belly, though the blade did not exist. "Bloodied gold," I interrupted, knowing what he would say.

"Aye!" he shouted. "But *worth* it! Shaine's war got me nothing but a dead son, the loss of my croft and the beggaring of my family. What else am I to do? Bellam offers gold—*bloodied gold*!—and I will take it. So will we all!"

"All?" I echoed, liking little of what I heard. Was all of Homana desiring to give me over to my enemy for his Solindish gold, my life was forfeit before the task was begun.

"Aye!" he shouted. "All! And why not? They are demons. Abominations. *Beasts*!"

The wind shifted. It threw ice into my face again, but I made no move to rid myself of it. I could not. I could only stare at the man in the snow, struck dumb by his admission.

And then I looked at Finn.

Like me, he was quite still. Silent. Staring. But then, slowly, he lifted his head and looked directly at me. I saw the shrinking of his pupils so that the yellow of his eyes stood out like a beacon against the storm. Yellow eyes. Black hair. The gold that hung at his left ear, bared by the wind that blew the hair from his face. His alien, predator's face.

I looked at him with new eyes, as I had not looked at

him for five years, and realized again what he was. Cheysuli. Shapechanger. *A man who took on the form of a wolf at will.*

And the reason for the attack.

Not me. Not me at all. I was insignificant. The prisoner did not know that my head—delivered to Bellam—would give him more gold than he could imagine. By the gods, he did not even know who I was!

Another time, I might have laughed at the irony. Been amused by my conceit, that I thought all men knew me and my worth. But here, in this place, my identity was not the issue. Finn's race was.

"Because of me," he said, and that only.

I nodded. Sickened by the realization, I nodded. What we faced now was more impossible than ever. Not only did we come home to Homana after five years of exile to raise an army and win back my stolen throne, but we had to do it in the face of Homanan prejudice. Shaine's purge— the Cheysuli call it *qu'mahlin*—was little more than the pretty vengeance of a mad king, and yet it had not ended even with the sundering of his realm.

They had not come to slay me or even take me prisoner. They had come for Finn, because he was Cheysuli.

"What did they do to you?" I asked. "The Cheysuli. What did this man do to you?"

The Homanan stared up at Finn in something akin to astonishment. "He is a shapechanger!"

"But what did he *do* to you?" I persisted. "Did he slay your son? Take your croft? Rape your daughter? Beggar your family?"

"Do not bother," Finn said. "You cannot straighten an ill-grown tree."

"You can chop it down," I returned. "Chop it down and into pieces and feed it to the fire—" I wanted to say more, but I stopped. I saw his face, with its closed, private expression, and I said nothing more. Finn was not one for sympathy, or even anger expressed in his behalf. Finn fought his own battles.

And now there was this one.

"Can he be turned?" I asked. "His need I understand—a desperate man will do desperate things—but his target I will not tolerate. Go into his mind and turn him, and he can go home again."

Finn's right hand came up. It was empty. But I saw the clenching of his fingers, as if he sought to clasp a knife. He was asking for my approval. He was liege man to the Prince of Homana, and he asked to mete out a death.

"No," I said. "Not this time. Use your magic instead."

The man spasmed against the snow. "Gods, no! No! *No sorcery—*"

"Hold him," I said calmly, as he tried to leap up and run.

Finn was on him at once, though he did not slay him. He merely held him on his knees, pressing him into the snow, on one knee himself with an arm thrust around the throat and the other gripping the head. One twist and it would be done.

"Mercy!" the dead man cried. But could I do it, I would leave him alive.

Finn would not ask again. He accepted my decision. I saw the hand tighten against the Homanan's head and the look of terror enter the brown eyes. And then they were empty, and I knew Finn had gone in to do as I had ordered.

It shows in the eyes. I have seen it in the faces and eyes of others Finn has used his magic on. But I also saw it in Finn's eyes each time: the total immersion of his soul as he sought the gift of compulsion and used it on another. He went away, though his body remained. That which was Finn was elsewhere; he was not-Finn. He was something less and something awesomely more. He was not man, not beast, not god. Something—apart.

The man wavered and sagged, but he did not fall. Finn's arm remained locked around his throat. The hand was pressed against his skull, but it did not break it. It did not snap the neck. It waited.

Finn twitched and jerked. The natural sunbronzing of his face was suddenly gone; he was the color of death. All gray and ivory, with emptiness in his eyes. I saw the slackening of his mouth and heard the rasp in his throat. And then, before I could say a word, he broke the man's neck and threw the body down.

"Finn!" I was off my horse at once, thrusting my sword blade down into the snow. I left it there, moving toward Finn, and reached out to grab what I could of his leathers and furs. "Finn, I said *turn* him, not slay him—"

But Finn was lurching away, staggering in the snow, and I knew he had not heard me. He was not himself. He was still—elsewhere.

"Finn." I caught his arm and steadied him. Even beneath the thickness of winter furs I could feel the rigidity in his arm. His color was still bad; his pupils were nothing but specks in a void of perfect yellow. *"Finn—"*

He twitched again, and then he was back. He swung his head to look at me, and only then realized I held his arm. At once I released it, knowing he was himself again, but I did not relax my stance. It was only because he was Finn that I had left my sword behind.

He looked past me to the body in the snow. *"Tynstar,"* he said. "I touched—*Tynstar.*"

I stared. *"How?"*

He frowned and pushed a forearm across his brow, as if he sweated. But his face was dusted with snow, and he shivered from the cold. Once, but it gave away his bewilderment and odd vulnerability. "He was—*there.* Like a web, soft but sticky . . . and impossible to shed." He shook himself, like a dog shaking off water.

"But—if he and the others were hunting Cheysuli and not the Prince of Homana . . ." I paused a moment. "Would Tynstar meddle in the *qu'mahlin?*"

"Tynstar would meddle in anything. He is Ihlini."

I nearly smiled. But I did not, because I was thinking about Tynstar. Tynstar, called the Ihlini, because he ruled (if that is the proper word) the race of Solindish sorcerers. Much like the Cheysuli were the magical race of Homana, the Ihlini sprang from Solinde. But they were evil and did the bidding of the demons who served the netherworld. There was nothing of good about the Ihlini. They wanted Homana, and had aided Bellam to get her.

"Then he does not know we are here," I said, still thinking.

"We are in Ellas," Finn reminded me. "Homana is but a day or two away, depending on the weather, and I do not doubt Bellam has spies to watch the borders. It may well be these men were sent to catch Cheysuli—" he frowned, and I knew he wondered what tokens Bellam required as proof of a Cheysuli kill. Probably the earring, perhaps the armbands as well. —"but it may be they sought Homana's exiled prince." He frowned again. "I cannot be sure. I had no time to learn his intent."

"And now it is too late."

Finn looked at me levelly. "If Tynstar is meddling with Homanans and sending them out against the Cheysuli, they must be slain." For a moment he looked at the body again. Then his eyes came back to me. "It is a part of my service to you to keep you alive. Can I not do the same for myself?"

This time I looked at the body. "Aye," I said finally, harshly, and turned back to retrieve my sword.

Finn moved to his dead horse and stripped him of the saddlepacks. I mounted my horse and slid the sword home in the scabbard, making certain the blade was clean of blood. The runes ran silver in the white light of the storm. Cheysuli runes, representing the Old Tongue which I did not know. A Cheysuli sword for a Homanan prince. But then that was another thing the prophecy claimed: one day a man of all blood would unite, in peace, four warring realms and two magic races. Perhaps it would no longer be a Cheysuli sword in the hand of a Homanan prince. It would merely be a sword in the hand of a king.

But until then, the golden hilt with its rampant, royal lion and the huge brilliant ruby in the prong-toothed pommel would remain hidden by leather wrappings. At least until I claimed the Lion Throne again and made Homana free.

"Come up," I told Finn. "You cannot walk in all this snow."

He handed up his saddlepacks but did not move to mount behind me. "Your horse carries enough bulk, with all of you." He grinned. "I will go on as a wolf."

"If Storr is too far ahead—" I stopped. Though the shapechange was governed by the distance between warrior and *lir*, it was obvious this time there was no impediment. The peculiar detached expression I knew so well came over Finn's face. For a moment his body remained beside my horse, but his mind did not. It was elsewhere, answering an imperative call; his eyes turned inward and blank and empty, as if he conversed with something—or *someone*—no one else could hear.

And then he was back, grinning in genuine pleasure and the attack on us both forgotten. "Storr says he has found us a roadhouse."

"How far?"

"A league, perhaps a bit more. Close enough, I think, after days without a roof over our heads." He ran a hand through his black hair and shook free the powdery snow. "There are great advantages to *lir*-shape, Carillon. I will be quicker—and certainly *warmer*—than you."

I ignored him. It was all I could ever do. I turned my horse back to the track and went on, leaving behind three dead men and one dead horse—the others had run away. I cursed the storm again. My face was numb from the ice in my beard. Even the wrappings did not help.

When Finn at last went past me, it was in wolf-shape: yellow-eyed, ruddy-furred, fleet of foot. And warmer, no doubt, than I.

TWO

The common room was crowded with men seeking respite from the storm. Dripping candles puddled into piles of cooling, waxy fat on each table, shedding crude light and a cruder pall of smoke into the low beamwork of the roadhouse. The miasma was thick enough to make me choke against its acrid odor, but there was warmth in abundance. For that I would share any stench.

The door hitched against the hardpack of the frozen earthen floor. I stopped short, ducking to avoid smacking my head against the doorframe. But then few roadhouse doors are built to accommodate a man of my height; the years spent in exile had made me taller than I had been five years before and nearly twice as heavy. Still, I would not complain; did the added height and weight—and the beard—keep me unknown on my journey home, I would not care if I knocked myself silly against Ellasian doorframes.

Finn slipped by me into the room as I wrestled with the door. I broke it free, then swung it shut on half-frozen leather hinges, swearing as a dog ran between my legs and nearly upset me. For a moment I thought of Storr, seeking shelter in the forest. Then I thought of food and wine.

I settled the latch-hook into place and marked absently how the stout iron loops were set for a heavy crossbeam lock. I could tell it was but rarely used, but I marked it nonetheless. No more did I have room in my life for the ease of meaningless friendships found in road- and alehouses.

Finn waited at the table. Like the others, it bore a single candle. But this one shed no light, only a clot of thick smoke that fouled the air where the flame had glowed a moment before. Finn, I knew. It was habit with us both.

I joined him, shedding furs and leathers. It felt good to be man again instead of bear, and to know the freedom of movement. I sat down on a three-legged stool and glanced around the common room even as Finn did the same.

No soldiers. Ellas was a peaceful land. Crofters, most of them, convivial in warmth and the glow of liquor. Travelers as well, bound east or west: Ellasians; Homanans; Falians too, by their accents. But no Caledonese, which meant Finn and I could speak Ellasian with a Caledonese twist and no one would name us other.

Except those who knew a Cheysuli when they saw one, and in Ellas that could be anyone.

Ellasians are open, gregarious folk, blunt-speaking and plain of habits. There is little of subterfuge about them, for which I am grateful. I have grown weary of such things, though I have, of necessity, steeped myself in it. It felt good to know myself accepted for what I appeared in the roadhouse: a stranger, foreign, accompanied by a Cheysuli, but welcome among them regardless. Still, it was to Finn they looked twice, if only briefly. And then they looked away again, dismissing what they saw.

I smiled. Few men dismiss a Cheysuli warrior. But in Ellas they do it often. Here the Cheysuli are not hunted.

And then I recalled that Homanans had come into Ellas hunting Cheysuli and I lost my smile entirely.

The tavern-master arrived at last, wiping greasy hands on a frayed cloth apron. He spoke with the throaty, blurred accent of Ellas, all husky and full of phlegm. It had taken me months to learn the trick, but I had learned. And I used it now.

"Ale," he said, "or wine. Red from Caledon, a sweet white from Falia, or our own fine Ellasian vintage." His teeth were bad but I thought the smile genuine.

"Have you *usca*?" I asked.

The grizzled gray brows rose as he considered the question. "*Usca*, is't? Na, na, I have none. The plainsmen of the Steppes have naught of trade wi' us now, since Ellas allied wi' Caledon in t'last war." His pale brown eyes marked us Caledonese; my accent had won us that much. Or *me*; Finn did not in the least resemble a Caledonese. "What else would you have?"

Finn's yellow eyes were almost black in the dim candlelight, but I saw the glint in them clearly. "What of Homanan honey brew?"

At once the brows drew down into a scowl. The Ellasian's hair, like his eyebrows, was graying, close-cropped against his head. A blemish spread across one cheek; some childhood malady had left him scarred. But there was no suspicion or distrust in his eyes, only vague disgust.

"Na, none of that, either. 'Tis Homanan, as you have said, and little enough of Homana comes across our borders now." For a moment he stared at the gold earring shining in Finn's black hair. I knew what the Ellasian thought: little enough of Homana crossed the borders, unless you counted the Cheysuli.

"No trade, then?" I asked.

The man picked at snags in his wine-stained apron. He glanced around quickly, judging the needs of his customers out of long practice. "Trade, after a fashion," he agreed in a moment, "but not wi' Homana. Wi' Bellam instead, her Solindish king." He tipped his head in Finn's direction. "*You* might know."

Finn did not smile. "I might," he said calmly. "But I left Homana when Bellam won the war, so I could not say what has befallen my homeland since."

The Ellasian studied him. Then he leaned forward, pressing both hands flat against the table. "*I* say 'tis a sad thing to see the land brought down so low. The land chafes under that Solindish lord. *And* his Ihlini sorcerer."

And so we came to the subject I had wanted to broach all along, knowing better than to bring it up myself. Now, did I say nothing and ask no questions, I made myself out a dullard, and almost certainly suspect. The man had proved talkative; I had best not disabuse him of that.

"Homana is not a happy land?" My tone, couched in Caledonese-tinged Ellasian, was idle and incurious; strangers passed time with such talk.

The Ellasian guffawed. "*Happy?* Wi' Bellam on her throne

and Tynstar's hand around her throat? Na, not happy, never happy . . . but helpless. We hear tales of heavy taxes and over-harsh justice. The sort of thing that troubles us little enough in Ellas, under our good High King." He hawked and turned his head to spit onto the earthen floor. "They do say Bellam desires an alliance with Rhodri himself, but he'll not be agreeing to such a miscarriage of humanity. Bellam's a greedy fool; Rhodri is not. He has no need of't, wi' six fine sons." He grinned. "I hear Bellam offers his only daughter to the High Prince himself, but I doubt there will be a match made. Cuinn has better thighs to part than Electra of Solinde's."

And so the talk passed to women, as it will among men. But only until the Ellasian left to see about our food, and then we said nothing more of women, thinking of Homana instead. And Bellam, governed by Tynstar.

"Six sons," Finn mused. "Perhaps Homana would not now be under Solindish rule, had the royal House proved more fertile."

I scowled at him. I needed no reminders that the House of Homana had been less than prolific. It was precisely because Shaine the Mujhar had sired no son at all—let alone *six* of them!—that he had turned to his brother's only son. Ah, aye, fertility and infertility. And how the issues had shaped my life, along with Finn's. For it was Shaine's infertility—except for a defiant daughter— that had left an enormous legacy to his nephew, Carillon of Homana, and the Cheysuli shapechanger who served him. The Lion Throne itself, upon the Mujhar's death, and now a war to fight.

As well as a purge to end.

The tavern-master arrived bearing bread for trenchers and a platter of steaming meat, which he set in the center of the table. Behind him came a boy with a jug of Ellasian wine, two leathern mugs and a quarter of yellow cheese. I saw how the boy looked at Finn's face, so dark in the amber candlelight. I saw how he stared at the yellow eyes, but he said not a single word. Finn was, perhaps, his first Cheysuli. And worth a second look.

Neither boy nor man lingered, being too pressed by other custom, and Finn and I set to with the intentness of starving men. We were nct starving, having eaten at the break of day, but stale journey-loaf eaten in a snowstorm is not nearly as toothsome as hot meat in a warm roadhouse.

I unsheathed my knife and sliced off a chunk of venison, dumping it onto my trencher. It was a Caledonese knife I used now in place of my own, a bone-handled blade wrought with runes and scripture. The hilt had been cut from the thigh of some monstrous beast, or so the king of Caledon had told me upon presentation of it. The blade itself was bright steel, finely honed; the weight of it was perfect for my hand. Still, it was not my own; that one—Cheysuli-made—was hidden in my saddlepacks.

I ate until I could hardly move upon my stool, and ordered a second jug of wine. And then, even as I poured our mugs full again, I heard the hum of rising conversation. Finn and I both looked instantly for the cause of the heightened interest.

The harper came down the ladder with his instrument clasped under one long arm. He wore a blue robe belted at the waist with linked silver, and a silver circlet held back the thick dark hair that curled on his shoulders. A wealthy harper, as harpers often are, being hosted by kings and gifted with gold and gems. This one had fared well. He was tall, wide-shouldered, and his wrists—showing at the edges of his blue sleeves—were corded with muscle. A powerful man, for all his calling was the harp instead of the sword. He was blue-eyed, and when he smiled it was a professional smile, warm and welcoming.

Two men cleared space for him in the center of the room and set out a stool. He thanked them quietly and sat down, settling harp against hip and thigh. I knew at once the instrument was a fine one, having heard so many of the best with my uncle in Homana-Mujhar. It was of rich honey-gold wood, burnished to a fine sheen with years of use. A single green stone was set into the top. The strings glowed gossamer-fine in the smoke and candlelight. They glinted, promising much, until he touched them and fulfilled that promise with the stroke of a single finger.

Like a woman it was, answering a lover's caress. The music drifted throughout the room, soft and delicate and infinitely seductive, and silenced the voices at once. There is no man alive who cannot lose himself in harpsong, unless he be utterly deaf.

The harper's voice, when he spoke, was every bit as lovely as the harp. It lacked the feminine timbre of many I had heard, yet maintained the rich liquid range the art requires. The modulation was exquisite; he had no need to speak loudly to reach all corners of the room. He merely spoke. Men listened.

"I will please you as I please myself," he said quietly, "by giving you what entertainments I can upon my Lady. But there is a task I must first perform." From the sleeve of his robe he took a folded parchment. He unfolded it, smoothed it, and began to read. He did not color his tone with any emotion, he merely read. But the words were quite enough.

> *"Know ye all men that Bellam the Mujhar,*
> *King of Solinde and Mujhar of Homana;*
> *Lord of the cities Mujhara and Lestra;*
> *Sets forth the sum of five hundred gold pieces*
> *to any man bringing sound word of Carillon,*
> *styling himself Prince of Homana,*
> *and wrongful claimant to the Lion Throne.*

> *"Know ye all men that Bellam the Mujhar*
> *desires even more the presence of the pretender,*
> *offering one thousand gold pieces*
> *to any man bringing Carillon—or his body—*
> *into Homana-Mujhar."*

The harper, when finished, folded the parchment precisely as it had been and returned it to his sleeve. His blue eyes, nearly black in the smoky light, looked at every man as if he judged his thoughts. All idleness was gone; I saw only shrewd intensity. He waited.

I wondered, in that moment, if he recruited. I wondered if he was Bellam's man, sent out with the promise of gold. I wondered if he counted the pieces for himself. Five hundred of them if he knew I was here. One thousand if he brought me home to Homana-Mujhar.

Home. For disposal as Bellam—or Tynstar—desired.

I saw what they did, the Ellasian men. They thought of the gold and the glory. They thought of the task and the triumph. They considered, for a moment, what it might be to be made rich, but only for a moment, for then they considered their realm. Ellas. Not Homana. Rhodri's realm. And the man who offered such gold had already swallowed one land.

The Ellasians, I knew, would do nothing for Bellam's gold. But there were others in the room, and perhaps they would.

I looked at Finn. His face was a mask, as ever; a blank, sun-bronzed mask, with eyes that spoke of magic and myth and made them both quite real.

The harper began to sing. His deep voice was fine and sweet, eloquently expressing his intent. He sang of the bitterness of defeat and the gut-wrenching carnage of war. He sang of boys who died on bloodied fields and captains who fell beneath Solindish and Atvian swords. He sang of a king who hid himself in safety behind the rose-red walls of Homana-Mujhar, half-mad from a crazed obsession. He sang of the king's slain brother, whose son was trapped in despair and Atvian iron. He sang of the same boy, now a man and free again, who lived his life in exile, fleeing Ihlini retribution. He sang my life, did this stranger, and brought the memories alive.

Oh gods . . . the memories . . .

How is it that a harper can know what was? How is it that he captures the essence of what happened, what I am, what I long to be? How is it that he can sing my song while *I* sit unknowing, knowing only it is true, wishing it were otherwise?

How is it done?

The poignancy nearly shattered me. I shivered once convulsively, then stared hard at the scarred wooden table while the shackle weals beneath the sleeves of my leather shirt ached with remembered pain. I could not look at the harper. Not while he gave me my history, my heritage, my legacy, and the story of a land—*my* land—in her death struggle.

"By the gods—" I murmured before I could stop.

I felt Finn's eyes on me. But he said nothing at all.

THREE

"I am Lachlan," said the harper. "I am a harper, but also a priest of Lodhi the All-Wise, the All-Father; would you have me sing of Him?" Silence met his question, the silence of reverence and awe. He smiled, his hands unmoving upon the harp. "You have heard of the magic we of Lodhi hold. The tales are true. Have you not heard them before?"

I looked over the room. Men sat silently on their benches and stools, paying no mind to anyone save the harper. I wondered again what he intended to do.

"The All-Father has given some of us the gift of song, the gift of healing, the gift of words. And fewer of us claim all three." He smiled. It was an enigmatic, eloquent smile. "I am one, and this night I will share what I can with you."

The harp's single green stone cast a viridescent glow as his fingers danced across the strings, stirring a sound that at once set the flesh to rising on my bones. His eyes passed over each of us again, as if he sought to comprehend what each one of us was about. And still he smiled.

"Some men call us sorcerers," he said quietly. "I will not dispute it. My Lady and I have traversed the leagues of this land and others, and what I have seen I have learned. What I will give you this night is something most men long for: a return to the innocent days. A return to a time when cares were not so great and the responsibilities of manhood did not weigh so heavily. I will give you your greatest day." The blue eyes swelled to black. "Sit you still and listen, hearing only my Lady and myself, and I will give you the gift of Lodhi."

I heard the music begin. For a moment I thought nothing of it: it was harpsong as ever, boasting nothing more than what I had already heard. And then I heard the underscore moving through the melody. A strange, eerie tone, seemingly at odds with the smoother line. I stared at the harper's hands as he moved them in the strings, light glittering off the strands. And then I felt him inside my head.

Suddenly I was nothing but music. A single, solitary note. A string plucked and plucked again, my use dictated by the harper whose hands were on my soul. I stared at the eloquent fingers moving, caressing, plucking at the strings, and the music filled my head.

The colors of the room spilled away, like a wineglass tipped and emptied. Everything was gray, dark and light, with no blacks and no whites. I saw a harper in a gray robe with gray eyes and grayish hair. Only the harp held true: honey-gold and gleaming, with a single emerald eye. And then even that was gone . . .

No more war—no more blood—no more wishing for revenge. Only the sense of other days. Younger days, and a younger Carillon, staring with joy and awe at the great chestnut warhorse his father had gifted him on his eighteenth birthday. I recalled the day so well, and what I had thought of the horse. I recalled it all, for on that day I was named Prince of Homana, and heir to the Lion Throne.

Again I clattered down the winding staircase at Joyenne, nodding at servants who gave me morning greeting, thinking only of the promised gift. I had known it was to be a horse, a warhorse, but not which one. I had hoped—

—and it was. The great red stallion had gotten a matching son on my father's best mare, and that son was mine at last. Full-grown and fully trained, ready for a warrior. I was not so much a warrior then, knowing only the practice chamber and tourney-fields, but I was more than ready to prove what I could of my skill. And yet I could not have wished for that chance to come so soon.

I saw then the underside of the harper's spell. It was true he gave me my innocent days, but with those days came the knowledge of what had followed. He could not have summoned a more evocative memory had he tried for it; I think he did it purposely. I think he reached into my mind, digging and searching until he found the proper one. And then he gave it to me.

The memory altered. No more was I the young prince reaching out to touch the stallion. No. I was someone else entirely: a bloodied, soiled, exhausted boy in a man's body, his sword taken from him and his wrists imprisoned in Atvian iron. Taken by Thorne himself, Keough's son, who had ordered the iron hammered on.

All my muscles knotted. Sweat broke out on my flesh. I sat in a crowded common room of a roadhouse in the depths of an Ellasian storm, and I sweated. Because I could not help myself.

And then, suddenly, the colors were back. The grays faded. Candlewicks guttered and smoked, turning faces light and dark, and then I realized I sat still upon my stool with Finn's hand imprisoning my right wrist. It was not iron, it was flesh and bone, holding my arm in place. And then I saw why. In my fist was gripped the bone-handled knife, the blade pointing toward the harper.

"Not yet," Finn said quietly. "Perhaps later, when we have divined his true intent."

It made me angry. Angry at Finn, which was wrong, but I had no better target. It was the harper I wanted, for manipulating me so, but it was Finn who was too near.

I let go the knife. Finn let go the hand. I drew it in to my body, massaging the ridges of scar tissue banding my wrist as if it bore iron still. And I glared at him with all the anger in my eyes. "What did he give *you*? A Cheysuli on the throne?"

Finn did not smile. "No," he said. "He gave me Alix."

It took the breath from my chest. Alix. Of course. How better to get to Finn than to remind him of the woman he had wanted badly enough to steal? The woman who had turned her back on him to wed Duncan, his brother.

The woman who was my cousin, that I wanted for myself.

I laughed bitterly. "A skillful harper indeed . . . or more likely a sorcerer, as he claims." I stared across at the blue-robed man who was calmly refusing to sing again. "Ihlini, do you think? Sent from Bellam to set a trap?"

Finn shook his head. "Not Ihlini; I would know. And I have heard of this All-Father god." He grimaced in distaste. "An Ellasian deity, and therefore of less importance to me, but powerful nonetheless." He shifted slightly on the stool, leaning forward to pour himself more wine. "I will have a talk with him."

He had named himself Lachlan, and now he moved around the room to gather up his payment in coin and baubles and wine. He carried his harp tucked into the crook of one arm and a cup in his other hand. Light glittered off the silver links around his waist and the circlet on his brow. He was a young man still, perhaps my own age, and tall, but lacking my substantial height and weight. Still, he was not slight, and I thought there was strength in those shoulders.

He came last to our table, as I expected, and I pushed the winejug forward so he would know to help himself. And then I kicked a stool toward him. "Sit you down. Please yourself with the wine. And this." I drew forth from my belt-purse a jagged piece of gold, stamped with a crude design. But it was good gold, and heavy, and few men would look askance at its crude making. I slid it across the table with a forefinger, pushing it around the bone-handled knife.

The harper smiled, nodded and sat down upon the stool. His blue eyes matched the rich hue of his robe. His hair, in the dim candlelight, showed no color other than a dull dark brown. It looked as if the sun had never touched it, to bleach it red or blond. Dyed, I thought, and smiled to myself.

He poured wine into the cup he held. It was a fine silver cup, though tarnished with age. The house cup for a harper, I thought, seeing little use. I doubted it was his own.

"Steppes gold." He picked up the coin. "I do not often see payment of this sort." His eyes flicked from the coin to my face. "My skill is not worth so much, I think; you may have it back." He set the coin on the table and left it.

The insult was made calmly and clearly, with great care. Its intent was unknown, and yet I recognized it regardless. Or was it merely a curious man gone fishing for an outsize catch? Perhaps an exiled prince.

"You may keep it or not, as you wish." I picked up my own mug. "My companion and I have just returned from the Caledonese war against the plainsmen of the Steppes— alive and unharmed, as you see—and we are generous because of it." I spoke Ellasian, but with a Caledonese accent.

The harper—Lachlan—swirled wine in his tarnished cup. "Did it please you," he said, "my gift?"

I stared at him over my mug. "Did you mean it to?"

He smiled. "I mean nothing with that harpsong. I merely share my gift—*Lodhi's* gift—with the listener, who will make of it what he will. They are *your* memories, not mine; how could I dictate what you see?" His eyes had gone to Finn, as if he waited.

Finn did not oblige. He sat quietly on his stool, seemingly at ease, though a Cheysuli at ease is more prepared than any man I know. He turned his mug idly on the table with one long-fingered hand. His eyes were hooded slightly, like a predator bird's, but the irises showed yellow below the lids.

"Caledon." The harper went on as if he realized he would get nothing from Finn. "You say you fought with Caledon, but you are not Caledonese. I know a Cheysuli when I see one." He smiled, then glanced at me. "As for you—you speak good Ellasian, but not good enough. You have not the throat for it. But neither are you Caledonese; I know enough of them." His eyes narrowed. "Solindish, perhaps, or Homanan. You lack the lilt of Falia."

"Mercenaries," I said clearly, knowing it was—or had been—the truth. "Claiming no realm, only service."

Lachlan looked at me. I knew he saw the thick beard and the uncut, sunstreaked hair that tangled on my shoulders. I had hacked off the mercenary's braid I had worn for five years, bound with crimson cord, and went as a free man again, which meant my sword was available. With a

Cheysuli at my side, I would be a valuable man. Kings would pay gold for our service.

"No realm," he said, and smiled. Then he pushed away from the table and got to his feet, cradling the harp. He picked up the blackened silver cup and nodded his thanks for the wine.

"Take your payment," I said. "It was made in good faith."

"And in good faith, I refuse it." He shook his head. "You have more need of it than I. I have no army to raise."

I laughed out loud. "You misunderstand mercenaries, harper. We do not raise armies. We *serve* in them."

"I said precisely what I meant." His face was solemn, eyes flicking between us shrewdly. And then he turned away.

Finn put out his hand and gathered up his knife. No, not his precisely; like me, he hid his away. He carried instead a knife taken from a Steppes plainsman, and it served its purpose. In Finn's hand, any knife did.

"Tonight," he said quietly, "I will have conversation with that harper."

I thought fleetingly of the Ellasian god the harper claimed to serve. Would Lodhi interfere? Or would Lachlan cooperate?

I smiled. "Do what you have to do."

Because the storm had driven so many inside for the evening, the roadhouse was crowded to bursting. There were no private rooms. The best I could do was give gold to the tavern-master for two pallets on the floor of a room already occupied by three others. When I went in alone, later than I had intended, they already slept. I listened silently just inside the open door, to see if anyone feigned sleep to lure me into a trap, but all three men were deep asleep. And so I shut the door, set my unsheathed sword on the lice-ridden pallet as I stretched out my legs, and waited for Finn to come in.

When he did, it was without sound. Not even the door squeaked, as it had for me. Finn was simply in the room.

"The harper is gone," he said. It was hardly a sound, but I had learned how to hear it.

I frowned into the darkness as Finn knelt down on the other pallet. "In this storm?"

"He is not here."

I sat back against the wall, staring thoughtfully into the darkness. My right hand, from long habit, touched the leather-wrapped hilt of my sword. "Gone, is he?" I mused. "What could drive a man into an Ellasian snowstorm, unless there be good reason?"

"Gold is often a good reason." Finn shed a few of his furs and dropped them over his legs. He stretched out upon his pallet and was silent. I could not even hear him breathe.

I bit at my left thumb, turning things over in my mind. Questions arose and I could answer none of them. Nor could Finn, so I wasted no time asking him. And then, when I had spent what moments I could spare considering the harper, I slid down the wall to stretch full length upon the lumpy pallet and went to sleep.

What man—even a prince with gold upon his head— need fear for his safety with a Cheysuli at his side?

It was morning before we could speak openly, and even then words were delayed. We went out into the ethereal stillness of abated storm, saddled and packed our horses and walked them toward the rack. The snow lay deep and soft around my boots, reaching nearly to my knees. The track was better, packed and shallow, and there I waited while Finn went into the trees and searched for his *lir*.

Storr came at once, bounding out of the trees like a dog, hurling himself into Finn's arms. Finn went down on one knee, ignoring the cold, and cast a quick, appraising look toward the roadhouse. I thought it highly unlikely anyone could see us now. Satisfied, Finn thrust out an arm and slung it around Storr's neck, pulling the wolf in close.

What their bond is, I cannot say precisely. I know only what Finn has told me, that Storr is a part of his heart and soul and mind; half of his whole. Without the wolf, Finn said, he was little more than a shadow, lacking the gifts of his race and the ability to survive. I thought it an awesomely gruesome thing, to claim life only through some sorcerous link with an animal, but I could not protest what so obviously worked. I had seen him with the wolf before during such greetings, and it never failed to leave me feeling bereft and somehow empty. Jealous, even, for what they shared was something no other man could claim save the Cheysuli. I have owned dogs and favorite horses, but it was not the same. That much I could tell, looking at them, for Finn's face was transfigured when he shared a reunion with Storr.

Finn's new horse, a dark brown gelding purchased from the tavern-master, pulled at the slack reins. I pulled him back again and got his reins untangled from those of my little Steppes pony. When I looked again at Finn I saw him slap Storr fondly on the shoulder, and then he was pushing back through the snow toward me.

I handed the reins to him. "How does he fare?"

"Well enough." The fond half-smile remained a moment, as if he still conversed with the wolf. I had thought once or twice that his expression resembled that of a man well-satisfied by a woman; he wore it now. "Storr says he would like to go home."

"No more than I." The thought of Homana instead of foreign lands knotted my belly at once. Gods, to go home again . . . I looped my horse's reins over his ears, pulled them down his neck and mounted. As ever, the little gelding grunted. Well, I am heavier than the plainsmen who broke him. "I think we can reach Homana today, does the sky remain clear." I looked skyward and squinted out of habit. "Perhaps we should go to the Keep."

Finn, settling into his saddle, looked at me sharply. He went hoodless as I did, and the early dawn light set his earring to glinting with a soft golden glow. "This soon?"

I laughed at him. "Have you no wish to see your brother?"

Finn scowled. "You know well enough I am not averse to seeing Duncan again. But I had not thought we would go openly into Cheysuli land so soon."

I shrugged. "We are nearly there. The Keep lies on the border, which we must cross. And, for all that, I think we both wish to see Alix again."

Finn did not meet my eyes. It was odd to realize the

time away from Homana had not blunted his desire for his brother's wife. No more than it had mine.

He looked at me at last. "Do you wish to take *me* to her, or go for yourself?"

I smiled and tried not to show him my regret. "She is wed now, and happily. There is no room for me in her life except as a cousin."

"No more for *me* except as a *rujholli*." Finn laughed bitterly; his eyes on me were ironic and assessive as he pushed black hair out of his dark, angular face. "Do you not find it strange how the gods play with our desires? You held Alix's heart, unknowing, while she longed for a single word from your mouth. Then I stole her from you, intending to make her my *meijha*. But it was Duncan, ever Duncan . . . he won her from us both." Grimly he put out his hand and made the gesture I had come to hate, for all its infinite meaning.

"*Tahlmorra*," I said sourly. "Aye, Finn, I find it passing strange. And I do not like it overmuch."

Finn laughed and closed his hand into a fist. "*Like* it? But the gods do not expect us to like it. No. Only to serve it."

"*You* serve it. I want none of your Cheysuli prophecy. I am a Homanan prince."

"And you will be a Homanan king . . . with all the help of the Cheysuli."

No man, born of a brief history, likes to hear of another far greater than his own, particularly when his House has fallen into disarray. The Homanan House had held the Lion Throne nearly four hundred years. Not long, to Cheysuli way of thinking. Not when their history went back hundreds of centuries to a time with no Homanans. Only the Firstborn, the ancestors of the Cheysuli, with all their shapechanging arts.

And the power to hand down a prophecy that ruled an entire race.

"This way, then." Finn gestured and kicked his horse into motion.

"You are certain?" I had no wish to get myself lost, not when I was so close to Homana at last.

Finn cast me a thoroughly disgusted glance. "We go to

the Keep, do we not? I should know the way, Carillon. Once, it was my home."

I subsided into silence. I am silent often enough around him. Sometimes, with Finn, it is simply the best thing *to* do.

FOUR

The weather remained good, but the going did not. We had left behind the beaten track that led westward into Homana, seeking instead the lesser-known pathways. Though the Cheysuli were welcome within Ellas, they kept to themselves. I doubted High King Rhodri knew much of the people who sheltered in his forests. They would keep themselves insular, and therefore more mysterious than ever. There would be no well-traveled tracks leading to the Keep.

At last, as the sun lowered in the sky, we turned into the trees to find a proper campsite, knowing Homana and the Keep would have to wait another day. We settled on a thick copse of oaks and beeches.

Finn swung off his mount. "I will fetch us meat while you lay the fire. No more journey-loaf for me, not when I have tasted real meat in my mouth again." He threw me his reins, then disappeared into the twilight with Storr bounding at his side.

I tended the horses first, untacking them, then hobbling and graining them with what dwindling rations remained. Once the horses were settled I searched for stones, intending to build us a proper firecairn. We had gone often enough without a fire, but I preferred hot food and warmth when I slept.

I built my cairn, fired the kindling we carried in our saddlepacks and made certain the flames would hold. Then

I turned to the blankets I had taken from the horses. Pelts, to be precise; each horse was blanketed with two. The bottom rested hair-down against the horse, the top one hair-up, to pad the saddle. At night the pelts became blankets for Finn and me, smelling of sweat and horsehair, but warm. I spread them now against the snow; after we ate we could thrust the hot stones beneath them to offer a little heat.

As I spread the blankets I heard the muffled movement in the snow. My hand was on my sword instantly, ripping it from the sheath at my left hip. I spun, leveling the blade, and saw the flash of setting sunlight turn the runes to blinding fire.

Three men before me, running at me out of the thickening shadows. More than that behind me. I wondered where was Finn, and then I did not, for I had no time.

I took the first one easily enough, marking the expression of shock on his face as I swung my blade and cut through leather and furs and flesh, shearing the bone of his arm in two just below the shoulder. The momentum of the blade carried it farther yet, into his ribs, and then he fell and I wrenched the sword free to use it on yet another.

The second fell as well, thrust through the lungs, and then the others did what they should have done at the first. They came at me at once, en masse, so that even did I try to take yet a third the others could bear me down. I did not doubt I would account for at least another death before I died, perhaps even two—Finn and adversity had taught me well enough for that—but the result would be the same. I would be dead, and Bellam would have his pretender-prince.

I felt the cold kiss of steel at the back of my neck, sliding through my hair. Yet another blade was at my throat; a third pressed against the leather and furs shielding my belly. Three men on me, then; two were dead, and the last man—the sixth—stood away and watched me. Blood was splattered across his face, but he bore no wound.

"Stay you still," he told me at once, and I heard the fear in his voice. As well as the Homanan words.

I gestured toward my belt-purse. "My gold is there."

"We want none of *your* gold," he said quickly. "We

came for something more." He smiled. "But we will take it, since you offer."

I still held my sword in my right hand. But they did not let me keep it. One man reached out and took it from me, then tossed it aside. I saw how it landed across the firecairn, clanging against the stone. I saw how the hilt was in the flames, and knew the leather would burn away to display the golden lion.

"Whose gold do you want, then?" I spoke Homanan, since they did, but I kept my Caledonese accent.

"Bellam's," he confided, and grinned.

Inwardly I swore. The Solindish usurper had caught me easily enough. And I had not even reached Homana.

Still, I forced a bewildered frown. "What does Bellam want with a mercenary? Can he not *buy* hundreds of them?"

"You travel with a shapechanger," he stated flatly.

Still I frowned. "Aye. What of it? Has Bellam declared it unlawful? I am not Homanan, I am Caledonese. I choose my companions where I will." I looked at the sword hilt and saw how the leather turned black and crisp. In a moment it would peel away, and I would be unmasked. If I were not already.

"Cheysuli are under sentence of death," the Homanan said. "That is one policy Bellam has kept intact since the days of Shaine."

I allowed surprise to enter my face. "You welcome Bellam as king, then? Though you be Homanan?"

He glanced at the others. They were all familiar: I had seen them in the roadhouse the night before. And they had heard Bellam's message the harper had read. But I wondered how I had given myself away.

The man spat into the snow. "We welcome Bellam's gold, since we get none of it another way. While he offers payment for each Cheysuli slain, we will serve him. That is all."

I kept my surprise from showing. Once more, it was not me they sought. Finn again. But it was me they had caught, and worth more—to Bellam—than five hundred Cheysuli warriors.

Except there were not five hundred Cheysuli left in all the world. My uncle had seen to that.

"You have come across the border hunting Cheysuli?" I asked.

He smiled. "They are hard to find in Homana. But the Ellasian king gives them refuge, so we seek them here. How better to earn the gold?"

"Then why," I asked very calmly, "do you disarm *me?* I have no stake in this."

"You came in with the shapechanger. By taking you, we take him. He will not turn beast with your life in our hands."

I laughed. "You count on a bond that does not exist. The Cheysuli and I met on the trail; we owe each other nothing. Taking me wins you nothing except a meaningless death." I paused. "You *do* mean to slay me, do you not?"

He glanced at the others. For a moment there was hesitation in his blue eyes, and then he shrugged. His decision had been made. "You slew two of us. You must pay."

I heard the jingle of horse trappings. The blades pressed closer against my neck, throat and belly as the man rode out of the trees. In his bare hands was a harp, and the single note he plucked held us all in thrall.

"You will slay no one," the harper said. "Fools, all of you, when you have Carillon in your hands."

The Homanans did not move. They could not. Like me, they were prisoners to the harp.

Lachlan looked at me. "They are Homanans. Did you tell them your name, they might bend knee to you instead of baring steel."

His fingers tangled in the strings and brought forth a tangle of sound. It allowed me to speak, but nothing more. "I am a mercenary," I said calmly. "You mistake me for someone else."

He frowned. His eyes were on me intently, and the sound of the harp increased. I felt it inside my head, and then he smiled. "I can conjure up your life, my lord. Would you have me show it to us all?"

"To what purpose?" I inquired. "You will do what you will do, no matter what I say."

"Aye," he agreed.

I saw how his fingers played upon the strings, drawing from the harp a mournful, poignant sound. It conjured up memories of the song he had played the night before, the lay that had driven a blade into my belly with the memories of what had happened. But it was not the same. It had a different sound. His Lady sang a different song.

The blades moved away from my neck, my throat, my belly. The Homanans stepped away, stumbling in the snow, until I stood alone. I watched, mute, as they took up the men I had slain and bore the bodies away into the trees. I was alone, except for the harper, but as helpless as before.

"Ah," I said, "you mean to claim the gold yourself."

"I mean to give you what men I can," he reproved. "I sent them home to wait until you call them to your standard."

I laughed. "Who would serve a mercenary, harper? You have mistaken me, I say."

Quite calmly he set the harp into its case and closed it up, hooking it to his saddle. Lachlan jumped down from his horse and crossed the snow to me. He knelt swiftly, pulled thick gloves from his belt and folded them, then pulled my sword from the firecairn. The leather had burned away, and in the last rays of the setting sun the ruby glowed deep crimson. The lion was burnished gold.

Lachlan rose. He held the blade gingerly, careful of the heat even through the gloves, but his smile did not fade. He turned to look at me with subtle triumph in his eyes. "I have leather in my packs," he said quietly. "You will have to wrap it again."

Still I could not move. I wondered how long he meant to hold me. I wondered if he would take me all the way to Mujhara in his ensorcellment, so that Bellam would see me helpless. The thought set my teeth to gritting.

And then I smiled. As Lachlan turned to go to his horse—for the harp, no doubt—Finn stepped around the horse's rump and blocked Lachlan's path. Around the other side came Storr. And the ensorcellment was broken.

I reached out and closed my gloved hand upon the blade of my sword, still in Lachlan's careful grasp. I felt the heat, but it was not enough to burn me. Simply enough to remind me what had so nearly happened.

Lachlan stood quite still. His hands were empty of everything now save the gloves he held, folded in his palms. He waited.

Finn moved closer. Storr followed. I could feel Lachlan's tension increase with every step they took. My own was gone at last; I felt calm, at ease, content to know the confrontation was firmly in our hands. No more in a sorcerous harper's.

"The others are dead." Finn stopped in front of Lachlan.

The harper started. "You *slew* them? But I gave them a task—"

"Aye," Finn agreed ironically. "I prefer to take no chances."

Lachlan opened his mouth to protest, then shut it again. I saw how rigid was his jaw. After a moment he tried again. "Then you have taken five men from Carillon's army. Five men you will miss."

Finn smiled. There was little of amusement in it. "I would sooner take five men from Carillon's army than Carillon himself."

Lachlan looked sharply at me. "You disbelieve me when I say I wish only to aid you. Well enough, I understand it. But he is Cheysuli. He can compel the truth from me. I know of his gifts; I have my own."

"And, having them, you may withstand mine," Finn commented.

Lachlan shook his head. "Without my harp, I have no magic. I am at your disposal. And I am not Ihlini, so you need fear no loss of your own power."

Finn's hands were a blur, reaching to catch the harper's head before Lachlan could move away. He held the skull between both palms, cradling it, as if he sought to crush it, but he did not. Lachlan's own hands came up, reaching to peel Finn's fingers away, but they stopped. The hands fell to his sides. Finn held him there, and went into his mind.

After a moment, when some sense came back to Finn's

eyes, he looked at me. "He is a harper, a healer and a priest. That much I can touch. But nothing else. He is well shielded, no matter that he wishes to claim his innocence."

"Does he serve Bellam or Tynstar?"

"He does not *appear* to." The distinction was deliberate.

I looked upon my sword and methodically rubbed the ash and charring from its hilt. "If he is neither Bellam nor Tynstar's man, whose man is he? He had his chance to slay me with that harp, or to take my mind from me. Bellam would give him his gold for a body or a madman." I grimaced. "He might even have used the Homanans as a guard contingent—he has the power with that harp. But he did none of those things."

"Shall I slay him for you?"

I squinted at the ruby, darkening as the sun went down. "Harpers are traditionally immune from such things as assassination. Petty intrigue they cannot help—I think it is born in them even as the harping is born—but never have I known one to clothe himself in murder."

"Gold can buy any man."

I grinned at him, brows lifting. "A Cheysuli, perhaps?"

Finn scowled. With the fortune in gold on his arms and in his ear, more would hardly tempt him. Or any other warrior. "He is not Cheysuli," was all he said, and the meaning was quite clear.

"No," I agreed, sighing. "But perhaps he is only a spy, not a hired assassin. Spies I can deal with; often they are useful. How else could we have led Bellam this merry dance for five years?" I smiled again. Bellam had sent spies to track us down. Five had even found us. Those we had stripped of their task, giving them a new one instead: to take word to Bellam that we were elsewhere in the world. Usually hundreds of leagues away from where we were. It had worked with three of them.

The others we had slain.

"Then you mean to use him." His tone was perfectly flat, but I knew he was not pleased.

"We will take him with us and see what he means to do."

"You tread a dangerous path, Carillon."

I smiled. "It is already dangerous. This will add a fillip."
I laughed at his expression. "It will also keep you in
practice, *liege man*. You were slow in coming to my aid."

"I had five men to slay before I could reach the harp."
But he frowned a little, and I knew he was not immune to
the knowledge that he *had* been slow. Faster than anyone
else, perhaps, but slow for a Cheysuli warrior.

"You are getting old, Finn." I gestured. "Set our harper
free. Let us see what he intends to do."

Finn released Lachlan. The harper staggered a moment, then caught himself, touching his head with a tentative hand. His eyes were blurred and unfocused. "Have
you done?"

"More than done," I agreed. "Now tell us why you wish
to aid me."

He rubbed his brow, still frowning slightly. "It is a
harper's life to make songs out of heroes and history. You
are both, you and your Cheysuli. You should hear the
stories they tell." He grinned, his senses restored. "A
harper gains his own measure of fame by adding to the
fame of others. I could do worse than to ride with Carillon
of Homana and his equally infamous liege man."

"You could," I agreed, and let him make of that what he
would.

After a moment Lachlan gestured. "Your fire has gone
out. Do you wish it, I can give it life again."

I glanced down at the firecairn. Snow had been kicked
into the fire during the scuffle with the Homanans and the
weight had finally doused it. "I have flint and steel," I
said.

"Your kindling is damp. What I do will take less effort."
Lachlan turned to go to his horse for the harp, but Storr
was in his way. After a moment a gray-faced harper looked
back at me.

I smiled. "Storr does Finn's bidding, when he does not
do his own. Look to him."

Lachlan did not move. He waited. And finally Storr
moved away.

The harper took down his case from the horse and
turned, cradling it against his chest. "You fear I will use
sorcery against you?"

"With reason," I declared.

"I will not." He shook his dull, dark head. "Not again. I will use it *for* you, do you wish it, but not against. Never against. We have too much in common."

"What," I asked, "does a mercenary have in common with a harper?"

Lachlan grinned. It was the warm, amused expression I had seen the evening before, as if he knew what I could not, and chose to keep it that way. "I am many things," he said obliquely. "Some of them you know: harper, healer, priest. And one day I will share the rest with you."

I lifted my sword. With great deliberation I set the tip against the lip of the sheath and let Lachlan see the runes, hardly visible in the dying light. Then I slid the sword home with the hiss of steel filling the shadows. "Do you admit to complicity," I said softly, "take care."

Lachlan's smile was gone. Hugging his harp case, he shook his head. "Were I to desire your death, your Cheysuli would give me my own." He cast a quick, flickering glance at Finn. "This is Ellas. We have sheltered the Cheysuli for some years, now. Do you think I discount Finn's skill? No. You need not be wary of me, with him present. I could do nothing."

I gestured. "There is that in your hands."

"My Lady?" He was surprised, then smiled. "Oh, aye, there is her magic. But it is Lodhi's, and I do not use it to kill."

"Then show us how you *can* use it," I bid him. "Show us what other magic you have besides the ability to give us our memories, or to lift our wills from us."

Lachlan looked at Finn, almost invisible in the deepening shadows. "It was difficult, with you. Most men are so shallow, so transient. But you are made of layers. Complex layers, some thin and easily torn away, but in tearing they show the metal underneath. Iron," he said thoughtfully. "I would liken you to iron. Hard and cold and strong."

Finn abruptly gestured toward the firecairn. "Show us, harper."

Lachlan knelt down by the firecairn. Deftly he unsealed the harp case—boiled leather hardened nearly to stone by some agent, padded thickly within—and took from it his Lady. The strings, so fragile-seeming, gleamed in the remaining light. The wood, I saw, was ancient, perhaps from some magical tree. It was bound with spun gold. The green stone—an emerald?—glowed.

He knelt in the snow, ignoring the increasing cold, and played a simple lay. It was soft, almost unheard, but remarkable nonetheless. And when his hands grew blurred and quick I saw the spark begin, deep in the damp, charred wood, until a single flame sprouted, swallowed it all, and the fire was born again.

The song died upon the harp. Lachlan looked up at me. "Done," he said.

"So it is, and myself unscathed." I reached down a gloved hand, caught his bare one and pulled him to his feet. His was no soft grasp, no woman's touch designed to keep his harper's fingers limber.

Lachlan smiled as we broke the grip. I thought he had judged me as quickly as I had him. But he said nothing; there was nothing at all to say. We were strangers to one another, though something within me said it would not always be so.

"You ride a blooded horse," I said, looking at the dapple-gray.

"Aye," Lachlan agreed gravely. "The High King likes my music. It was a gift last year."

"You have welcome in Rheghed?" I asked, thinking of the implications.

"Harpers have welcome anywhere." He tugged on his gloves, hunching against the cold. "I doubt not Bellam would have me in Homana-Mujhar, did I go."

He challenged me with his eyes. I smiled, but Finn did not. "Aye, I doubt not." I turned to Finn. "Have we food?"

"Something like," he affirmed, "but only if you are willing to eat coney-meat. Game is scarce."

I sighed. "Coney is not my favorite, but I prefer it to none at all."

Finn laughed. "Then at least I have taught you something in these past years. Once you might have demanded venison."

"I knew no better, then." I shook my head. "Even princes learn they have empty bellies like anyone else, when their titles are taken from them."

Lachlan's hands were on his harp as he set it within its case. "Which title?" he asked. "Prince or Mujhar?"

"Does it matter? Bellam has stolen them both."

When the coneys were nothing but gristle and bone— and Storr demolished the remains quickly enough—Lachlan brought out a skin of harsh wine from his saddlepacks and passed it to me. I sat cross-legged on my two pelts, trying to ignore the night's cold as it settled in my bones. The wine was somewhat bitter but warming, and after a long draw I handed it to Finn. Very solemnly he accepted it, then invoked his Cheysuli gods with elaborate distinction, and I saw Lachlan's eyes upon him. Finn's way of mocking another man's beliefs won him few friends, but he wanted none. He saw no sense in it, with Storr.

Lachlan retrieved the skin at last, drank, then passed it on to me. "Will you tell me what I must know, then? A saga is built out of fact, not fancy. Tell me how it was a king could destroy the race that had served him and his House so well."

"Finn would do better to tell it." If he would.

Finn, sitting on his pelts with Storr against one thigh, shrugged. The earring glinted in the firelight. In the shadows he seemed more alien than ever, part of the nighttime itself. "What is there to say? Shaine declared *qu'mahlin* on us for no good reason . . . and we died." He paused. "Most of us."

"*You* live," Lachlan commented.

Finn's smile was not precisely a smile, more a movement of his lips, as if he would bare his teeth. "The gods saw another way for me. My *tahlmorra* was to serve the prophecy in later years, not die as a helpless child." His hand went out to bury itself in Storr's thick hair.

Lachlan hesitated, cradling his harp case. "May I have the beginning?" he asked at last, with careful intonation.

Finn laughed. There was no humor in it. "What is the beginning, harper? I cannot say, and yet I was a part of it." He looked at me a moment, fixedly, as if the memories had swallowed him.

I swallowed, remembering too. "The fault lay in a man's overweening pride." I did not know how else to begin. "My uncle, Shaine the Mujhar—who wanted a son and had none—tried to wed his daughter to Ellic of Solinde, Bellam's son, in hopes of ending the war. But that daughter sought another man: Cheysuli, Shaine's own liege man, turning her back on the alliance and the betrothal. She fled her father, fled Homana-Mujhar, and with her went the warrior."

"My *jehan*," Finn said before I could continue. "Father, you would say. Hale. He took Lindir from her *tahlmorra* and fashioned another for them both. For us all; it has resulted in disaster." He stared into the fire. "It took a king in the throat of his pride, strangling him, until he could not bear it. And when his *cheysula* died of a wasting disease, and his second bore no living children, he determined the Cheysuli had cursed his House." His head moved slightly, as if to indicate regret. "And he declared *qu'mahlin* on us all."

Lachlan frowned intently. "A woman, then. The catalyst of it all."

"Lindir," I agreed. "My cousin. Enough like Shaine, in woman's form, to be a proper son. Except she was a daughter, and used her pride to win her escape."

"What did she say to the result?"

I shook my head. "No one knows. She came back to her father eight years later when she was heavy with Hale's child, because he was dead and she had no other place to go. Shaine took her back because he needed a male heir; when the child was born a girl he banished her to the woods so the beasts could have their shapechanger halfling. But Alix lived because Shaine's arms-master—and the Queen of Homana herself—begged the Mujhar to give her to man instead of beast." I shifted on my pelts. "Lindir died bearing Alix. What she thought of the *qu'mahlin* I could not say, but it slew her warrior and nearly destroyed his race."

Lachlan considered it all. And then he looked at Finn.

"How is it, then, you serve Carillon? Shaine the Mujhar was his uncle."

Finn put out his hand and made the familiar gesture. "Because of this. *Tahlmorra*. I have no choice." He smiled a little. "You may call it fate, or destiny, or whatever Ellasian word you have for such things . . . we believe each child is born with a *tahlmorra* that must be heeded when the gods make it known. The prophecy of the First-born says one day a man of all blood shall unite, in peace, four warring realms and two magic races. Carillon is a part of that prophecy." He shook his head, solemn in the firelight. "Had I a choice, I would put off such binding service, but I am Cheysuli, and such things are not done."

"Enemies become friends." Lachlan nodded slowly, staring fixedly into the fire as if he already heard the music. "It would make a fine lay. A story to break hearts and rend souls, and show others that hardships are nothing compared to what the Cheysuli have suffered. Do you give me leave, Finn, I will—"

"—do what?" Finn demanded. "Embellish the truth? Change the story in the interests of rhyme and resonance? *No*. I deny you that leave. What I have suffered—and my clan—is not for others to know."

My hands, hooked loosely over my knees, curled into fists that dug the bluntness of my nails into the leather of my gloves. Finn rarely spoke of his past or his personal feelings, being an intensely private man, but as he spoke I heard all the pain and emotion in his voice. Raw and unfettered, in the open at last.

Lachlan met his eyes. "I would embellish nothing, with such truth," he said quietly. "I think there would be no need."

Finn said something in the Old Tongue, the ancient language of the Cheysuli. I had learned words and phrases in the past years, but when Finn resorted to it out of anger or frustration—or high emotions—I could understand none of it. The lyrical syllables became slurred and indistinct, yet managed to convey his feelings just the same. I winced, knowing what Lachlan must feel.

But Finn stopped short. He never yelled, having no

need, but his quietness was just as effective. Yet silence was something altogether different, and I thought perhaps something had stopped him. Then I saw the odd detached expression in his face, and the blankness of his eyes, and realized Storr conversed with him.

What the wolf said I cannot guess, but I saw Finn's face darken in the firelight with heavy color, then go pale and grim. Finally he unlocked his jaw and spoke.

"I was a boy." The words were so quiet I could hardly hear them over the snap and crackle of the flames. "Three years old." His hand tightened in the silver fur of Storr's neck. I wondered, with astonishment at the thought, if he sought support from his *lir* to speak of his childhood clearly. It was not something he had said to me before, not even when I had asked. "I had sickened with some childish fever, and kept to my *jehana's* skirts like a fool with no wits." His eyes hooded a little, but he smiled, as if the memory amused him. Briefly only; there was little of amusement in the tale. "Sleep brought me no peace, only bad dreams, and it was hot within the pavilion. It was dark, so dark, and I thought the demons would steal my soul. I was so hot." A heavy swallow rippled the flesh of his throat. "Duncan threw water on the fire to douse it, thinking to help, but he only made it smoke, and it choked me. Finally he fell asleep, and my *jehana*, but I could not."

I glanced at Lachlan. He was transfixed.

Finn paused. The firelight filled his eyes. "And then the Keep was full of the thunder of the gods, only the thunder came from men. The Mujhar's men. They swept into our Keep like demons from the netherworld, determined to destroy us all. They set fire to the pavilion."

Lachlan started. "With *children* inside?"

"Aye," Finn said grimly. "Ours they knocked down with their horses, then they dropped a torch on it." His eyes flicked to Lachlan's astonished face. "We paint our pavilions, harper. Paint burns very quickly."

Lachlan started to speak, as if to halt the recital. Finn went on regardless, perhaps purging his soul at last.

"Duncan pulled me from the fire before it could consume us all. My *jehana* took us both into the trees, and there we hid until daylight. By then the men were gone, but so was most of our Keep." He took a deep breath. "I was young, too young to fully understand, but even a child of three learns how to hate." The eyes came around to me. "I was born two days before Hale went away with Lindir, and still he took her. Still he went from the Keep to Homana-Mujhar, and helped his *meijha*, his mistress, escape. And so Shaine, when he set his men upon us, made certain Hale's Keep was the first."

Lachlan, after a long moment of silence, shook his head. "I have gifts many men do not, because of Lodhi and my Lady. But even *I* cannot tell the tale as you do." His face was very still. "I will leave it to those who can. I will leave it to the Cheysuli."

FIVE

When at last we drew near the Keep a day later, Finn grew pensive and snappish. It was unlike him. We had dealt well together, though only after I had grown used to having a Cheysuli at my side, and after *he* had grown accustomed to riding with a Homanan. Now we had come home again, at least to his mind; home again, would Finn put off his service?

It set the hairs to rising on my neck. I had no wish to lose Finn. I needed him still. I had learned much in the years of exile, but I had yet to learn what it was to lay claim to a stolen throne. Without Finn, the task would be close to impossible.

He pulled up his mount sharply, hissing invectives beneath his breath. And then his face went blank with the uncanniness of the *lir*-bond and I knew he conversed with the wolf.

Lachlan, wise harper, said nothing. He waited as I did. But the tension that was a tangible thing did not appear to touch him.

Finn broke free of the contact at last. I had watched his face; had seen it grow hard and sharp and bleak, like his eyes. And now I grew afraid.

"What is it?" I hissed.

"Storr sends a warning." Finn shivered suddenly, though the sunlight that glittered off his earring was warm upon our shoulders. "I think I feel it myself. I will go in. Keep yourself here." He looked at Lachlan a moment, considering something, by the look in his eyes. Then he shrugged, dismissing it. "Keep yourself here, as I said, until I come back for you."

He spoke lightly enough, no doubt for Lachlan's benefit, but I could not wait for subterfuge. I caught the rein of his horse and held him still. "Tell me. What is it?"

Finn looked again at Lachlan, and then he looked at me. "Storr can touch no *lir*."

"*None*?"

"Not even Alix."

"But—with her Old Blood—" I stopped. He need say no more. Could Storr touch no *lir* at all, the situation was grave indeed. "There may be danger for you as well," I told him quietly.

"Of course. So I go in *lir*-shape." He dropped off his horse at once, leaving me with a skittish animal at the end of a leather rein. "*Tahlmorra lujhala mei wiccan, cheysu*," he said to me, shrugging, and then he was no longer a man.

I watched Lachlan. As the space in which Finn stood emptied, swallowed instead by the void, Lachlan's eyes stretched wide. And then they narrowed as he frowned, staring as if he would learn it himself. His fingers dropped to the harp case at his knee, touching it as if to reassure himself he was awake, not asleep. By the time I looked back at Finn the man-shape was completely gone, replaced by the blurred outline of a wolf. I felt the familiar rolling of my belly, swallowed against it, as always, and looked at Lachlan again. His face had taken on a peculiar greenish hue. I thought he might vomit up his fear and shock, but he did not.

The ruddy wolf with Finn's yellow eyes flicked his tail and ran.

"They do not merit fear," I told Lachlan clearly, "unless you have done something to merit their enmity." I smiled as his eyes turned to me, staring as if he thought I too might be a wolf, or something equally bestial. "You are an innocent man, you have said: a harper . . . what have *you* to fear from Finn?"

But a man does not stop fearing the specter of childhood

nightmares so easily, no matter how innocent he is. Lachlan—with, perhaps, more guilt than he claimed—might have better reason to fear what he saw. He stared after Finn, seeing nothing now, but the greenish pallor had been replaced by the white of shock and apprehension. "*Wolves* cannot know reason! Does he know you in that shape?"

"Finn, in that shape, knows everything a man knows," I said. "But he also claims the wisdom of a wolf. A double threat, you might say, for one who deserves careful consideration." I shifted in the saddle, half my mind with Finn and the other half knowing what Lachlan felt. I had felt it myself, the first few times. "He is not a demon or a beast. He is a man who claims a god-gift in his blood, much as you claim it in yours. It is only his gods manifest their presence a little differently." I thought of the magic he made with his music, and then I laughed at his horrified expression. "Think you he worships Lodhi? Not Finn. Perhaps he *worships* no god, or gods, but he serves his own better than any man I have ever known. How else do you think he would keep himself to my side?" Finn's horse tried to wander, searching for grass in the snow, and I pulled him back. "You need have no fear he might turn on you, wolflike, and tear your throat from your body. He would do that only if you gave him reason." I met the harper's eyes steadily, keeping my tone light. "But then you have no wish to betray me, have you? Not with your saga at stake."

"No." Lachlan tried to smile, but I could see the thoughts in his head. No man, seeing the shapechange for the first time, forgets it so quickly. If at all. "What was it he said to you, before he changed himself?"

I laughed. "A philosophy, of sorts. Cheysuli, of course, and therefore alien to Homanans or Ellasians." I quoted the words: "*Tahlmorra lujhala mei wiccan, cheysu*. It means, roughly, the fate of a man rests always within the hands of the gods." I made the gesture, being very distinct as I lifted my right hand and spread my fingers. "It is usually shortened to the word *tahlmorra*, which says more than enough quite simply."

Lachlan shook his head slowly. "Not so alien to me, I

think. Do you forget I am a priest? Admittedly my god is singular, and far different from those Finn claims, but I am trained to understand the faith a man holds. More than trained; I believe it with all my heart, that a man may know and serve his deity." His hand tapped the harp case. "My gift is there, Carillon. Finn's is elsewhere, but just as strong. And he is just as devout, perhaps more so, to give himself up to his fate." He smiled. "*Tahlmorra lujhala mei wiccan, cheysu*. How eloquent a phrase."

"Have you any like it?"

Lachlan laughed. "You could never say it. You lack an Ellasian throat." He thumped the harp case. "This one is not so hard: *Yhana Lodhi, yffennog faer*." He smiled. "A man walks with pride forever when he walks with Lodhi, humble."

And then Finn was back, two-legged and white-faced, and I had no more time for philosophy. I held out the rein as Finn reached for it, but I could ask none of the questions that crowded my mouth. Finn's face had robbed me of my voice.

"Destroyed," he said in a whisper. "Torn down. *Burned*." His pallor was alarming. "There is no Keep."

I was over the broken stonework before I realized what it was, setting my horse to jumping though he lacked the legs to do it. He stumbled, scrabbling at the snow-cloaked heaps of mortared stone, and then I knew. The wall, the half-circle wall that surrounded every Keep. Shattered and broken upon the ground.

I pulled up at once, saving the horse, but also saving myself. I sat silently on the little gelding, staring at what remained of the Keep. Bit by bit I looked, allowing myself one portion at a time; I could not bear to see it all at once.

Snow covered nearly everything, but scavenger beasts had dug up the remains. I saw the long poles, some snapped in two, some charred. I saw scraps of soiled cloth frozen into stiffness, colors muted by time and harsh weather. The firecairns that had stood before each pavilion lay in tumbled fragments, spilled by hostile feet and destructive hooves. All of it gone, with only ragged remnants of a once-proud Keep.

In my mind I saw it as I had seen it last: undressed,

unmortared stone standing high to guard the Keep; billowing pavilions of varied hues emblazoned with painted *lir*. The perches and pelts existing for those *lir*, and the children who feared nothing of the wild. Save, perhaps, for those who knew to fear Homanans.

I cursed. It came viciously out of my mouth along with the spittle. I thought of Duncan, clan-leader of his Keep, but mostly I thought of Alix.

I rode on then. Directly to the proper place. I knew it well enough, though nothing remained to mark it. And there I slid off my horse, too stiff to dismount with any skill or grace, and fell down upon my knees.

One pole pierced its way through snow to stab out of the ruins like a standard. A scrap of fabric, stiff from freezing, still clung to the wood. I tugged at it and it came away, breaking off in my hand. Slate-colored, with the faintest blur of gold and brown. For Cai, Duncan's hawk.

Not once had I thought they might be dead. Not once, in all the time spent in exile, had I thought they might be gone. They had been the one constant in my life, along with Finn. Always I had recalled the Keep and the clan-leader's pavilion, filled with Duncan's pride and Alix's strength, and the promise of the unborn child. Never once had I even considered they might not be here to greet me.

But it was not the greeting I missed. It was the conviction of life, no matter where it existed. Nothing lived here now.

I heard the sound behind me and knew at once it was Finn. Slowly, suddenly old beyond my years, I stood up. I trembled as if with illness, knowing only a great sorrow and rage and consuming grief.

Gods . . . they could not be dead—

Lachlan made a sound. I looked at him blindly, thinking only of Alix and Duncan, and then I saw the expression of realization in his eyes.

Finn saw it also. As he leaped, still in human form, I caught him in mid-stride. "Wait—"

"He knew."

The words struck me in the face. But still I held Finn.

"Wait. Do you slay him, we will learn nothing from him. *Wait*—"

Lachlan stood rooted to the earth. One hand thrust outward as if to hold us back. His face was white. "I will tell you. I will tell you what I can."

I let go of Finn when I knew he would do nothing more. At least until he had better reason. "Then Finn has the right of it: you knew."

Lachlan nodded stiffly. "I knew. Have known. But I had forgotten. It was—three years ago."

"Three years." I stared around the remains of the Keep. "Harper—what happened?"

He looked steadily at me. "Ihlini."

Finn hissed something in the Old Tongue. I merely waited for further explanation. But I said one thing: "This is Ellas. Do you say Tynstar has influence here?"

Dull color came up into Lachlan's face. "I say nothing of that. Ellas is free of Ihlini domination. But once, only once, there was a raid across the border. Ihlini and Solindish, hunting the Cheysuli who sheltered in this realm, and they came here." A muscle ticked in his jaw. "There have been songs made about it, but it is not something I care to recall. I had nearly forgotten."

"Remember," Finn said curtly. "Remember it all, harper."

Lachlan spread his hands. "The Ihlini came here. They destroyed the Keep. They slew who they could of the Cheysuli."

"How many?" Finn demanded.

"Not all." Lachlan scrubbed a hand across his brow, as if he wished to free himself of the silver circlet of his calling. "I—do not know, perhaps, as much as I should."

"Not enough and too much, all at once," Finn said grimly. "Harper, you should have spoken earlier. You knew we came to the Keep."

"How am I to know them *all?*" Lachlan demanded. "The High King gives the Cheysuli shelter, but he does not count them, old or young. I doubt *Rhodri* can say how many Keeps or how many Cheysuli are in Ellas. We merely welcome them all."

This time it was Finn who colored, but only for a moment. The grief and tension were back at once, etching lines into his face. He wore his mask again, the private mask, stark and hard in his insularity. "They may all be dead. And that would leave only me—" He broke off.

Lachlan took a deep breath. "I have heard that those who survived went back into Homana. North. Across the Bluetooth River."

Finn frowned. "Too far," he muttered, looking at Storr. "Too far even for the *lir*-link."

I looked directly at Lachlan. "You have heard much for a man who recalls so little. To Homana, you say. North, across the Bluetooth. Are you privy to information we have no recourse to?"

He did not smile. "Harpers are privy to much, as you should know. Had you none in Homana-Mujhar?"

"Many," I said briefly. "Before Bellam silenced the music."

Finn turned his back. He stared again at the remains of Duncan's slate-gray pavilion. I knew he meant to master himself. I wondered if he could.

"May I suggest," Lachlan began, "that you use my harp skill in trying to rouse your people? I could go into taverns and sing *The Song of Homana,* to test how the people feel. How better to learn their minds, and how they will answer their rightful king's call?"

"*The Song of Homana?*" Finn said doubtfully, turning to stare at Lachlan.

"You have heard it," the harper said, "and I saw what it did to you. It has a magic of its own."

He spoke the truth. Did he go into Homanan taverns and play that song on his Lady, he would know sooner than anyone else what my people were capable of. Had Bellam cowed them, it would take time to rebuild their spirit. Were they merely angry, I could use it.

I nodded at Lachlan. "The horses require tending."

For a moment he frowned, baffled, and then he understood. Silently he took away our horses and gave us room to speak freely, without fear he might overhear.

"I give you leave to go," I told Finn simply.

Something flickered in his eyes. "There is no need."

"There is. You must go. Your clan—your kin—have gone north across the Bluetooth. Home to Homana, where we are bound. You must go and find them, to set your soul at peace."

He did not smile. "Healing Homana is more important than seeking out my clan."

"Is it?" I shook my head. "You told me once that clan- and kin-ties bind more closely than anything else in Cheysuli culture. I have not forgotten. I give you leave to go, so I can have you whole again." I held up a silencing hand. "Until you know, it will eat at your soul like a canker."

The flesh of his face was stiff. "I will not leave you in companionship to the enemy."

I shook my head. "We do not know if he is an enemy."

"He knows too much," Finn said grimly. "Too much and too little. I do not trust him."

"Then trust me." I put out my gloved hand and spread my fingers, palm up. "Have you not taught me all you can in the art of staying alive, even in dire adversity? I am no longer quite the green princeling you escorted into exile. I think I may have some control over my life." I smiled. "You have said it is my *tahlmorra* to take back the Lion Throne. If so, it will happen, and nothing will gainsay it. Not even this time apart."

He shook his head slowly. "*Tahlmorras* may be broken, Carillon. Do not mislead yourself into believing you are safe."

"Have more faith in me," I chided. "Go north and find Alix and Duncan. Bring them back." I frowned a moment. "Bring them to Torrin's croft. It was Alix's home, and if he is still alive it will be a place of sanctuary for us all."

He looked at the ruined pavilion, buried under snow. And then he looked at Storr. He sighed. "Rouse your people, my lord of Homana. And I will bring home the Cheysuli."

SIX

Mujhara. It rose out of the plains of Homana like an eagle on an aerie, walled about with rose-red stone and portcullised barbican gates. Homana-Mujhar was much the same: walled and gated and pink. The palace stood within the city on a hill. Not high, but higher than any other. Lachlan and I rode through the main gate into Mujhara, and at once I knew I was home.

Save I was not. My home was filled with Solindish soldiers, hung about with ringmail and boiled leather and glinting silver swords. They let us in because they knew no better, thinking Homana's rightful lord would never ride so willingly into his prison.

I heard the Solindish tongue spoken in the streets of Mujhara more than I heard Homanan. Lachlan and I spoke Ellasian merely to be safe. But I thought I could say anything and be unacknowledged; Bellam's soldiers were bored. After five years and no threat from without, they lived lazily within.

The magnificence was gone. I thought perhaps it was my own lack of discernment, having spent so long in foreign lands, but it was not. The city, once so proud, had lost interest in itself. It housed a Mujhar who had stolen his throne, and the Homanans did not care to praise his name. Why should they praise his city? Where once the windows had glittered with glass or glowed with horn, now the eyes were dark and dim, smoked over, puttied at corners with dirt and grime. The white-washed walls were dingy and gray, some fouled with streaks of urine. The cobbled streets had crumbled, decayed until the stench hung over it like a miasma. I did not doubt Homana-Mujhar remained fit for a king, but the rest of the city did not.

Lachlan looked at me once, then again. "Look not so angry, or they will know."

"I am sick," I said curtly. "I could vomit on this vileness. What have they done to my city?"

Lachlan shook his head. "What defeated people do everywhere: they live. They go on. You cannot blame them for it. The heart has gone out of their lives. Bellam exacts overharsh taxes so no one can afford to eat, let alone wash their houses. And the streets? Why clean dung when the great ass sits upon the throne?"

I glanced at him sharply. He did not speak as Bellam's man, saying what he should to win my regard. He spoke like a man who understood the reasons for Mujhara's condition—disliking it, perhaps, as much as I, but tolerating it better. Perhaps it was because he was Ellasian, and a harper, with no throne to make his own.

"I am sorry you must see it this way," I told him with feeling. "When *I*—" I broke it off at once. What good lies in predicting something that may not happen?

Lachlan gestured. "Here, a tavern. Shall we go in? Perhaps here we will find better fortune than we found at the village taverns."

We had better. Failure rankled, though I understood it. It is difficult to ask poor crofters to give up what little they have to answer the call of an outlawed prince. It was soldiers I needed first, and then what other men I could find.

I stared at the tavern grimly. It looked like all the others: gray and dingy and dim. And then I looked at Lachlan.

He smiled, but it lacked all humor, a hooking down of his mouth. "Of course. We will go on to another . . . one you will choose for yourself."

I jumped off my horse, swore when I slipped in some

muck, and scraped my boot against a loosened cobble. "This will do well enough. Come in, and bring your harp."

Lachlan went in before me when he had taken his Lady from his saddle. I paused to let him enter alone, then went in behind him, shoving open the narrow, studded door.

At once I ducked. The beamwork of the dark roof was low, so low it made me wince against its closeness. The floor beneath my feet was earthen, packed, but bits of it had been scraped into ridges and little piles of dirt, as if the benches and tables had been dragged across it to rest in different places. I put up a hand to tear away the sticky webbing that looped down from the beam beside my head. It clung to my fingers until I scrubbed it off against the cracked, hardened leather of my jerkin.

A single lantern depended from a hook set into the central beam, painted black with pitch. It shed dim light over the common room. A few candles stood out on the tables, fat and greasy and stinking. There was little light in the place, just a sickly yellow glow and the haze of ocherous smoke.

Lachlan, with his harp, was welcomed at once. There were perhaps twenty men scattered around the common room, but they made way for him at once, drawing up a stool and bidding him begin. I found a table near the door and sat down, asking for ale when the tavern-master arrived. It was good brown ale when it came, hearty and woody; I drank the first cup down with relish.

Lachlan opened with a sprightly lay to liven them up. They clapped and cheered, urging him on, until he sang a sad song of a girl and her lover, murdered by her father. It brought a less exuberant response but no less a liking for Lachlan's skill. And then he picked out the opening notes of *The Song of Homana*.

He got no more than halfway through the tale. Abruptly a soldier in Solindish ringmail and too much wine pushed to his feet and drew his sword. "Treason!" he shouted. He wavered on his feet, and I realized how drunk he was. "You sing *treason!*" His Homanan was poor, but he was clearly understandable. So was his implication as he raised the shining sword.

I was on my feet at once. My own sword was in my hand, but other men had already seized the soldier and forced him down on his stool, relieving him of his sword. It clanged to the floor and was kicked away. Lachlan, I saw, had set down his Lady in the center of a table, and his hand was near his knife.

Four men held the soldier in place. A fifth moved to stand before him. "You are alone here, Solindishman," he said. "Quite *alone*. This is a Homanan tavern and we are all Homanans; we invite the harper to finish his lay. You will sit and listen . . . unless I bid you otherwise." He jerked his head. "Bind him and stop up his mouth!"

The soldier was instantly bound and gagged, propped upon the stool like a sheep held down for shearing. With less tenderness. The young man who had ordered him bound cast an assessive glance around the room. I saw his eyes on me, black in the dimness of the candlelight. They paused, oddly intent though seemingly indifferent, and moved on.

He smiled. He was young, eighteen or nineteen, I thought, with an economy of movement that reminded me of Finn. So did his black hair and the darkness of his face. "We have silenced this fool," he said calmly. "Now we shall let the harper finish."

I sheathed my sword and sat down slowly. I was aware of the men who had moved in behind me, ranging themselves along the wall. The door, I saw, was barred. This was not an unaccustomed occurrence, then; the Solindish were the hunted.

The knowledge made me smile.

Lachlan completed his lay. The final note, dying out, was met with absolute silence. I felt a trickle of forboding run quickly down my spine; I shivered, disliking the sensation. And yet I could not shake it from me.

"Well sung," the black-eyed young man said at last. "You have a feel for our plight, it seems. And yet you are Ellasian."

"Ellasian, aye." Lachlan raised a cup of water to his mouth and sipped. "But I have traveled many lands and have admired Homana for years."

"What is left to admire?" the Homanan demanded. "We are a defeated land."

"For now, aye, but do you not wait only for your prince to return?" Smiling, Lachlan plucked a single string of his Lady. The sound hung in the air a moment, and then it faded away. "The former glory you aspire to have again . . . it may come."

The young man leaned forward on his stool. "Tell me— you travel, as you say—do you think Carillon hears of our need? Do you sing this song wherever you go, surely you have had *some* response!"

"There is fear," Lachlan said quietly. "Men are in fear of Solindish retribution. What army could Carillon raise, were he to come home again?"

"Fear?" The other nodded. "Aye, there is fear. What else could there be in this land? We need a lord again, a man who can rouse this realm into rebellion." He had all the dedication of the fanatic, and yet there was little of the madness in him, I thought. He was desperate; so was I. "I will not lie and say it would be easy, harper, but I think Carillon would find more than a few ready to rally to his standard."

I thought of the crofters, muttering into their wine and ale. I thought of what little success we had had in learning if Homana desired my return.

"What would you do," Lachlan asked, "were he to come home again?"

The other laughed with a bitterness older than his years. "Join him. These few you see. Not many, but a beginning. Still, there are more of us yet. We meet in secret, to plot, and to aid Carillon however we may. In hopes he will come home."

"Bellam is powerful," Lachlan warned, and I wondered what more he knew.

The Homanan nodded. "He is indeed strong, and claims many troops who serve him well. And with Tynstar at his side, he is certainly no weak king. But Carillon brought the Cheysuli into Homana-Mujhar before, and nearly defeated the Ihlini. This time he might succeed."

"Only with help."

"He will have it."

Lachlan nodded idly. "There are strangers among you. Even I, Ellasian though I may be."

"You are a harper." The young man frowned. "Harpers have immunity, of course. As for the soldier, he will be slain."

Lachlan looked at me across the room. "And the other?"

The Homanan merely smiled. And then the men were at my back, asking for my knife and sword. After a moment's hesitation, I gave them into their hands. Two men remained behind me, another at my left side. The young man was taking no chances. "He will be slain, of course."

Of course. I smiled at Lachlan, who merely bided his time.

The knife was given to the young man. He looked at it briefly, frowning over the Caledonese runes and scripture, then set it aside on the nearest table. The sword was given to him then, and he did not at once put it down. He admired the edge, then saw the runes set into the silver. His eyes widened. "Cheysuli-made!" He glanced sharply at me. "How did you get this?" For a moment something moved in his face. "Off a dead man, no doubt. Cheysuli swords are rare."

"No," I said. "From a live one. And now, before you slay me, I bid you do one thing."

"*Bid* me?" He stared, brows rising beneath the black hair. "Ask, perhaps . . . but it does not mean I will answer."

I did not move. "Cut the leather free."

His hands were on the hilt. I saw him look down at the leather, feeling the tautness of it. I had wrapped it well, and would do so again.

"Cut the leather free."

His stare challenged me a moment. And then he drew his knife and did precisely as I asked.

The leather fell free of his hand. He stared at the hilt: the rampant, royal lion of purest Cheysuli gold, the burnished grip, the massive ruby clutched in curving prongs. The magnificent Mujhar's Eye.

"Say what it is, so all will know," I told him quietly.

"The lion crest of Homana." His eyes moved from the hilt to my face, and I smiled.

"Who carries this sword, this crest?"

Color had left his face. "The blood of the House of Homana." He paused. Then, in a rush of breath and words, "But you might have *stolen* this sword!"

I glanced pointedly at my guards. "You have disarmed me. Say I may come forward."

"Come, then." Color was back in his face. He was young, and angry, and afraid of what he thought he might hear.

I rose, pushing away my stool. Slowly I walked forward, looking only at the young man, and then I stopped before him. He was tall, Cheysuli-tall, but I was taller still.

I pushed back the sleeve on my left arm, showing him the scar that ringed my wrist. "See you that? I have another exactly like it, on my right. You should know them both, Rowan." He flinched in surprise. "You were prisoner to Keough of Atvia, as I was. You were flogged because you spilled wine on Keough himself, even though I asked them to spare you. Your back must show signs of the flogging, even as my arms show the mark of the iron." I let go the sleeve. "May I have my sword back, now?"

Stiffly, he lowered his head to look at it in his hands. And then, as if realizing the history of the blade, he thrust it out to me. I accepted it, feeling safer almost at once, and then he dropped to his knees.

"*My lord,*" he whispered. "Oh, my lord . . . forgive me!"

I slid the sword home in its sheath. "There is nothing to forgive. You have done what you should have done."

He stared up at me. I saw how his eyes were yellow in the candlelight; I had always thought him Cheysuli. It was Rowan who denied it. "How soon do we fight, my lord?"

I laughed at his eagerness. "It is late winter now. It will take time to gather what men we can. In true spring, perhaps, we can begin the raiding parties." I gestured. "Get up from there. This is not the place. I am not the Mujhar quite yet."

He remained where he was. "Will you formally accept my service?"

I reached down and caught his woollen shirt and leather jerkin, pulling him to his feet. "I told you to get up from the floor," I said mildly, startled to find him so grown. He had been but thirteen the last time I had seen him.

Rowan straightened his clothing. "Aye, my lord."

I turned to the other men. Rowan's, all of them, intent upon rebellion. And now intent upon the scene before them; not quite believing the prince he had promised had come into their midst.

I cleared my throat. "Most of you are too young to recall Homana before the days of the *qu'mahlin*, when my uncle the Mujhar ordered every Cheysuli slain. You have grown up fearing and distrusting them, as I did myself. But I learned differently, and so must you." I put up a silencing hand. "They are not demons. They are not beasts. They serve nothing of the netherworld; they serve *me*." I paused. "Has any of you ever even *seen* a Cheysuli warrior?" There was a chorus of denials, even from Rowan. I looked at each man, one by one. "I will have no bloodshed among my men. The Cheysuli are not your foes."

"But—" one man began, then squirmed beneath my eye.

"It is not easy to forget a thing you have been taught to believe," I went on, more quietly. "I know that better than you think. But I also think, once you have got over your superstitious fears of something you cannot comprehend, you will see they are no different from any other." I paused. "You had *better*."

Rowan, behind me, laughed once. I thought there was relief in his tone.

"Will you serve me," I asked, "even with the Cheysuli by my side?"

Agreement. No denials. I searched for reluctance and found none.

"And so the *Song* continues," murmured Lachlan, and at that I laughed aloud.

It was Rowan who told me of my kin, what remained of it: my mother and my sister. We sat alone at a corner table, speaking of plans for the army we must gather. He spoke clearly and at length, having spent much of his time considering how best it could be done, and I was grateful for his care. He would make the preparation much easier.

But when at last he chanced to say, off-handedly, that my mother no doubt missed my sister's company, I raised my hand to stop him.

"Is Tourmaline not at Joyenne?"

Rowan shook his head. "Bellam took her hostage. Years ago; I think it was not long after you escaped from Homana-Mujhar."

Escaped—Tynstar had *let* me go. I picked at the scarred wood of the table and bid Rowan to continue.

He shrugged, at a loss for what to tell me. "The Lady Gwynneth is kept at Joyenne, well-guarded. Princess Tourmaline, as I said, is at Homana-Mujhar. Bellam seeks to hold anything that might bring you to him. He dares not allow either of them freedom, for fear they could be used as a rallying point for the rebellion."

"Instead of me?" I ran a hand through my beard to scratch the flesh beneath. "Well, Bellam will be busy with me. There is no need for him to hold two women."

"He will," Rowan asserted. "He will never let them go." He stopped a moment, eyeing me tentatively. "There is even talk he will wed the lady, your sister."

I spat out an oath and nearly stood up, hand to my re-wrapped sword hilt. Instead I sat down again and hacked at the table with my knife, adding yet more scars to the wood. "Torry would not allow it," I said flatly, knowing she would have little to say about it. Women did not when it came to their disposal.

Rowan smiled. "I had heard she was not an acquiescent hostage. And with two women in one castle—" He laughed aloud, genuinely amused.

"Two?"

"His daughter, the Princess Electra." Rowan frowned. "There is talk she is Tynstar's light woman."

"*Tynstar's.*" I stared at him, sitting upright on my stool. "Bellam gives his daughter over to *that*?"

"I heard it was Tynstar's price." Rowan shifted on his bench. "My lord, there is little I can tell you. Most is merely rumor. I would not dare claim any of it as truth."

"There is some truth in rumor," I said thoughtfully, taking up my ale again. "If she is Tynstar's light woman, there is a use for her in my plans."

"You wish to use a woman against the *sorcerer*?" Rowan shook his head. "Begging your pardon, my lord, I think you are mistaken."

"Princes are never mistaken." I grinned at his instant discomfort. "*All* men can be mistaken, and fools if they think not. Well enough, we shall have to consider a plan. Two of them—to wrest my mother from Joyenne, and Torry from Homana-Mujhar." I frowned, wishing Finn were with me. To set a trap without him—I focused on Rowan again. "For a man who swears he is not Cheysuli, you are the perfect image of a warrior."

Dark color moved through Rowan's face. "I know it. It has been my bane."

"There is no danger in it, with me. You could admit it freely—"

"I admit nothing!" I was pleased he did not hide his anger, even before his prince. Treacherous are men who are all obsequious nods and bows, never letting me see their hearts. "I have said I am not Cheysuli," he repeated. "My lord."

I laughed at his stiff, remembered formality. And then the laughter died away, for I heard Lachlan harping in the background. Making magic with his Lady.

I turned to look at my enigmatic ally. Ellasian. A stranger who wished to be my friend, he said. Bellam's man? Or Tynstar's? Or merely his own, too cunning to work for another? I still doubted him.

Slowly I rose. Rowan rose with me, out of courtesy, but I could see the puzzlement in his eyes. I went across the room and stopped at Lachlan's table, seeing how his blue eyes were black in the yellow light of the tavern.

He stopped playing at once, his fingers still resting upon the gleaming strings. His clustered audience, seeing my face, moved away in silence.

I drew my sword from its sheath. I saw the sudden flaring of fear in Lachlan's eyes. A sour, muted note sang from his harp and then stilled, but the candles and lantern guttered out.

Darkness. But not so dark there was no light. Merely shadows. And the sorcerous green stone in Lachlan's Lady gave off enough brilliance to see by.

His fingers were in the strings. But so was the tip of my sword.

I saw it in his face: the fear I would harm his harp. Slay it, like an animal, or a man. As if the wood and wire lived.

"Put her down—your Lady," I said gently, having felt her magic twice.

He did not move. The stoneglow washed across the blade of my sword, setting the runes to glinting in its light. And in that light I knew power, ancient and strong and true.

The blade was parallel to the strings, touching nothing. Slowly I turned it. One string whined its protest, but I held it back from death.

Lachlan bent forward a little, sliding the harp free of my sword. Carefully he set his Lady in the center of the table and took his hands away. He waited then, quietly, his arms empty of his harp.

I put my left hand on my sword, on the blade below the crosspiece. I took my right hand off the hilt. That I offered to Lachlan.

"The Solindish soldier," I said calmly. "Slay him for me, harper."

SEVEN

"Forgive me, my lord," Rowan said quietly. "Is it wise you should go, and alone?"

I sat upon a rotting tree stump, high on the hill behind Torrin's croft. Alix's foster father was indeed still alive, and he had been astonished to find me the same when I had arrived at his dwelling some weeks before. He had given me the story of the Ihlini attack much as Lachlan had, verifying that what remained of the clan had gone north across the Bluetooth. So now, using Torrin's croft as a temporary headquarters, I gathered what army I could. Here I was safe, unknown; the army camped in the sheltering forest in the hills behind the valley, practicing with swords and knives.

I stirred, knocking snow off my boots by banging heels against the tree stump. The day was quite clear; I squinted against the sunlight. "Wise enough, does no one find me out." I glanced at Rowan, standing three steps away, in the attitude of a proper servant. I thought it would ease with time, so that he served through desire instead of rigid dedication. "I have told no one but you and Torrin of my plan."

Rowan nodded as the color came and went in his sun-bronzed face. He was not accustomed to being in my confidence. It rested ill with him, who thought himself little more than a servant no matter how often I said he was much more. "There is the harper," he offered quietly.

I grunted, shifting my seat on the rotting stump. "Lachlan believes he has proven his worth by slaying the soldier. I will let him think it. He has, to some extent . . . but not all." I bent and scooped up a stone, idly tossing it through the trees. "Say what is in your mind, Rowan. At my behest."

He nodded, head bowed in an attitude of humility. His hands were behind his back. His eyes did not look at me but at the snow-covered ground beneath his boots. "You distrust the harper, still, because you do not know him well enough. My lord—I say you know me little better."

"I know enough," I said. "I recall the thirteen-year-old boy who was captive of the Atvians along with me. I recall the boy who was made to serve the Lord Keough himself, though he be cuffed and struck and tripped." Rowan's eyes came up to mine, stricken. "I was in the tent also, Rowan. That you must surely recall. And I saw what they did to your back."

His shoulders moved, tensing, rippling beneath the leather and wool. I knew what he did, flinching from the lash. He could not help it, no more than I at times, when I recalled the iron upon my wrists.

At that, the flesh twinged. I rubbed at both wrists, one at a time, not needing to feel the ridges to know they were there. "I know what it was, Rowan," I said unevenly. "No man, living through that, would willingly serve the enemy. Not when his rightful lord is come home."

He stared again at the ground. I saw the rigidity in his shoulders. "I will do whatever you require." His voice was very quiet.

"I require you to wait here while I go, and to be vigilant in your watching." I smiled. "Lachlan may fool us all, in the end, by being precisely what he claims, but I would know my enemy before I give him my back. I trust to you and Torrin in this. See to it the harper does not leave and make off for Mujhara, to carry Bellam word of my where-abouts. See to it he cannot give any of us away."

Through the trees came the clashing of swords and the angry shout of an arms-master. The men drilled and drilled until they would drop, cursing the need for such practice even while they knew it was necessary. They had been gone from war too long, most of them; some of them had never known it. Men came from crofts and cities and even distant valleys, having heard the subtle word.

Carillon, it said. *Carillon is come home*.

I stood up, slapping at my leather breeches. The snow was slushy now, almost sodden; I thought the thaw would come soon. But not yet. I prayed not yet. We were nowhere close to being an army, and in spring I wanted to start my campaign against Bellam's men.

I smiled. In spring, when the planting began, so no one would be expecting battle. I would anticipate a summer campaign, and throw Bellam into disarray.

I hoped.

"He will know," Rowan said, "the Solindish king. He will send men."

I nodded. "Take the army deeper into the forest. Leagues from here. Leave no one with Torrin; I do not wish to endanger him. I want no fighting now. Better to hide like runaway children than give ourselves over to Bellam's men. See they do it, Rowan."

He crossed his arms and hugged his chest, as if he were suddenly cold. "My lord—take you care."

I grinned at him. "It is too soon to lose me yet. Does it come, it will come in battle." I turned away to my horse and untied his reins from a slender sapling. The same little dun Steppes gelding, still shaggy and ragged and ugly. Nothing like the warhorse my father had given me five years before.

Rowan's face was set in worried, unhappy lines. All his thoughts were in his eyes: he thought I would die and the rebellion come to an end.

I mounted and gathered in my reins. "She is my lady mother. I would have her know I live."

He nodded a little. "But to have to go where you know there are soldiers—"

"They will be expecting an army, not a single man." I touched the hilt of my sword, wrapped once again and scabbarded at my saddle. "I will be well enough."

I did not look back as I rode away from the young man I had learned to trust. But I knew he stood in the shade of the trees, squinting against the sun.

* * *

The walnut dye turned my hair dark and stiff and dull.
Grease made it shiny and foul. One braid, bound with a
leather lace, hung before my left ear. The beard was
already dark, and unknown to any who had seen me at
eighteen.

My teeth were good and I still boasted all of them. I
rubbed a resinous gum into them to turn them yellow and
foul my tongue. My clothes were borrowed, though I
doubted I would return them; the man who wore mine no
doubt preferred them to his, they being much better than
his rags. What I wore now was a threadbare woollen tunic,
once dark green, now brown with mud and grease. Matching woollen trews bagged at my knees, reaching only
halfway to my ankles. I had put off my boots and replaced
them with leather buskins.

Leather bracers hid my wrist scars, something a guard
might look for. No doubt Bellam had described me as tall,
tawny-dark and blue-eyed, with shackle scars on both
wrists. I was still tall, but now walked stooped, hitching a
leg, one shoulder crooked down as if a broken bone had
been improperly set. There was nothing of Bellam's
pretender-prince about me as I walked toward the village
surrounding Joyenne. Not even the sword and the bow,
for both could give me away. Both I had buried in the
snow beneath a rowan tree, marked with a lightning gash.
I carried only the knife, and that was sheathed beneath
my tunic against my ribs.

I scuffed through snow and slush, kicking out at the
dogs who ran up to see the stranger. Joyenne-town was
little more than a scattered village grown up because of
the castle. There were no walls, only dwellings, and the
people passing by. They took no note of me.

I could smell the stink of myself. More than that, I
could smell the stink of a broken homeland. The village I
had always known had been a good place, full of bustle
and industry. Like all villages it claimed its share of repro-
bates, but the people had mostly been happy. I had known
some of it well, as young men will, and I recalled some of
the women who had been happy to show favor to their

lord's tall son. And I wondered, for the first time in my life, whether I had gotten children on any of them.

The main track led directly to the castle. Joyenne proper, built upon a hill, with walls and towers and the glittering glass of leaded, mullioned casements. My father had taken great joy in establishing a home of which to be proud. Joyenne was where we lived, not fought; it was not a bastion to ward off the enemy but a place in which to rear children. But the gods had seen fit to give them stillborn sons and daughters, until Torry and then myself.

Joyenne was awash with sunlight, gold and bronze and brown. The ocher-colored stone my father had chosen had bleached to a soft, muted color, so that the sunlight glinted off corners and trim. Against the snowy hill it was a great blot of towered, turreted stone, ringed by walls and ramparts. There was an iron portcullis at the frontal gate, but rarely was it ever brought down. At least in my father's day. Joyenne had been open to all then, did they need to converse with their lord.

Now, however, the great mortar mouth was toothed with iron. Men walked the walls with halberds in their hands. Ringmail glinted silver in the sunlight. Bellam's banner hung from the staffs at each tower: a rising white sun on an indigo field.

Because I was a poor man and fouled with the grime of years, I did not go to the central gate. I went instead to a smaller one, stooped and crooked and hitching my leg along. The guards stopped me at once, speaking in poor Homanan. What was it, they asked, I wanted?

To see my mother, I said civilly, showing stained and rotting teeth. The scent of the gum was foul and sent them, cursing, two steps back. My mother, I repeated in a thick and phlegmy voice. The one who served within the castle.

I named a name, knowing there was indeed a woman who served the hall. I could not say if still she lived—she had been old when I had gone to war—but a single question would tell the men I did not lie. She had had a son, I knew, a son twisted from childhood disease. He had gone away to another village—her everlasting shame—but now, I thought, he would come back. However briefly.

The guards consulted, watching me with disgusted, arrogant eyes. They spoke in Solindish, which I knew not at all, but their voices gave them away. My stink and my grease and my twisted body had shielded me from closer inspection.

Weaponed? they asked gruffly.

No. I put out my hands as if inviting them to search. They did not. Instead they waved me through.

And thus Carillon came home again, to see his lady mother.

I hitched and shuffled and stooped, wiping my arm beneath my nose, spreading more grease and fouling my beard. I crossed the cobbled bailey slowly, almost hesitantly, as if I feared to be sent away again. The Solindishmen who passed me looked askance, offended by my stink. I showed them my yellowed, resined teeth in the sort of grin a dog gives, to show his submission; to show he knows his place.

By my appearance, I would be limited to the kitchens (or the midden.) It was where the woman had served. But my lady mother would be elsewhere, so I passed by the kitchens and went up to the halls, scraping my wet buskins across the wood of the floor.

There were few servants. I thought Bellam had sent most of them away in an attempt to humble my mother. For him, a usurper king, it would be important to wage war even against a woman. Gwynneth of Homana had been wed to the Mujhar's brother; a widow now, and helpless, but royal nonetheless. It would show his power if he humbled this woman so. But I thought it was unlikely he had succeeded, no matter how many guards he placed on the walls; no matter how many Solindish banners fluttered from the towers.

I found the proper staircase, winding in a spiral to an upper floor. I climbed, sensing the flutter in my belly. I had come this far, so far, and yet a single mistake could have me taken. Bellam's retribution, no doubt, would see me kept alive for years. Imprisoned and humiliated and tortured.

I passed out of the staircase into a hall, paneled in honey-gold wood. My father's gallery, boasting mullioned windows that set the place to glittering in the sun. But the beeswax polish had grown stale and dark, crusted at the edges. The gallery bore the smell of disuse and disinterest.

My hand slipped up between the folds of my soiled tunic, sliding through a rent in the cloth. I closed my fingers around the bone-handled hilt of my Caledonese knife. For a moment I stood at the polished wooden door of my mother's solarium, listening for voices within. I heard nothing. It was possible she spent her time elsewhere, but I had learned that men or women, in trying circumstances, will cling to what they know. The solar had ever been a favorite place. And so, when I was quite certain she was alone, I swung open the oiled panel.

I moved silently. I closed the door without a sound. I stood within the solar and looked at my mother, and realized she had grown old.

Her head was bent over an embroidery frame. What she stitched there I could not say, save it took all her attention to do it. The sunlight burned through the mullioned panes of the narrow casement nearest her and splashed across her work, turning the colored threads brilliant in the dimness of the room. I noticed at once there was a musty smell, as if the dampness of winter had never been fully banished by the warmth of the brazier fires. This had ever been a warm, friendly room, but now it was cold and barren.

I saw how she stitched at the fabric. Carefully, brows furrowed, in profile to me. And her hands—

Twisted, brittle, fragile things, knobbed with buttons of flesh at her knuckles and more like claws than fingers. So painstakingly she stitched, and yet with those hands I doubted she could do little more than thrust needle through fabric with little regard for the pattern. Disease had taken the skill from her.

I recalled then, quite clearly, how her hands had pained her in the dampness. How she had never complained, but grew more helpless with each month. And now, looking at her, I saw how the illness had destroyed the grace my father had so admired.

She wore a white wimple and coif to hide her hair, but a single loop escaped to curve down the line of her cheek.

Gray, all gray, when before it had been tawny as my own. Her face was creased with the soft, fine lines of age, like crumpled silk.

She had put on indigo blue, ever a favorite color with her. I thought I recognized the robe as an old one she had given up more than seven years before. And yet she wore it now, threadbare and thin and hardly worthy of her station.

Perhaps I made a sound. She lifted her head, searching, and her eyes came around to me.

I went to her and knelt down. All the words I had thought to say were flown. I had nothing but silence in my mouth and a painful cramping in my throat.

I stared hard at the embroidery in her lap. She had let it fall, forgotten, and I saw that the pattern—though ill-made—was familiar. A tall, bearded soldier on a great chestnut stallion, leading the Mujhar's army. I had loved it as a child, for she had called the man my father. It seemed odd that I would look now and see myself.

Her hand was on my head. At first I wanted to flinch away, knowing how foul the grease and dye had made me, but I did not move. With her other hand she set her fingers beneath my chin and turned up my face, so she could look upon me fully. Her smile was brilliant to see, and the tears ran down her face.

I reached out and caught her hands gently, afraid I might break them. They were so fragile in my own. I felt huge, overlarge, much too rough for her delicacy.

"Lady." My voice came out clogged and uneven. "I have been remiss in not coming to you sooner. Or sending word—"

Fingers closed my mouth. "No." She touched my beard lingeringly, then ran both hands through my filthy hair. "Was this through choice, or have you forgotten all the care I ever taught you?"

I laughed at her, though it had a hollow, brittle sound. "Exile has fashioned your son into another sort of man, I fear."

The lines around her eyes—blue as my own—deepened. And then she took her hands away as if she had finished with me entirely. I realized, in that instant, she was sacrificing the possessiveness she longed to show me. In her eyes I saw joy and pride and thankfulness, and a deep recognition of her son as a man. She was giving me my freedom.

I rose unsteadily, as if I had been too long without food. Her smile grew wider. "Fergus lives on in you."

I walked to the casement, overcome for the moment, and stared out blindly to watch the guards upon the ramparts. When I could, I turned back. "You know why I have come."

Her chin lifted. I saw the delicate, draped folds of the silkin wimple clustered at her throat. "I was wed to your father for thirty-five years. I bore him six children. It was the gods who decreed only two of those children would live to adulthood, but I am quite certain they have learned, both of them, what it is to be part of the House of Homana." The pride made her nearly young again. "Of course I know why you have come."

"And your answer?"

It surprised her. "What answer is there to duty? You *are* the House of Homana, Carillon—what is left for you to do but take back your throne from Bellam?"

I had expected no different, and yet it seemed passing strange to hear such matter-of-factness from my mother. Such things from a father are never mentioned, being known so well, but now I lacked a father. And it was my mother who gave me leave to go to war.

I moved away from the window. "Will you come with me? Now?"

She smiled. "No."

I made an impatient gesture. "I have planned for it. You will put on the clothes of a kitchen servant and walk out of here with me. It can be done. *I* have done it. It is too obvious for them to suspect." I touched my fouled, bearded face. "Grease your hair, sully your skirts, affect the manners of a servant. It is your life at risk—you will do well enough."

"No," she said again. "Have you forgotten your sister?"

"Torry is in Homana-Mujhar." I thought it answer enough as I glanced out the casement again. "It is somewhat more difficult for me to get into Homana-Mujhar, but once we are safely gone from here, then I will turn my plans to Torry."

"No," she repeated, and at last she had my complete attention. "Carillon, I doubt not you have thought this out well, but I cannot undertake it. Tourmaline is in danger. She is hostage to Bellam against just this sort of thing; do you think he would sit and do nothing?" I saw the anguish in her eyes as she looked into my frowning face. "He would learn, soon enough, I had gotten free of his guards. And he would turn to punish your sister."

I crossed to her at once, bending to catch her shoulders in my hands. "I cannot leave you here! Do you think I could live with myself, knowing you are here? You have only to look at this room, stripped bare of its finery and left cold, no doubt to freeze your bones. Mother—"

"No one harms me," she said clearly. "No one beats me. I am fed. I am merely kept as you see me, like a pauper-woman." The twisted hands reached up to touch my leather-clad wrists. "I know what you have risked, coming here. And were Tourmaline safe, I would come with you. But I will not give her over to Bellam's wrath."

"He did it on purpose, to guard against my coming." That truth was something I should have realized long ago, and had not. "Divide the treasure and the thieves are defeated." I cursed once, then tried to catch back the words, for she was my lady mother.

She smiled, amused, while the tears stood in her eyes. "I cannot. Do you understand? I thought you were dead, and my daughter lost. But now you are here, safe and whole, and I have some hope again. Go from here and do what you must, but go without me to hinder you." She put out her hands as I sought to speak. "See you how I am? I would be a burden. And that I refuse, when you have a kingdom to win back."

I laughed, but there was nothing of humor in it. "All my fine plans are disarranged. I thought to win you free of here and take you to my army, where you would be safe. And then I would set about planning to take Torry—or take Homana-Mujhar." I sighed and shook my head, sensing the pain of futility in my soul. "You have put me in my place."

"Your place is Homana-Mujhar." She rose, still clasping my hands with her brittle, twisted fingers. "Go there. Win your throne and your sister's freedom. And then I will go where you bid me."

I caught her in my arms and then, aghast, set her aside with a muttered oath. Filthy as I was—

She laughed. She touched the smudge of grease on her crumpled-silk face and laughed, and then she cried, and this time when I hugged her I did not set her at once aside.

EIGHT

I went out of Joyenne as I had gone in: with great care. Stooping and hitching I limped along, head down, making certain I did not hasten. I went out the same gate I had come in, muttering something to the Solindish guards, who responded with curses and an attempt to trip me into a puddle of horse urine pooling on the cobbles. Perhaps falling would have been best, but my natural reflexes took over and kept me from sprawling as the leg shot out to catch my ankle. I recalled my guise at once and made haste to stumble and cry out, and when I drew myself up it was to laughter and murmured insults in the Solindish tongue. And so I went away from my home and into the village to think.

My mother had the right of it. Did I take her out of Joyenne, Bellam would know instantly I had come back, and where. Who else would undertake to win my mother free? She had spent five years in captivity within her own home and no one had gotten her out. Only I would be so interested as to brave the Solindish guards.

It is a humbling feeling to know all your plans have been made for naught, when you should have known it at the outset. Finn, I thought, would have approached it differently. Or approached it not at all.

I retrieved my horse from the hostler at a dingy tavern and went at once, roundabout, to the rowan tree to unearth my sword and bow. It felt good to have both in my hands again, and to slough off the tension my journey into Joyenne had caused me. I hung my sword at my hips again, strapped on the Cheysuli bow, and mounted the gelding once more.

I rode out across the snowfields and headed home again. To a different home, an army, where men planned and drilled and waited. To where Homana's future waited. And I wondered how it had come to pass men would claim a single realm their own, when the gods had made it for all.

I thought of Lachlan then, secure within his priesthood. He had told me how it was for him; how Lodhi's service did not require celibacy or cloistering or the foolishness of similar things. His task, he had said, was merely to speak of Lodhi to those who would listen, in hopes they would learn the proper way. I had acknowledged his freedom to do so, knowing my own lay in other gods, but he had never pressed me on it, and for that I was grateful indeed.

The sun burned yellow in an azure sky, reflecting from the snow. The horse sweated and so did I; the grease stank so badly I wanted to retch and rid myself of its stench. But until I had time to bathe myself I would have to remain as I was.

I saw them then, silhouetted against the skyline. Four men atop a hill, shapes only, with sunlight glittering off their ringmail. All save one, who wore dark clothes instead. No mail. No sword at all.

My heart moved within my chest in the squirm of sudden foreboding. Intentionally I kept my hand from my sword, riding onward along the narrow track beaten into the slushy snow. Men had the freedom to come and go as they pleased; Solindish or not, they had the right to ride where they would. And I had better not gain their attention with a show of arms or strength.

The hill lay to my right, and ahead. I rode on doggedly, round-shouldered and slumped, affecting no pride or curiosity. The four waited atop the hill, well-mounted and silent, still little more than shapes at this distance, yet watching. Watching always.

I did not quicken the gelding's pace. I made no movement to call attention, and yet I could feel their eyes as they watched me, waiting, as I passed the crest of their hill. Still it lay to my right, bulging up out of a rift through which ran the smallest of snow-melt streams. That stream lay to my left; I rode between water and men. The gelding snorted, unimpressed, but I thought he sensed my tension.

The ringmail blazed in the brilliant sun. Solindishmen, I knew. Homanan mail was darker, duller, radiating less light in the sun. Showing less light in the starlit darkness when armies moved to set an ambush. It was something my father had taught me; perhaps Bellam was too sure of his men and saw no need for such secrecy.

I rode on. And so did they.

Three of them. The men in mail. They came directly down the hill toward me, moving to cut me off, and I saw them draw their swords. This was no parley, no innocent meeting of strangers. It was blood they wanted, and I had none to spare.

I doubted I could outrun them. The snow was thick and slushy, treacherous footing to any horse, but to mine in particular: short-legged and slighter of frame. Still, he was willing, and when I set him to a run he plunged through the heavy going.

Snow whipped into the air in a fine, damp spray, churned up beneath driving hooves. I bent low and forward, shifting weight over the moving shoulders. I heard the raspy breathing of my horse and the shouts of men behind me.

The gelding stumbled, recovered, then went down to his knees. Riding forward as I was, the fall pitched me neatly off over his head. It was not entirely unexpected; I came up at once, spinning to face the oncoming men, and stripped the bow from my back.

The arrow was nocked. Loosed. It took the first soldier full in the throat, knocking him off his horse. The next shaft blurred home in the second man's chest, but the third one was on me and there was no more time for a bow.

The sword slashed down to rip the bow from my hands. I stumbled, slipping to my knees in the slushy snow, and wrenched free the sword in my scabbard. Both hands clamped down on the leather-wrapped hilt. I pushed myself up to my feet.

The Solindishman swung back, commanding his horse with his knees. I saw the sunlight flashing off his blade as the man rode toward me. I saw also the badge he wore: Bellam's white sun on an indigo field.

The soldier rode me down. But he paused to deliver what he thought was the death-blow; I ducked it at once and came up with my blade, plunging it into the horse's belly. The animal screamed and staggered at once, floundering to his knees. The soldier jumped off instantly and met me on common ground.

His broadsword was lifted high to come down into my left shoulder. I caught his blade on my own and swung it up diagonally from underneath, wrist-cords tightening beneath the leather bracers. He pulled away at once, dropping to come under my guard; I met his blow with a downward stroke across my body. He changed then, shifting his stance to come at me another way, but I broke his momentum and slid under his guard with ease, plunging my sword to the hilt through his ribs. Steel blade on steel mail shrieked in disharmony a moment, and then I freed my sword as the body slumped to the snow.

I turned at once, searching for the man who wore no ringmail or sword, but saw no one. The crest of the hill was empty. I listened, standing perfectly still, but all I heard was the trickling of the tiny streamlet as it ran down through its channel.

The Solindish warhorse was dead. The horses belonging to the two soldiers dead of arrows had gone off, too far for me to chase. I was left with my shaggy Steppes horse, head hanging as he sought to recover from his flight.

I sheathed my sword, reclaimed my bow and mushed over to him through the snow, cursing the wet of my buskins and the chill of ice against my flesh. The ragged clothing I wore was soaked through from the flight and the fight. And I still stank.

I put out my hand to catch dangling reins and felt something crawl against the flesh of my waist. I slapped at it at once, cursing lice and fleas; slapped again when the tickling repeated itself. I set my hand against the hilt of my Caledonese knife and felt it move.

I unsheathed it at once, jerking it into the sunlight. For

a moment I stared at it, seeing blade and bone, and then I saw it move.

Every muscle tensed. The horse snorted uneasily behind me. I stood there and stared, fascinated as the bone reshaped itself.

It was growing. In my hand. The smooth, curving hilt lengthened, pulling itself free of the blade's tang. The runes and scripture melted away into the substance of the bone, as if the pieces carved away to make the shapes were replacing themselves.

And then I knew I was watched.

I looked up at once, staring at the low ridge of the hill from which the Solindishmen had come. There, dark against the blue of the sky, was the fourth man. The one without ringmail or sword. Too far for me to discern his features, save I knew he watched and waited.

Ihlini, I knew instantly.

I threw the knife away in a convulsive, sickened movement. I reached at once for my bow, intending to loose an arrow. But I stopped almost at once, because an arrow against sorcery claims no strength.

The bone. The thighbone of a monstrous beast, the king of Caledon had said. And the Ihlini had conjured the source of the bone, placing it before me in the snowfields of Homana.

The bones knit themselves together. From one came another, then another, until they ran together and built the skeleton. The spine, ridged and long. Massive shoulder joints. And the skull, pearly white, with gaping orbits for eyes.

Then, more quickly, the viscera. The brain. The vessels running with blood. The muscles, wrapping themselves into place, until the flesh overlay it all. And the hide on top of that.

I gaped at the beast. I knew what it was, of course; my House had used it forever as a crest, to recall the strength and courage of the mythical beast, long gone from the world.

The lion of Homana.

It leaped. It gathered itself and leaped directly at the horse, and took him down with the swipe of one huge paw. I heard the dull snap of a broken neck, then saw the beast turn toward me.

I dropped my bow. I ran. So did the lion run. It was a huge flash of tawny golden-yellow; black-maned past his shoulders, tail wiry as if it lived. I ran, but I could not outrun it. And so I turned, unsheathing my sword, and tried to spit the lion on it.

It leaped. Up into the air it leaped, hind legs coiling to push it off the ground, front paws reaching out. My ears shut out the fearful roar so that I heard only the pounding of my blood as it ran into my head.

One paw reached out and caught me across the head. But I ducked most of the weight; in ducking, I saved my life. The blow, had it landed cleanly, would have broken my neck at once. As it was part of the paw still caught me, knocking me down, so that I feared my jaw was shattered. Blood ran freely from my nose.

Even as I went down I kept my sword thrust up. I saw the blade bite into the massive chest, tearing through the hide. It caught on bone, then grated as the lion's leap carried it past.

I was flat on my back in the snow. I was up almost at once, too frightened to take refuge in the pain and shock. My head rang and blood was in my mouth. My sword was no use against the lion unless I hit a vital spot. To try for that would put me too close, well within its range. I did not relish feeding it on my flesh.

The lion's snarl was a coughing, hacking sound. Its mane stood out from the hide, black and tangled. But the muscles rippled cleanly against the tawny-gold; the wound had done nothing to gainsay it. Blood flowed, but still it came on.

I knew, instinctively, it would not die. I could not slay it by conventional means. The beast had been summoned by a sorcerer.

My foot came down on something hard as I backed away from the lion. I realized I had run in a circle, so that I was back where I had begun. The horse lay where the lion had put it. And the bow lay under my feet.

I dropped the sword at once and caught up the bow. I

snatched an arrow from my quiver. As the beast leaped yet again I nocked the arrow and spun—

—let fly. But not at the lion. At the man.

The shaft went home in the sorcerer's chest. I saw him stagger, clutching the arrow, then he slumped down to his knees. He was abruptly haloed in a sphere of purple fire that sprung up around his body. And then the arrow burst into brilliant crimson flames and he was dead.

I swung back. The beast was nothing but bone. A single, hilt-shaped bone, lying in the snow.

I sank down to my knees, slumping forward, until only my arms braced stiffly against the snow held me up. My breath came from deep in my chest in wheezing gasps, setting my lungs afire. Blood still ran from my nose, staining the snow, and my head ached from the blow. I spat out a tooth and hung there, spent, to let my body recover.

When at last I could stand again I weaved like a man too far gone in wine. I shook in every bone. I stumbled to the snow-melt stream and knelt there, scooping cold water and ice to cleanse my face and mouth of blood and filth and my mind of the blanking numbness.

I pushed to my feet again. Slowly, moving like an old, old man, I gathered up bow and sword. The knife hilt I left lying in the snow. That I would never carry again.

The Ihlini was quite dead. His body was sunken within his clothing, as if the arrow had somehow loosed more than life, but a force as well; released, its shell had shrunk. It was a body still, but not much of a man.

The Ihlini's horse stood part way down the backside of the ridge. It was a dark brown gelding, not fine but good. An Ihlini's horse, and ensorcelled?

I caught the reins from the ground and brought the horse closer. Taller than the dun. Shedding his winter hair. He had kind eyes, clipped mane and short tail. One spot of white was on his face. I patted his jaw and mounted.

I nearly fell off again. My head spun and throbbed with renewed ferocity; the lion had rattled my senses. I huddled in the saddle a long moment, eyes shut, waiting for the pain and dizziness to diminish.

Carefully I touched my face and felt the swollen flesh.,

No doubt I would purple by nightfall. But my nose, for all it ached, was whole. And then, done marking my numerous aches, I turned the horse and rode eastward.

Torrin's dog ran out to meet me. In the weeks since we had come he had grown, now more dog than pup, but his ebullience was undiminished. He loped along next to my horse and warned Torrin of my presence. It was not necessary; Torrin was at the well fishing up the bucket.

In five years, Torrin had not changed much. His gray hair was still thinning, still cropped against his head. He still bore seams in his flesh and calluses on his hands. Crofting had changed his body from the bulk of an armsmaster's to the characteristic slump of a man who knew sheep and land, but I could still see his quiet competence. He had been born to blades, not the land, and yet for Alix's sake he had given all of that up. Because Shaine had wanted to be rid of her, and Torrin could not bear to see the infant left to die.

I rode up slowly. The horse made his way to the well and put his head into the bucket Torrin held. Torrin, looking up at me from brown eyes couched in fleshy folds, shook his head. "Was that Solindish-done?"

He meant my face. I touched it and said no. "Ihlini. He summoned a beast. A lion."

The color changed in his leathered cheeks. "Bellam knows—"

I shook my head before he could finish. "He may not. The men who sought to slay me are dead. I have no doubt he knows I am back—most people do—but there is no one left to tell him where I am. I think we will be safe a little longer."

He looked troubled, but I had no more time to wonder at it. I bent forward and swung off the horse slowly, wincing from the bruises. I left the horse with Torrin and slowly made my way to the croft. Wood smoke veiled the air.

"My lord, I think—"

I turned back before the door, interrupting in my weariness. "You have a half-cask, do you not? Clothes I left with you. Soap and water? Hot. I wish to boil myself free of this stench."

He nodded, brow furrowed. "Do you wish me to—"

"No." I lifted a hand in a weary wave. "I will see to it myself." It was something I had learned in exile. I needed no servants to fetch and carry.

"My lord—" he tried again, but I went into the croft.

And stopped. It was Alix.

She stood by the table before the fire, with her arms plunged into a bubble of bread dough set out on a board. Flour reached to her elbows. I saw at once her dark brown hair had grown long enough to braid, pinned against her head with silver clasps that glittered in the sunlight slanting in the open door.

I saw again the girl I had befriended, when a prince had so few real friends. I saw again the girl who had been the reason for my capture by Finn and his raiding party. I saw again the girl whose Cheysuli *tahlmorra* was so firmly linked with my own Homanan fate.

But mostly I saw the girl who had become a woman, and I hated the time I had lost.

There was a question in her eyes, and bafflement. She knew me not, in my foul and filthy state, bearded and greased and bruised. I thought of what kind of man I had been five years before, and what I was now, and I laughed.

And then, as her mouth shaped my name, I crossed the tiny room and caught her in my arms.

She hugged me as tightly as I hugged her, saying my name again and again. She smelled of bread dough and wood smoke, and laughed as if she could not stop.

"So *filthy*—" she said, "and so *humble*—"

I had never been that. But I laughed with her, for what she saw was true if, perhaps, to a lesser extent than she thought. Or for different reasons. I was humbled, it was true, by the very thing that elevated so many men: I wanted her. And so, unable to help myself, I cupped her head in my hands and kissed her.

Only once had I kissed her before, and under such circumstances as she could claim it a token of my thanks. I had meant that, then, too, but more as well. But by then, when she rescued me from the Atvians, she had already pledged herself to Duncan. She had carried his child in her belly.

Now, she did not rescue me. There was nothing of gratefulness about what I was feeling; she could not construe it as such. In five years I had had time to think of Alix, and regret what had not happened between us, and I could not hide my feelings.

And yet there was Duncan, still, between us.

I let her go. I still longed to touch her, but I let her go. She stood quietly before me, color high in her face, but there was a calmness in her eyes. She knew me better than I did.

"That much you may have, having taken it already," she said quietly, "but no more."

"Are you afraid what might grow up from this beginning?"

She shook her head once. "Nothing can grow up from this beginning. There is nothing—here." She touched her left breast, indicating her heart. Her gaze was perfectly steady.

Almost I laughed. It was so distinct a change. She had gained understanding and comprehension, aware of what she was. Gone was the virgin, confused by body and emotions. Now she was woman, wife and mother, and she knew. I was not enough.

"I have thought of you for years," I said. "All those nights in exile."

"I know." Her tone did not waver for an instant. "Had you been Duncan, I would have felt the same. But you were—and are—not. You are yourself. You are special to me, it is true, but it is far too late for more. Once, perhaps . . . but all of that time has passed."

I took a deep breath and tried to regain my composure. "I did not—did not mean to do this. I meant only to greet you again. But it seems I cannot keep my hands from you now any more than I ever could." I smiled wryly. "An admission few men would make to a woman who will not have them."

Alix smiled. "Finn said much the same. His greeting was—similar."

"And Duncan?"

"Duncan was—elsewhere. He is not an insensitive man."

"Nor ever was." I sighed and scratched my jaw beneath the beard. "Enough of this. I came in to wash, as you see."

"Good." Some of the tension vanished and the light came into her eyes. The warm, amber eyes I recalled so well—so perfect a melding of Cheysuli and Homanan, more beautiful to me than either. "I doubt I could stand your stink one more moment." She turned away at once to the fire in the low stone fireplace, kneeling to add wood, then glanced over her shoulder at me. "Perhaps you would fill the cauldron with water?" And then color blazed up high in her face, as if she recalled I was royal and above such lowly things.

I grinned. "I will fetch it and set out the cask. Do you forget?—I have been with Finn all these years. I am not quite the same as you knew me." I left her then, having caught up the heavy cauldron, and went out to fill it with water.

Torrin sat on the edge of the stone-ringed well, smoking his clay pipe. His grizzled eyebrows rose. "I thought to warn you she was here," he said around the stem.

I grunted as I began to crank up the bucket. "I had not thought it was so obvious to everyone."

"To me." Torrin got up to steady the bucket as it came up from the water. He caught it and poured its contents into the cauldron. "She was so young when first you met her. Then so new to her heritage, knowing little of royal things. And finally, of course, there was Duncan."

The name dropped into my soul like a stone. "Aye . . . he had more sense than I. He saw what he wanted and took it."

"He *won* it," Torrin said quietly. "My lord—do you think to win her back from him, think again. I was her father for seventeen years. Even now, I feel she is mine. I will not have her hurt, or her happiness harmed. She loves him deeply." He dropped the bucket down when it was emptied and met my eyes without the flicker of an eyelid. As he had, no doubt, met my uncle's unwavering stare. "You are the Mujhar, and have the right to do what you will, even with the Cheysuli. But I think you have more sense than that."

For most of my life I had been given what I wanted, including women. Alix I had lost before I knew how much I wanted her. And now, knowing it keenly, I knew how much it hurt to lose.

Especially to Duncan.

Alix came to the door of the white-washed, thatch-roofed croft with its gray stone chimney. "The fire is ready." Around her neck shone the golden torque made in the shape of a flying hawk, wings outspread and beak agape, with a chunk of amber caught in the clutching talons. A *lir*-torque and Cheysuli bride-gift. Made for her by Duncan.

I hoisted the cauldron and lugged it inside, hanging it from the iron hook set into the stone of the blackened fireplace. I sat on a stool and waited, aware of her every movement, and stared at the fire as she kneaded the dough again.

"When did you come?" I asked at last.

"Eight days ago. Finn brought us here." A warm, bright smile shone on her face.

"He is back?" I felt better almost at once.

"He brought us down from the North." The silver pins in her coiled braids glittered in the sunlight as she worked. The folds of her moss-green gown moved as she moved, shifting with the motion of her body. The overtunic, with sheepskin fleece turned inward, was dyed a pale, soft yellow, stitched in bright green yarn. It hung to her knees, belted at her waist with brown leather and a golden buckle. Cheysuli finery, not Homanan; she was all Cheysuli now.

I scratched at my itching face. "He is well?"

"Finn? Oh, aye—when is he not? He is Finn." She smiled again, beating the dough with her hands. "Though I think he has another thing to occupy himself with, now."

"A woman," I predicted. "Has he found someone among the clan?"

She laughed. "No, not a woman. My son." Her smile widened into a grin. "There are times Donal is more like his *su'fali* than his *jehan*. And now they have become close friends as well, I have only Finn to blame for my son's little indescretions. One was bad enough; now there are two."

"Two Finns?" I thought about it, laughing, and saw Alix shake her head.

"Shall I bid them come?" she asked, still kneading. "I have only to speak to Cai and Storr."

I thought again of the power she held, the boundless magic that ran in her veins. Old Blood, it was, a gift reborn of the gods. Alix, and only Alix, could converse with any *lir*. Or take any shape at will.

"No," I said. "I will go up myself, when I have shed my weight of dirt." I checked the water and found it nearly hot. Then I asked for the half-cask; Alix told me where it was and I dragged it out of the tiny antechamber, if a croft could be said to have a proper one. The half-cask was bound with hammered copper. It still smelled faintly of cider, betraying its original purpose. In Homana-Mujhar I had bathed in oak-and-silver cask-tubs polished smooth, so no splinters threatened my flesh. I doubted this one was as good, but it would serve. In exile I had learned to be grateful for anything.

I rolled the cask into Torrin's tiny bedchamber, containing a pallet, chest and chair. There I tipped the cask on its end, then began filling it from the cauldron. When at last it stood ready I went seeking cloth and soap.

Alix gave me both. "Torrin has changed nothing since I left," she said with a nostalgic smile, and I wondered if she recalled the day Finn had stolen us both.

How could she not? I did. Too well. And the changes that had occurred since then.

I looked at her a long moment, my hands full of threadbare cloth and hard brown soap. I wished there was more I could say. And then I said it anyway. "I will insult neither you nor your husband by pursuing you where I am not wanted."

Color flared in her face again. I marked how the years had melted away the flesh of youth, leaving her with the characteristic angular, high-planed Cheysuli face. Her face was more like Finn's than ever before; the children showing the father's blood.

"There was no need to say it," she told me softly.

"There was. Otherwise I could not account for my actions." Briefly I touched her face with the backs of two fingers. "Alix—once we might have shared so much. Let us keep of it what we can." I took my hand away and went into the gloomy bedchamber where the water steamed in the air. I pulled the curtain closed and stripped out of my filthy garb.

I could not put her from my mind. I thought of her in the other room, kneading away, knowing she had Duncan close at hand. I thought of her with him, at night. I thought of her as I had known her: a young, sweet-natured girl with coltish grace and an integrity few men possess.

And I thought how odd a thing it is that two people can inhabit a single room, each knowing how the other one feels, and knowing there is no good in it.

No good at all. Only pain.

NINE

The half-cask, unfortunately, did not accommodate a man of my size. It was an awkward bath. I sat with my knees doubled up nearly beneath my chin and my spine crushed against the wood. But it was wet and hot and I scrubbed with every bit of strength I had, ridding myself of all the dirt and grease. Even that in my hair and beard.

When at last I could breathe again, stripped of the stench of my disguise, I relaxed. I hung my legs outside of the cask and sat back, tipping my head against the wooden rim. The flesh of my face still ached from the lion's blow; the rest of my body hurt as much. I felt older than my years. The lion had drained my strength; that, and the knowledge of Ihlini sorcery.

The water cooled, but not so fast I could not take my time getting out. And so I did. I let go of all my breath, let my muscles turn to rags, and promptly went to sleep.

"Carillon."

I jerked awake. My spine scraped against the rough wood and I cursed, staring in some confusion at Finn, who stood just inside the doorway with the curtain pulled closed behind him. Thoughtful of my modesty, for once; perhaps it was Alix who elicited such care.

I sat upright and pulled my legs back in, scowling at him. Finn merely smiled, amused to find me in such a state, and leaned back against the wall with bare arms folded across his chest. He had put off his winter leathers in deference to the thaw; I saw again the heavy gold that banded his arms above the elbows. Wide, beautiful things, embossed with runes and wolf-shape. He wore snug leathers again: leggings and a sleeveless jerkin. At his belt hung the Steppes knife, and I thought again of the sorcery I had seen.

"When did you get back?" he asked quite calmly.

I stood up, dripping, and reached for the blanket he tossed me from Torrin's pallet. "Not so long ago that I have had time to fill my belly."

"But time for a bath." His tone was perfectly flat, but I had little trouble discerning his intent. I had not had that trouble for some years now.

"Had you seen me—or *smelled* me—you would have pushed me in yourself." I climbed out of the cask and pulled on the dark brown breeches, then bent to jerk on the knee boots. My shirt was green. I put a brown jerkin over it and belted it with leather and bronze. "I thought I would go up to the army. Will you come?"

"Ah, the army." Finn smiled his ironic smile. "Do you wish to call it that."

I scowled at him, combing my fingers through my wet hair. It tangled on my shoulders and dampened the fabric of shirt and jerkin. "Rowan has done what he can to assemble men willing to fight. I will use what I can. Do you expect me to gather the thousands Bellam has?"

"It makes no difference." Finn followed me through to the other room, where Alix knelt to hang the pot of bread dough over the fire. "You will have the Cheysuli, and that is enough, I think." He put out a hand to Storr, seated by the table.

I scoffed. "I have *you*. And no doubt Duncan, and perhaps those he has managed to persuade to join me in the name of the prophecy." I scooped up a clay jug of Torrin's sour wine and poured myself a cup, pouring a second for Finn as he nodded willingness to drink.

"You have more than a few." He accepted the cup without thanks and swallowed half the wine at once. "How many would you ask for, could you have a larger number?"

I returned the jug to its place on the sideboard near the fireplace and perched upon the table as I drank. "The

Cheysuli are the finest fighting men in all of Homana." He did not smile at my compliment; it was well known. "And with each warrior I would gain a *lir*, so double the number at once." I shrugged. "A single warrior is worth at least five of another, so with a *lir* it is ten to one." I shook my head. "It is folly to wish for what I cannot have. Nonetheless, I would be more than pleased with one hundred."

"What of *three* hundred?" Finn smiled. "Perhaps even more."

I stared at him, forgoing my wine altogether. "Have you turned sorcerer, to conjure up false men?"

"No." Finn tossed his empty cup to Alix, who caught it and put it with the jug. "I have conjured up men I thought long dead. Shaine, you see, did not slay as many as we feared."

I set my cup down very precisely in the center of the table. "Are you saying—?"

"Aye." He grinned. "While searching for my clan, I found others. The Northern Wastes boast many places where a clan may hide, and I found several of them. It took time, but we have gathered together every warrior we could find." He shrugged. "All the clans are here; we are building a Keep beyond the hill."

He said it so simply: "*All the clans are here; we are building a Keep beyond the hill.*"

I stared at him. A Keep. *With three hundred warriors and their lir.*

I whooped. And then I was on my feet, clasping him in my arms as if I could not let him go. No doubt too demonstrative for Finn's sensibilities, but he knew the reason. And he smiled, stepping away when I was done.

"My gift to you," he said lightly. "Now, come with me and I will show you."

We went out at once, leaving Alix to tend her bread, and Finn gave me back my Ihlini horse. His eyes were on it, for he had known me to ride the dun, but he waited until we were free of the croft and riding toward the hill before he asked me about it, and then obliquely.

"Torrin said you had gone to Joyenne."

"Aye. To get my lady mother out."

"You did not succeed?"

"No, but only because she refused to come." The sunlight was bright in our eyes. I put up a hand to block the stunning brilliance. "Bellam holds Tourmaline, my sister. He has for some time. I do not doubt he keeps her safe, being who she is, but I want her free of him." I swore suddenly as the anger boiled over. "By the gods, the man threatens to wed her!"

We rode abreast with Storr leading the way. Finn, frowning, nodded, saying little. "It is the way of kings. Especially usurper kings."

"He will not usurp my *sister*!"

"Then do you mean to dance into Homana-Mujhar as easily as you did into Joyenne?"

And so I knew what he thought of my actions. I scowled at him blackly. "I got in and got out with little trouble. I was careful. No one knew me."

"And did you yourself put those bruises on your face?"

I had nearly forgotten. My hand went to my jaw and touched the sore flesh. "The Ihlini did this. Or rather: his conjured beast."

"Ah." Finn nodded in apparent satisfaction. "No trouble at Joyenne, you say, but an Ihlini set a beast on you." He sighed, shaking his head. "Why should I concern myself with your welfare? All you manage to do is tangle with one of Tynstar's minions."

His irony, as ever, galled me. "Enough. It was not my fault the men found me. They could have found me here."

"*Men?* First it was an Ihlini and his beast. Now there are more." He gestured to direct me up the hill.

I glared at him. "Why not just compel me to tell you the truth, as you did Lachlan?"

"Because I had believed you knew enough to tell me willingly."

I sighed and leaned forward as my horse climbed the hill toward the treeline. "You should not worry. I slew them all, even the Ihlini."

"I have no reason to worry," he agreed. "What have I done, save swear a blood-oath to serve you always?" For the first time a hint of anger crept into his voice. "Do you think I waste my time? Do you wish to do this alone? Think how many times over you would have been slain without me. And now, when I leave you to seek my clan—at your behest—you place yourself in such jeopardy even a child knows better."

"Finn—enough."

"*Not* enough." He glared at me openly now. "There is some little of my life invested in you. *All of it*, now. What we do is not entirely for you, Carillon, and for Homana, but for the Cheysuli as well." His mouth tightened as he reined his horse back even with mine. "Were you to die now, in some foolish endeavor of your own devising, the rebellion would fail. Bellam would rule forevermore. He would likely wed your sister, get new sons on her, and put *them* on the throne behind himself. Is that what you wish?"

I reached out and caught his reins, jerking his horse to a halt. All the anger and frustration came pouring out as pride. "I am your *prince!*"

"And I your liege man!" He ignored the jerk of the reins against his hands. "Do you think it is so easy for me to watch you as a father with a son? I am not your *jehan*, Carillon, merely your liege man. And a cousin, of a sort, because my *jehan* saw fit to lie with a haughty Homanan princess when he had a *cheysula* at home!"

He had never said so much before. Had coming home done it? I knew the differences in myself. Perhaps there were some in Finn as well.

I let go his reins and minded my own, though I did not start up the hill quite yet. "Does the service grow so tedious, seek another," I suggested bitterly.

His laugh was a short bark of sound. "How? The gods have tied me to you. Better yet: they have set iron around your neck as well as mine, and locked them together, like oxen in a yoke."

I sat in the blinding gold of the late afternoon sun and said nothing for a long moment. And then when I did, I asked a question I had not thought to ask before: "What do you want from this life?"

He was surprised. I could see it in his eyes. He understood perfectly well what I asked, and probably why, but he went on to step around the question. "I want you on the throne of Homana."

"Given that," I agreed, "what more?"

"The Cheysuli free to live as they would again."

"Given that." Had I to do it, I would ask him until the moon came up.

Finn squinted into the sun, as if the light would shield his feelings from me, or lessen the pain of the question. He appeared to have no intention of answering me, but this once I would make him.

"Finn," I said patiently, with all the solemnity I could muster, "were the gods to give you anything, *anything* at all, what would you ask for?"

At last he looked directly at me. The sunlight, striking through the trees like illuminated spears, was my unwitting servant. All of Finn's soul was bared to me in the light. This once, just once, but enough for me to see it. "You have not met Donal, have you?"

I thought it a question designed to lead me away from the quarry, like a dog led away by a clever fox. "Alix's son? No. I have only just got here. *Finn*—"

But he was serious. "Could I have it, I would ask for a son." He said it abruptly, as if the admission endangered the hope, and then he rode away from me as if he had shared too much.

There were no tracks to mark an army, no pall of smoke hanging above the treeline to mark the army's presence. There was nothing Bellam could use to seek me out. Finn took me into the forest away from the valley and I knew the army was safe. Rowan had done my bidding by taking them deeper into cover; even I could not say there was an army near, and it was mine.

The forest was overgrown with vines and creepers and brambles and bushes. Ivy fell down from the trees to trip the horses and foul the toes of my boots. Mistletoe clustered in the wooden crotches and a profusion of flowers hailed our passing. Homana. At last. Home again, for good, after too long a time spent in exile.

Sunlight spilled through the leaves and speckled the forest floor into goldens, greens and browns. Finn, riding before me, broke a pheasant from cover and I heard the whirring of its wings as it flew, whipping leaves and stirring sunmotes in its passage to the sky. I thought, suddenly, of the last time I had supped on pheasant: in Homana-Mujhar, feasting a guest, when my uncle had been pleased with a new alliance made. Too long ago. Too long being mercenary instead of prince.

I heard the harp and nearly stopped. There was nothing else save the threshing of the horses tearing through the brush and vines and creepers. But the harpsong overrode it all, and I recognized the hand upon the strings. "Lachlan," I said aloud.

Finn, reining in to ride abreast of me, nodded. "He has come each day, sharing his music with us. Once I might have dismissed it as idle whimsy, but no more. He has magic in that harp, Carillon—more even than we have seen. Already he has begun to give the Cheysuli what we have lacked these past years: peace of spirit." He smiled, albeit wryly. "Too long have we forgotten the music of our ancestors, thinking instead of war. The Ellasian has reminded us; he has given us some of it back again. I think there will be music made in the Keep again."

We passed through the final veil of leaves and vines and into the Keep. And yet it was no proper Keep, lacking the tall stone wall that circled the pavilions ordinarily. This was not a true Keep at all, not as I had known it, but a wide scattering of tents throughout the forest. There was no uniformity, no organization.

Finn ducked a low branch, caught it and held it back as I rode by. He saw the expression on my face. "Not yet. It will come later, when Homana is made safe again for such things as permanent Keeps." He released the branch and fell in next to me. "This is easily defensible. Easily torn down, do we need to move on again."

The tents huddled against the ground, like mushrooms beneath a tree. They were the colors of the earth: dark green, pale moss, slate-gray, rust-red, brown and black and palest cream. Small and plain, without the *lir*-symbols I remembered: tents instead of pavilions. But a Cheysuli Keep, for all its odd appearance.

I smiled, though it pained my injured face. I could not count them all. I could not see them all, so perfectly were they hidden, even though I knew how to look. And Bellam?

No doubt his men, if they came so far, would miss the Keep entirely.

Defensible? Aye—when an enemy does not see until too late. Torn down fast? Oh, aye—requiring but a moment to collapse the earth-toned fabric. A perfectly portable Keep.

And full of Cheysuli.

I laughed aloud and halted my horse. Around me spread the Keep, huddled and subtle and still. Around me spread my strength, equally subtle and silent and still. With the Cheysuli and an army besides, Bellam could never stop me.

"*Tahlmorra lujhalla mei wiccan, cheysu*," I said softly. *The fate of a man rests always within the hands of the gods.*

Finn, so silent beside me, merely smiled. "You are welcome to Homana, my lord. And to the homeplace of my people."

I shook my head, suddenly overcome. "I am not worthy of it all . . ." In that moment, I was certain of it. I was not up to the task.

"Are you not," my liege man said simply, "no man is."

When I could, I rode farther into the Keep. And thanked the gods for the Cheysuli.

TEN

The harpsong filled the forest. The melody was so delicate, so fragile, and yet so strong. It drew me as if it were a woman calling me to her bed; Lachlan's Lady, and I a man who knew her charm. I forgot the warriors Finn had promised and followed a song instead, feeling its magic reach out to touch my soul.

I found him at last perched upon the ruin of a felled beech, huge and satin-trunked. The tree had made its grave long since, but it provided a perfect bench—or throne—for the harper. The sunlight pierced the surrounding veil of branches and limbs like enemy spears transfixed upon a single foe: the harp. His Lady, so dark and old and wise, with her single green eye and golden strings. Such an eloquent voice, calling out; such a geas he laid upon me. I reined in my horse before the beech and waited until he was done.

Lachlan smiled. The slender, supple fingers grew quiet upon the glowing strings, so that music and magic died, and he was merely a man, a harper, blessed with Lodhi's pleasure.

"I knew you would come," he said in his liquid, silken voice.

"Sorcerer," I returned.

He laughed. "Some men call me so. Let them. You should know me better now." For a moment there was a glint of some unknown emotion in his eyes. "Friend," he said. "No more."

I realized we were alone. Finn I had left behind. And that, by itself, was enough to make me fear the Ellasian harper.

He saw it at once. Still he sat unmoving upon the beech trunk, his hands upon his Lady. "You came because I wished you to, and because *you* wished it," he said quietly. "Finn I did not require; not yet. But he will come, and Duncan." The sunlight was full upon his face. I saw no guile there, no subterfuge. Only honesty, and some little dedication. "I am a harper," he said clearly. "Harpers require men of legend in order to do what they do. You, my lord, are legend enough for most. Certainly for me." He smiled. "Have I not proven my loyalty?"

"Men will slay whom they are told to, do they have reason enough for it." I remained upon my horse, for I did not fully trust him with that harp held in his hands. "You slew the man I bid you to, but a spy would do so easily enough, merely to maintain his innocence."

He took his hands from the harp and spread them. "I am no spy. Save, perhaps, your own."

"*Mine.*" I said nothing more; for the moment he had made me speechless. And then I looked deeper into his eyes. "Would you, an Ellasian, serve me, a Homanan, in anything I bid you?"

"Providing it did not go against my conscience," he said at once. "I am a priest of the All-Father; I will not transgress any of His teachings."

I made a dismissing gesture. "I would ask no man to go against his lights. Not in something such as his gods. No. I mean, Lachlan, to see just how loyal you are."

"Then bid me," he returned. "I am here because I wish to be, not because some Ihlini sorcerer or Solindish king has sent me. And if they had, would I not take them the news they wish to hear? Would I still be here, when I could tell them the location of the Cheysuli and your army?"

"A wise spy, spies," I told him flatly. "The hare that breaks too soon is caught quickly by the fox."

He laughed. Lachlan's laugh is warm, generous, a true

casement of his soul. "But it is not a fox I fear, my lord . . . it is a wolf. A Cheysuli wolf." His eyes went past me. I did not turn, knowing who stood there.

"What would you do, then?" I asked.

The laughter had died. He looked at me directly. "Spy for you, Carillon. Go into Mujhara, to the palace itself, and see what Bellam does."

"Dangerous," Finn said from behind me. "The hare asks to break."

"Aye," Lachlan agreed. "But who else could do it? No Cheysuli, that is certain. No Homanan, for whom would Bellam admit without good reason? But I, *I* am a harper, and harpers go where they will."

It is true harpers are admitted to places other men cannot go. I knew from my own boyhood, when my uncle had hosted harpers from far and wide within Homana-Mujhar. A harper would be a perfect spy, that I did not doubt.

And yet—"Lachlan of Ellas," I said, "what service would you do me?"

His fingers flew against the strings. It was a lively tune, evocative of dance and laughter and youth. It conjured up a vision before my eyes: a young woman, lithe and lovely, with tawny-dark hair and bright blue eyes. Laughter was in her mouth and gaiety in her soul. My sister, Tourmaline, as I recalled her. At nineteen, when I had seen her last, though she would be twenty-four now.

Tourmaline, hostage to Bellam himself. And Lachlan knew it well.

I was off my horse at once, crossing to the beech in two long steps. My hands went out to stop his fingers in the strings, but I did not touch them after all. I felt a sudden upsurge of power so great it near threw me back from the man. I took a single step backward against my will, all unexpected, and then I stood very still.

His fingers slowed. The tune fell away until only an echo hung in the air. And then that, too, was gone, and silence built a wall between us.

"No," he said quietly. "No man gainsays the truth."

"You do not ensorcell *me!*"

"*I* do not," he agreed. "What power there is comes of

Lodhi, not His servant. And do you seek to injure my Lady, she will injure you." He did not smile. "I mean you no harm, my lord, nor my harp; yet harm may come to the man who means *me* harm."

I felt the upsurge of anger in my chest until it filled my throat. "I meant you no harm," I said thickly. "I merely wanted it to *stop*—"

"My Lady takes where she will," he said gently. "It is your sister who lives within you now, because of Bellam's power. I merely wished to show it to you, so you would know what I can do."

Finn was at my side. "What would you do?" he asked. "Free his sister from Bellam?"

Lachlan shook his head. "I could not do so much, not even with all of Lodhi's aid. But I *can* take her any word you might wish to give her, as well as learn what I can of Bellam's and Tynstar's plans."

"Gods!" The word hissed between my teeth. "Could I but trust you . . ."

"Do, my lord," he said gently. "Trust your liege man, if not me. Has he not questioned my intent?"

I let out my breath all at once, until my chest felt hollow and thin. I looked at Finn and saw the solemnity in his face. So much like Duncan, I thought, and at such odd times.

He looked directly at Lachlan. The sunlight set his *lir*-gold to shining like the strings in the harper's Lady. Neither man said a word, as if they judged one another; I found my own judgment sorely lacking, as if I had not the mind to discern what should be done. I was weary and hungry and overcome, suddenly, with the knowledge of what I must do.

"Trust him," Finn said finally, as if disliking the taste. "What is the worst he could do—tell Bellam where we are?" His smile held little humor. "Does he do that, and Bellam sends soldiers, we will simply slay them all."

No doubt he could do it, with three hundred Cheysuli warriors. And no doubt Lachlan knew it.

He stood up from the beech with his Lady clasped in his arms. Slowly he went down on one knee, still hugging the harp, and bowed his head a little. A proud man,

Lachlan; the homage was unexpected. It did not suit him, as if he were meant to receive it instead of offer. "I will serve you in this as I would have you serve me, were the roles reversed." His face was grimly set, and yet I saw the accustomed serenity in his eyes. That certainty of his fate.

Like Finn and his *tahlmorra*.

I nodded. "Well enough. Go you to Homana-Mujhar, and tend my service well."

"My lord." He knelt a moment longer, supplicant to a king instead of a god, and then he rose. He was gone almost at once, hidden by the shrubbery, with no word of parting in his mouth. But the harpsong, oddly, lingered on, as if he had called it from the air.

"Come," Finn said finally, "Duncan waits."

After a moment I looked at him. "Duncan? How does he know I have come?"

Finn grinned. "You are forgetting, my lord—we are in a Keep, of sorts. There are *lir*. And gossiping women, I do not doubt." The grin came again. "Blame me, or Storr, or even Cai, whom Storr tells me is the one who told Duncan you had come. He waits, does my *rujho*, somewhat impatiently."

"Duncan has never been impatient in his life." In irritation I turned back to my horse and swung up into the saddle. "Do you come? Or do I go without you?"

"*Now* who is impatient?" He did not wait for an answer, which I did not intend to give; he mounted and led the way.

I saw Duncan before he saw me, for he was intent upon his son. I thought it was his son; the boy was small enough for a five-year-old, and his solemnity matched that I had seen so often on his father's face. He was a small Cheysuli warrior, in leathers and boots but lacking the gold, for he was not a man as yet and had no *lir*. That would come in time.

The boy listened well. Black hair, curly as was common in Cheysuli childhood, framed his dark face with its inquisitive yellow eyes. There was little of Alix in the boy, I thought, and then he smiled, and I saw her, and realized how much it hurt that Donal was Duncan's son instead of mine.

Abruptly Duncan bent down and caught the boy in his arms, sweeping him up to perch upon one shoulder. He turned, smiling a wry, familiar smile—Finn's smile—and I realized there was much of Duncan I did not know. What I had seen was a rival, a man who sought the woman I sought; the man who had won her, when I could not. The man who had led an exiled race back from the edge of death to the promise of life again. I had given him little thought past what he had been to me. Now I thought about what he was to the Cheysuli . . . and to the boy he carried on his shoulder.

The boy laughed. It was a pure soprano tone, girlish in its youth, unabashed and without the fear of discovery. No doubt Donal knew what it was to hide, having hidden for all of his short life, but he had not lost his spirit with it. Duncan and Alix had seen to it he had his small freedoms.

The Keep suddenly receded. The humming of voices and the laughter of other children became an underscore to the moment. I knew, as I looked at Duncan and his son, I looked upon the future of Homana. From the man had come the son, who would no doubt rule in his father's place when Duncan's time was done. And would my son rule alongside him? Homanan Mujhar and Cheysuli clan-leader. Under them would a nation be reborn from war and purge into life again. Better, stronger than ever.

I laughed. It rang out, bass rather than Donal's soprano, and for just a moment the voices mingled. I saw the momentary surprise on Duncan's face and then the recognition, and finally the acknowledgment. He swung his son down from his shoulder and waited, while I got off my horse.

It was Donal I went to, not his father. The boy, so small beside the man, and so wary of me suddenly. He knew enough of strangers to know they sometimes brought danger with them.

I dwarfed him, taller even than Duncan. At once I went down on one knee so as not to loom over him like a hungry demon. It put us on a level: tall prince, small boy; warriors both, past, present and future.

"I am Carillon," I told him, "and I thank the gods you are here to give me aid."

The wariness faded, replaced by recognition. I saw wonder and confusion and uncertainty, but I also saw pride. Donal detached his hand from his father's and stood before me, frowningly intent, with color in his sun-bronzed cheeks. He was a pretty boy; he would make a handsome man. But then the Cheysuli are not an ugly race.

"My *jehan* serves you," he said softly.

"Aye."

"And my *su'fali*."

I thought of Finn, knowing he was behind me. "Aye. Very well."

Donal's gaze did not waver. There was little of indecision in him, or hesitation. I saw the comprehension in his face and knew he understood what he said, even as he said it. "Then I will serve you also."

Such a small oath, from so small a boy. And yet I doubted none of its integrity, or his honor. Such things are in all of the Cheysuli, burning in their blood. Donal was years from being a warrior, and yet I did not doubt his resolve.

I put both hands on his slender shoulders. I felt suddenly overlarge, as I had with my mother, for there was little of gentleness about me. And nothing at all of fatherhood.

But honor and pride I know, and I treasured it from him. "Could I have but one Cheysuli by my side, it would be you," I told him, meaning it.

He grinned. "You already have my *su'fali*!"

I laughed. "Aye, I do, and I am grateful for him. I doubt not I will have him for a long time. But should I need another, I know to whom I will come."

Shyness overcame him. He was still a boy, and still quite young. The intimacy had faded; I was a prince again, and he merely Duncan's son, and the time for such oaths was done.

"Donal," Finn said from behind me, "do you wish to serve your lord as I do, you might see to his mount. Come and tend it for him."

The boy was gone at once. I turned, rising, and saw the light in his face as he ran to do Finn's bidding. My horse's reins were taken up and the gelding led away with great

care toward the picket-string in the forest. Finn, like
Donal, walked, and I saw the calm happiness in his face as
he accompanied the boy. Indeed, he needed a son.

"You honor me with that," Duncan said.

I looked at him. His voice held an odd tone; a mixture,
I thought, of surprise, humility and pride. What had he
expected of me? A dismissal of the boy? But I could do
nothing so cruel, not to Alix's son.

And then I realized what he meant. He had forgotten
none of what lay between us; perhaps he had even dreaded
our first meeting. No, not dreaded; not Duncan, who
knew me too well for that. Perhaps he had merely anticipated antipathy.

Well, there was that. Or would be. There was still Alix
between us.

"I honor you with that," I agreed, "but also the boy
himself. I have not spent five years with Finn without
learning a little of your customs, and how you raise your
children. I will not dishonor Donal by dismissing him as a
child, when he is merely a warrior who is not fully grown."

Duncan sighed. I saw a rueful expression leach his face of
its customary solemnity. He shook his head. "Forgive me,
Carillon, for undervaluing you."

I laughed, suddenly light-hearted. "You have your brother
to thank for that. Finn has made me what I am."

"Not in his image, I hope."

"Could you not stand two?"

"Gods," he said in horror, "two of Finn? One is too
much!" But I heard the ring of affection in his tone and
saw the pleasure in his face; I realized, belatedly, he had
undoubtedly missed Finn as much as Finn had missed
him. No matter how much they disagreed when they were
together.

I put out my hand to clasp his arm in the familiar
Cheysuli greeting. "I thank you for him, Duncan. Through
him, you have saved my life many times."

His hand closed around my upper arm. "What Finn
knows, he learned elsewhere," he retorted. "Little enough
of me is in him. Though the gods know I tried—" He
grinned, forgoing the complaint. "He did not lie. He said
you had come home a man."

That got me laughing. "He would not say that within *my* hearing."

"Perhaps not," Duncan conceded, "but he said it within mine, and now I have told it to you."

Men judge men by handclasps. We held ours a moment, remembering the past, and there was no failing in his grasp, nor none in mine. There was much between us, and neither of us would forget.

We broke the clasp at last, two different men, I thought, than we had been before. Some unknown communication had passed between us: his recognition of me as someone other than I had been, when he had first known me, and my recognition of what he was. Not a rival, but a friend, and a man I could trust with my life. That is not so easy a thing to claim when a king has set gold on your head.

"My tent is too small for Mujhars," he said quietly, and when I looked harder I saw the glint of humor in his eyes. "My tent is particularly too small for *you*, now. Come with me, and I will give you a throne better suited, perhaps, than another. At least until you have slain the man who makes it his."

I said nothing. I had heard the grim tone in his voice and realized, for the first time, Duncan probably hated as well as I did. I had not thought of it before, so caught up in my own personal—and sometimes selfish—quest. I wanted the throne for myself as well as Homana. Duncan wanted me to have it for his own reasons.

He took me away from the tents to a pile of huge granite boulders, gray and green and velveted with moss. The sunlight turned the moss into an emerald cloak, thick and rich and glowing, like the stone in Lachlan's Lady. The throne was one rump-sized stone resting against another that formed a backrest. The moss offered me a cushion. Gods-made, Finn would say; I sat down upon it and smiled.

"Little enough to offer the rightful Mujhar." Duncan perched himself upon a companion rock. The veil of tree limbs hanging over us shifted in a breeze so that the sunlight and shadow played across his face, limning the planes and hollows and habitual solemnity. Duncan had always been less prone to gaiety than Finn; steadier, more serious, almost dour. Seeming old though he was still young by most men's reckoning. Young for a clan-leader, I knew, ruling because his elders were already dead in Shaine's *qu'mahlin*.

"It will do, until I have another," I said lightly.

Duncan bent and pulled a single stalk of wild wheat from the soggy ground. He studied the lime-green plant as if it consumed his every interest. It was unlike Duncan to prevaricate, I thought; unless I had merely gotten old enough to prefer the point made at once.

"You will have trouble reconciling the Homanans with Cheysuli."

"Not with all." I understood him at once. "Some, perhaps; it is to be expected. But I will have no man who does not serve willingly, whether it be next to a Cheysuli or myself." I sat forward on my dais of moss and granite. So different from the Lion Throne. "Duncan, I would have this *qu'mahlin* ended as soon as may be. I will begin with my army."

He did not smile. "There is talk of our sorcery."

"There will ever be talk of your sorcery. It is what made them afraid in the first place." I recalled my uncle's rantings when I was young; how he had said all of Homana feared the Cheysuli, because he had made them feared. How the shapechangers sought to throw down the House of Homana to replace it with their own.

Their own. In Cheysuli legend, their own House had built Homana herself, and gave her over to mine.

"There is Rowan," he said quietly.

I did not immediately take his meaning. "Rowan serves me well. I could not ask for a better lieutenant."

"Rowan is a man caught between two worlds." Duncan looked at me directly. "You have seen him, Carillon. Can you not see his pain?"

I frowned. "I do not understand. . . ."

A muscle ticked in his jaw. "He is Cheysuli. And now the Homanans know it."

"He has ever denied—" I halted the unfinished comment at once. It was true he had always denied he was Cheysuli. And I had ever wondered if he were regardless, with his Cheysuli coloring.

"Cai has confirmed it," Duncan said. "I called Rowan here and told him, but he denies it still. He claims himself Homanan. How a man could do that—" He broke it off at once, as if knowing it had nothing to do with the subject. "I bring Rowan up because he illustrates the troubles within your army, Carillon. You have Homanans and Cheysuli, and you expect them to fight together. After *thirty years* of Shaine's *qu'mahlin*."

"What else can I do?" I demanded. "I need men—*any* men—and I must have you both! How else can I win this war? Bellam cares little who is Cheysuli and who is Homanan—he will slay *everyone*, do we give him the chance! I cannot afford to divide my army because of my uncle's madness."

"It has infected most of Homana." Duncan shook his head, his mouth a flat, hard line. "I do not say *all* of them hate us. Does Torrin? But it remains that you must fight your own men before Bellam, do you let this hostility flourish. Look to your army first, Carillon, before you count your host."

"I do what I can." I felt old suddenly, and very tired. My face ached from its bruising. "Gods—I do what I can . . . what else is there *to* do?"

"I know." He studied his stalk of wheat. "I know. But I have put my faith in you."

I sighed and clumped down against my mossy throne, feeling the weight of my intentions. "We could lose."

"We could. But the gods are on our side."

I laughed shortly, with little humor in the sound. "Ever so solemn, Duncan. Is there no laughter in you? And do you not fear the Ihlini gods are stronger than your own?"

He did not smile. His eyes appraised me in their quiet, competent way, and I knew again the chafing of youth before an older, wiser man. "I will laugh again when I do not fear to lose my son because his eyes are yellow."

I flinched beneath the bolt as it went cleanly home in my soul. In his place, I might be like him. But in *my* place, what would he do?

"Were you Mujhar—" I began, and stopped when I saw the flicker in his eyes. "Duncan?"

"I am not." No more than that, and the flicker was gone.

I frowned at him, sitting upright again on my rock. "I will have an answer from you: were you Mujhar, what would you do?"

He smiled with perfect calm. "Win back my throne. We are in accord, my lord—you have no need to fear your throne is coveted. You are welcome to the Lion."

I thought of the throne. The Lion Throne, ensconced within Homana-Mujhar. In the Great Hall itself, crouched down upon the marble dais, dark and heavy and brooding. With its crimson cushion and gilt scrollwork, set so deeply in the old, dark wood. How old? I could not say. Ancient. And older still.

"Cheysuli," I said, without meaning to.

Duncan smiled more warmly. The smile set creases around his eyes and chased away the gravity, stripping his face of its age. "So is Homana, my lord. But we welcomed the unblessed, so long ago. Will you not welcome us?"

I set my face against my hands. My eyes were gritty; I scrubbed at them and at my skin, so taut with worry and tension. So much to do—and so little time in which to do it. Unite two warring races and take a realm; a realm held by sorcery so strong I could not imagine the power of it.

"You are not alone," Duncan said quietly. "Never that. There is myself, and Finn . . . and Alix."

I sat hunched, eyes shut tightly against the heels of my hands as if the pressure might carry me past all the pain, past all the battles, past all the necessities of war to the throne itself. Could it be done, I would not have to face the risks and the losses and the fears.

But it could not be done so easily, and a man learns by what he survives, not by passing o'er it.

I felt a hand on my shoulder. I turned my face away from my hands and looked into Duncan's eyes, so wise and sad and compassionate. Compassion, from him; for a man who wished to be his king. It made me small again.

"*Tahlmorra lujhalla mei wiccan, cheysu,*" he said quietly, making the gesture with his right hand. "Now, my lord, come and sup with me. Wars are lost on empty bellies."

I pushed myself off the rock with a single thrust of my hand. *The fate of a man rests always within the hands of the gods.*

My gods? I wondered. Or Bellam's?

ELEVEN

Cai sat upon a polished wooden perch sunk into the ground next to Duncan's slate-gray tent. His massive wings were folded with perfect precision; not a single feather was out of place. The great hooked beak shone in the dim firelight and the red glow of the setting sun: dark and sharp and deadly. And his eyes, so bright and watchful, missed not a single movement within the Keep.

I stood outside the tent. Duncan, Finn and the boy remained within, finishing what supper there was: hot stew, fresh bread, cheese and Cheysuli honey brew. And Alix, who had come up from Torrin's croft with the bread, had gone off to another tent.

I had put on a Cheysuli cloak, wrapping myself in the harsh woollen folds to ward off the chill of dusk. The fabric was so deep a green I melted into the surrounding darkness, even with the light from the firecairns on me. No longer did I wonder how the Cheysuli achieved their secrecy; a man, standing still, can hide himself easily enough. He need only affect the proper coloration and wait, and the enemy will come to him.

Cai turned his head. The great hawk looked directly at me, dark eyes glittering in the dying light. He had the attentiveness of a man in his gaze, and yet more, for he was a *lir* and a *lir* is better than a man, or so the Cheysuli claim. I had no reason to dispute it. I had known Storr

long enough to acknowledge his virtues, and be thankful
for his service.

I shivered, though it was not from the evening chill. It
was from the pervasive sense of destiny within the Cheysuli
Keep, for a Keep is where a man is, with his *lir*, and here
sat a *lir* beside me. Cai, the great dark hawk with the
wisdom of the ages, and the knowledge of what was to
come. Divulging it never, to no man, not even Duncan,
who served his gods better than any I had known. Such a
harsh service, I thought, requiring death and sacrifice.
What the Cheysuli bore in their bones was a weight I
could not carry. The shapechange was magic indeed, but I
would not pay its price.

I turned away and pulled aside the doorflap. The dim
light from the small iron brazier filled the tent with shadows, and I saw three pairs of yellow eyes fixed upon my
face.

Beast eyes. . . .

Even friendship does not dampen the residual fear en-
gendered by such eyes.

"I will go up to the army encampment. I have spent
enough time away from my men."

Finn rose at once, handing his cup to Duncan. The light
glittered off the Steppes knife in his belt, and suddenly I
recalled I had none to wear at my own. The bone-hilted
Caledonese weapon lay in the snowfields near Joyenne.

Finn caught up a night-black cloak and hung it over his
shoulders. It hid the gold on his arms entirely, turning
him black from brown in the dim glow of light. His hair
swung forward to hide his earring, and all I saw was the
yellow of his eyes. Suddenly, in the presence of three
Cheysuli, I found myself lacking, and I the Prince of
Homana.

Finn smiled. "Do we go?"

I needed no weapon, with him. He was knife and bow
and sword.

"We go." I looked past him to Duncan with his son by
his side. "I will think well on what you have said. I will
speak to Rowan and see what pain is in his heart, so I may
have a man beside me free of such cares."

He smiled. In the dim light he seemed older, but the

boy by his side made him young again. The future of his race. "Perhaps it will be enough for Homana to know her Mujhar again."

I stepped aside and Finn came out. Together we walked through the darkness to our horses, still saddled at the picket line. The Cheysuli trust no one this close to Mujhara; nor do I.

"The army will not be far." Finn ducked a low branch. "I think even Homanans know the value in three hundred Cheysuli."

"They will when we are done with them."

He laughed softly, nearly invisible in the deepening night.

I untied and mounted my dark Ihlini horse. Finn was up on his mount a moment later, heading through the trees, and I followed. Storr slipped along behind me, guarding my back as Finn preceded his lord. It is an exacting service, and one they perform with ease.

The moon rose full above us, above the stark black, skeletal trees: a silver plate in the dark night sky. I looked through the screen of trees that arched over my head. Beyond the screen were the white eyes of the stars, staring down. I heard the snap of twigs and branches broken by the hooves and the soft thunk of iron shoe against turf track. The forest sang with scent and the nightsounds I had so long taken for granted. Crickets called out our passage: a moth fluttered by my face on its journey toward the light. But there was no light. Not here, so deep among the trees.

And then such joy at being in Homana again rose up in my chest that I could hardly breathe. It did not last, and for a moment I was taken aback, but then I gave myself over to it. Finn was welcome to his *lir*-bond and the magic of his race, I longed only for Homana. Even an exiled Mujhar can find joy in such exile, does it bring him home again.

We rode along the crest of a hill, rising upward through the trees, and then down it, like water down a cobbled spillway. Finn took me down into a tiny bowl of a valley, skirting the edges so the trees gave cover. Clustered amid the night and darker shadows were pinpoints of flickering

light. Tiny lights, little more than the luminance shed by
the flame moths. Like the Cheysuli, my army kept itself to
subtle warmth and illumination. One would have to look
hard to see it; expecting it, it was not so hard for me to
discover. A pinpoint here and there, lost within the shadows, screened by trees and brush.

A circlet of light rimmed the bowl-like valley. It crowned
the crests like a king's fillet crusted with glowing gem-
stones, glittering against the darkness. We rode closer,
still clinging to the trees, and then I learned how well-
guarded was the army.

"Hold!" shouted a voice. I heard the rustling in the
leaves and placed each man; a semi-circle of five, I thought.
"Say who is your lord." The order was clipped off, lacking
the smoothness of aristocratic speech, but Homanan all
the same.

"Carillon the Mujhar," I said quietly, knowing Finn's
accent would give away his race. In the darkness, the men
might slay him out of hand.

"How many?" came the voice.

"Three." I smiled. "One Homana, one Cheysuli . . .
and one *lir*."

I felt the indrawn breath in five throats, though I heard
nothing. Good men. I was grateful for that much, even
though I grew cold upon my horse.

"You are Homanan?"

"I am. Would you have me speak more for you, to
discern my accent?" I thought it a worthwhile test; the
Solindish speech does not mimic ours and would give
away an enemy.

"You have said enough. What weapons do you bring?"

"A sword and a bow, and a Cheysuli warrior. Weapons
enough, I think."

A grunt. "Come ahead, with escort."

We went on, Finn first, surrounded by the men. Not
enough to gainsay Finn did he seek to slay them all; I
could account for at least two myself, possibly three. And
Storr a few more. It would take ten to stop us, perhaps
more. I found I liked such odds.

More rustles in the bushes and the crunching of night-
crisped snow. At last we halted near the outer rim of a

firecairn's light, and I saw the glint of weapons. Silent, shadowed men, grave-faced and wary-eyed, watching. Storr they watched the most, as any man will, knowing only a wolf. And Finn, cloaked in black with raven hair, dark-faced and yellow-eyed. Me they hardly marked at all, save perhaps to note my size.

The leader stepped forward into the firelight. He wore a long-knife in his belt and a sword upon a baldric. He was squat, well-proportioned, with close-cropped, graying red hair and bright green eyes. His body cried out for a soldier's leather and mail, though he wore only wool. He had the calm authority of a born leader; I knew at once he was a veteran of my uncle's wars against Solinde.

Other men had gathered around the tiny firecairn. There was not enough light to see them all clearly, merely arms and legs and faces, shadowed in the darkness. Silence and waiting and wariness, the mark of hunted men. Bellam had made them so.

"What do you call yourself?" I asked the leader.

"Zared," he said calmly. "And you?"

I grinned. "Mercenary. And Finn, with Storr the wolf." I shifted in the saddle and saw hands move to hilts. "Put up your weapons, for I am Homanan-born and wish only to go to war. I am impressed by your competence, but enough of it for now." I paused. "I am Carillon."

Zared's green eyes narrowed. "Come down from that horse."

I did so and stood before the man while he looked closely at my face.

"I fought with Prince Fergus, Carillon's father," he said abruptly. "I saw the son taken by Throne himself. Do you tell me you are that boy?"

His tone was dubious, but there was no humor in that moment. I put out both hands and pushed back the sleeves from my wrists. In the dim firelight the scars were nearly black; ridged bracelets in my flesh. Zared's eyes were on them, then rose to my face again. They narrowed once more. "Stories have it you were slain in exile."

"No. I am as you see me." I put my arms down again. "Is there more proof you would see?"

"Many men have been chained." An odd argument, but I understood him.

"Take the sword from my saddle."

He flicked a finger. One man stepped to the far side of my horse and unhooked the scabbard, then brought it to Zared. He pulled the blade partway free of the sheath so the runes writhed upon the metal, but the hilt, wrapped again in taut leather, looked an unmade thing.

"Cut it free," I said, yet again.

He did so with his knife, freeing the gold at last. The rampant lion clawed upon the metal as the shadows shifted upon it. The lion of Homana. And in the pommel glowed the ruby.

"That I know," he said in satisfaction. And he gave the sword to me.

"If you thought I was dead, why did you join the army?" I asked curiously.

"I am a soldier," he said simply. "I serve Homana. Even without a Mujhar to follow—a *Homanan* Mujhar—I will fight to defend my land. But I could not do it alone, and before now few were willing to risk themselves." He smiled a little, and it put lines in his rough-worked face. "Now we have more than a thousand men, my lord, and at last a prince to lead them."

I saw the others staring at me. They had just heard their leader admit I was their lord. It is sometimes an awesome thing for men to see who rules, when often he is only a name.

I turned back to my horse and hooked my scabbarded blade to it again. "Direct me to Rowan."

"Rowan?" Zared sounded surprised. "You wish to speak to *him*?"

"Why should I not? It was he who began this army." I swung up into the saddle again. "Would you have it said another has done it, when it was Rowan?"

Dull color flushed his face. "My lord—it is said he is Cheysuli . . . Cheysuli do not lead Homanans." The tone was harsh, the words clipped off; he did not look at Finn.

The nakedness of it stunned me. Zared I judged a fair man, a good soldier, worthy of any rank I chose for him.

And he, even knowing the skill of the Cheysuli, could continue to resent their presence.

I drew in a steadying breath and spoke exceedingly calmly. "We will dismiss any man who chooses to hate the Cheysuli. *Any* man. We will not argue with what my uncle's purge has put into your mind—he worked hard enough to do it—but we do not have to tolerate it in our army. Those of you who wish to continue Shaine's policy of Cheysuli extermination may leave now. We will have none of you with us."

Zared stared, openly stunned. *"My lord—"*

"We want none of you," I repeated. "Fight Bellam and Tynstar, but no other. Not Cheysuli. They serve us too well." I gathered in my reins. "Direct us to Rowan at once."

Zared pointed toward a distant flicker. "There, my lord. There."

"Think on what I have said," I told him. "When we have won this war the Cheysuli will know freedom again. We will begin *that* policy now."

"My lord—"

I heard nothing more of his comment, for I left his fire as fast as the horse would take me.

Rowan sat alone by his tiny firecairn. He was surrounded by clustered trees, as if he had gathered about himself a royal guard, stolid and silent. And yet within his guard he was a man alone, untouched by all save his grief. He had been found out, and no more was the secret kept.

The firecairn was not enough to warm him, I knew; probably not enough to warm the leathern cup of wine he held in rigid fingers. But the tiny light threw illumination over his face in the thick darkness, and I saw the gaunt expression of loss.

I swung off my horse and moved toward the cairn so that he had to acknowledge me. His head came up. For a moment he stared, still lost in his reverie, and then slowly he moved forward onto his knees. It was an old man's ungainly movement.

I saw past the shock. I saw past the outer shell of loss to the resignation beneath.

He had known.

"How long?" I asked. "And why did you hide it from me?"

"All my life," he said dully, still kneeling on the ground. "As for hiding it from you—what choice did I have? Few Homanans are like you, my lord . . . I thought they would revile me. And they *have*."

I dropped the reins and moved closer yet, motioning him up from his knees. Slowly he sat again upon the campstool. The cup in his hands shook. "Tell me," I said calmly.

He shut his eyes a moment. In the stark light he was the image of a childhood demon. *Cheysuli*.

"I was five," he said quietly. "I saw the Mujhar's men murder my kin. All save me." A quiver passed over his young face. "They came on us in the trees, shouting they had found a nest of demons. I ran. My *jehan* and *jehana*— and my *rujholla*—could not run in time. They were slain."

The Cheysuli words from Rowan's mouth were a shock to me. He had always spoken with the accent of Homana, lacking the Old Tongue entirely—and now I knew he had more claim to it than most.

I heard Finn come up beside my horse. I did not look at him, but Rowan did. They were as much alike as two leaves from the same vine; like enough to be father and son. Perhaps they were even kin.

"I had no choice," Rowan said. "I was found by a couple who had no children. They were Ellasian, but they had come to live in Homana. The valley was distant, insular, and there were none there who had seen Cheysuli. I was safe. And I kept myself so, until I came here."

"You must have known you would be discovered."

He shrugged. "I knew there was the chance. In Mujhara, I was careful. But the men interested in fighting Bellam were young, like myself, and they had never seen a Cheysuli shapechanger. So I named myself Homanan, and they believed it. It has been so long since the Cheysuli were free to go where they choose—much of Homana does not know her ancient race." Briefly he looked at me. "Aye. I have known what I am. And what I am not." He turned his face to the fire. "I have no *lir*."

I did not fully understand. And then I thought of Finn's link with Storr and the price it carried, and I knew what Rowan meant. "You cannot mean you will seek out your death!"

"There is no need for that," Finn said. He swung down from his horse and came into the firelight with Storr pacing at his side. "He never had a *lir*, which is somewhat different from losing one. Where there is no loss, a man is not constrained to the death-ritual."

Rowan's face was leached of color, painted bleak by the firelight. "The ritual is already done, though it be a Homanan one. I am named shapechanger, and stripped of what honor once I had."

I thought of the men in the tavern where Lachlan and I had found Rowan. Those men had followed him willingly. It was Rowan who had gathered most of those who were here. Word of mouth had gathered the others and still did, but Rowan had begun it all.

"Not all of them," I told him, ignoring Zared's attitude. "Those who are men, know men. They do not judge by eyes and gold." I realized, too, he wore no *lir*-gold. He had not earned the right.

"The gods are blind to you," Finn said quietly.

I stared at him in shock. "Do you seek to destroy what is *left* of him?"

"No. I tell him what he knows. You have only to ask him." Finn's voice and eyes were implacable. "He is *lirless*. Unwhole. Half a man, and lacking a soul. Unblessed, like you, though he be Cheysuli instead of Homanan." He went on, ignoring the beginnings of my protest. "He is not a warrior of the clan, lacking a *lir*. He will have no passage to the old gods."

My hand was on his arm. I felt the hard sinews beneath his flesh as my fingers clamped down. I had never before put my hand on him in anger.

He stopped speaking. He waited. And when I took my hand away he explained the words to me. "He gave it up willingly, Carillon. Now he must suffer for it."

"Suffer!"

"Aye." His eyes flicked down to Rowan's hunched figure. "Had it been me with the choice, I would have taken the risk."

"And *died*," I returned angrily.

"Oh, aye," he said matter-of-factly, "but I could not have lived with it, else."

"Do not listen," I told Rowan wearily. "Finn sometimes speaks when he would do better to hide his sentiments."

"Let him speak," Rowan said wearily. "He says what I have expected all my life. My lord—there is much of the Cheysuli you do not know. Much *I* do not know, having given up my soul." A bitter, faint smile twisted his mouth into a travesty of the expression. "Oh aye, I know what I am. Soulless and *lirless*, unwhole. But it was the choice I made, too frightened to seek my death. And I thought I *would* die, when the time for the *lir*-bond came."

"You knew?" I stared at him. "You knew when the time had come?"

"How could I not? I was sick for days, until my foster parents feared I would die. The longing, the need, the emptiness within me." A terrible grimace twisted his face. "The pain in the denial—"

"You had only to answer that need," Finn said harshly. "The gods fashioned a *lir* for you, and you gave it over into death. *Ku'reshtin!* You should have died for what you did."

"Enough!" I shouted at him. "Finn—by the gods!—I want support from you! Not condemnation for a man I need."

Finn's hand stabbed out to point at Rowan's lowered head. "He lived, while the *lir* died. Can you not see what it makes him? A murderer, Carillon—and what he slew was a gift of the gods themselves—"

"Enough," I repeated. "No more."

"Look at Storr," Finn snapped. "Think how your life would have been had *I* ignored my chance to link with him. He would have died, for a *lir* who does not link when the need is upon him gives himself over to death. It is the price *they* pay, as a warrior does when his *lir* is slain." His teeth showed briefly in a feral baring, like a wolf prepared to leap.

A wolf—Finn.

"Leave Rowan be," I said at last. "You have said more than was required."

"I would say it all again, and more, did I think it would make him see what he has done."

"I *know* what I have done!" Rowan was on his feet at last, his arms coming up as if to ward off the words Finn said. "By the gods, do you think I have not suffered? Do you think I have not cursed myself? I live with it each day, *shapechanger!* The knowledge will never go away."

I saw then that each suffered. Rowan, for what he never had; Finn, for what he could not comprehend: that a Cheysuli could give up his birthright and continue to survive. It was not Rowan who was left out, but myself. Carillon. The Homanan, who could not possibly know what it was to have a *lir*, or what it was to give one up.

"I need you both," I told them finally as they faced one another across the firelight. "I will have no disharmony among my men. Neither Cheysuli-Homanan conflict, nor that between men of a single race, blessed or not." I sighed, suddenly disgusted. "By the gods, do I know anything at all of the Cheysuli? I begin to think I *cannot*."

"*This* much I know," Rowan said, still looking at Finn. "No man, unblessed, can ever know the grace of the gods or understand the prophecy."

Finn laughed, though it had a harsh sound. "Not so soulless after all, are you? You have enough blood in you for that much."

The tension lessened at once. They still faced one another like predatory beasts: one a wise wolf, the other a man who lacked the gifts of the *lir*-bond, and yet claimed all the eerie charisma of the race.

"Unblessed," I growled. "By the gods, now there are *two* of you prating this nonsense. . . ." I turned away to my horse, my Ihlini horse, who was as much a stranger as I to the world of the Cheysuli.

I mustered my forces in the valley the following day, Cheysuli and Homanan alike. I watched them come, silent upon my horse, and waited until they filled the bowl-shaped valley. It was a small place and made my army look smaller still; I had so few men beneath my standard. And yet more came each day, trickling in with the thaw.

I thought of haranguing them with all the arguments and commands until all went away with the taste of Carillon in their mouths. I was angry enough that my Homanans could disregard the Cheysuli when we needed every man; did they wish to lose this war? And yet I understood, for I too had been raised to hate and fear the race. I had learned my lesson, and well, but only in adversity. Many of the Homanans I faced had lacked the teacher I had.

Instead of haranguing, I talked. Shouted, rather, since I could not reach them all by merely speaking, but I left my anger behind. I told them what we faced; told them how badly we were outnumbered. I would have none of them saying later I had led them unknowing into war. Did a man go to his death, I wanted him to know the risks.

I broke them into individual units, explaining my strategy to them. We could not afford the pitched battles we had ever known before, there being too few of us, and none I could spare in such futile attacks. Instead we would go in bit by bit, piece by piece, harrying Bellam's patrols. They would be fewer now, with harvest, and we would stand a better chance of catching them unawares.

The units I kept separate, knowing better than to mix Cheysuli with Homanan. Many of our Homanans were veteran enough to recall the days before the *qu'mahlin*, and they readily accepted the Cheysuli as expert fighting men; these men I put in charge of raiding parties. I counted on them to quash the rumbles of discontent. All men knew the ferocity and incredible abilities of the Cheysuli; I thought, in the end, they would prefer to have them with us than against us.

Few questions were asked. I wondered how many men came out of a true conviction of my goal, or merely desiring a change from daily life. Some, I did not doubt, were like Zared in their desire to free Homana from Bellam's rule. But others likely sought a release from what they had known, wanting merely a different life. I could promise them that much. They would go home vastly different, did they go home at all.

I named my captains. Rowan was one of them. Him I

placed with the men he had gathered in the tavern, knowing he could not lead other Homanans until he had proved himself. The Cheysuli would not accept him either, I thought, judging by Finn's reaction.

I dismissed the men into their units, tasking the captains with the goal I wanted: superior raiding parties. Men willing to sweep down quickly on Solindish patrols, slaying as they could, and sweeping away again as quickly as they had come. No time wasted; fewer lives lost. Cheysuli warfare, and more effective than most. I knew it could work, if they were willing to act as I desired.

"You have mastered them." This from Finn, sitting behind me on his horse.

I smiled, watching the army depart. "Have I? Then you are deaf to all the mumbled complaints."

"Men will ever complain. It is the nature of the beast." He kneed his mount forward and came up next to me. "I think you have won their hearts."

"I need that *and* their willingness to fight."

"And I think you will have it." He pulled something from his belt and held it out. A knife. A Cheysuli long-knife hilted in silver, with a gleaming wolf's-head pommel. It was my own, given to me by Finn so many years before. "I took it from your things," he said quietly. "A Mujhar ever carries one."

I thought of the one I had left behind. The piece of bone. I thought of the one I had replaced it with: a Homanan knife of army issue, when there was my own. But I had hidden it so long— Abruptly I put out my hand and accepted the Cheysuli knife. And then I told Finn how it was I had lost the other. I told him of the sorcerer, and of the lion-beast.

His brows drew down as he listened. Gone was the calm expression of the loyal liege man, although even then there was the hint of mockery. Now he listened, thinking even as I spoke, and when I was done with words he nodded a little, as if I had told him nothing new.

"Ihlini," he said on a sigh, as if there were need for nothing more.

"That was obvious."

For a moment his eyes were on me, but he saw something more than myself. Then his gaze cleared and he looked at me, smiling in a grim parody of the Finn I knew. "So obvious? —no. That he was Ihlini, no doubt—but not that he had used so much of his sorcery."

"So much?" It puzzled me. "There are degrees in it?"

He nodded, shifting in the saddle. "There is much of the Ihlini I do not know. They hide themselves in mystery. But it *is* known they have gifts similar to our own."

I stared at him, struck by the revelation. "Do you mean to say they shift their shapes?"

"No. That is a Cheysuli thing." His thoughtful frown was becoming a scowl. "But they can alter the shapes of other things, such as weapons." He looked at the Cheysuli knife I held in my hand. "Had you borne *that*, he could have conjured no beast. Do you see? He touched that which was not alive—nor made of Cheysuli skill—and fashioned it into an enemy for you." He shook his head. "I had heard . . . but I have never seen it."

I felt my gorge rise. I had faced the lion, knowing it was a sorcerous thing, and yet I had fought it as if it had been real, a thing Homanan-born, to be slain before it slew me. I had known it had grown out of the Caledonese bone hilt—how else would it have appeared?—but somehow I had ignored the implications of it. If the Ihlini had such power over objects, I faced a more dangerous foe than I had thought.

"What else can they do?" I demanded. "What magic should I expect?"

A stray breeze lifted a lock of black hair from Finn's left shoulder. The earring glittered. Seated on his dark horse in his dark leathers, he reminded me of the stories I had heard of man-horses, half of each, and inseparable. Well, so was Finn inseparable. From his *lir*, if not from his horse.

"With the Ihlini," he said, "expect anything."

The last of the Homanans disappeared into the trees to gather with their captains. To plan. To do as I wished, which was to strip Bellam of men and power until I could steal it all back from him.

I felt a roll of trepidation in my belly. "I am afraid," I said flatly, expecting ridicule—or worse—from him.

"No man, facing what you face, denies his fear," Finn said calmly. "Unless he lies. And you are not a liar."

I laughed, albeit oddly. "No, not a liar. A fool, perhaps, but not a liar." I shook my head, tasting the sharp tang of apprehension in my mouth. "What we face—"

"—we face," he finished. "As the gods desire." He made the familiar gesture. "*Tahlmorra*, my lord. It will go on." He closed his hand abruptly, the gesture banished. His hand was a fist, a hard brown fist of flesh and bone, and the promise of death to come.

TWELVE

Our first strikes against Bellam were successful. My raiding parties caught the Solindish patrols by complete surprise, as I had intended, slaying everyone rapidly and then departing more quickly than they had come. But Bellam was no fool; soon enough he put up a defense. In two months the Solindish patrols had cut down many of my men. But still more flocked to join me, won over by the knowledge I had come home at last to take back my throne. In those first days I had had thirteen hundred men, Cheysuli and Homanan alike. Now the number was four times that many, and still more came.

Carefully I split my raiding parties and sent them out to harry Bellam from all directions. I took several of my best captains, experienced veterans all, and dispatched them with their men to distant parts of Homana. Slowly, from all four directions, they would work their way toward Mujhara and Bellam's principal forces. Little by little they would gnaw their way inward, chewing holes in Bellam's martial fabric, until the cloth was weakened. Even a large army can be defeated by small insects.

Much of my time was taken up with army matters, allowing me small chance to do any fighting myself, but I was not unready to take the field and I did whenever I could. Finn fought with me, and Storr, along with Rowan and his men. And when I could not fight, too busy with other matters, I practiced when I could against sword and bow and knife.

Zared was often my partner, for the red-haired soldier had proved an invaluable fighter. He had come to me not long after the first few strikes, offering apology for his words concerning Rowan. I had listened in silence, allowing him what he would say, and then ordered Rowan fetched so Zared could say it again to the one who deserved the words. Rowan had come, listened in a silence similar to mine, and accepted the apology. I thought he felt better for it.

Since then Zared and I had been on friendly terms, and I had come to know him better. He knew much of war, having fought for years under my father, and for that alone I was grateful. There were not many left who could recall the man who sired me, for with him had perished thousands. The memory still hurt, for I had been spared where my father had not. And all because I was heir to Shaine the Mujhar. Unexpendable, while my father was not.

Zared and I, between strikes against Bellam's patrols, sparred within a clearing in the forest. We did not maintain the camp in the same place for longer than a few days at the most, knowing more permanency would make us easier to track down. We moved constantly but with little grumbling. The army understood that our safety remained in secrecy.

I had stripped to breeches and boots, bare-chested in the late spring warmth and extra activity. Zared wore little enough as well, concentrating on footwork; I outweighed him considerably and towered over him, so though to most we seemed unevenly matched, it merely afforded us a chance to fight against different styles. He was a superb swordsman, and I still had need of such tutors. Finn had taught me nothing of the sword, for the Cheysuli do not believe in using a sword where a knife will do. What I had learned I had learned from arms-masters within Homana-Mujhar, and from exile in foreign lands.

The bout had gone on for a considerable length of time. My thighs burned and my arms ached. And yet I dared not call halt, or Zared would claim himself the victor. More often than not I won, being younger and stronger, but when he took a bout it was with great finesse and much shouting to let the others know he had beaten his Mujhar. My pride stood it well enough, after the first time, but my battered body did not like it so much. I fought to win.

Zared, on the point of thrusting at me with his sword, suddenly fell back. I followed with a counterthrust, nearly drove the blade through when he did not move to deflect, and stopped short. Zared remained in one spot, staring past me. His sword drooped in his hand. I saw the expression—shock and awe and utter desire—and turned to see what had caused it.

A woman. Women are not unheard of in an army camp—even I had taken my ease in camp followers—but this one was different. This one was no light woman or crofter's daughter seeking a soldier in her bed.

I forgot I held a sword. I forgot I was half-naked and sweaty, wet-haired and smelling of exertion. I forgot who I was entirely, knowing only I was a man, and a man who wanted that woman.

I felt the fist knot up deep in my belly, making me aware of what I needed. Wanted, aye, but needed as well. With the sudden recognition of such things, I knew I wanted to bed the woman before the day was done.

She had not come of her own volition. That much was clear. Finn held her arm roughly, and he brought her to me with infinite satisfaction in his demeanor. I had never seen him so pleased before, and yet his pleasure was not something others—certainly not the woman—could see. It showed only in the deep feral light in his eyes and the set of his mouth, too calm for Finn. He did not smile, but I saw the laughter in his soul.

He brought her to me. I remembered all at once what it was she saw, and for once I was displeased with my liege man. No doubt the woman was a prisoner, but surely he could have done me the courtesy of allowing me time to put on fresh clothing and wipe the sweat from my face. It dripped from my hair and beard to trickle down my bare chest.

She was stiff and clumsy with rage. White-blond hair spilled free of its sheer silken covering, tumbling past slender shoulders clad in slate-gray velvet. Her gown was torn and stained; flesh showed through the rents, but her pride was undiminished. Even as she stood before me in obvious disarray, in the open for all to see, the sight of her pride struck the smile from my face.

Her eyes fixed themselves upon me. Wide-spaced eyes, gray and cool as water, long-lidded and filled with virulent scorn. An apt emotion for the man who stood before her, rank from exertion, a bared blade in his callused hand.

I saw again the wild light in Finn's eyes. "We took a procession out of Mujhara, bound for Solinde."

I looked at the woman again. Her skin was pale as death, but that changed as color crept into her face. Anger, I knew, and defiance.

And then she spoke. "Do you mean to tell me, shape-changer, *this* man is the pretender-prince?"

"Carillon of Homana," I informed her, and a suspicion formed in my mind. I looked at Finn for confirmation and saw his satisfied smile. At that I had to add my own. "Pretender-prince, am I? When I was born to that throne? I think not, lady. I think it is your father who pretends. A usurper king, and you his daughter." I laughed then, into her angry face. "Electra!" I said. "Oh, aye, you are well come to this camp. And I thank the gods for their gift."

Her teeth showed briefly in a faint, feral baring, much as I had seen in Finn from time to time. But there was nothing of the Cheysuli in her. She was pale, so pale, like winter snow. White on white, with those ice-gray eyes. Gods, what a woman was this!

"Electra," I said again, still smiling. Then I gestured toward Finn. "Take her to my tent. Guard her well—we dare not lose this woman."

"No, my lord." I saw the appraisal in his eyes. No doubt it was obvious what I wanted. To her as well as him.

I watched her move away with him, one slim arm still caught in his sun-bronzed hand. The torn gown hid little of her body. It was with great effort that I dispatched Zared for cloth and fresh wine. When he came back I dried myself as best I could, drank down two cups of harsh red wine and put on my shirt and leather jerkin. Little in my apparel made me a prince, but I thought it would not matter. There was more on my mind than rank.

I went into my tent at last. Electra stood precisely in the center, resolutely turned away from Finn, and now myself. The tent boasted little of fine things, being a field pavilion. There was a rude bed, a table and stool, tripod and brazier. There was little room for more.

Except, perhaps, Electra.

Finn turned. He was unsmiling now, but I saw something in the set of his mouth and the tautness of his face. I wondered what she had said or done to set him so on edge. I had seen him like this rarely, especially with a woman.

We measured each other in that moment. But it was Electra who broke the silence by turning to face us both. "This is ill-done, Homanan. You take me from my women and leave him to the shapechangers."

"See to your men," I told Finn briefly. "You may leave her with me."

He knew dismissal when he heard it. More often than not we played at lord and liege man, being better friends than most men of such rank, but this time he heard the command. I had not meant it to come out so baldly, but there was nothing for it. There was no room for Finn in this.

He smiled grimly. "Beware your weapon, my lord Mujhar."

The euphemism brought crimson flags to her face as he left and I wondered how much she knew of men. No doubt Bellam claimed his daughter a virgin, but I thought it unlikely. She did not look at me with any of the virgin's fear or curiosity. She was angry still, and defiant, but there was also the look of a woman who knows she is wanted by a man.

The tent was of thin, pale fabric. Though the doorflap hung closed, enough light crept through the gap to lend a dusky daylight to the interior. The roof draped down from the ridgepole, nearly brushing my head, and the breeze billowed the side panels. She stood very still in the center, head raised and arms at her sides, keen-edged as any blade. It reminded me that I bore a sword, unsheathed, and no doubt she took it as a threat.

I moved past her to the table and set the blade upon it. I turned back, watching as she turned, and saw the seductiveness in her movements. She knew well enough what she did: she watched me as well as I watched her.

"Electra." Her eyes narrowed as I spoke. "Do you know what men call you?"

Her head, on her pale, slender neck, lifted. Gold glimmered in her ears and at her throat. She smiled back at me slowly, untouched by the insinuation in my tone. "I know."

I poured a cup of wine and deliberately kept it for myself, offering her none. She made no indication she cared, and suddenly I felt ludicrous. I set down the cup so hard the wine slopped over the rim and spilled, crawling across the parchment map upon the table like a crimson serpent seeking its lair.

"Tynstar's light woman," I said, "An Ihlini's whore."

Her pale eyes were still and cool in her flawless face. She appraised me from head to toe, even as I assessed her, and I felt the heat creep up from my belly to engulf my face. It was all I could do to keep my hands from her.

"You are a princess of Solinde," I reminded her, perhaps unnecessarily. "I know it, even if you have forgotten. Or is it that Bellam does not care what men say about his daughter?"

Electra smiled. Slowly she reached out and took up the forgotten wine cup, lifting it to her mouth. She held my eyes with her own and drank three sips, then threw down the cup with a gesture of condescension. The red wine colored her lips and made me all the more aware of her, when I needed no reminding.

"What else have they said, my lord?" Her tone was husky and slow. "Have they said I am more witch than woman?"

"You are a woman. Do you require more witchcraft than that?" I had not meant to say it. It had given her a weapon, though perhaps she had held it all along.

She laughed deep in her throat. Her accent was exquisite. "Aye, pretender-prince, perhaps it is. But I will tell you anyway." One slender, fine-boned hand smoothed a pale strang of hair away from her face. "How old am I, Carillon?"

The Solindish accent made the syllables of my name sing. Suddenly I wanted her to say it again, in my arms, in my bed, as she assuaged the knot in my belly. "How old?" I asked, distracted.

"Surely you can give me an age."

The vanity of women. "Perhaps twenty."

Electra laughed. "When Lindir of Homana—your cousin, I believe?—was promised to my brother, I was ten years old." She paused. "In case you cannot count, my lord—that was thirty years ago."

The grue slid down my spine. "No."

"Aye, Carillon." Two fingers traced the gold around her throat. It was a twisted piece of wire, simple and yet elegantly suitable. "Are not Tynstar's arts impressive?"

My desire began to spill away like so much unwanted seed. Tynstar's arts—Tynstar's light woman. Gods. "Electra." I paused. "I think you have a facile tongue. But you undervalue my intelligence."

"Do I? Do you disbelieve me?" The velvet on her shoulders wrinkled in a shrug. "Ah well, believe as you will. Men do, for all they claim themselves an intelligent race." She smiled. "So—this is what you face: this poor little tent, in your desire to seek my father's throne."

"*My* throne, lady."

"Bellam took it from Shaine," she said calmly. "It belongs to the House of Solinde."

I smiled with a confidence I did not entirely feel, facing her. "And I will take it back."

"Will you? How? By selling me?" Her cool eyes narrowed. The expression did not suit their long-lidded, somnolent slant. "What will you do with me, my lord?"

"I have not decided."

"Ransom me? Slay me?"

I frowned. "*Slay* you—I? Why should I desire your death?"

"Why not? I am your enemy's daughter."

I laughed. "And a woman such as I have never seen.

Slay you? Never. Not when there is so much I would rather do."

I saw the subtle change in her mouth; in the shape of her jaw. She had me, not I her, and she knew it. She smiled. It was a faint, slow, seductive smile, and went straight to the knot in my belly. The long-lidded eyes took their measure of me, and I wondered if she found me lacking somehow.

Electra moved swiftly, diving for the Cheysuli sword on the table next to me. I spun and caught her waist as she slipped by; she clawed for the sword even as my hands closed on her. She had it in her hands, both hands, jerking it from the table. The blade flashed in the pale, muted light and I caught her wrist, knocking her arm against my upraised leg. She hissed in pain and lost the sword, dropping it to the hard-packed earth.

The white-blond hair was a curtain across her face, hiding it from me as the fine strands snagged on the leather of my jerkin. I released one of her arms and smoothed away the hair from her angry face, drawing her inexorably closer. And then, even as she caught my neck in her arms, I ground my mouth onto hers.

She was like the finest wine, subtle and heady and powerful. She went straight to my head, blurring my senses and addling my wits. I could do nothing but drown, drinking more even as I drowned, wanting only to take her with me. I could not think of letting her go. And she did not insist upon it, reaching up to catch my damp hair in two doubled fists. But her teeth sank into my bottom lip, tearing, and I cursed and jerked my face free.

"Rape?" she demanded.

"Who rapes?" I asked. "You or I? I think you have as much interest in this as I."

I had not let her go. I did not, even as I set the back of one hand against my bleeding lip. The other hand was caught in the fabric of her gown, one arm locked around her spine. I could feel every line of her body set so hard against mine. Gods, but it would be easy to simply bear her down and take her here—

"Electra," I said hoarsely, "are you Tynstar's light woman?"

"Does it matter?" Her breasts rose against my chest. "Does it matter so much, pretender-prince?"

My lip still bled. And yet I cared little enough for the pain. I wanted to share it with her. "Oh aye, it matters. For he will pay dearly for you."

She stiffened at once. "Then you will seek ransom—"

"I seek what I can get," I told her bluntly. "By the gods, woman, what do *you* seek to do? Ensorcell me?"

She smiled. "I do what I can." She touched my lip with a gentle finger. "Shall I take the pain away?"

"Witch," I accused.

"Woman." This time she was the aggressor as much as I, and she did as she had offered. She took the pain from my mouth and centered it much deeper, where I could not control myself.

"How much will you ask for me?" she whispered against my mouth.

"My sister."

Her head rose. "Tourmaline?"

"Aye. I care little enough for gold. It is my sister I want."

"My father will never pay it."

"He will. I would." And I knew as I said it, she had had the truth from me.

Electra laughed. "Carillon, oh Carillon—such words from you already? Do you give in to my witchcraft so soon?"

I set her away with effort. I felt unsteady, as if sickening from some fever. I was hot and cold and ringing with the tension as well as the demand.

I realized, with a sense of astonishment, that the sword still lay on the ground between us. I had not recovered it. It had lain there, blade bare, as if in promise of what might lie between us in the future.

Electra stood by the table. Her mouth was still red from the wine and stained by my blood. The long-lidded eyes regarded me calmly, assessively, as if she judged me within her mind. I dared not ask what she saw; I had not the courage.

I bent and picked up the sword. Slowly I slid it home in the scabbard and set it on the table. Within reach. She had only to pick it up again.

Electra laughed. "You are too quick for me, my lord, and far too strong. You are a man, you see, and I merely a woman."

"Merely," I said in disgust, and saw her contented smile. "No rape," I told her, "though I doubt—judging by what I have tasted—you would be so unwilling. But no rape." I smiled. "I do not rape what I will have in marriage."

"*Marriage!*" she shouted, and I knew I had broken through her guard at last.

"Aye," I agreed calmly. "When I have slain your father—and Tynstar—and once again hold *my* throne . . . I will make you Queen of Homana."

"No!" she shouted. "I will not *allow* it!"

"Do you think I care what you will allow?" I asked her gently. "I will take you to wife, Electra. None can gainsay me, now."

"*I* will gainsay you!" She was so vividly angry I could scare draw breath. "You puling fool, *I* will gainsay you!"

I merely smiled at her, and offered more wine.

Finn, seated on a stool within my tent, nearly dropped his cup of wine. "You will do *what*?"

"Wed her." I sat on the edge of my army cot, boots kicked off and wine in my wooden cup. "Would you have a better idea?"

"Bed her," he said curtly. "Use her, but do not *wed* her. The Mujhar of Homana wed to Bellam's daughter?"

"Aye," I agreed. "That is how alliances are made."

"Alliance!" he lashed. "You are here to take back the throne from the man who usurped it, not win his approval as a husband for his daughter. By the gods, what has put this foolishness in your head?"

I scowled at him. "You name *me* a fool? Are you blind? This is not just a thing between a man and a woman, but between realms and people as well." I shifted on the cot. "We cannot force war on Homana forever. When I have slain Bellam and won back the Lion, there will still be Solinde. The realm is large and strong, and I would prefer not to fight it forever. Do I wed Electra to cap my victory, I may well settle a lasting peace."

It was Finn's turn to scowl. His wine was untouched. "Do you recall, *my lord*, how it was the *qu'mahlin* was begun?"

"I recall it well enough," I snapped impatiently. "And I do not doubt Electra will also refuse to wed with me, as Lindir refused to wed with Ellic, but she will have no choice when the throne is mine."

Finn said something in a tone of deep disgust, but it was in the Old Tongue and I could not understand it. He reached down and tugged at one of Storr's ears as if seeking guidance. I wondered what the wolf told him.

"I know what I am doing," I said quietly.

"Do you? How do you know she is not Tynstar's minion? How do you know she will not slay you in your wedding bed?"

It was my turn to swear, though I did it in Homanan. "When I am done with this war, Tynstar will be dead."

"What will you do with her now?"

"Keep her here. Bellam will send word concerning Torry's release, and then we shall see to returning his daughter to him." I smiled. "If he is not dead by then himself."

Finn shook his head. "Keeping her I can see, for it is a tool to use against your *rujholla's* captivity. But wedding her? No. Seek your *cheysula* elsewhere."

"Would you have me wed a Cheysuli, then?" I scoffed. "The Homanans would never allow it."

"Cheysuli women wed Cheysuli men," he said flatly. "No woman would look outside her clan."

"What of the men?" I asked. "I have not seen the warriors keeping to their clan. Not even you." I smiled at his wary expression. "There was Alix, only half Cheysuli, and not knowing it at all." I paused. "And now, perhaps, Electra?"

He sat upright so quickly wine slopped over the rim of his cup and splashed across Storr's head. The wolf sat up as quickly as Finn, shaking his head to send droplets flying in all directions. The look he flashed Finn was one of such grave indignation I could not help but laugh, though Finn found little humor in it.

He rose and set the cup down on the table, still scowling. "I want none of Electra."

"You forget, I know you. I have seen you with women before. She touched you, Finn, as much as she touched me."

"I want none of her," he repeated.

I laughed at him. And then the laughter died, and I frowned. "Why is it we are attracted by the same women? There was Alix first, and the red-haired girl in Caledon, and now—"

"A liege man knows his place." The comment overrode me. "Do you truly think he seeks what woman his lord will make his queen?"

"Finn." I rose as he turned away. "Finn, I know you better than that."

"Do you?" His face was uncommonly grave. "I think not. I think not at all."

I put down my cup of wine. "I take her to wife because she is worthy of that much. I will not get her another way."

"Put out your hand and take her," Finn said. "She will come to you like a cat to milk."

The wall went up between us, brick by brick. Where once its name had been Alix, now it was Electra. And, though I thought what he felt for Electra was closer to dislike than anything akin to love, I could not see the way of tearing it down again. Kingdoms take precedence even over friendships.

"There are things a king must do," I said quietly.

"Aye, my lord Mujhar." This time he did leave, and the wolf went with him.

THIRTEEN

I jerked aside the doorflap and went out, buckling on my swordbelt with its weight of Cheysuli gold. No longer did I wrap the hilt in leather to hide the crest and ruby. All men knew I had come at last—including Bellam—and no longer did I wish to hide my presence or my identity.

Finn stood waiting with the horses. He, like myself, wore his warbow slung across one shoulder. But he wore no ringmail or boiled leather, trusting instead to his skill to keep him free of harm. No Cheysuli wore armor. But perhaps I too would leave it off, did I have the chance to wear an animal's form.

I took the reins from him and turned to mount. But I stopped the motion and turned back as Rowan called to me.

"My lord—wait you!" He hastened toward me in a rattle of mail and sword. Like us, he prepared to lead an attack against one of Bellam's patrols. "My lord, the lady is asking for you." He arrived at last, urgency in face and voice.

"Electra asks for nothing," I told him mildly. "Surely you mean she has *sent*."

Color rose in his face. "Aye," he said, "she has sent." He sighed. "For you."

I nodded. Electra sent for me often, usually two or more times in a single day. Always to complain about her captivity and to demand her immediate release. It had become a game between us—Electra knew well enough what she did to me when I saw her. And she played upon that effect.

In the six weeks since Finn had captured her, nothing had been settled between us except out mutual attraction. She knew it as well as I. Ostensibly enemies, we were also eventual bedmates. It was simply a matter of time and circumstance. Did I wish to, I could have her before her internment was done. But I gambled for higher stakes—permanency, in reign and domesticity—and she knew it. She used it. And so the courtship rite went on, bizarre though it was.

"She waits," Rowan reminded me.

I smiled. "Let her." I swung up on my horse and gathered the reins, marking how my men waited. And then I was gone before Rowan could speak again.

Finn caught up to me not far from the camp. Behind us rode our contingent of soldiers: thirty Homanans armed to the teeth and ready for battle once more. Scouts had already brought reports of three Solindish patrols; I would take one, Rowan another, Duncan the third. Such warfare had worked well in the past months; Bellam already shouted impotent threats from his stolen throne.

"How much longer do we keep her?" Finn asked.

No reference was necessary. "Until I have Torry back." I squinted against the sun. "Bellam's last message said he would send Torry out of Mujhara with an escort—and Lachlan also. Electra will be back with her father soon enough."

"Will you let her go?"

"Aye," I said calmly. "It will be no hardship to let her go when I will have her back so soon."

He smiled. "No more hedging, from you. No more modesty."

"No," I agreed, grinning. "I have come home to take my uncle's throne, and I have every intention of doing it. As for Bellam, we have harried him long enough. In a month, or two or three, he will come out of Mujhara to fight. This thing will be settled then."

"And his daughter?"

I looked directly at him, tasting the dust of warfare in

my mouth as we moved toward our battle. "She is Tynstar's light woman, by all accounts—including her own. For that alone, I will make her mine."

"Revenge." He did not smile. "I understand that well enough, Carillon, having tasted it myself—but I think it is more than that."

"Political expediency," I assured him blandly. "She is a valuable tool."

A scowl pulled his face into grim lines. "In the clans, it is not the same."

"No," I agreed quietly. "In the clans you take women as you will and care little enough for the politics of the move." I glanced back at my soldiers. They followed in a tight unit, bristling with swords and knives and ringmail. "Men have need of such things as wives and children," I told him quietly. "*Kings* have need of more."

"More," he said in disgust, and his eyes were on Storr. The wolf loped by Finn's horse, silver head turned up so their eyes locked: one pair of eerie, yellow eyes; one pair of amber, bestial eyes. And yet I could not say who was truly the beast.

Or if either of them were.

Our attack swept down on Bellam's patrol and engulfed the guardsmen. I halted my horse some distance from the melee and set about loosing arrow after arrow into selected targets. The Atvian longbow, for all its range was good, lacked the power of my Cheysuli bow; until my arrows were gone, I would be well-nigh invincible.

Or so I thought, until one Atvian arrow, half-spent, struck the tender flesh of my horse's nose and drove him into a frenzy of pain. I could not control him. Rather than lose myself to a pain-crazed horse in place of an Atvian arrow, I jumped from the horse and set about doing what I could on foot.

My Homanans fought well, proving their worth. There was no hesitation on their part, even facing the archers who had so badly defeated them six years before. But we were greatly outnumbered. Bellam's men turned fiercely upon my own, slashing with swords, stabbing with knives, screaming like utter madmen as they threw themselves into the fight. So many times we had swarmed upon them like gnats; at last they swatted back.

I discarded my bow when my arrows were gone, turning instead to my sword. I waded into the nearest knot of men, slashing at the enemy. Almost instantly I was engaged by an Atvian wielding a huge broadsword. I met blade with blade and gasped as the jar ran up through my arms to my shoulders, lodging in knotted muscles. I disengaged, counterthrust, then sank my own blade deep in his chest.

The man went down at once. I wrenched my sword free and staggered across the body, ducking another scything sweep near my head, swung around and cut loose the arm that swung the blade. The Solindishman went down screaming, spraying blood across matted grass already boggy with gore. One glance showed me the battle had turned decidedly in Solindish favor.

The trick was now to get out. My horse had been left behind. But most of the enemy was on foot as well, since we struck first at their mounts, and a foot race is more commonly won by men with greater reason to run. I had reason enough.

I looked for Finn and found him not far from me, as ever, shouting something as he closed with a Solindish soldier. He wore his human form, eschewing the savagery that accompanies the shapechange in the midst of battle. It was a matter of balance, he had told me once; a Cheysuli warrior remains himself even in *lir*-shape, but should he ever lose himself in the glory of a fight, he could lose himself forever. It was possible a warrior, crossing over the boundaries of balance, might remain a beast forever.

I did not care to think of Finn locked into his wolf-shape. Not forever. I needed him too much as himself.

And then I saw Storr running between two men. His tail was straight out as he streaked across the bloodied field. His ears were pinned back against his head and his teeth were bared. I knew then he ran to aid Finn, and I knew he was too late.

The sword came down and bit into the wolf's left shoulder. His yelp of pain pierced through the din of battle like a scythe. Finn heard it at once, or else he heard something more within the link. Helplessly I watched him turn away from his enemy to look for Storr.

"No!" I roared, trying to run through the slippery grass. "Finn—look to *yourself*!"

But he did not. And the Atvian spear drove into his right leg and buried itself in the hillside.

I threw myself over dead and wounded, enemy and Homanan alike. Finn was sprawled on his back against the ground, trying to wrench the spear from his thigh. But it had gone straight through, pinning him down, even as he sought to break the shaft with his hands.

The Atvian spearman, seeing his advantage, pulled his knife from its sheath and lunged.

I brought down my sword from the highest apex of its arc, driving it through leather and mail and flesh. The body toppled forward. I caught it before it fell across Finn and dragged it away, tossing it to one side. And then I cursed as I saw the damage that had already been done; how he had laid open the flesh of Finn's face with his knife. The bloody wound bisected the left side from eye to jaw.

I broke the spear in my hands and rolled Finn onto one side, grateful he was unconscious. I pulled the shaft free as the leg twitched and jumped beneath my hands. Blood ran freely from the wound, pooling in the matted, trampled grass. And then I pulled my liege man from the ground and carried him from the field.

Finn screamed Storr's name, lunging upward against my restraining hands. I pressed him down against the pallet, trying to soothe him with words and wishes alone, but he was too far gone in fever and pain. I doubted he heard me, or even knew I was there.

The tiny pavilion was rank with heat and the stench of blood. The chirurgeons had done what they could, stitching his face together again with silk thread and painting it with an herbal paste, but it was angry and swollen and ugly. The wound in his thigh they had drained and poulticed, but one man had gone so far as to say he thought it must come off. I had said no instantly, too shocked to consider the amputation, but now that some time had passed I understood the necessity of the suggestion.

Did the leg fill with poison, Finn would die. And I did not wish to give him over to such pain.

I knelt rigidly at his side, too stiff and frightened to move away. The doorflap hung closed to shut out the gnats and flies; the air was heavy and stifling. Rowan stood beside me in the dimness of the tent, saying nothing, but I knew he felt his own measure of shock and apprehension. Finn had ever seemed invincible, even to those he hardly knew. To those of us who knew him best of all—

"He is Cheysuli." Rowan meant to reassure me.

I looked down on the pale, sweating face with its hideous wound. Even stitched closed, the thing was terrible. It snaked across his face from eye to jaw, puckering the flesh into a jagged, seeping serpent. Aye, he was Cheysuli.

"They die," I said in a ragged tone. "Even Cheysuli die."

"Less often then most." He moved forward a little. Like me, he was splattered with blood. Rowan and his men had gotten free without losing a single life. I had lost most of my unit, and now perhaps Finn as well. "My lord—the wolf is missing."

"I have dispatched men to search. . . ." I said nothing more. Storr's body had not been found upon the field. And I myself had seen the sword cut into his shoulder.

"Perhaps—once he is found—"

"For a Cheysuli, you know little enough of your customs." Abruptly I cursed myself for my curtness. It was not my place to chastise Rowan for what he could not help. I glanced up at his stricken face, realized he risked as much as I in this endeavor, and tried to apologize.

He shook his head. "No. I know what you say. You have the right of it. If the wolf is already slain—or dies—you will lose your liege man."

"I may lose him anyway." It seemed too much to hope he would live. And if I gave the order to take his leg—

"Carillon." It was Alix, pulling aside the doorflap, and I stared in blank astonishment. "They sent for me." She came into the tent, dropping the flap behind her, and I saw the pallor of her face. "Duncan is not here?"

"I have sent for him."

She moved closer and knelt down at my side, amber eyes fixed on Finn. Seeing him again through her vision, I nearly turned away. He wore a death's-head in place of his own.

Alix put out her hand and touched his bare arm. The *lir*-gold with its wolf-shape was smeared with blood, dulled by grime; it seemed a reflection of his death. But she touched his arm and then clasped his slack hand, as if she could not let him go.

I watched her face. She knelt at his side and held his hand so gently. There was a sudden horrified grief in her eyes, as if she realized she would lose the man who had given her over to her heritage, and that realization broke down the wall between them. Ever had they been at one another's throats, cutting with knives made of words and swords made of feelings. They were kin and yet more than that, so much more, and I think she finally knew it.

She tipped back her head. I saw the familiar detached expression enter her eyes, making them blank and black and odd. Suddenly Alix was more Cheysuli than I had ever seen her, and I sensed the power move into her soul. So easily she summoned it, and then she released a sigh.

"Storr is alive."

I gaped at her.

"He is sorely hurt. Dying." Grief etched lines into her smooth face. "You must go. Fetch him back at once, and perhaps we can save them both."

"Where?"

"Not far." Her eyes were on Finn again and still she clasped his hand. "Perhaps a league. Northwest. There is a hill with a single tree upon it. And a cairn marker." She shut her eyes a moment, as if she drew upon the memory of the power. "Carillon—go *now* . . . I can reach Duncan through Cai."

I stood up at once, hardly aware of the protests of my body. I did not need to tell her to tend him well. I merely went out in my bloody, crusted leather-and-mail and ordered a horse at once.

*　　*　　*

Rowan came out of the pavilion as I rode up with Storr clasped in my arms. I dismounted carefully, loath to give the wolf over to anyone else, and went in as Rowan pulled aside the doorflap. It was then I was conscious of the harpsong and Lachlan's nimble fingers.

He sat on a campstool at Finn's side. His Lady was set against his chest, resting on one knee, and he played. How he played. The golden notes, so sweet and pure, poured forth from the golden strings. His head was bowed and his eyes were shut. His face was rigid with concentration. He did not sing, letting the harp do it for him, but I knew what magic he sought.

A healer, he had called himself. And now he tried to heal.

I knelt down and set Storr at Finn's side as gently as I could. Carefully I placed one limp brown hand into the stiffened silver fur, then moved back. The harpsong played on, dying away, and at last there was silence again.

Lachlan shifted a little, as if he awoke. "He is—beyond my aid. Even Lodhi's, I fear. He is Cheysuli—" He stopped, for there was little left to say.

Alix was in the shadows. She had left Finn's side as I entered, making room for Storr, and now she stood in the center of the tent. Her braids were coiled and pinned against her head but glittered not, for it seemed there was no light within the tent. No light at all.

"Duncan comes," she said softly.

"In time?"

"I cannot say."

I crossed my arms and hugged my chest as if I could keep the pain from showing on my face. "Gods—he is my right hand! I need him still—"

"We all need him." Her quiet words reproved me for my selfishness, though I doubt she meant them to.

A single note rang out from the harp as Lachlan shifted again on his stool. He silenced it at once, very grave of face. "How do *you* fare, Carillon?"

"Well enough," I said impatiently, and then I realized he referred to the blood on my mail. "I am unharmed. It was Finn they struck instead." The wolf lay quietly at his side, still breathing; so, thank the gods, was Finn.

"My lord." It was Rowan's tentative voice. "Shall I tell the princess the harper is come?"

For a moment I could not understand him. And then I knew. Lachlan had come from Bellam to direct the exchange. Electra for Tourmaline. And now I could hardly think.

Lachlan's eyes were on me. "Your sister is well, Carillon. Somewhat weary of being held in Bellam's command, but she has taken no harm. None at all." I was aware of an odd note in his voice. "She is well indeed . . . and lovely."

I looked more sharply at him. But I had no time to untangle the subtleties I heard, or the emotions of the moment. There were other things more pressing. "Where is she?"

"Not far from here. Bellam sent her out with a Solindish guard, and myself. They wait with her. I am to bring the Princess Electra, and then escort Torry back." He caught himself at once. "The Princess Tourmaline."

I did not wish to think of Electra, nor even Tourmaline. And yet I must. Impatiently I nodded at Rowan. "Tell her Lachlan is come, and to ready herself. When there is time, the exchange will be made."

Rowan bowed and left at once, perhaps grateful for a task. There is nothing so helpless as a man who must watch another die.

The flap was ripped aside. Duncan stood in the opening, backlighted by the sunlight, and suddenly the pavilion was filled with illumination. He was a silhouette against the brilliance until he came in, and then I saw how harshly set was his face.

"Alix." She went to him at once. Duncan hardly looked at me, for his attention was fixed on Finn. "Harper," he said, "I thank you. But this is Cheysuli-done."

Lachlan took the dismissal with good grace, rising instantly from the stool and moving out of the way. Duncan pushed the campstool away and knelt down with Alix at one side. He said nothing at all to me.

"I have never done this." There was fear in Alix's voice.

The heavy gold on Duncan's arms glowed in the shadows, reflecting the light that crept in through the gaps in the door-flap. "You have the Old Blood, *cheysula*. You need fear nothing of this. It is the earth magic we seek. You need only ask it to come, and it will use you to heal Finn. And Storr." Briefly he cupped her head in one hand and pressed it against one shoulder. "I promise you—it will be well done."

She said nothing more. Duncan released her and set one hand against the wound in the wolf's side. Of the two, Storr seemed to have a more fragile hold on life. And if he died before they healed Finn, the thing was futile indeed.

"Lose yourself," Duncan said. "Go down into the earth until there is nothing but the currents of life. You will know it—be not afraid. Tap it, Alix, and let it flow through you into the wolf. He is *lir*. He will know what we do for him."

I watched the changes in Alix's face. At first she was hesitant, following Duncan's lead, and then I saw the first indication of her own power. She knelt beside the wolf with her hands clasped lightly in her lap, eyes gone inward to face her soul. For a moment her body wavered and then it straightened. I saw the concentration and the wonder as she slipped from this world into another.

I nearly touched her then. I took two steps, intending to catch her in my arms, but the knowledge prevented me. What she did was beyond my ken—what she *was*, as well—but I knew Duncan. I knew he would never risk her. Not even to save his brother.

A tiny sound escaped her mouth, and then she was gone. Her body remained, so still and rigid, but Alix was gone. Somewhere far beneath the earth she roamed, seeking the healing arts her race claimed as their own, and Duncan was with her. I had only to look at his face and see the familiar detachment. It was profoundly moving, somehow, that a man and woman could link so deeply on a level other than sexual, and all to save a wolf.

Cheysuli magic goes into the earth, taps the strength of the ancient gods and lends it to the one who requires the healing. The sword wound in Storr's shoulder remained, but it lacked the unhealthy stink and appearance. His breathing steadied. His eyes cleared. He moved, twitching once all over, and came into the world again.

Alix sagged. Duncan caught her and clasped her against

his chest, much as Lachlan clasped his Lady. I saw the
fear and weariness etched in his face and wondered if he
had lied to her, saying it was safe when such magic took a
part of the soul away. Perhaps, for Finn, he *would* risk
Alix.

It made me profoundly angry. And then the anger died,
for I needed them both. I needed them all.

"No more," Duncan told her. "Storr is well enough. But
now it is my task to heal Finn."

"Not alone!" She sat up, pulling out of his arms. "Do
you think I will give you over to *that* when I have felt it
myself? No, Duncan—call the others. Link with them all.
There is no need for you to do this alone."

"There is," he told her gently. "He is my *rujho*. And I
am not alone . . . there is Cai." He smiled. "My thanks for
your concern, but it is unwisely spent. Save it for Finn
when he wakens."

And then he slipped away before she could protest,
sliding out of our hands like oil. The shell we knew as
Duncan remained, but he was gone. Whatever made him
Duncan had gone to another place, and this time he was
gone deeper and longer, so deep and so long I thought we
had lost them both.

"Alix!" I knew she meant to follow. I bent to pull her
from the ground.

She turned an angry face to me. "Do not keep me from
him, Carillon! Do you think I could bear to lose him like
this? Even for Finn—"

"You risked yourself for me, once, when I did not wish
you to," I told her harshly. "When I lay chained in Atvian
iron, and you came as a falcon to free me. Do you think I
would have given you permission for such a thing?" I
shook my head. "What Duncan does is for him to do. Did
he want you with him, he would have asked it."

She wrenched her head around to stare again at her
husband. He knelt by Finn's side, there and yet not. And
Finn, so weak upon the pallet, did not move.

"I could not make a choice," she said in a wavering
voice. "I ever thought I would say Duncan before anyone
else, but I could not. I want them *both*. . . ."

"I know. So do I. But it is for the gods to decide."

"Has Lachlan turned you priest?" She smiled a little, bitterly. "I never knew you to prate of such things."

"I do not prate of them now. Call it *tahlmorra,* if you will." I smiled and made the gesture. "What is there for us to do but wait and see what will happen?"

Duncan said something then. It was garbled, tangled up in the Old Tongue and his weariness, but it was a sound. He moved as if to rise, could not, and fell back to knock his head against the campstool. Lachlan set down his Lady and knelt at once to give him support, even as Alix wrenched herself free of me.

"You fool," Finn said weakly. "It is not for a man to do alone."

I stared at him, unsure I had heard him correctly. But it was Finn, white as death, and I saw tears in his eyes.

Duncan pushed himself upward with Lachlan's help. He sat half-dazed, legs sprawled, as if he could not come back to himself. Even as Alix knelt down before him he seemed not to know her.

I saw Finn push an elbow against the pallet to lever himself up. And again it was myself who pushed him down. "Lie you still."

"Duncan—" he said thickly, protesting ineffectively.

"Come back!" Alix shouted. "By the gods, you fool—" And she struck Duncan hard across the face with the flat of her hand.

It set up brilliant color in his face, turning his cheek dark red. But sense was in his eyes again. He looked at Alix, at me, at Finn, and then he was Duncan again. "Gods," he said weakly. "I did not know—"

"No," Finn agreed, with my hand upon his shoulder in case he moved again. "You did not, you fool. Did you think I would wish to trade your life for mine?" He grimaced then, and instantly hissed as the expression pulled the stitches against his swollen flesh. "By the gods—that Atvian—"

"—is slain," I finished. "Did you think I would let him finish what he had begun?"

Finn's hand was in Storr's matted pelt. His eyes were shut in a gray-white face. I thought he had lost consciousness again.

"*Rujho*," Duncan said, "there is something you must do."

"Later," Finn said through the taut line of his mouth.

"Now." Duncan smiled. "You owe thanks to Carillon."

I looked at him in surprise. Finn's eyes opened a slit, dilated black and glittering with the remnants of his fever. "It was *you* who—"

"Aye," Duncan interrupted, "but it was Carillon who carried you from the field. Else you would still be there, and dead."

I knew what he did. Finn has never been one for showing gratitude, though often enough I knew he felt it. I myself had trouble saying what I meant; for Finn it was harder still. I thought of protesting, then let Duncan have his way. He it was who had had the raising of Finn, not me.

Finn sighed. His eyes closed again. "He should have left me. He should not have risked himself."

"No," Duncan agreed, "but he did. And now there are the words to be said."

I thought Finn was asleep. He did not move; did not indicate he heard. But he had. And at last he looked at me from beneath his heavy lids. "*Leijhana tu'sai*," he muttered.

I blinked. And then I laughed. "In the Old Tongue, I would not know if you thanked me or cursed me."

"He thanked you," Duncan said gravely. And then, "*Leijhana tu'sai*, Carillon."

I realized I was the only one standing. Even Lachlan knelt, so close to Duncan, with his Lady gleaming on the table. It was an odd sensation to have such people in such postures, and to know one day it would be expected.

I looked at Lachlan. "We have an exchange to conduct."

He rose and gathered his harp. But before we left the tent I glanced back at Finn.

He slept. "*Leijhana tu'sai*," I said, "for living instead of dying."

FOURTEEN

I left the tent, my legs trembling with the aftermath of fatigue and tension. I stopped just outside, letting the doorflap fall shut behind me. For a moment I could only stare blankly at the few pavilions scattered across the turf in apparent confusion, lacking all order. I had taken the idea from the Cheysuli, although here we lacked the trees to hide ourselves adequately, We had camped on a grassy plain, leaving the forests behind as we moved closer to Mujhara; closer to Bellam and my throne. The encampment was little more than a scattering of men with cookfires here and there. But it had served us well.

I sucked in a deep breath, as deep as I could make it, filling my lungs with air. The stink of the army camp faded to nonexistence as I thought how close I had come to losing Finn. I knew perfectly well that had my chirurgeons pressed to take his leg, he would have found another way to die. A maimed warrior, he had told me once, was of little use to his clan. In Finn's case, it was worse; he would view himself as useless to his Mujhar as well, and that would pervert his *tahlmorra* and his very reason for living.

Lachlan slipped through the entrance. I heard the hiss of fabric as he moved, scraping one hand across the woven material. Few of us had tents to claim as shelter; I, being Mujhar, had the largest, but it was not so much. This one served as a temporary infirmary; the chirurgeons had kept all others free of it when I had brought Finn. He would be nursed in private.

Lachlan's arms were empty of harp for once. "Finn will live. You need fear no more."

"Have you consulted Lodhi?"

He made no indication my comment bothered him. "There is no need for that. I asked His help before, but there was nothing in Finn I could touch. He was too far from this world, too lost in his pain and Storr's absence. But when Duncan and Alix worked their magic—" He broke off, smiling a little. "There is much I cannot understand. And until I know more of the Cheysuli, I cannot hope to make songs of them."

"Most men cannot understand the Cheysuli," I told him. "As for songs—I doubt they would wish it. There are legends enough about them." I stared at the tiny field pavilion farthest from where we stood. It was guarded by six soldiers. "How many men are with my sister?"

"Bellam sent a guard of fifty with her." His face was grave. "My lord—you do not intend to go *yourself*—"

"She is my sister." I set off toward the saffron-colored tent as Lachlan fell in beside me. "I owe Tourmaline what honor there is, and of late there is little. I will send no man in my place."

"Surely you will take some of your army with you."

I smiled, wondering if he sought the information for simple curiosity's sake. "No."

"Carillon—"

"If it is a trap, the teeth will close on air." I signaled to the soldiers guarding Electra's tent. They stepped away at once, affording me privacy, though they remained within earshot. "*You* would know, perhaps, what Bellam intends for me."

Lachlan smiled as I paused before the tent. "He did not divulge his plans to me, unfortunately. He welcomed me as a harper, not a confidant. I cannot say he sends men to take you, but I think it very likely." His eyes went past me to study the scattered encampment. "You would do well to take a substantial escort."

"No doubt," I said blandly.

I turned and pulled aside the doorflap, but did not go in

at once. I could not. The sunlight was brilliant as it slashed into the interior, illuminating the woman who sat within. She wore a dark brown gown laced with copper silk at throat and cuffs. A supple leather belt, clay-bleached to a soft yellow, bound her slender waist, fastened with a copper buckle. The gown was from Alix, fashioned by her own hands, given freely to replace the soiled gray velvet Electra had worn the day Finn caught her. The new one fit well enough, for they were of a like size, though nothing like in coloring.

Electra waited quietly, seated on a three-legged camp-stool with the folds of her dark skirts foaming around her feet like waves upon a shore. She sat erect, shoulders put back, so that the slender, elegant line of her neck met the jaw to emphasize the purity of her bones. She had braided her hair into a single loose-woven rope that hung over one shoulder to spill into her lap, coiled like a serpent. The smooth, pale brow cried out for a circlet of beaten gold, or—perhaps better—silver, to highlight the long-lidded, magnificent eyes.

I knew Rowan had been here to tell her. She waited, hands clasped beneath the rope of shining hair. Silently she sat upon the stool as the sunlight passed through the weave of the saffron-colored tent to paint her with a pastel, ocherous glow. She wore the twisted gold at her throat, and it shone.

By the gods, so did she. And I wanted so much to lose myself in it. In her. Gods, but what a woman can do to a man—

Even the enemy.

Forty years, this woman claimed. And I denied it, as ever.

I put out my hand to raise her from the stool. Her fingers were still, making no promises, though I had had that of her, as well.

"You have been in battle." Her voice was cool as ever, with its soft, Solindish cadence.

I had not put off the blood-crusted leather-and-mail. My hair, dried now from the sweat of my exertions, hung stiffly against my shoulders. No doubt I smelled of it as well, but I wasted no time on the niceties of such things while I had a war to fight. "Come, lady—your father waits."

"Did you win your battle?" She allowed me to lead her from the tent, making no move to remove her hand from my grasp.

I shook my head. Rowan stood outside with four horses. I saw no good in gaming with her, denying my loss to gain a satisfaction that would not last. I *had* lost, but Bellam still lacked his pretender-prince.

Electra paused as she saw the empty saddles. Four horses only, and no accompaniment. "Where are my women?"

"I sent them back long ago." I smiled at her. "Only you were brought here. But then you were compromised the moment Finn took you captive. What should it matter, Electra—you are an Ihlini's light woman."

Color came into her face. I had not expected to see it, from her. She was a young woman suddenly, lacking the wisdom of experience, and yet I saw the glint of knowledge in her eyes. I wondered, uneasily, if Tynstar's arts *had* given her youth in place of age. "Does it grate within your soul?" she asked. "Does it make you wish to put your stamp upon me, to erase Tynstar's?" She smiled, a mere curving of the perfect mouth. "You fool. You could not begin to take his place."

"You will have the opportunity to know." I boosted her into the saddle without further comment, and felt the rigid unyielding in her body. I had cut her, somehow: but then she had cut me often enough. I nodded at Rowan. "Send for Zared, at once."

When Zared came he bowed respectfully. His gray-red hair was still cropped closely against his head, as was common in soldiery. I had not taken up the custom because it had been easy enough, in Caledon, to braid it and bind it with the scarlet yarn of a mercenary. It had been what I was.

"See to it the camp is dispersed," I told him. "I want no men here to receive Bellam's welcome, for you may be quite certain his daughter will tell him where we have been." I did not look at her, having no need; I could sense

her rigid attention. "When I am done with this exchange,
I will find the army."

"Aye, my lord Mujhar." He bowed, all solemn servi-
tude, and stepped away to follow orders.

Lachlan mounted next to me, and Rowan next to Electra.
She was hemmed in on both sides, closely kept. It would
not do to lose her now, before I claimed my sister.

Electra looked at us all. "No army to escort you?"

"Need I one?" I smiled. I glanced to Lachlan and saw
his gesture. Westward, toward Mujhara, and Tourmaline,
my sister.

The sun beat down upon our heads as we waited on the
hilltop. We silhouetted ourselves against the horizon, a
thing I had not done in the long months of bitter war, but
now I did it willingly. I wanted Tourmaline to see us
before the exchange was made, so she would know it was
us in truth, and not some trick of Bellam's.

The plains stretched below us. No more spring; it was
nearly midsummer. The sun had baked the green from the
land, turning it yellow and ocher and amber, and the dust
rose from the hooves of more than fifty horses to hang in
the air like smoke. Through the haze I could see the men,
in Solindish colors, glittering with ringmail and swords. A
troop of men knotted about a single woman like a fist
around a hilt.

I could not see Tourmaline well. But from time to time
I saw the dappled gray horse and the slender, upright
figure, wearing no armor but a gown instead, an indigo-
colored gown and no traveling mantle to keep the dust off
her clothing. Even her head was bared, and her tawny-
dark hair hung down freely to tangle across the horse's
gray rump.

I heard Lachlan's quiet, indrawn breath. I heard my
own as well, but it lacked the note I heard in his. I
glanced at him a moment, seeing how avidly he watched
the troop approach; how intent were his eyes upon the
woman. Not my sister, in that instant, but a woman.

I knew then, beyond any doubt at all, that Lachlan plot-
ted no treachery, no betrayal. I was certain of it, in that
instant. To do so would endanger Tourmaline, and that he

would never countenance. I had only to look at his face as he looked for hers, and at last I had my answer.

If for nothing else, he would be loyal to me out of loyalty to my sister. And what a weapon he gave me, did I find the need to use it.

The Solindish troop stopped at the foot of the hill. The sun glittered off their trappings; off their ringmail; off their intention. Fifty men bent on taking Bellam's enemy. And that enemy with only a token escort at his side.

It was warm on the hilltop. The air was quite still; the silence was broken only by the jingle and clash of horse trappings and the buzzing hum of an occasional insect. The dust was dry in my mouth and nose; I tasted the flat, bitter salt of summer-swept plains. Come fall, turf would spring up beneath a gentler sun. Come winter, snow would blanket the world. Come spring, I should be King.

If not before.

I looked through the clustered troop to the treasure they guarded so closely. Tourmaline, a princess of Homana. The woman Bellam had threatened to wed; the woman he could not because I had taken his daughter. A princess for a princess.

She sat quite still upon her horse, her hands holding the reins. But she was not entirely free. A soldier flanked her directly on either side; a lead-rope tied her horse to a man who rode before her. They meant not to lose her so easily, did I give them cause to fight.

Lachlan's breath was audible in his throat. It rasped, sliding through the constriction slowly, so that Rowan glanced at him. There was curiosity in Rowan's eyes; knowledge in Electra's. She would know. She would know what he felt: a man in love with a woman, looking at her with desire.

"Well?" I said at last. "Are we to confront one another in silence all day, or is there a thing I must do?"

Lachlan wrenched his attention back to me. "I am to escort Electra down, and bring Torry back with me."

"Do it."

He rubbed at the flesh beneath the silver circlet on his brow. "Nothing more?"

"Am I to think you seek to warn me of some treachery?"

I smiled. "Do what you have said must be done. I want my sister back."

His jaw tightened. Briefly he glanced at Electra. She sat very still on her horse, like Torry, hardly moving her hands upon the reins. But I saw her fingers tense and the subtle shift of her weight. She meant to run, with Tourmaline still held.

I reached out and caught one of her wrists, clamping down tightly. "No," I said calmly. "Do you forget I have a bow?"

Her eyes went to the Cheysuli bow at once. And my quiver, freshly filled. "You might slay some," she conceded coolly, "but I doubt you could slay them all before they took you."

"No," I agreed, "but have I spoken of slaying *men*?"

She understood at once. I saw the color move into her face swiftly, setting flags of anger into her cheeks. The somnolent, ice-gray eyes were blackened with frustration, but only for a moment. She smiled. "Slay me, then, and you purchase your fate from Tynstar."

"I do not doubt I have done so already," I told her calmly. "I think my sister is worth dying for. But are you?"

"So long as *you* do the dying." She did not look at me. She looked instead at the troop of men her father had sent to fetch her.

I laughed and released her wrist. "Go, then, Electra. Tell your father—and your sorcerer—whatever you wish to say. But remember that I will have you as my wife."

Loathing showed on her face. "You will have nothing, pretender-prince. Tynstar will see to that."

"My lord." Rowan sounded uneasy. "They are fifty to our three."

"So they are." I nodded to Lachlan. "Take her down, and bring my sister back."

Lachlan put out his hand to grasp Electra's rein. But she did not let him. She pulled the horse away and set him to walking down the hill. Lachlan fell in close beside her almost at once, and I watched as they rode toward the troop. I unstrapped the bow so the captain could see it, though I did not intend to use it. I did not think I would need it.

Electra was swallowed almost at once by the Solindish soldiers and I was left without a target. Unless one counted the captain and his men. But Electra had the right of it; I could not slay them all. Even with Rowan at my side.

He shifted in his saddle. "My lord—"

"Be patient," I chided gently.

Lachlan waited at the edge of the hard-eyed throng. The sun on his dyed hair treated it poorly, turning it dull and lifeless. Only the glint of silver on his brow lent him authenticity, and that only won through his harp. I wondered again what made him the man he was, and how it was to be a priest.

The troop parted. Tourmaline came forward on her dappled gray horse. Like Electra, she did not hasten, but I saw the tension in her body. Doubtless she feared the trade would not be finished.

Well, it was not finished yet.

Lachlan put out his hand to her. Briefly she held it tightly with her own, as if thanking him for his care; I watched in bemusement. It was all well and good for a harper to love a princess—that happened with great regularity, to judge by the content of their lays—but I was not certain Tourmaline's apparent regard for him pleased me one whit. He was a harper, and she was meant for a prince.

"They come," Rowan said softly, more to himself than to me.

They came. Side by side, no longer clasping hands, their shoulders rigid against the Solindish guard. Dust rose up from the ground and enveloped them in a veil; Tourmaline's eyes were squinted against it as she came yet closer to me. And then she was laughing, calling out my name, and kicked her horse into a run.

I did not dismount, for all it would have been an easier greeting on the ground. She set her horse into mine, but gently, and our knees knocked as she reached out to hug my neck. It was awkward on horseback, but we got it done. And then, as she opened her mouth to speak again, I waved her into silence.

"My lord!" It was Rowan as Lachlan rode up. "They come!"

And so they did. Almost all fifty of them, charging up the hill, to swallow us within their ringmailed fist.

I smiled grimly, unsurprised. I saw the frustrated, impotent anger on Rowan's young face as he put his hand to his sword; he did not draw it because he saw no reason to. We were too soundly caught.

Lachlan said something in his Ellasian tongue. A curse, I thought, not recognizing it, or perhaps a plea to his All-Father; whatever it was, it sounded like he meant to chew up their bones, did they bother to come close enough.

Tourmaline, white-faced, shot me a glance that said she understood the brevity of our greeting. What fear I saw in her face was not for herself, but for me. Her brother, who had been sought for six long years, was home at last. And caught.

The Solindish captain wore a mail coif that hid all of his head but his face. A wide, hard, battle-scarred face, with brown eyes that had undoubtedly seen everything in war, and yet now expressed a bafflement born of disbelief. His Homanan was twisted by his Solindish accent, but I understood him well enough. "Surely a *boy* would know better."

My horse stomped beneath me, jarring my spine against the saddle. I did not answer.

"Carillon of Homana?" the captain asked, as if he could not believe he had caught the proper quarry.

"The Mujhar," I agreed calmly. "Do you mean to take us to the usurper on his stolen throne?"

Tourmaline drew in a sudden breath. Lachlan moved his horse closer to my sister's, as if to guard her. It was for me to do, not him, but I was occupied at the moment.

"Your sword," the captain said. "There is no hope of escape for you."

"No?" I smiled. "My sword is my own to keep."

The first shadow passed over my face, moving on quickly to blot out the captain's face. Then another. Yet a third, and the ground was suddenly blotched with moving darkness, as if a plague of shadows had come to settle across us all. All men, save me, looked up, and saw the circling birds.

There were dozens of them. Hawks and eagles and falcons, owls and ravens and more. With wings outstretched and talons folded, they danced upon the air. Up, then down, then around and around bent upon some goal.

Rowan began to laugh. "My lord," he said at last, "forgive me for doubting you."

They stooped. They screamed. They slashed by the enemy and slapped wings against staring eyes, until the Solindish soldiers cried out in fear and pain. No man was slain; no man was even wounded, but their skill and pride and dignity was completely shredded. There are more ways of overcoming the enemy than merely by slaying him. With the Cheysuli, half the defeat comes from knowing what they are.

Half the birds broke away. They dipped to the ground with a rustle of outspread wings; the soughing of feathers folded away. They were birds no more, but men instead, as the shapechange swallowed them all.

I heard the outcries of utter panic from the Solindish troop. One or two retched and vomited against the earth, too frightened to hold it in. Some dealt with horses threatening to bolt. Others sat perfectly still in their saddles, staring, with no hands upon their weapons.

I smiled. With Rowan, my sister and Lachlan at my back, I broke passage through the enemy to the freedom outside the shattered fist. And when we were free again, guarded against attack by more than half a hundred warriors, I nodded. "Put them to death," I said. "All but five. They may escort the lady to her father."

"My lord?" It was Rowan, questioning the need for sparing even five Solindishmen to fight us another day.

"I want Bellam to know," I said. "Let him choke upon what I have done."

"Do you leave him his daughter?" Lachlan asked.

I looked past the silent troop to the five men who guarded Electra so closely at the bottom of the hill. I saw the tension in their bodies. Hands rested on their swords. Electra, too distant for me to make out her expression, sat equally still. No doubt she thought I would take her back. No doubt she knew I wanted to.

"I leave him his daughter," I said at last. "Let her spend her time in Homana-Mujhar wondering when I will come." I looked at the Cheysuli warriors surrounding the captured Solindish. Horses trembled; so did men. I thought it a fitting end.

And then I saw Duncan. He stood to one side with Cai upon his shoulder. The great hawk sat quietly, a mass of gold and brown next to the blackness of Duncan's hair. The clan-leader seemed to support him effortlessly, though I could imagine the weight of the bird. In that instant I thought back to the time, six years before, when I had been imprisoned by the Cheysuli; when Finn had held and taunted me. Duncan it was who had ruled, as the Cheysuli are ruled, by numbers instead of a single man. But there was no doubting who held the power in the clan. There was no doubting it now.

Cai lifted and returned to the air, stirring the fine veil of dust with his great outspread wings, and soared into the heavens along with the other *lir*. The shadows continued to blotch the land and the fear continued to live.

Duncan was unsmiling. "Shall I begin with the captain?"

I released a breath and nodded. Then I looked at Tourmaline. "It is time we found the camp."

Her eyes, blue as my own, were wide and staring as she looked upon the Cheysuli. I recalled she had seen none before, though knew of them as I had for so many years. To her, no doubt, they were barbaric. To her, no doubt, they were worse than beasts.

She said nothing, knowing better than to speak freely before the enemy, but I did not doubt she would when we were free.

"Come," I said gently, and turned her horse away.

FIFTEEN

The wind came up at sunset as we rode into the newly
settled encampment. It blew dust in our faces and tangled
Tourmaline's hair, until she caught it in one hand and
made it tame, winding it through her fingers. Lachlan
muttered something in his Ellasian tongue—it had to do
with Lodhi, as usual—and Rowan blinked against the grit.
As for me, I relished it. The wind would blow away the
taste of blood and loss. For I had led my men into death,
and I would not forget.

"A storm," Torry said. "Rain, do you think?"

The cookfires, which pocked the open landscape, whipped
and strained against the wind. I smelled the aroma of
roasting meat and it set my mouth to watering. I could not
recall when last I had eaten—surely it was this morning?

"No rain," I said finally. "Only wind, and the smell of
death."

Tourmaline looked at me sharply. I saw a question
forming in her face, but she asked nothing. She glanced
instead at Lachlan, seeking some assurance, then turned
her attention to her horse as I led them to my pavilion
when I had asked directions of a passing soldier.

I jumped from my horse by the doorflap and turned to
Torry's mount. She slid out of the saddle and into my
arms, and I felt the weariness in her body. Like me, she
was in need of rest, sustenance and sleep. I thought to set
her down and take her inside, to get her properly settled,

but she wrapped her arms around my neck and hugged with all her strength. There were tears, warm against my flesh, and I knew she cried for us both.

"Forgive me," she whispered into my sweat-dried hair. "I prayed all these years that the gods would let you live, even as Bellam sought you, yet when you come I give you thoughtless welcome. I thought you grown harsh and cruel when you ordered them slain, but I—of all—should know better. Was not our father a soldier?"

"Torry—"

She lifted her head and looked me in the face, for while I held her she was nearly as tall as I. "Lachlan told me what odds you face, and how well you face them; it is not my place to reprove you for your methods. Harsh times require harsh measures, and the gods know war is not for gentle men."

"You have not reproved me. As for gentle, no. There is little room in me for that." I set her on her feet and reached out to tousle her hair. It was an old game between us, and I saw she recalled it well. Ever the older sister telling the youngest child what to do. Except the boy had grown up at last.

"In my heart," she said softly, "I reproved. It is my fault for having expectations. I thought, when you came, it would be the old Carillon, the one I used to tease. But I find it is the new one, and a different man who faces me."

There were strangers among us, though I knew their names, and we could not say precisely what we wished. But for the moment it was enough to see her again and know her safe, as she had not been safe for years. So I said something of what I felt. "I am sorry. I should have come home sooner. Somehow, I should have come—"

She put her hand across my mouth. "No. Say nothing. You are come home now." She smiled the brilliant smile of our mother and the lines of tension were washed from her face. I had forgotten the beauty of my sister, and I saw why Lachlan was smitten.

The wind cracked the folds of the pavilion beside us. Lachlan's horse stepped aside uneasily; he checked it with a tightened rein. I looked up at Rowan and squinted against the dust. "See you she has food and wine. It will be your task to make certain she is well."

"My lord," he said, "your pavilion?"

"Hers, now." I smiled. "I have learned these past years what it is to make my bed upon the ground."

Lachlan, laughing, demurred at once. "Are you forgetting harpers are given their own sort of honor? Pavilions are part of it. Does it not ruffle your Mujhar's pride and dignity, you may share mine with me."

"It ruffles nothing," I retorted. "And will not, so long as you refrain from singing—or praying—in your sleep." I looked at Torry again. "This is an army encampment, rude and rough. There is little refinement here. I must ask you to forgive what you hear."

She laughed aloud with the pleasure of her retort. "Well enough, I shall forgive your men. But never you."

The wind blew a lock of her unbound hair against my chest. It caught on the links of my ringmail, snagging, and I sought to free it without tearing the strands. I felt the clean silk against my callused, blood-stained hands, and knew again what manner of man her brother had become.

It was no wonder she had reproved me, even in her heart.

I pulled aside the doorflap and gestured her within. "Rowan will bring food and wine, and anything else you might require. Sleep, if you will. There will be time for talking later."

I saw the questions in her eyes and her instant silencing of them. She nodded and ducked inside, and I saw the glow of a lighted candle. She would not be left in darkness.

I glanced up at Lachlan, who watched her disappear as the flap dropped down behind her. Inwardly I smiled, knowing the edge of the weapon; outwardly I was casual. "No doubt she would welcome company."

His face colored, then blanched. He had not realized how easily I saw his feelings. His hands touched his silver circlet as if to gather strength. "No doubt. But yours, I think, not mine."

I let it go, knowing I might use it later to bind him to me. Through Tourmaline, at least, I could know the harper's intentions. "Come, then. We must tell Finn what has happened. It was his plan, not mine, and he should know."

Rowan started. "His?"

I nodded. "We made it in Caledon one night, or something like it, when we had nothing better to do." I smiled with the memory. "It was a summer night, like this one, but lacking the wind, and warmer. The evening before a battle. We spoke of plots and plans and strategies, and how it would be a fitting trick to set loose in Bellam's midst." My smile faded. "But that night we did not know if we would one day come home again, or if there would be so many Cheysuli."

Again the pavilion fabric cracked. Lachlan stepped down from his horse, hair tamed by the circlet. "But there *are* Cheysuli, my lord . . . and you have come home again."

I looked at him and saw again the dull brown hair. I thought of him in love with my sister. "Will you harp for me tonight?" I asked. "Give me *The Song of Homana*."

It was the harp I saw first as I entered the infirmary tent; Lachlan's Lady, with her brilliant green eye. She stared at us both as the doorflap fell behind us, and I thought, oddly, the harp was like a *lir*. That Lachlan served her I did not wonder; that she served Lachlan, I knew. I had felt the magic before when they wove it between them.

"Ah," said Finn, "he has not forgotten me. The student recalls the master."

I grinned, relieved past measure to hear his voice so full of life. Yet even as I looked at him I could not help but wince, at least inwardly; the stitches held his face together, but the scar would last forever. It would be *that* men—and women—saw before anything else.

Lachlan slipped past me to gather his harp into his arms. He had spent much of the day without his Lady; I wondered if it hurt.

As for Finn, he did not smile. But, knowing him, I saw the hint of pleasure in his eyes and, I thought, relief. Had he thought I would not come back?

"Have they all left you alone?" I hooked the stool over with a foot.

Finn's laugh was a breath of sound. He was weak still, I could see it. But I thought he would survive. The magic had given him that much, even had it not made him fully well. "Alix has spent all day with me. Only now have I managed to send her away." He shifted slightly on the pallet, as if the leg yet pained him. "I told her I needed time alone, and I do. There is no need to coddle me."

"Alix would hardly coddle *you*." I looked more closely at his face and saw the sallow tinge. It was better than the ashy hue of death, but he lacked the proper color. There was no fever, that much I could tell, but he was obviously weary. "Is there aught I might bring you?"

"A Mujhar, serving me?" This time there was a smile, though it was very faint. "No, I am well. Alix has done more than enough. More than I ever expected."

"Perhaps it is her way of compensation," I suggested without a smile.

"Perhaps," he agreed in his ironic manner. "She knows what she lacks. I have impressed it upon her on several occasions."

Lachlan, leaning against the table, struck a note on his harp. "I could put it to song. How you wooed and lost a maiden; how the brother was the victor."

Finn cast him a scowl, though it lacked its usual depth. "Harper, you would do well to think of your own women, and leave mine to me."

Lachlan's smile froze, then grew distracted, and I knew he thought of Torry. His fingertips brushed the glowing golden strings and I heard the breath of sound. It conjured up the grace and elegance in a woman, and I thought at once of Electra. No doubt *he* thought of my sister; Finn—no doubt Finn remembered Alix. Alix before she knew Duncan.

"The exchange was accomplished," I said quietly. "My sister is safe, and Electra returns to her father."

"I thought you might keep her."

I scowled at the ironic tone. "No. I have set my mind to winning the throne before I win the woman. Did it come to a choice, you know which one I would take."

Finn's brows lifted a bit. "There have been times, of late, I have not been so sure." He shifted a little, restless, and I saw the twinge cross his face. Storr, lying next to him, settled his body closer. One brown arm with its weight of gold cradled the wolf as if Finn feared to release him.

"Will you be well?" I asked it more sharply than I intended. "Has the earth magic not healed you fully?"

He gestured briefly with a limp hand. "It does not always restore a body completely, it merely aids the healing. It is dependent on the injury." For a moment tentative fingers touched the bandage binding the thigh. "I am well enough—for a man who should have died."

I took a deep breath and felt the slow revolution of the shadows in the tent. I was so tired . . . "The plan we made was ideal. Duncan brought all the winged *lir*. The Solindish stood no chance."

"No," he agreed. "It is why I suggested it."

Lachlan laughed softly. "Does Carillon do nothing without your suggestion?"

For a moment Finn's expression was grim, for a face that was mostly ruined by swelling and seeping stitches. "There are times he does too much."

"As when I decide whom to wed." I smiled at Lachlan's expression of surprise. "The lady who goes to her father will become the Queen of Homana."

His eyebrows rose beneath the circlet. "Bellam might not be willing."

"Bellam will be dead when I wed his daughter." I rolled my head to and fro, popping the knots in my neck. My back was tense as well, but there was no help for that. I would have to work it out with proper sleep and exercise; the former I would not see, no doubt, but the latter was a certainty.

"I had heard she was offered to High King Rhodri's heir." Lachlan's fingers brought a singing cadence from the strings.

I shrugged. "Perhaps Bellam offered, but I have heard nothing of Rhodri's answer. You, being Ellasian and his subject, might know better."

Lachlan's mouth twisted thoughtfully. "I doubt he would stand in your way. What I know of Cuinn I have learned mostly first-hand, from being hosted in the castle. The

High Prince is an idle sort, though friendly enough, with no mind to marriage so soon." He shrugged. "Rhodri has strength of his own; I doubt he will demand his heir's marriage as yet. But then who am I to know the minds of kings?" He grinned at me. "There is only you, my lord, and what do I know of you?"

"You know I have a sister."

His face went very still. "Aye. I do." Briefly he glanced at Finn. "But if we speak of it more, you will set your liege man to laughing."

Finn smiled. "Has a princess caught your eye? But what else?—you are a harper."

The golden notes poured forth, and yet Lachlan did not smile. "So I am, with thanks to Lodhi's power. But there are times I could wish myself more . . ."

So a princess might look his way? No doubt. But though harpers hold high honor in the courts of kings, they do not have enough to wed a woman of Torry's rank.

I leaned forward a moment and scrubbed at my gritty, burning eyes. And then I heard the scream.

Finn tensed to rise and then fell back; no doubt he feared it was Alix. But at once I knew it was not. The sound belonged to my sister.

I do not recall how I got from Finn's tent to my own, nor do I recall Lachlan at my side holding his gleaming harp. He was simply there, clasping his Lady, and the curses poured from his mouth. I hardly heard them. Instead I heard the echo of Torry's scream and the pounding of my blood.

Men stood around my pavilion. Someone had pulled the doorflap aside and tied it. I saw shadows within, and silhouettes; I tore the throng apart and thrust myself inside, not caring whom I hurt.

Tourmaline stood in one corner, clutching a loose green robe of my own around her body. A single candle filled the tent with muted, smoky light; it painted her face rigid and pale and glowed off the gold in her hair.

She saw me and put up a hand at once, as if to stay me. As if to tell me she had suffered no harm. It passed through my mind then that my sister was a stronger woman than I had supposed, but I had no more time for that. It was Rowan I looked at, and the body he bent over.

"Dead?" I demanded.

Rowan shook his head as he reached down to pull a knife from the man's slack hand. "No, my lord. I struck him down with the hilt of my sword, knowing you would have questions for him."

I moved forward then, reaching to grasp the leather-and-mail of the man's hauberk. The links bit into my hands as I jerked him over and up, so I could see him clearly. I nearly released him then, for the light fell on Zared's face.

He was half-conscious. His eyes blinked and rolled in his head, which lolled as I held him up. "Well?" I asked of Rowan. "You were set to guard her."

"Against Zared?" His tone was incredulous. "Better to guard against *me*."

I felt the burn of anger in my belly. "Does even *that* need doing, I will do it! Answer the question I asked!"

The color fell out of his face. I heard Tourmaline's sound of protest, but my attention was taken up with Rowan. For a moment there was a flare of answering anger in his yellow Cheysuli eyes, and then he nodded. He did not seem ashamed, merely understanding, and accepting. It was well; I did not want a man who put his tail between his legs.

"I heard her cry out," he said. "I came in at once and saw a man standing over the cot, in the darkness. He held a knife." Rowan lifted a hand and I saw it. "And so I struck him down. But it was not until he fell that I saw it was Zared."

"Tourmaline?" I asked, more gently than I had of Rowan.

"I had put the candle out, so I could sleep," she told me quietly. "I heard nothing; he was very quiet. And then suddenly there was a presence, and a shape, and I screamed. But I think, before that last moment, he knew it was not you."

Zared roused in my hands and I tightened my grip. The ring-mail was harsh against my fingers but I did not care. I dragged him up, thrust him out of the pavilion and saw him tumble through the throng. He was left alone to fall;

they closed him within a circle of glittering, ringmailed leather but did not touch. They waited for me to act.

Zared was fully conscious. He shifted as if to rise, then fell back to kneel upon the ground as the throng took a single step forward. He knew the mettle of the men. He knew me.

He touched fingers to the back of his neck where Rowan had struck him. Briefly he looked at Torry, standing in the open doorflap, and then he looked at me. "I did not mean to harm the lady," he told me calmly. "I admit freely: it was you I wanted."

"For that, my thanks," I said grimly. "If I thought it was my sister you meant to slay, your entrails would be burning."

"Get it done," he returned instantly. "Give me over to the gods."

I looked at him, kneeling there. At the compact, powerful veteran of my uncle's Solindish wars. My father's man, once, and now he sought to slay his son. "After an explanation," I agreed.

He turned his head and spat. "*That* for your explanation." He sucked in a breath as the gathered men muttered among themselves. "I owe you nothing. I *give* you nothing. There will be no explanation."

I took a step forward, angry enough to strike him as he knelt, but Lachlan's hand was on my arm. "No," he said, "let *me—*"

He said nothing more. He did not need to. His fingers had gone into the strings of his Lady, plucking them, and the sound silenced us all.

The pavilion cracked behind me. I heard the breath of the wind as it whipped at nearby fires. Torry said a word, a single sound, and then not another one was made.

The harp music took us all. I felt it more than heard it as it dug within my soul, and there it stayed. So did I. The wind blew dust into my eyes, but I not blink. I felt the beating of grit against my face, but did not move to wipe it away. I stood quite still as the others did, and listened to Lachlan's soft promise.

"You misjudge, Zared," he said. "But how you misjudge

my Lady. She can conjure visions from a blind man . . . words from a dumb man. And put madness in its place. . . ."

Zared cried out, cringing, and clapped his hands to his ears. The song went on, weaving us all in its spell. His fingers dug rigidly into his flesh, as if he could block the sound. But it sang on, burrowing into his mind even as it blanked ours out.

"Lachlan," I said, but no sound came out of my mouth.

Zared's hands fell away from his head. He knelt and stared, transfixed as any child upon an endless wonder: jaw sagging, drool falling, eyes bulging open in a terrible joy.

The harp sang on, a descant to the wind. So subtle, seductive and sly. Lachlan himself, with his dyed hair blowing and his blue eyes fixed, smiled with incredible power. I saw his face transfigured by the presence of his god; he was no more the harper but an instrument of Lodhi, perhaps the harp herself, and a locus for the magic. Pluck him and she sounded, sharp and sweet. Pluck her and he quivered, resonating in the wind.

I shivered. It ran over me like a grue, from scalp to toes, and I shivered again. I felt the hair stand up from my flesh and the coldness in my soul. "Lachlan," I begged, "*no—*"

The harpsong reached out and wrapped Zared in a shroud. And there he sat, soundless, as it dug into his mind and stripped it bare, to make his memories visible.

A pavilion. The interior. Ocher and amber and gray. One candle glowed in the dimness. It glinted off the ringmail hauberk and tarnished sword hilt. The man stood in silence with his ruddy head bowed. He dared not look upon the lady.

She moved into the light. She wore a brown gown and a yellow belt. She glowed at throat and wrists from the copper-dyed silk. But it was the hair that set her apart, that and her unearthly beauty.

She put up a hand. She did not touch him. He did not look at her. But as she moved her fingers they took on a dim glow. Lilac, I thought. No—purple. The deep purple of Ihlini magic.

She drew a rune in the air. It hissed and glowed,

clinging to the shadows, spitting sparks and tails of flame. Fearfully Zared raised his head.

His eyes fastened upon it. For a moment he tried to look away, to look at her, but I could see he had not the power. He could stare only at the rune. The delicate tracery of purest purple glowed aginst the air, and as Electra bid him he put up his hand.

"*Touch it*," she said. "*Take it. Hold it. It will give you the courage you need.*"

Zared touched a trembling fingertip to the rune. Instantly it spilled down across his flesh, consuming his hand in livid flame, until he cried out and shook his arm as if to free it. But by then it was done. I saw the rune, so lively and avid, run up his arm to his face, his nose, and then it slid into his nostrils.

He cried out, but it was a noiseless sound. His body was beset by tremors. His eyes bulged out and blood ran from his nose, two thin trails of blackened blood. And then, as he reached for his knife, the trembling was gone and Electra touched his hand.

"*It is done*," she said calmly. "*You have watched me so long, desiring me so, that I could not help but give you your wish. I will be yours, but only after this thing is done. Will you serve me in this?*"

Zared merely nodded, eyes transfixed on her face. And Electra gave him his service.

"*Slay him*," she said. "*Slay the pretender-prince.*"

The harp music died. Lachlan's Lady fell silent. I heard the wind strike up the song and the echo in my soul. So easily she had done it.

Zared sat slumped against the earth. His head sagged upon his chest as if he could not bear to meet my eyes. Perhaps he could not. He had meant to slay his lord.

I felt old. Nothing worked properly. I thought to cross to the man and speak to him quietly, but the muscles did not answer my intentions. And then I heard the harp again, and the change in the song, and saw the change in Lachlan's eyes.

"Lachlan!" I cried, but the thing was already done.

He conjured Electra before us. The perfect, fine-boned face with its fragile planes and flawless flesh. The winged brows and ice-gray eyes, and the mouth that made men weak. Lachlan gave us all the beauty, and then he took it from her.

He stripped away the flesh. He peeled it from the bone until it fell away in crumpled piles of ash. I saw the gaping orbits of vanished eyes, the ivory ramparts of grinning teeth. The hinge of the jaws and the arch of her cheeks, bared for us all to see. And the skull, so smooth and pearly, stared upon us all.

No man moved. No man could. Lachlan had bound us all.

The music stopped, and with it Zared's heart.

I wavered, caught myself, and blinked against the dust. I put a hand to my face to wipe it free of grit, and then I stopped, for I saw the tears on Lachlan's face.

His hands were quite still upon the strings. The green stone in the smooth dark wood was dim and opaque. And his eyes looked past me to Torry.

"Could I undo it, I would," he said in toneless despair. "Lodhi has made me a healer, and now I have taken a life. But for you, lady, for what he nearly did to you . . . there seemed no other way."

Torry's hand crept up to crush a fold of the green woolen robe against her throat. Her face was white. But I saw the comprehension in her eyes.

"Lachlan." My voice was oddly cramped. I swallowed, clearing my throat, then tried again to speak. "Lachlan, no man will reprove you for what you have done. Perhaps the method was—unexpected, but the reasons are clear enough."

"I have no dispute with that," he said. "It is only that I thought myself above such petty vengeance." He sighed and stroked two fingers along his Lady, touching the green stone gently. "Such power as Lodhi bestows can be used for harm as well as good. And now you have seen them both."

I cast an assessive glance around at the staring throng. There was still a thing to be said. "Is there yet a man who would slay me? Another man willing to serve the woman's power?" I gestured toward Zared's body on the ground. "I charge you to consider it carefully when you think to strike me down."

I thought there was need for nothing more, though something within me longed to cry out at them all, to claim myself inviolate. It was not true. Kings and princes are subject to assassination more often than death from old age. And yet I thought it unlikely more would strike now, after what had just occurred.

I looked at the body. It resembled that of a child within the womb, for I had seen a stillbirth once; the arms were wrapped around the double-up knees, fingers clawed. The feet were rigid in their boots. Zared's head was twisted on his neck and his eyes were open. Staring. I thought I might get myself the reputation of a man surrounding himself with shapechangers and Ellasian sorcerers, and I thought it just as well. Let any man who thought to slay his king think twice upon the subject.

"Go," I said, more quietly. "There are yet battles to be fought, and winejugs to be emptied."

I saw the smiles. I heard the low-voiced comments. What they had seen would not be forgotten, used instead to strengthen existing stories. They would drink themselves to sleep discussing the subject of death, but at least they would sleep. I thought it unlikely I would.

I touched Lachlan on the shoulder. "It was best."

But he did not look at me. He looked only at my sister while she stared at Zared's corpse.

"Does it please you," asked Finn, "to know how much the woman desires your death?"

I spun around. He was pale and sweating, white around the mouth, and his lips were pressed tightly closed. I saw immense tension in the line of his shoulders. The stitches stood out like a brand upon his face. He stood with such rigidity I dared not touch him, even to help, for fear he might fall down.

"It does not please me," I answered simply. "But it does not surprise me, either. Did you really think it would?" I shook my head. "Still . . . I had not known she held such power."

"She is Tynstar's *meijha*," Finn said clearly. "A whore, to keep from dirtying the Old Tongue with her name. Do

you think she will let you live? Be not so blind, Carillon—
you have now seen what she can do. She will fill your cup
with bitter poison when you think to drink it sweet."

"Why?" Torry asked sharply. "What is it you say to my
brother?"

I lifted a hand to wave him into silence, then let it drop
back to my side. Finn would never let silence rule his
tongue when there was something he wished to say.

"Has he not told you? He means to wed the woman."

The robe enveloped her in a cloud of bright green wool
as she came from the tent to me. Her hair spilled down
past her waist to ripple at her knees, and she raised a
doubled fist. "You will do no such thing! *Electra?* Carillon—
have sense! You have seen what she means to do—Electra
desires your death!"

"So does Bellam and Tynstar and every other Solindishman in Homana. Do you think I am blind?" I reached out
and caught her wrist. "I mean to wed her when this war is
done, because to do so will settle peace between two lands
that have warred too long. Such things are often done, as
you well know. But now, Tourmaline, *now*—perhaps we
can make it last."

"Alliance?" she asked. "Do you think Solinde will agree
to any such thing? With Bellam dead—"

"—Solinde will be without a king," I finished. "She
will have me instead, and no more Ihlini minions. Think
you what Shaine meant to do when he betrothed Lindir
to Ellic! He wanted a lasting peace that would end these
foolish wars. Now it is within *my* grasp to bring this peace
about, and I have every intention of accomplishing it. I
will wed Electra, just as you, one day, will wed a foreign
prince."

Her arm went slack in my hand. Color drained from her
face. "Carillon—wait you—"

"We will serve our House, Tourmaline, as all our ancestors have done," I said clearly. "Shall I name them for
you? Shaine himself wed Ellinda of Erinn, before he took
Homanan Lorsilla. And before that—"

"I *know!*" she cried. "By the gods, Carillon, I am older
than you! But what gives you the right to say whom I will
have in marriage!"

"The right of a brother," I said grimly, disliking to hurt her so. "The right of the last surviving male of our House. But most of all . . . the right of the Mujhar."

Her arm was still slack in my hand. And then it tightened and she twisted it free of my grasp. "Surely you will let me have some *choice*—"

"Could I do it, I would," I said gently. "But it is the Mujhar of Homana the envoys will approach, not his spinster sister." I paused, knowing how much I hurt her, and knowing whom she wanted, even as he heard me. "Did you think yourself free of such responsibility?"

"No," she said finally. "No . . . not entirely. But it seems somewhat precipitate to discuss whom I will wed when you still lack the Lion Throne."

"That is a matter of time." I rubbed at my aching brow and shifted my attention to Finn. "If I give you an order, will you obey it?"

One black brow rose slightly. "That is the manner of my service . . . usually."

"Then go to the Keep as soon as you are able." He opened his mouth to protest, but this time I won. "I am sending Torry, so she will be safe and free of such things as she has encountered tonight." I did not say she would also be separated from Lachlan, whom I thought might offer too much succor for his sake as well as hers. "You I want healed," I went on. "Alix will no doubt wish to return to Donal, so she can give Torry proper escort. Remain until you are fully recovered. And there, my liege man, is the order."

He was not pleased with it, but he did not protest. I had taken that freedom from him. And then, before I could put out a hand to aid him as I intended, he turned and limped away.

The wind rippled Torry's hair as we watched him go. I heard surprise and awe in her voice, and recalled she knew little of the Cheysuli. Only the legends and lays. "That," she said, "is strength. And such pride as I have never seen."

I smiled. "That," I said merely, "is Finn."

SIXTEEN

It was bright as glass as I sat outside my pavilion, and the sunlight beat off my head. I sat on a three-legged camp-stool with my legs spread, Cheysuli sword resting across my thighs. I squinted against the brilliant flashes of the mirrored blade and carefully checked its edges. From elsewhere, close by, drifted the curl of Lachlan's music.

> Come, lady, and sit down beside me,
> settle your skirts in the hollowed green hills
> and hear of my song
> for I am a harper
> and one who would give of himself
> to you.

Rowan stood at my right, waiting for my comment. He had spent hours honing and cleaning the blade. At first I had not thought to set him to the task, for in Caledon I had learned to tend my weapons as I tended my life, but this was not Caledon. This was Homana, and I must take on the behaviors of a king. Such things included in that were having men to tend my weapons, mail and horse. Still, it had been only this morning that I had trusted my sword to another.

The ruby, the Mujhar's Eye, glowed brilliantly in the pommel. The gold prongs holding it in place curved snuggly around it, like lion's claws; apropos, I thought, since it was the royal crest. The rampant beast depicted in the hilt gleamed with a thorough cleaning, and I thought overall it would do. I touched fingertips to the runes, feeling the subtle ridges beneath my flesh, and nodded. "Well done, Rowan. You should have been an arms-master."

"I prefer being a captain," he said, "so long as it is you I serve."

I smiled and used a soft cloth to rub the oil of my fingers from the glory of the steel. "I am not a god, Rowan. I am as human as you."

"I know *that*." Some of his awe had faded, that was obvious. "But given the choice, I would continue to serve the Mujhar. Human or not." I glanced up and saw his smile.

A thin veil of dust hung in the air to layer the men who caused it. I heard the sound of arms-practice, wrestling, argument and laughter. But I also heard the harp, and Lachlan's eloquent voice.

> *Come, lady, and hear of my harp;*
> *I will sing for you, play for you,*
> *wait for you, pray for you*
> *to say you love me, too . . .*
> *as much as I love you.*

I lifted my swordbelt from the ground and set the tip of the blade against the lip of the sheath. Slowly I slid it home, liking the violent song. Steel against leather, boiled and wrapped; the hissing of blade against sheath. Better, I thought, than the chopping of blade hacking flesh or the grate of steel against bone.

"Hallooo the camp!" called a distant voice. "A message from Bellam!"

The dust cloud rolled across the encampment. Four men rode in: three were guards, the fourth a Homanan I had seen only once before, when I had set him to his task.

The guards brought him up, taking away his horse as he jumped from the mount and dropped to one knee in a quick, impatient gesture of homage. His eyes sparkled with excitement as I motioned him up. "My lord, I have word from Mujhara."

"Say on."

"It is Bellam, my lord. He desires a proper battle, two armies in the field, with no more time and blood spent in pointless skirmishes." He grinned; he knew what I would say.

I smiled. "Pointless, are they? So pointless now he begs me hold back my men, because we have undermined his grip upon Homana. So pointless he wishes to settle the thing at last." I felt the leap of anticipation within my chest. At last. *At last.* "Is there more?"

He was winded, trying to catch his breath. I had taken up the practice of posting men in relays along the major roads, ostensibly iternerants or crofters or traders; anything but soldiers. Some had even been sent to Mujhara to learn what they could firsthand, and to expand on the insight Lachlan had given us as to Bellam's mind.

"My lord," the man said, "it seems Bellam is angry and impatient. He is determined to bring you down. He challenges you, my lord, to a battle near Mujhara. A final battle, he claims, to end the thing at last."

"Does he?" I grinned at Rowan. "No doubt there were assorted insults to spice these words of his."

The messenger laughed. "But of course, my lord! What else does a beaten man do? He blusters and shouts and threatens, because he knows his strength is failing." Color stood high in his face. "My lord Carillon, he claims you fight such skirmishes because you are incapable of commanding an entire army within a proper battle. That you rely on the Cheysuli to ensorcel his patrols, having no skill yourself. My lord—do we fight?"

His eagerness was manifest. I saw others gathering near; not so close as to intrude, but close enough to hear my answer. I did not mind. No doubt all my men felt some of the impatience that nipped at Bellam's heels.

"We will fight," I agreed, rising from my stool. The cheer went up at once. "Seek you food and rest, and whatever wine you prefer. Tonight we will feast to Bellam's defeat, and tomorrow we shall plan."

He bowed himself away and went off to do my bidding. Others hastened away as well to spread the word; I knew

the army grapevine would do what I could not, which was
speak to every man. There were too many now.

Rowan sighed. "My lord—it is well. Even I would relish
a battle."

"Though you may die in it?"

"There is that chance each time I lead a raid," he
answered. "What difference to me whether I die with
twenty men or two hundred? Or even twenty thousand?"

The hilt of my sword was warm against my palm and the
royal ruby glowed. "What difference, indeed?" I stared
across the encampment with its knots of clustered men.
"Is a Mujhar's strength measured by the number of men
whose blood is spilled—or merely that it spills?" Then I
frowned and shook the musing away. "Find me Duncan.
Last I saw, he was with Finn, now that his brother is back.
There are things we must discuss."

Rowan nodded and went off at once. I buckled on my
swordbelt and turned to go inside my pavilion, intending
to study my maps, but I paused instead and lingered.

> *Come, lady, and taste of my wine,*
> *eat of my fruit*
> *and hear of my heart,*
> *for I long for you, cry for you,*
> *ache for you, hate for you*
> *to say you will not come.*

I grimaced and scrubbed fingers through my beard to
scratch my tight-set jaw. It was not Torry who was saying
she would not come, but her brother commanding it. And
in the eight weeks since I had sent her to the Keep,
Lachlan had kept himself to his thoughts and his Lady,
forgoing the confidences we once had shared.

"A fool," I muttered. "A fool to look so high . . . and
surely a harper knows it."

Perhaps he had, once. He had spent his time with
kings. But a man cannot always choose where he will love,
no more than a princess may choose what man she will
wed.

The harpsong died down into silence. I stood outside

my pavilion and heard the hissing of the wind across the sandy, beaten ground. And then I cursed and went inside.

"Carillon."

It was Finn at the doorflap, but when I called to him to enter, he merely pulled the flap aside. He stood mostly in shadow with the darkness of full night behind him.

I sat up, awake at once—for I had hardly slept in the knowledge I would face Bellam at last—and lighted my single candle. I looked at Finn and frowned. Of a sudden he was alien to me, eerie in his intensity.

"Bring your sword and come."

I glanced at the sword where it lay cradled in its sheath. It waited for me now as much as it waited for the morning; *the* morning. And, knowing Finn did nothing without sound reason, I put on my boots and stood up, fully clothed as was common in army camps. "Where?" I pulled the sword from its sheath.

"This way." He said nothing more, merely waited for me to follow. And so I went with him, following Storr, to the hollow of a hill. We left the encampment behind, a dim, smoky glow across the crest of the hill, and I waited for Finn to explain.

He said nothing at first. I saw him look down at the ground, searching for some mark or other indication, and then I saw it even as he did.

Five smooth stones, set in a careful circle. He smiled and knelt, touching each stone with a fingertip as if he counted, or made himself known to all five. He said something under his breath, some unknown sentence; the Old Tongue, and more obscure than usual. This was not the Finn I knew.

Kneeling, he glanced up. Up and up, until he tipped back his head. It was the sky he stared at, the black night sky with its carpet of shining stars, and the wind blew his hair from his face. I saw again the livid scar as it snaked across cheek and jaw, but I also saw something more. I saw a man gone out of himself to some place far beyond.

"*Ja'hai*," he said. "*Ja'hai, cheysu, Mujhar.*"

The wolf walked once around the circle. I saw the

amber glint of his eyes. Finn glanced at him briefly with the unfocused detachment of *lir*-speech, and I wondered what was said.

The night was cool. The wind blew grit against my face, catching in my beard. I put one hand to my mouth, intending to wipe my lips clean, but Finn made a gesture I had never seen and I stopped moving altogether. I looked up, as he did, and saw the garland of stars.

Five of them. In a circle. Like a torque around a woman's neck. A moment before they had been five among many, lost in the brilliance of thousands, and now they stood apart.

Finn touched each stone again with a gentle fingertip. Then he placed one palm flat against the earth as if he gave—or sought—a blessing, and touched the other hand to his heart.

"Trust me." I realized this time he spoke to me.

It took me a moment to answer. The very stillness made me hesitate. "When have I not trusted you?"

"Trust me." I saw the blackness of his eyes, swollen in the darkness.

I swallowed down my foreboding. "Freely. My life is yours."

He did not smile. "Your life has ever been mine. For now, the gods have set me a further task . . ." For a moment he closed his eyes. In the moonlight his face was all hollows and planes, leached free of its humanity. He was a shadow-wraith before me, hunched against the ground. "You know what we face tomorrow." His eyes were on my face. "You know the odds are great. You know also, of course, that should we fail—and Bellam keeps Homana—it is the end of the Cheysuli race."

"The Homanans—"

"I do not speak of Homanans." Finn's tone was very distant. "We speak now of the Cheysuli, and the gods who made this place. There is no time for Homanans."

"*I* am Homanan—"

"You are a part of our prophecy." For a moment he smiled the old, ironic smile. "Doubtless you would prefer it otherwise, given a choice—no more than I, Carillon— but there is none. If you die tomorrow; if you die within a week in Bellam's battles, Homana and the Cheysuli die with you."

I felt the slow churning in my belly. Finn—you set a great weight upon my shoulders. Do you wish to bow me down?"

"You are Mujhar," he said softly. "That is the nature of the task."

I shifted uneasily. "What is it you would have me do? Strike a bargain with the gods? Only tell me the way."

There was no answering smile. "No bargain," he said. "They do not bargain with men. They offer; men take, or men refuse. Men all too often refuse." He set one hand against the ground and thrust himself to his feet. The earring winked in the moonlight. "What I tell you this night is not what men prefer to hear, particularly kings. But I tell you because of what we have shared together . . . and because it will make a difference."

I took a deep, slow breath. Finn was—not Finn. And yet I knew no other name. "Say on, then."

"That sword." He indicated it briefly. "The sword you hold is Cheysuli-made, by Hale, my *jehan*. For the Mujhar it was said he made it, and yet in the Keep we knew differently." His face was very solemn. "Not for Shaine, though Shaine was the one who bore it. Not for you, to whom Shaine gave it on your acclamation. For a Mujhar, it is true . . . but a Cheysuli Mujhar, not Homanan."

"I have heard something of the sort before," I said grimly. "It seems these words—or similar ones—have been often in Duncan's mouth."

"You fight to save Homana," Finn said. "*We* fight to save Homana as well, and the Cheysuli way of life. There is the prophecy, Carillon. I know—" he lifted a hand as I sought to speak— "I know, it is not something to which you pay mind. But *I* do; so do we all who have linked with the *lir*." His eyes were on Storr, standing so still and silent in the night. "It is the truth, Carillon. *One day a man of all blood shall unite, in peace, four warring realms and two magic races.*" He smiled. "Your bane, it appears, judging by your expression."

"What are you leading to?" I was grown impatient with

his manner. "What has the prophecy to do with this sword?"

"That sword was made for another. Hale knew it when he fashioned the blade from the star-stone. And the promise was put in there." His fingers indicated the runes running down the blade. "A Cheysuli sword, once made, waits for the hand it was made for. That hand is not yours, and yet you will carry the sword into battle."

I could not suppress the hostility in my tone. "Cheysuli sufferance?" I demanded. "Does it come to this again?"

"Not sufferance," he said. "You serve it well, and it has kept you alive, but the time draws near when it will live in another man's hands."

"My son's," I said firmly. "What *I* have will be my son's. That is the nature of inheritance."

"Perhaps so," he agreed, "do the gods intend it."

"Finn—"

"Lay down the sword, Carillon."

I faced him squarely in the darkness. "Do you ask me to give it up?" I weighted my words with care. "Do you mean to take it from me?"

"That is not for me to do. When the sword is given over to the man for whom it was made, it will be given freely." For a moment he said nothing, as if listening to his words, and then he smiled. Briefly he touched my arm with a gesture of comradeship I had seen only rarely before. "Lay down the sword, Carillon. This night it belongs to the gods."

I bent. I set the sword upon the ground, and then I rose again. It lay gleaming in the moonlight: gold and silver and crimson.

"Your knife," Finn said.

And so he disarmed me. I stood naked and alone, for all I had a warrior and wolf before me, and waited for the answers. I thought there might be none; Finn only rarely divulged what was in his mind, and this night I thought it unlikely I would get anything from him. I waited.

He held the knife in his hand, the hand which had fashioned the weapon. A Cheysuli long-knife with its wolf's-head hilt; no Homanan weapon, this. And then I understood.

This night he was all Cheysuli, more so than ever before. He put off his borrowed Homanan manners like a soldier slipping his cloak. No more the Finn I knew but another, quieter soul. He was full of his gods and magic, and did I not acknowledge what he was I would doubtless regret it at once. As it was, I had not seen him so often in such a way as to lose my awe of him.

Suddenly I stood alone on the plains of Homana with a shapechanger waiting before me, and I knew myself afraid.

He caught my left wrist in one hand. Before I could speak he bared the underside to the gods and cut deeply into the flesh.

I hissed between my teeth and tried to pull back the arm. He held me tightly, clamping down on the arm so that my hand twitched and shook with the shock of the cutting.

I had forgotten his strength, his bestial determination that puts all my size to shame. He held me as easily as a father holds a child, ignoring my muttered protest. He forced my arm down and held it still, and then he loosened his fingers to let the blood well free and fast.

It ran down my wrist to pool in my palm, then dropped off the rigid fingers. Finn held the arm over the patch of smooth earth with its circle of five smooth stones.

"Kneel." A pressure on the captive wrist led me downward, and I knelt as he had ordered.

Finn released my wrist. It ached dully and I felt the blood still coursing freely. I lifted my right hand to clamp the cut closed, but the look on Finn's face kept me from it. There was more he wanted of me.

He took up my sword from the ground and stood before me. "We must make this yours, for a time," he said gently. "We will borrow it from the gods. For tomorrow, for Homana . . . you must have a little magic." He pointed at the bloodied soil. "The blood of the man; the flesh of the earth. United in one purpose—" He thrust the sword downward until the blade bit into the earth, sliding in as if he sheathed it, until the hilt stood level with my face as I knelt. The clean, shining hilt with its ruby eye set so firmly in the pommel. "Put your hand upon it."

Instinctively I knew which hand. My left, with its bloody glove.

I touched the hilt. I touched the rampant lion. I touched the red eye with the red of my blood, and closed my hand upon it.

The blood flowed down the hilt to the crosspiece and then down upon the blade. The runes filled up, red-black in the silver moonlight, until they spilled over. I saw the scarlet ribbon run down and down to touch the earth where it merged with the blood-dampened soil, and the ruby began to glow.

It filled my eyes with crimson fire, blinding me to the world. No more Finn, no more me . . . only incarnadine fire.

"*Ja'hai,*" Finn whispered unevenly. "*Ja'hai, cheysu, Mujhar . . .*"

Five stars. Five stones. One sword. And one battle to be won.

The stars moved. They broke free of their settings and moved against the sky, growing brighter, trailing tails of fire behind them. They shot across the sky, arcing, like arrows loosed from bows, heading toward the earth. Shooting stars I had seen, but this was different. This was—"

"Gods," I whispered raggedly. "Must a man ever see to believe?"

I wavered on my knees. It was Finn who pulled me up and made me stand, though I feared I would fall down and shame myself. One hand closed over the cut and shut off the bleeding. He smiled a moment, and then the eyes were gone blank and detached, so that I knew he sought the earth magic.

When he took his hand away my wrist was healed, bearing no scar save the shackle wound from Atvian iron. I flexed my hand, wiggling my fingers, and saw the familiar twist to Finn's smile. "I told you to trust me."

"Trusting you may give me nightmares." Uneasily I glanced at the sky. "Did you see the stars?"

"Stars?" He did not smile. "Rocks," he said. "Only rocks."

He scooped them up and showed me. Rocks they were,

in his hand; I put out my own and held them, wondering what magic had been forged.

I looked at Finn. He seemed weary, used up, and something was in his eyes. I could not decipher the expression. "You will sleep." He frowned in abstraction. "The gods will see to that."

"And you?" I asked sharply.

"What the gods give me is my own affair." His eyes were back on the sky.

I thought there was more he wished to say. But he shut his mouth on it, offering nothing, and it was not my place to ask. So I put my free hand on the upstanding hilt and closed my fingers around the bloodied gold. But I knew, as I pulled it from the earth, I would not ask Rowan to clean it.

"Rocks," Finn murmured, and turned away with Storr.

I opened my hand and looked at the rocks. Five smooth stones. Nothing more.

But I did not drop them to the ground. I kept them, instead.

It was Rowan who held the tall ash staff upright in the dawn. The mist clung to it; droplets ran down the staff to wet the fog-dampened ground, as my blood had run down the sword. The banner hung limply from the top of the staff: a drapery of crimson cloth that did not move in the stillness. Within its silken folds slept the rampant black lion of Homana, mouth agape and claws extended, waiting for its prey.

The tip of the staff bit into the ground as Rowan pushed it. He twisted, worked the standard into the damp, spongy ground until the ash was planted solidly. And then he took his hands away, waiting, and saw it would remain.

A cheer went up. A Homanan cheer; the Cheysuli said nothing. They waited on foot at my back, separated from the Homanans, and their standard was the *lir* who stood at their sides or rested on their shoulders.

I tasted the flat, dull tang of apprehension tinged with fear in my mouth. I had never rid myself of the taste, no matter how many times I had fought. I sat on my horse with my sword in its sheath, ringmail shrouding my body, and knew I was afraid. But it was the fear that would drive me on in an attempt to overcome it; in doing so I would also, I prayed, overcome the enemy.

I turned my back on that enemy. Bellam's troops lay in wait for us on the plains, the dawning sunlight glittering off weapons and mail. They were too far to be distinct, were merely a huge gathering of men prepared to fight. Thousands upon thousands.

I turned my back so I could look at my army. It spread across the hill like a flood of legs and arms and faces. Unlike Bellam's hordes, we did not all boast ringmail and boiled leather. Many wore what they could of armor, that being leather bracers, stiff leather greaves and a leather tunic. A breastplate, here and there; perhaps a toughened hauberk. But many wore only wool, having no better, yet willing to fight. My army lacked the grandeur of Bellam's silken-tunicked legions, but we did not lack for heart and determination.

I pulled my sword from its sheath. Slowly I raised it, then closed my callused hand around the blade, near the tip. I thrust the weapon upright in the air so that the hilt was uppermost, and the ruby caught fire from the rising sun.

"Bare your teeth!" I shouted. "Unsheathe your claws! *And let the Lion roar!*"

SEVENTEEN

The sun, I knew, was setting. The field was a mass of crimson, orange and yellow. But I could not be certain how much of the crimson was blood or setting sun.

The ground was boggy beneath my knees, the dry grass matted, but I did not get up at once. I remained kneeling, leaning against my planted sword, as I stared into the Mujhar's Eye. The great ruby, perhaps, was responsible for the color. Perhaps it painted the plains so red.

But I knew better. The field was red and brown and black with blood, and the dull colors of the dead. Already carrion birds wheeled and settled in their eternal dance, crying their victory even as men cried their defeat. It was all merely sound, another sound, to fill my ringing head.

The strength was gone from my body. I trembled with a weakness born of fatigue that filled my bones, turning my limbs to water. There was nothing left in me save the vague realization the thing was done, and I was still alive.

A step whispered behind me. I spun at once, lifting the sword, and set the point at the man.

He stood just out of range, and yet close enough had I the strength to try for a lunge. I did not. And there was no need, since Finn was not the enemy.

I let the tip of the sword drop away to rest against the ground. I wet my bloodied lips and wished for a drink of wine. Better yet: water, to cool my painful throat. My voice was a husky shadow of my usual tone; shouting had leached it of sound.

"It is done," Finn said gently.

"I know it." I swallowed and steadied my voice. "I know it."

"Then why do you remain on your knees like a supplicant to Lachlan's All-Father creature?"

"Perhaps I am one . . ." I sucked in a belly-deep breath and got unsteadily to my feet. The exertion nearly put me down again, and I wavered. Every bone in my body ached and my muscles were shredded like rags. I shoved a mailed forearm across my face, scrubbing away the sweat and blood. And then I acknowledged what I had not dared say aloud before, or even within my mind. "Bellam is—defeated. Homana is mine."

"Aye, my lord Mujhar." The tone, as ever, was ironic and irreverent.

I sighed and cast him as much of a scowl as I could muster. "My thanks for your protection, Finn." I recalled how he had shadowed me in the midst of the day-long battle; how he had let no enemy separate me from the others. In all the tangle of fighting, I had never once been left alone.

He shrugged. "The blood-oath *does* bind me . . ." Then he grinned openly and made a fluid gesture that said he understood. Too often we said nothing to one another because there was no need.

And then he put out a hand and gripped my arm, and I accepted the accolade in silence only because I had not the words to break it.

"Did you think we would see it?" I asked at last.

"Oh, aye. The prophecy—"

I cut him off with a wave of one aching arm. "Enough. Enough of the thing. I grow weary of your prating of this and that." I sighed and caught my breath. "Still, there is Mujhara to be freed. Our liberation is not yet finished."

"Near enough," Finn said quietly. "I have come to take you to Bellam."

I looked at him sharply. "You have him?"

"Duncan—has him. Come and see."

We walked through the battlefield slowly. All around

me lay the pall of death; the stench of fear and futility. Men had been hacked and torn to pieces, struck down by swords and spears alike. Arrows stood up from their flesh. Birds screamed and shrieked as we passed, taking wing to circle and return as we passed by their bounty. And the men, enemy and companion alike, lay sprawled in the obscene intercourse of death upon the matted, bloody grass.

I stopped. I looked at the sword still clutched in my hand. The Cheysuli sword, Hale-made, with its weight of burning ruby. The Mujhar's Eye. Or was it merely *my* eye, grown bloody from too much war?

Finn put his hand on my shoulder. When I could, I sheathed the sword and went on.

Duncan and Rowan, along with a few of my captains, stood atop a small hill upon which stood the broken shaft of Bellam's standard, trampled in the dust. White sun rising on an indigo field. But Bellam's sun had set.

He was quite dead. But of such a means I could not name, so horrible was his state. He was no longer precisely a man.

Tynstar. I knew it at once. What I did not know was the reason for the death. And probably never would.

It—Bellam was no longer recognizably male—was curled tightly as if it were a child as yet unborn. The clothes and mail had been burned and melted off. Ash served as a cradle for the thing. Ringmail, still smoking from its ensorcelled heat, lay clumped in heaps of cooling metal. The flesh was drawn up tightly like brittle, untanned hide. Chin on knees; arms hugging legs; nose and ears melted off. Bellam grinned at us all from his lipless mouth, but his eyes were empty sockets.

And on the blackened skull rested a circlet of purest gold.

When I could speak again without phlegm and bile scraping at my throat, I said two words: "Bury it."

"My lord," Rowan ventured, "what do you do now?"

"Now?" I looked at him and tried to smile. "Now I will go into Mujhara to claim my throne at last."

"Alone?" He was shocked. "*Now?*"

"Now," I said, "but not alone. With me go the Cheysuli."

We met token resistance in the city. Solindish soldiers with their Atvian allies still fought to protect their stolen palace, but word spread quickly of Bellam's death and the grisly manner of it. It wondered at Tynstar's decision; surely the Solindish would hate and fear him for what he had done. Had he not broken the traditional bond between Bellam and the Ihlini? Or would the sorcery prove stronger even than fear, and drive the Solindish to follow him still?

The resistance at Homana-Mujhar broke quickly enough. I left behind the bronze-and-timber gates, dispatching Cheysuli and *lir* into the interior of the myriad baileys and wards to capture the turrets and towers along the walls, the rose-colored walls of Homana-Mujhar. I dismounted by the marble steps at the archivolted entrance and went up one step at a time, sword bare in my hand. By the gods, this place was *mine* . . .

By the gods, indeed. I thought of the stars again.

Finn and Duncan were a few steps behind me and with them came their *lir*. And then, suddenly, I was alone. Before me stood the hammered silver doors of the Great Hall itself. I heard fighting behind me but hardly noticed; before me lay my *tahlmorra*.

I smiled. *Tahlmorra*. Aye. I thought it was. And so I threw open the doors and went in.

The memories crashed around me like falling walls. Brick by brick by brick. I recalled it all—

—*Shaine, standing on the marble dais, thundering his displeasure . . . Alix there as well, beckoning Cai within the hall, and the great hawk's passage extinguishing all the candles. . . . Shaine again, my uncle, defying the Cheysuli within the walls they built so long ago, destroying the magic that kept the Ihlini out and allowing Homana's defeat* . . . My hand tightened on my sword. By the gods, I did recall that defeat!

I went onward toward the dais. I ignored the Solindish coats-of-arms bannering the walls and the indigo draperies with Bellam's crest. I walked beside the unlighted firepit as it stretched the length of the hall with its lofty hammer-beamed ceiling of honey-dark wood and its carven animal shapes. No, not animal shapes. *Lir*-shapes. The Cheysuli had gone from carving the *lir* into castles to painting them onto pavilions. The truth had been here for years, even when we called them liars.

I stopped before the dais. The marble, so different from the cold gray stone of the hall floor, was light-toned, a warm rose-pink with veins of gold within it. A proper pedestal, I thought, for the throne that rested on it.

The Lion. It hunched upon its curling paws and claws, its snarling face the headpiece upon the back of the throne. Dark, ancient wood, gleaming with beeswax and gilt within the scrollwork. Gold wire banded the legs. The seat was cushioned in crimson silk with its rampant black lion walking in its folds. That much Bellam had not changed. He had left the lion alone.

My lion; my Lion.

Or was it?

I turned, and he stood where I expected.

"Yours?" I asked. "Or mine?"

Duncan did not attempt to dissemble or pretend to misunderstand. He merely sheathed his bloodied knife, folded his arms, and smiled. "It is yours, my lord. For now."

I heard the shouts of fighting behind him. Duncan stood just inside the open doorway, framed by the silver leaves. His black hair hung around his shoulders, bloody and sweaty like mine, and he bore bruises on his face. But even for all the soiling of his leathers and the smell of death upon him, he outshone the hall he stood in.

The breath rasped in my throat. To come so far and know myself so insignificant— "The throne," I said hoarsely, "is meant for a Cheysuli Mujhar. You have said."

"One day," he agreed. "But that day will come when you and I are dead."

"Then it is like this sword—" I touched the glowing ruby. "Made for another man."

"The Firstborn come again." Duncan smiled. "There is a while to wait for *him*."

A soft, sibilant whisper intruded itself upon us. "And shall you wait a while for *me?*"

I spun around, jerking my sword from its sheath. Tynstar, *Tynstar*, came gliding out of the alcove so near the throne.

He put up his hand as Duncan moved. "Do not, shapechanger! Stay where you are, or I will surely slay him." He smiled. "Would it not grieve you to know you have lost your Mujhar the very day you have brought him to the throne?"

He had not changed. The ageless Ihlini was smiling. His bearded face was serene, untroubled; his hair was still thick—black touched with silver. He wore black leathers, and bore a silver sword.

I felt all the fear and rage and frustration well up within my soul. It was ever Tynstar, enforcing his will; playing with us like toys.

"Why did you slay Bellam?" When I had control of my voice, I asked.

"Did I?" He smiled. He *smiled*.

I thought, suddenly, of Zared, and how he had died. How Lachlan had harped him to death upon his Lady. I recalled quite clearly how Zared's corpse had looked, all doubled up and shrunken, as Bellam's had been.

For only a moment, I wondered. And then I knew better than to let Tynstar bait me. "Why?"

An eloquent shrug of his shoulders. "He was—used up. I had no more need of him. He was—superfluous." A negligent wave of the hand relegated Bellam to nonexistence. But I recalled his body and the manner of his going.

"What more?" I asked in suspicion. "Surely there was more."

Tynstar smiled and his black eyes held dominion. On one finger gleamed a flash of blue-white fire. A ring. A crystal set in silver. "More," he agreed. "A small matter of a promise conveniently forgotten. Bellam was foolish enough to desire an Ellasian prince for his lovely daughter, when she was already given to me." Amusement flickered across the cultered, guileless face. "But then, I did tell him he would die if he faced you this day. There are times your gods take precedence over my own."

The sword was in my hand. I wanted so to strike with it,

and yet for the moment I could not. I had another weapon. "Electra," I said. "Your light woman, I have heard. Well, I shall forget her past while I think of her future—as my wife and Queen of Homana."

Anger glittered in his eyes. "You will not take Electra to wife."

"I will." I raised the sword so he could see the glowing ruby. "How will you stop me, when even the *gods* send me aid?"

Tynstar smiled. And then, even as I thrust, he reached out and caught the blade. "Die," he said gently. "I am done with our childish games."

The shock ran through my arm to my shoulder. The blade had struck flesh, and yet he did not bleed. Instead he turned the sword into a locus for his power and sent it slashing through my body.

I was hurled back against the throne, nearly snapping my spine. The sword was gone from my hand. Tynstar held it by the blade, the hilt lifted before my eyes, and I saw the ruby go dark.

"Shall I turn this weapon against you?" His black eyes glittered as brightly as his crystal ring. "I have only to touch you—*gently*—with this stone, and poor Carillon's reign is done."

The sword came closer. *My* sword, that now served him. I slid forward to my knees, intending to dive and roll, but Tynstar was too fast.

And yet he was not. Even as the ruby, now black and perverted, touched my head, a knife flew home in Tynstar's shoulder. Duncan's, thrown from the end of the hall. And now Duncan was following the blade.

I found myself face-down against the marble. Somehow I had fallen, and the sword lay close at hand. But the ruby, once so brilliant, now resembled Tunstar's eyes.

Duncan's leap took Tynstar down against the dais, not far from where I lay. But Tynstar struggled up again, and Duncan did not. He lay, stunned by the force of his landing, sprawled across the steps. One bare brown arm with its gleaming *lir*-band stretched across the marble, gold on gold, and blood was staining the floor.

"*Tynstar!*"

It was Finn, pounding the length of the hall, and I saw the knife in his hand. How apropos, I thought, that Tynstar would die by a royal Homanan blade.

But he did not die. Even as Finn raced toward him, the Ihlini pulled Duncan's knife from his shoulder and hurled it down. Then he sketched a hurried rune in the air, wrapped himself in lavender mist, and simply disappeared.

I swore and tried to thrust myself upright. I failed miserably, flopping hard against the dais. And so I gave up and lay there, trying to catch my breath, as Finn knelt beside his brother.

Duncan muttered something. I saw him press himself up off the floor, then freeze, and it was Finn who kept him from falling. "A rib, I think," Duncan said between tight-locked teeth. "I will live, *rujho*."

"All this blood—"

"Tynstar's." Duncan winced as he settled himself upon the top step, one hand pressed to his chest. "The knife was mostly spent by the time it reached him, or he surely would have died." He glanced at me briefly, then gestured to his brother. "Finn—see to Carillon."

Finn heaved me up into a sitting position and leaned me against the throne. One curving, clawed paw supported my head. "I thought perhaps I could slay him," I explained, "and save us all the worry of knowing he is free."

Finn picked up the sword. I saw the color spill out of his face as he looked at the ruby. The black ruby. "He did *this*?"

"Something did." I swallowed against the weariness in my bones. "He put his hand on the blade and the stone turned black, as you see it."

"He used it to fix his power," Duncan said. "All of Carillon's will and strength was sucked out through the sword, then fed back with redoubled effect. It carried the sorcery with it." He frowned. "*Rujho*, the sword has ever been merely a sword. But for it to become accessible to Ihlini magic, it had to have its own. What do you know of this?"

Finn would not meet Duncan's eyes. I stared at him in

astonishment, trying to fathom his emotions, but he had put up his shield against us all.

"*Rujho*," Duncan said more sharply. "Did you seek the star magic?"

"He found it. He found *something*." I shrugged. "Five stones, and blood, and the stars fell out of the skies. He said—" I paused, recalling the words exactly. "—*Ja'hai, cheysu, Mujhar.*"

Duncan's bruised face went white. At first I thought it was fear, and then I saw it was anger. He spat something out in the Old Tongue, something unintelligible to me—which I thought best, judging by the fury in his tone. Having never seen Duncan so angry, I was somewhat fascinated by it. And pleased, very pleased, I was not the focus of it.

Finn made a chopping motion with his right hand, a silencing gesture I had seen only rarely, for it was considered rude. It did not have much effect on Duncan.

He did not shout. He spoke quietly enough, but with such violence in his tone that it was all the more effective. I shifted uneasily against the throne and thought to interrupt, but it was not my affair. It had become a thing between brothers.

Finn stood up abruptly. Still he held the sword, and the ruby gleamed dull and black. Even the runes seemed tarnished. "Enough!" he shouted, so that it echoed in the hall. "Do you seek to strip me *entirely* of my dignity? I admit I was wrong—I admit it!—but there is no more need to remind me. I did it because I had to."

"Had to!" Duncan glared at him, very white around the mouth, yet blotched from pain and anger. "Had the gods denied you—what then? What would we have done for a king?"

"King?" I echoed, seeing I had some stake in this fight after all. "What are you saying, Duncan?"

Finn made the chopping motion again. And again Duncan ignored it. "He asked the gods for the star magic. I am assuming they granted it, since you are still alive."

"Still *alive*?" I sat up straighter. "Do you say I could have died?"

Duncan was hugging his chest. "It is a thing only rarely

done, and then only because there is no other choice. The risk is—great. In more than six hundred years, only two men have survived the ceremony."

I swallowed against the sudden dryness in my mouth. "Three, now."

"Two." Duncan did not smile. "I was counting you before."

I stared at Finn. "*Why?*"

"We needed it for Homana." He looked at neither of us. His attention was fixed on the sword he held in his hands. "We needed it for the Cheysuli."

"You needed it for *you*," Duncan retorted. "You know as well as I only a warrior related by blood to the maker of the sword can ask the gods for the magic. It was your chance to to earn your *jehan's* place. Hale is gone, but Finn is not. So the son wished to inherit the *jehan's* power." Duncan looked at me. "The risk was not entirely your own. Had the petition been denied, the magic would have struck you both down."

I looked at Finn's face. He was still pale, still angered by Duncan's reaction, and no doubt expecting the worst from me. I was not certain he did not deserve it.

"Why?" I asked again.

Still he stared at the stone. "I wanted to," he said, very low. "All my life I have wanted to ask it. To see if I was my *jehan's* true son." I saw bitterness twist his face. "I had less of him than Duncan . . . his *bu'sala*. I wanted what I could get; to get it, I would take it. So I did. And I would do it all again, because I know it would succeed."

"How?" Duncan demanded. "There is no guarantee."

"This time there is. You have only to look at the prophecy."

Silence filled the hall. And then Duncan broke it by laughing. It was not entirely the sound of humor, but the tension was shattered at last. "Prophecy," he said. "By the gods, my *rujholli* speaks of the prophecy. And speaks *to* the gods." He sighed and shook his head. "The first I do often enough, but the second—oh, the second . . . not for a *bu'sala* to do. No. Only a blood-son, not a foster-son." For a moment Duncan looked older than his years, and very tired. "I would trade it all to claim myself Hale's blood-son. And *you* offer it up to the gods. A sacrifice. Oh Finn, will you never learn?"

Finn looked at his older brother. Half-brother. They shared only a mother, and yet looking at them I saw the father in them both, though he had sired only one.

I said nothing for a long moment. I could think of nothing to fill the silence. And then I rose at last and took my sword back from Finn, touching the blackened ruby. I returned the weapon to my sheath. "The thing is done," I said finally. "The risk was worth the asking. And I would do it all again."

Finn looked at me sharply. "Even knowing?"

"Even knowing." I shrugged and sat down in the throne. "What else was there to do?"

Duncan sighed. He put out his hand and made the familiar gesture: a spread-fingered hand palm-up.

I smiled and made it myself.

EIGHTEEN

I received the Solindish delegation dressed befitting my rank. Gone was the cracked and stained ringmail-and-leather armor of the soldier: in its place I wore velvets and brocaded satins of russet and amber. My hair and beard I had had freshly trimmed, smoothed with scented oil; I felt nearly a king for the first time in my life.

I knew, as the six Solindish noblemen paced the length of the Great Hall, they were not seeing the man they expected. Nearly seven years before, when Bellam had taken Homana, I had been a boy. Tall as a man and as strong, but lacking the toughness of adulthood. It seemed so long ago as I sat upon my Lion. I recalled when Keough's son had divested me of my sword and thrown me into irons. I recalled the endless nights when sleep eluded my mind. I recalled my complete astonishment when Alix had come to my aid. And I smiled.

The Solindishmen did not understand the smile, but it did not matter. Let them think what they would; let them judge me as I seemed. It would all come quite clear in time.

I was not alone within the hall. Purposely I had chosen a Cheysuli honor guard. Finn, Duncan and six other warriors ranged themselves on either side of the throne, spreading across the dais. They were solemn-faced. Silent. Watching from impassive yellow eyes.

Rowan, who had escorted the Solindish delegation into

the Homanan-bedecked hall, introduced each man. Duke this, Baron that; Solindish titles I did not know. He did it well, did my young Cheysuli-Homanan captain, with the proper note of neutrality in a tone also touched with condescension. We were the victors, they the defeated, and they stood within *my* palace.

Essien. The man of highest rank and corresponding arrogance. He wore indigo blue, of course, but someone had picked the crest from the left breast of his silken tunic. I could see the darker outline of Bellam's rising sun; a subtle way of giving me insult, so subtle I could do nothing. Outwardly he did not deny me homage. Did I protest, he could no doubt blame the coffer-draining war for the loss of better garments. So I let him have his rebellion. I could afford it, now.

His dark brown hair was brushed smoothly back from a high forehead, and his hands did not fidget. But his brown eyes glittered with something less than respect when he made his bow of homage. "My lord," he said in a quiet tone, "we come on behalf of Solinde to acknowledge the sovereignty of Carillon the Mujhar."

"You are aware of our terms?"

"Of course, my lord." He glanced briefly at the other five. "It has all been thoroughly discussed. Solinde, as you know, is defeated. The crown is—uncontested." I saw the muscles writhe briefly in his jaw. "We have no king . . . no *Solindish* king." His eyes came up to mine and I saw the bitterness in them. "There is a vacancy, my lord, which we humbly request you fill."

"Does Bellam have no heirs?" I smiled a small, polite smile that said what I wanted to say. A matter of form, discussing what all knew. "Ellic has been dead for years, of course, but surely Bellam had bastards."

"Aplenty," Essien agreed grimly. "Nonetheless, none is capable of rallying support for our cause. There would be—contention." He smiled thinly. "We wish to avoid such difficulties, now our lord is dead. You have proven— sufficient—for the task."

Sufficient. Essien had an odd way of speaking, spicing his conversation with pauses and nuances easily understood by one who had the ears to understand it. Having grown up in a king's court surrounded by his advisors and courtiers, I did.

"Well enough," I agreed, when I had made him wait long enough. "I will continue to be—*sufficient*—to the task. But there was another request we made."

Essien's face congested. "Aye, my lord Mujhar. The question of proper primogeniture." He took a deep breath that moved the indigo tunic. "As a token of Solinde's complete compliance with your newly won overlordship of our land, we offer the hand of the Princess Electra, Bellam's only daughter. Bellam's only surviving *legitimate* child." His nostrils pinched in tightly. "A son born of Solinde and Homana would be fit to hold the throne."

"Proper primogeniture," I said reflectively. "Well enough, we will take the lady to wife. You may tell her, for Carillon the Mujhar, that she has one month in which to gather the proper clothing and household attendants. *If she does not come* in that allotted time, we will send the Cheysuli for her."

Essien and the others understood quite clearly. I knew what they saw: eight warriors clad in leather and barbaric, shining gold, with their weapons hung about them. Knife and bow, and *lir*. They had only to look at the *lir* in order to understand.

Essien bowed his head in acknowledgment of my order. The conversation was finished, it seemed, but I had one final question to ask. "Where is Tynstar?"

Essien's head snapped up. He put one hand to his hair and smoothed it; a habitual, nervous gesture. His throat moved in a swallow, then again. He glanced quickly to the others, but they offered nothing. Essien had the rank.

"I do not know," he said finally, excessively distinct. "No man can say where the Ihlini goes; no man, my lord. He merely *goes*." He offered a thin smile that contained subtle triumph as well as humor . . . at my expense. "No doubt he plans to thwart you how he can, and he will, but I can offer you nothing of what he intends. Tynstar is—Tynstar."

"And no doubt he will be abetted," I said without inflection. "In Solinde, the Ihlini hold power—for now.

But their realm—*his* realm—shall be a shadow of what it was, for we have the Cheysuli now."

Essien looked directly at Finn. "But even in Solinde we have heard of the thing that dilutes the magic. How it is a Cheysuli loses his power when faced with an Ihlini." His eyes came back to me. "Is that not true?"

I smiled. "Why not ask Tynstar? Surely *he* could explain what there is between the races."

I watched his expression closely. I expected—*hoped*—I would see the subtleties of his knowledge, betraying what he knew. He should, if he knew where Tynstar was, give it away with something in his manner, even remaining silent. But I saw little of triumph in his eyes. Only a faint frown, as if he considered something he wished to know, and realized he could not know it until he discovered the source. He had not lied.

I moved my hand in a gesture of finality. "We will set a Homanan regency in the city of Lestra. Royce is a trusted, incorruptible man. He will have sovereignty over Solinde in our name, representing our House, until such a time as we have a son to put on the throne. Serve my regent well, and you will find we are a just lord."

Essien shut his teeth. "Aye, my lord Mujhar."

"And we send some Cheysuli with him." I smiled at the Solindman's expression of realization. "Now you may go."

They went, and I turned to look at the Cheysuli.

Duncan's smile was slow. "Finn has taught you well."

"And with great difficulty." The grin, crooked as usual, creased the scar on Finn's dark face. "But I think the time spent was well worth it, judging by what I have seen."

I got up from the throne and stretched, cracking the joints in my back. "Electra will not be pleased to hear what I have said."

"Electra will not be pleased by anything you have to say or do," Finn retorted. "But then, did you want a quiet marriage I doubt not you could have asked for someone else."

I laughed at him, stripping my brow of the golden circlet. It had been Shaine's once, crusted with diamonds and emeralds. And now it was mine. "A tedious marriage is no marriage at all, I have heard." I glanced at Duncan. "But you would know better than I."

For a moment he resembled Finn with the same ironic grin. Then he shrugged. "Alix has never been tedious."

I tapped the circlet against my hand, thinking about the woman. "She will come," I muttered, frowning. "She will come, and I will have to be ready for her. It is not as if I took some quiet little virgin to tremble in my bed . . . this is *Electra*."

"Aye," Finn said dryly. "The Queen of Homana, you make her."

I looked at Rowan. He was very silent, but he also avoided my eyes. The warriors avoided nothing, but I had never been able to read them when they did not wish it. As for Duncan and Finn, I knew well enough what they thought.

I will take a viper to my bed . . . I sighed. But then I recalled what power that viper had over men in general, myself in particular, and I could not suppress the tightening of my loins. By the gods, it might be worth risking my life for one night in her bed . . . well, I would.

I looked again at Finn. "It brings peace to Homana."

He did not smile. "Whom do you seek to convince?"

I scowled and went down the dais steps. "Rowan, come with me. I will give you the task of fetching my lady mother from Joyenne as soon as she can travel. And there is Torry to fetch, as well . . . though no doubt Lachlan would be willing to do it." I sighed and turned back. "Finn. Will you see to it Torry has escort here?"

He nodded, saying nothing; I thought him still disapproving of my decision to wed Electra. But it did not matter. I was not marrying Finn.

A sound.

Not precisely a noise, merely not silence. A breath of sound, subtle and sibilant, and I sat up at once in my bed.

My hand went to the knife at my pillow, for even in Homana-Mujhar I would not set aside the habit. My sword and knife had been bedfellows for too long; even within the tester bed I felt unsafe without my weapons. But as I jerked the draperies aside and slid out of the bed, I knew myself well taken. No man is proof against Cheysuli violence.

I saw the hawk first. He perched upon a chair back, unblinking in the light from the glowing torch. The torch was in Duncan's hand. "Come," was all he said.

I put the knife down. Once again, a Cheysuli summoned me out of the depths of a night. But this one I hardly knew; what I did know merely made me suspicious. "Where? And why?"

He smiled a little. In the torchlight his face was a mask, lacking definition. His eyes yellowed against the light, with pinpricks for pupils. The hawk-shaped earring glinted in his hair. "Would you have me put off my knife?"

I felt the heat and color running quickly into my face. "Why?" I retorted, stung. "You could slay me as easily without."

Duncan laughed. "I never thought you would *fear* me—"

"Not fear, precisely," I answered. "You would never slay me, not when you yourself have said how important a link I am in your prophecy. But I do suspect the motives for what you do."

"Carillon," he chided, "tonight I will make you a king."

I felt the prickle in my scalp. "Make *me* one?" I asked with elaborate distinctness, "or another?"

"Come with me and find out."

I put on breeches and shirt, the first things I could find. And boots, snugged up to my knees. Then I followed him, even as he bid Cai remain, and went with him as he led me through my palace.

He walked with utter confidence, as a man does who knows a place well. And yet I knew Duncan had never spent excess time in Homana-Mujhar. Hale had, I knew, brought him to the palace at least once, but he had been a child, too young to know the mazes of hallways and chambers. And yet he went on through such places as if he had been born here.

He took me, of course, to the Great Hall. And there he took down a second torch from its bracket on the wall, lighted it with his own and handed them both to me. "Where we are going," he said, "it is dark. But there will be air to breathe."

I felt the hair rise on the back of my neck. But I refrained from asking him where. And so I watched in silence and astonishment as he knelt by the firepit rim.

He began to pull aside the unlighted logs. Ash floated up to settle on his hair. Suddenly he was an old man without the wrinkles, gray instead of black, while the gold glowed on his arms. I coughed as the ash rose high enough to clog my nose, and then I sneezed. But Duncan was done rearranging my firepit quickly enough; he reached down and caught a ring of iron I had never seen.

I scowled, wondering what other secrets Duncan knew of Homana-Mujhar. And then I watched, setting myself to be patient, and saw him frown with concentration. It took both hands and all of his strength, but he jerked the ring upward.

It was fastened to a hinged iron plate that covered a hole. Slowly he dragged up the plate until the hole lay open. He leaned the cover, spilling its coating of ash, against the firepit rim, then grimaced as he surveyed the ruin of his leathers.

I leaned forward to peer into the hole. Stairs. I frowned. "Where—?"

"Come and see." Duncan took back his torch and stepped down into the hole. He disappeared, step by step. Uneasily, I followed.

There was air, as he had promised. Stale and musty, but air. Both torches continued to burn without guttering, so I knew we would be safe. And so I went down with Duncan, wondering how it was he knew of such a place.

The staircase was quite narrow, the steps shallow. I had to duck to keep from scraping my head. Duncan, nearly as tall, did as well, but I thought Finn would fit. And then I wished, with the familiar frisson of unease, that he was with me as well. But no. I had sent him to my sister, and left myself to his brother's intentions.

"Here." Duncan descended two more steps to the end of the staircase into a shallow stone closet. He put his fingers to the stone, and I saw the runes, old and green with dampness and decay. Duncan's brown fingers, now gray with ash, left smudges on the wall. He traced out the runes, saying something beneath his breath, and then he nodded. "Here."

"What do—" I did not bother to finish. He pressed one of the stones and then leaned against the wall. A portion of it grated and turned on edge, falling inward.

Another stairway—? No. A room. A vault. I grimaced. Something like a crypt.

Duncan thrust his torch within and looked. Then he withdrew it and gestured me to go first.

I regarded him with distinct apprehension that increased with every moment.

"Choose," Duncan said. "Go in a prince and come out a Mujhar . . . or leave now, and forever know yourself lacking."

"I lack nothing!" I said in rising alarm. "Am I not the link you speak about?"

"A link must be properly forged." He looked past me to the rising staircase. "There lies your escape, Carillon. But I think you will not seek it. My *rujholli* would never serve a coward or a fool."

I bared my teeth in a grin that held little of humor. "Such words will not work with me, shapechanger. I am willing enough to name myself *both*, does it give me a chance to survive. And unless you slay me, as you have said you would not do, I will come out of here a Mujhar even if I do *not* to into that room." I squinted as my torch sputtered and danced. "You are not Finn, you see, and for all I know I should trust you—we have never been easy with each other."

"No," he agreed. "But what kept us from that was a woman, and even Alix has no place here. This is for you to do."

"You left Cai behind." Somehow it incriminated him.

"Only because here, in this place, he would be a superfluous *lir*."

I stared at him, almost gaping. Superfluous *lir*? Had *Duncan* said this? By the gods, if he indicated such a willingness to dispense with the other half of his soul, surely I could trust him.

I sighed. I swallowed against the tightness in my throat, thrust the torch ahead of me, and went in.

Superfluous. Aye, he would have been. For here were all the *lir* of the world, and no need for even one more.

It was not a crypt. It was a memorial of sorts, or perhaps a chapel. Something to do with Cheysuli and *lir*, and their gods. For the walls were made of *lir*, *lir* upon *lir*, carved into the pale cream marble.

Torchlight ran over the walls like water, tracking the veining of gold. From out of the smooth, supple stone burst an eagle, beak agape and talons striking. A bear, hump-backed and upright, one paw reaching out to buffet. A fox, quick and brush-tailed, head turned over its shoulder. And the boar, tusks agleam, with a malevolent, tiny eye.

More. So many more. I felt my breath catch in my throat as I turned in a single slow circle, staring at all the walls. Such wealth, such skill, such incomparable beauty, and buried so deeply within the ground.

A hawk, touching wingtips with a falcon. A mountain cat, so lovely, leaping in the stone. And the wolf; of course, the wolf, Storr-like with gold in its eyes. Every inch, from ceiling to floor, was covered with the *lir*.

Superfluous. Aye. But so was I.

I felt tears burn in my eyes. Pain, unexpected, was in my chest. How futile it was, suddenly, to be Homanan instead of Cheysuli; to lack the blessings of the gods and the magic of the *lir*. How utterly insignificant was Carillon of Homana.

"*Ja'hai*," Duncan said. "*Ja'hai, cheysu, Mujhar.*"

I snapped my head around to stare at him. He stood inside the vault, torch raised, looking at the *lir* with an expression of wonder in his face. "What are those words?" I demanded. "Finn said those words when he talked to the gods, and even you said he should not have done it."

"That was Finn." The sibilants whispered in the shadows of the *lir*. "This is a clan-leader who says them, and a man who might have been Mujhar." He smiled as my mouth flew open to make an instant protest. "I do not want it, Carillon. If I did, I would not have brought you down here. It is here, within the *Jehana's* Womb, that you will be born again. Made a true Mujhar."

"The words," I repeated steadfastly. "What do they mean?"

"You have learned enough of the Old Tongue from Finn to know it is not directly translatable. There are nuances, unspoken words, meanings requiring no speech. Like gestures—" He made the sign of *tahlmorra*. "*Ja'hai, cheysu, Mujhar* is, in essence, a prayer to the gods. A petition. A Homanan might say: *Accept this man; this Mujhar*."

I frowned. "It does not sound like a prayer."

"A petition—or prayer—such as the one Finn made—and now *I* make—requires a specific response. The gods will always answer. With life . . . or with death."

Alarm rose again. "Then I might *die* down here—?"

"You might. And this time you will face that risk alone."

"You knew about it," I said suddenly. "Was it Hale who told you?"

Duncan's face was calm. "Hale told me what it was. But most Cheysuli know of its existence." A faint smile appeared. "Not so horrifying, Carillon. It is only the Womb of the Earth."

The grue ran down my spine. "What womb? What earth? Duncan—"

He pointed. Before, I had looked at the walls, ignoring the floor entirely. But this time I looked, and I saw the pit in the precise center of the vault.

Oubliette. A man could die in one of those.

I took an instinctive step back, nearly brushing against Duncan just inside the door, but he merely reached out and took the torch from my hand. I turned swiftly, reaching for a knife I did not have, but he set each torch in a bracket near the door so the vault was filled with light. Light? It spilled into the oubliette and was swallowed utterly.

"You will go into the Womb," he said calmly, "and when you come out, you will have been born a Mujhar."

I cursed beneath my breath. Short of breaking his neck—and I was not at all certain even I could accomplish that—I had no choice but to stay in the vault. But the Womb was something else. "Just—go in? How? Is there a rope? Hand holes?" I paused, knowing the thing was futile. Oubliettes are built to keep people in. This one would offer no aid in getting out.

"You must jump."

"Jump." My hands shut up into fists that drove my nails into my palms. "Duncan—"

"Sooner in, sooner out." He did not smile, but I saw the glint of amusement in his eyes. "The earth is like most *jehanas*, Carillon: she is harsh and quick to anger and sometimes impatient, but she ever gives of her heart. She gives her child life. In this case, it is a Mujhar we seek to bring into the world."

"I am *in* the world," I reminded him. "I have already been born once, birthed by Gwynneth of Homana. Once is more than enough—at least *that* one I cannot remember. Let us quit this mummery and go elsewhere; I have no taste for wombs."

His hand was on my shoulder. "You will stay. We will finish this. If I have to, I will *make* you."

I turned my back on him and paced to the farthest corner, avoiding the edge of the pit. There I waited, leaning against the stone, and felt the fluted wings of a falcon caress my neck. It made me stand up again.

"You are not Cheysuli," Duncan said. "You cannot *be* Cheysuli. But you can be made to better understand what it is to think and feel like a Cheysuli."

"And this will make me a man?" I could not entirely hide my resentment.

"It will make you, however briefly, one of us." His face was solemn in the torchlight. "It will not last. But you will know, for a moment, what it is to be Cheysuli. A child of the gods." He made the gesture of *tahlmorra.* "And it will make you a better Mujhar."

My throat was dry. "Mujhar is a Cheysuli word, is it not? And Homana?"

"Mujhar means *king,*" he said quietly. "Homana is a phrase: *of all blood.*"

"King of all blood." I felt the tension in my belly. "So, since you cannot put a Cheysuli on the throne—yet—you will do what else you can to make me into one."

"Ja'hai, cheysu," he answered. *"Ja'hai, cheysu, Mujhar."*

"No!" I shouted. "Will you condemn me to the gods? Duncan—I am *afraid*—"

The word echoed in the vault. Duncan merely waited. It nearly mastered me. I felt the sweat break out and run from my armpits; the stench of fear coated my body. A shudder wracked my bones and set my flesh to rising. I wanted to relieve myself, and my bowels had turned to water.

"A man goes naked before the gods."

So, he would have me strip as well. Grimly, knowing he would see the shrinking of my genitals, I pulled off my boots, my shirt, and lastly the snug dark breeches. And there was no pity in Duncan's eyes, or anything of amusement. Merely compassion, and perfect comprehension.

He moved to the torches. He took each from the brackets and carried them out into the stairway closet. The door to the vault stood open, but I knew it was not an exit.

"When I shut up the wall, you must jump."

He shut up the wall.

And I jumped—

NINETEEN

Ja'hai, cheysu, Mujhar—
The words echoed in my head.
Ja'hai, cheysu, Mujhar—
I fell. And I fell. *So far. . . .* Into blackness; into a perfect emptiness. *So far. . . .*
I screamed.
The sound bounced off the walls of the oubliette; the round, sheer walls I could not see. Redoubled, the scream came back and vibrated in my bones.
I fell.
I wondered if Duncan heard me. I wondered—I wondered—I did not. I simply fell.
Ja'hai, cheysu, Mujhar—
It swallowed me whole, the oubliette; I fell back into the Womb. And could not say whether it would give me up again—
Duncan, oh Duncan, you did not give me proper warning . . . But is there a proper way? Or is it only to fall and, in falling, learn the proper way?
Down.
I was stopped. I was caught. I was halted in mid-fall. Something looped out around my ankles and wrists. Hands? No. Something else; something else that licked out from the blackness and caught me tightly at wrists and ankles, chest and hips. And I hung, belly-down, suspended in total darkness.

I vomited. The bile spewed out of my mouth from the depths of my belly and fell downward into the pit. My bladder and bowels emptied, so that I was nothing but a shell of quivering flesh. I hung in perfect stillness, not daring to move, to breathe; praying to stay caught by whatever had caught me.

Gods—do not let me fall again—not again—

Netting? Taut, thin netting, perhaps, hung from some unseen protrusions in the roundness of the oubliette. I had seen nothing at the lip of the pit, merely the pit itself, yet it was possible the oubliette was not entirely smooth. Perhaps there was even a way out.

The ropes did not tear my flesh. They simply held me immobile, so that my body touched nothing but air. I did not sag from arms and legs because of the ropes at chest and hips. I was supported, in a manner of speaking, and yet remained without it.

A cradle. And the child held face-down to float within the Womb.

"Duncan?" I whispered it, fearing my voice would upset the balance. "Is it supposed to be this way?"

But Duncan was gone, leaving me completely alone, and I knew why he had done it. Finn had said little of Cheysuli manhood rites, since most warriors were judged fully grown by the bonding of the *lir*, but I thought there might be more. And I would remain ignorant of it, being Homanan and therefore unblessed, unless this was the way to discover what made the Cheysuli, Cheysuli.

Tonight I will make you a king.

A king? I wondered. Or a madman? Fear can crush a soul.

I did not move. I hung. I listened. I wondered if Duncan would return to see how I fared. I would hear him. I would hear the grate of stone upon stone, even the subtle silence of his movements. I would hear him because I listened so well, with the desperation of a man wishing to keep his mind. And if he came back, I would shout for him to let me out.

Probably I would beg.

Go in a prince and come out a Mujhar.

Gods, would it be worth it?

Air. I breathed. There was no flavor to it, no stench to make it foul. Just air. From somewhere trickled the air that kept me alive; perhaps there were holes I could use to escape.

I hung in total silence. When I turned my head, slowly, I heard the grating pop of spinal knots untying. I heard my hair rasp against my shoulders. Hardly sounds. Mostly whispers. And yet I heard them.

I heard also the beating begin: *pa-thump, pa-thump, pa-thump*.

Footsteps? No. Duncan? No.

Pa-thump, pa-thump, pa-thump.

I heard the wind inside my head, the raucous hissing roar. Noise, so much noise, hissing inside my head. I shut my eyes and tried to shut off my ears.

Pa-thump, pa-thump, pa-thump.

I hung. Naked and quite alone, lost within the darkness. The Womb of the Earth. A child again, I was; an unborn soul caught within the Womb. It was the beating of my own heart I heard; the noise of silence inside my head. A child again, was I, waiting to be born.

"*Duncannnn—!*"

I shut my eyes. I hung. The chill of fear began to fade. I lost my sense of touch; the knowledge I was held.

I floated.

Silence.

Floating—

No warmth. No cold. Nothingness. I floated in the absence of light, of sound, of touch, taste and smell. I did not exist.

I waited with endless patience.

Ringing. Like sword upon sword. Ringing. *Noise—*

It filled my head until I could taste it. I could smell it. It sat on my tongue with the acrid tang of blood. Had I bitten myself? No. I had no blood. Only flesh, depending from the ropes.

My eyes, I knew, were open. They stared. But I was blind. I saw only darkness, the absolute absence of light.

And then it came up and struck me in the face, and the light of the world fell upon me.

I cried out. Too much, too much—will you blind me with the light?

It will make you, however briefly, one of us.

"Duncan?"

The whisper I mouthed was a shout. I recoiled in my ropes and recalled I had a body. A body. With two arms, two legs, a head. Human. Male. Carillon of Homana.

You will know, for a moment, what it is to be Cheysuli.

But I did not.

I knew nothing.

I thought only of being born.

I heard the rustling of wings. The scrape of talons. Cai? No. Duncan had left him behind.

Soughing of wings spread, stretching, folding, preening. The pipping chirp of a falcon; the fierce shriek of a hunting hawk. The scream of an angry eagle.

Birds. All around me birds. I felt the breath of their wings against my face, the caress of many feathers. How I wanted to join them, to feel the wind against my wings and know the freedom of the skies. To dance. Oh, to dance upon the wind—

I felt the subtle seduction. I opened my mouth and shouted: "I am man, not bird! *Man*, not beast! *Man*, not shapechanger!"

Silence soothed me. *Pa-thump, pa-thump, pa-thump.*

Whispering.

DemonDemonDemon—

I floated.

DemonDemonDemon—

I stirred. *No.*

SHAPEchangerSHAPEchangerSHAPEchanger—

NoNoNo. I smiled. *ManManMan.*

YouShiftYouShiftYouShift—

Gods' blessing, I pointed out. *Cannot be denied.*

BeastBeastBeast—

No!No!No!

I floated. And I became a beast.

* * *

I ran. Four-legged, I ran. With a tail slashing behind me, I ran. And knew the glory of such freedom.

The warm earth beneath my paws, catching in the curving nails. The smells of trees and sky and grass and brush. The joyousness of playful flight; to leap across the creeks. The hot red meat of prey taken down; the taste of flesh in my mouth. But most of all the freedom, the utter, perfect freedom, to cast off cares and think only of the day. The moment. Not yesterday, not tomorrow; the day. The moment. *Now.*

And to know myself a *lir.*

Lir? I stopped. I stood in the shadow of a wide-boled beech. The glittering of sunlight through the leaves spattered gems across my path.

Lir?

Wolf. Like Storr: silver-coated, amber-eyed. With such grace as a man could never know.

How? I asked. *How is it done?*

Finn had never been able to tell me in words I could understand. *Lir* and warrior and *lir*, he had said, knowing no other way. To part them was to give them over to death, be it quick or slow. The great yawning emptiness would lead directly into madness, and sooner death than such an end.

For the first time I knew the shapechange. I felt it in my bones, be they wolf's or man's. I felt the essence of myself run out into the soil until the magic could be tapped.

The void. The odd, distorted image of a man as he exchanged his shape for another. He *changed his shape* at will, by giving over the human form to the earth. It spilled out of him, sloughing off his bones, even as the bones themselves altered. What was not needed in *lir*-shape, such as clothing, weapons and too much human weight, went into storage in the earth, protected by the magic. An exchange. Give over excess and receive the smaller form.

Magic. Powerful magic, rooted in the earth. I felt the heavy hair rise upon my hackles, so that I saw the transformation. Of soul as well as flesh.

I knew the void for what it was. I understood why it

existed. The gods had made it as a ward against the dazzled eyes of humans who saw the change. For to see flesh and bone before you melt into the ground, to be remade into another shape, might be too much for even the strongest to bear. And so mystery surrounded the change, and magic, and the hint of sorcery. No man, seeing the change for what it was, would ever name the Cheysuli *men*.

And now, neither could I.

The fear came down to swallow me whole and I recoiled against my ropes.

Ropes. I hung in the pit. A man, not a wolf; not a beast. But until I acknowledged what the Cheysuli were, I would never be Mujhar.

Homana was Cheysuli.

I felt the madness come out of my mouth. "Accept!" I shouted. "Accept this man; this Mujhar!"

Silence.

"*Ja'hai!*" I shouted. "*Ja'hai, cheysu, ja'hai—Ja'hai, cheysu, Mujhar!*"

"Carillon."

"*Ja'hai,*" I panted. "*Ja'hai!*" O gods, accept. O gods, acceptAcceptAccept—

"Carillon."

If they did not—if they did not—

"*Carillon.*"

Flesh on flesh. *Flesh on flesh.* A hand supporting my head.

"*Jehana?*" I rasped. "*Jehana? Ja'hai . . . jehana, ja'hai—*"

Two hands were on my head. They held it up. They cradled it, like a child too weak to lift himself up. I lay against the cold stone floor on my back, and a shadow was kneeling over me.

My blinded eyes could only see shape. Male. Not my *jehana*.

"*Jehan?*" I gasped.

"No," he said. "*Rujholli.* In this, for this moment, we are." The hands tightened a moment. "*Rujho,* it is over."

"*Ja'hai—?*"

"*Ja'hai-na,*" he said soothingly. "*Ja'hai-na Homana Mujhar.* You are born."

BornBornBorn. "*Ja'hai-na?*"

"Accepted," he said gently. "The king of all blood is born."

The Homanan was back on my tongue, but the voice was hardly human. "But I am not." Suddenly, I knew it. "I am only a *Homanan*."

"For four days you have been Cheysuli. It will be enough."

I swallowed. "There is no light. I can barely see you." All I *could* see was the darker shape of his body against the cream-colored walls, and the looming of the *lir*.

"I left the torch in the staircase and the door is mostly shut. Until you are ready, it is best this way."

My eyes ached. It was from the light, scarce though it was, as it crept around the opening in the wall. It gleamed on his gold and nearly blinded me with its brilliance; it made the scar a black line across his face.

Scar. Not Duncan. Finn.

"*Finn*—" I tried to sit up and could not. I lacked the strength.

He pressed me down again. "Make no haste. You are not—whole, just yet."

Not whole? What *was* I then—?

"Finn—" I broke off. "Am I out? Out of the oubliette?" It seemed impossible to consider.

He smiled. It chased away the strain and weariness I saw stretching the flesh of his shadowed face. "You are out of the Womb of the Earth. Did I not say you had been born?"

The marble was hard beneath my naked body. I drew up my legs so I could see my knees, to see if I was whole. I was. In body, if not in mind. "Am I gone mad? Is that what you meant?"

"Only a little, perhaps. But it will pass. It is not—" He broke off a moment. "It is not a thing we have done very often, this forcing of a birth. It is never easy on the infant."

I sat up then, thrusting against the cold stone floor. Suddenly I was another man entirely. Not Carillon, Something else. Something drove me up onto my knees. I knelt, facing Finn, staring into his eyes. So yellow, even in the darkness. So perfectly *bestial*—

I put up a hand to my own. I could not touch the color. They had been blue . . . I wondered now what they were. I wondered what *I* was . . .

"A man," Finn said.

I shut my eyes. I sat very still in the darkness, knowing light only by the faint redness across my lids. I heard my breathing as I had heard it in the pit.

And *pa-thump, pa-thump, pa-thump*.

"*Ja'hai-na*," Finn said gently. "*Ja'hai-na Homana Mujhar*."

I reached out and caught his wrist before he could respond. I realized it had been the first time I had out-thought him, anticipating his movement. My fingers were clamped around his wrist as he had once clasped mine, preparing to cut it open. I had no knife, but he did. I had only to put out my other hand and take it.

I smiled. It was flesh beneath my fingers, blood beneath the flesh. He would bleed as I had bled. A man, and capable of dying. Not a sorcerer, who might live forever. Not like Tynstar. Cheysuli, not Ihlini.

I looked at his hand. He did not attempt to move. He merely waited. "Is it difficult to accomplish?" I asked. "When you put your *self* into the earth, and take out another form? I have seen you do it. I have seen the expression on your face, while the face is still a face, and not hidden by the void." I paused. "There is a need in me to know."

The dilation turned his eyes black. "There are no Homanan words—"

"Then give me Cheysuli words. Say it in the Old Tongue."

He smiled. "*Sul'harai*, Carillon. That is what it is."

That I had heard before. Once. We had sat up one night in Caledon, lost in our jugs of *usca*, and spoke as men will about women, saying what we liked. Much had not been said aloud, but we had known. In our minds had been Alix. But out of that night had come a single complex word: *sul'harai*. It encompassed that which was perfect in the union of man and woman, almost a holy thing. And though the Homanan language lacked the proper words for him, I had heard it in his tone.

Sul'harai. When a man was a woman and a woman a man, two halves of a whole, for that single fleeting instant. And so at last I knew the shapechange.

Finn moved to the nearest wall and sat against it, resting his forearms on his drawn-up knees. Black hair fell into his face; it needed cutting, as usual. But what I noticed most was how he resembled the *lir*-shapes upon the wall, even in human form. There is something predatory about the Cheysuli. Something that makes them wild.

"When did you come back?"

He smiled. "That is a Carillon question; I think you are recovered." He shifted. Behind him was a hawk with open wings. The stone seemed to encase his shoulders so that he appeared to be sprouting wings. But no, that was his brother's gift. "Two days ago I came. The palace was in an uproar: the Mujhar, it was said, had gone missing. Assassination? No. But it took Duncan to tell me, quite calmly, he had brought you here to be born."

I scrubbed an arm across my head. "Did you know about this place?"

"I knew it was here. Not where, precisely. And I did not know he had intended such a thing." His brow creased. "He reprimanded me because I had risked you in the star magic, and yet he brought you down here and risked you all over again. I do not understand him."

"He might have been Mujhar," I said reflectively, feeling the rasp in my throat. "Duncan, instead of me. Had the Homanans never ruled . . ."

Finn shrugged. "But they—you—did. It does not matter what might have been. Duncan is clan-leader, and for a Cheysuli it is enough."

I put up a hand and looked at it. It was flesh stretched over bone. Callused flesh. And yet I thought it had been a paw. "Dreams," I murmured.

"Divulge nothing," Finn advised. "*You* are the Mujhar, not I; you should keep to yourself what has happened. It makes the magic stronger."

The hand flopped down to rest across my thigh. I felt too weak to move. "What magic? I am Homanan."

"But you have been born again from the Womb of the Earth. You lack the proper blood, it is true, and the

lir-gifts as well . . . but you share in a bit of the magic."
He smiled. "Knowing what you survived should be magic
enough."

Emptiness filled my belly. "Food. Gods, I need food!"

"Wait you, then. I have something for you." Finn rose
and went away, stepping out of the vault. I stared blankly
at all the walls until he came back again. A wineskin was in
his hand.

I drank, then nearly spat it out. "*Usca!*"

"*Jehana's* milk," he agreed. "You need it, now. Drink.
Not much, but a little. Stop dribbling like a baby."

Weakly I tried to smile and nearly failed in the attempt.
"Gods, do I not get *food*—"

"Then put on your clothes and we will go out of here."

Clothes. Unhappily, I looked at the pile. Shirt, breeches,
boots. I doubted I could manage even the shirt.

And then I recalled how I had lost control of my body in
the oubliette, and the heat rushed up to swallow my
flesh.

"Gods," I said finally, "I cannot go like *this*—"

Finn fetched the clothing, brought it back and began
putting it on me, as if I were a child. "You are too big to
carry," he said when I stood, albeit wobbly, in my boots.
"And it might somewhat tarnish your reputation. Carillon
the Mujhar, drunk in some corner of his palace. What
would the servants say?"

I told him, quite clearly, what I thought of servants
speaking out of turn. I did it in the argot of the army we
had shared, and it made him smile. And then he grasped
my arm a moment.

"*Ja'hai-na*. There is no humiliation."

I turned unsteadily toward the door and saw the light
beyond. I wavered on my feet.

"Walk, my lord Mujhar. Your *jehana* and *rujolla* are
here."

"Stairs."

"Climb," he advised. "Unless you prefer to fly."

For a moment, just a moment, I wondered if I could.
And then I sighed, knowing I could not, and started to
climb the stairs.

TWENTY

I stared back at myself from the glitter of the polished silver plate set against the wall. My hair was cut so that no longer did it tangle on my shoulders, and the beard was trimmed. I was less unkempt than I had been in years. I hardly knew myself.

"No more the mercenary-prince," Finn said.

I could see him in the plate. Like me, he dressed for the occasion, though he wore leathers instead of velvet. White leathers, so that his skin looked darker still. And gold. On arms, his ear, his belt. And the royal blade with its rampant lion. Though at a wedding no man went armed save the Mujhar with his Cheysuli sword, the Cheysuli were set apart. Finn more so than most, I thought; he was more barbarian than man with all his gold; more warrior than wedding guest.

"And you?" I asked. "What are you?"

He smiled. "Your liege man, my lord Mujhar."

I turned away from the plate, frowning. "How much time?"

"Enough," he returned. "Carillon—do not fret so. Do you think she will not come?"

"There are hundreds of people assembled in the Great Hall," I said irritably. "Should Electra choose to humiliate me by delaying the ceremony, she will accomplish it. Already I feel ill." I put one hand against my belly. "By the gods—I should never have agreed to this—"

Finn laughed. "Think of her as an enemy, then, and not merely a bride. For all that, she *is* one. Now, how would you face her?"

I scowled and touched the circlet on my head, settling it more comfortably. "I would sooner face her in bed than before the priest."

"You told me it was to make peace between the realms. Have you decided differently?"

I sighed and put my hand on the hilt of my sword. A glance at it reminded me of what Tynstar had done; the ruby still shone black. "No," I answered. "It must be done. But I would sooner have my freedom."

"Ah," His brows slid up. "Now you see the sense in a solitary life. Were you *me*—" But he broke off, shrugging. "You are not. And had I a choice—" Again he shrugged. "You will do well enough."

"Carillon." It was Torry in the doorway of my chambers, dressed in bronze-colored silk and a chaplet of pearls. "Electra is nearly ready."

Something very akin to fear surged through my body. Then I realized it *was* fear. "Oh gods—what do I do? How do I go through with this?" I looked at Finn. "I have been a fool—"

"You are often that," Torry agreed, coming directly to me to pry my hand off the sword. "But for now, you will have to show the others you are not, *particularly* Electra. Do you think she will say nothing if you go to her like this?" She straightened the fit of my green velvet doublet, though my body-servant had tended it carefully.

Impatiently, I brushed her hands aside. "Oh gods, there is the gift. I nearly forgot—" I moved past her to the marble table and pushed back the lid on the ivory casket. In the depths of blue velvet winked the silver. I reached in and pulled out the girdle dripping with pearls and sapphires. The silver links would clasp Electra's waist very low, then hang down the front of her skirts.

"Carillon!" Torry stared. "Where did you find such a thing?"

I lifted the torque from the casket as well, a slender silver torque set with a single sapphire with a pearl on either side. There were earrings also, but I had no hands for those.

Finn's hand shot out and grabbed the torque. I released it, surprised, and saw the anger in his eyes. "Do you know what these are?" he demanded.

Tourmaline and I both stared at him. Finally I nodded. "They were Lindir's. All the royal jewels were brought to me three weeks ago, so I could choose some for Electra. I thought these—"

"*Hale* made these." Finn's face had lost its color, yet the scar was a deep, livid red. "My *jehan* fashioned these with such care as you have never known. And now you mean them for *her*?"

Slowly I settled the girdle back into the ivory casket. "Aye," I said quietly. "I am sorry—I did not know Hale made them. But as for their disposition, aye. I mean them for Electra."

"You cannot. They were Lindir's." His mouth was a thin, pale line. "I care little enough for the memory of the Homanan princess my *jehan* left us for, but I do care for what he made. Give them to Torry instead."

I glanced at my sister briefly and saw the answering pallor in her face. Well, I did not blame her. Without shouting, he made his feelings quite clear.

I saw how tightly his fingers clenched the torque. The silver was so fine I thought he might bend it into ruin. Slowly I put out my hand and gestured with my fingers.

"Carillon—" Torry began, but I cut her off.

"Give it over," I told Finn. "I am sorry, as I have said. But these jewels are meant for Electra. For the *Queen*."

Finn did not release the torque. Instead, before I could move, he turned and set it around Torry's throat. "There," he said bitterly. "Do you want it, take it from your *rujholla*."

"No!" It was Torry, quite sharply. "You will not make me the bone of contention. Not over *this*." Swiftly she pulled the torque from her throat and put it into my hands. Their eyes locked for a single moment, and then Finn turned away.

I set the torque back into the casket and closed the lid. For a moment I stared at it, then picked it up in both hands. "Torry, will you take it? It is my bride-gift to her."

Finn's hands came down on the casket. "No." He shook his head. "Does anyone give over the things my *jehan* made, it will be me. Do you see? It has to be done this way."

"Aye," I agreed, "it does. And is it somehow avoided—"

"It will not be." Finn bit off the words. "Am I not your liege man?" He turned instantly and left my chambers, the casket clutched in his hands. I put my hand to my brow and rubbed it, wishing I could take off the heavy circlet.

"I have never seen him so angry," Torry said finally. "Not even at the Keep when Alix made him spend his time in a pavilion, resting, when he wished to hunt with Donal."

I laughed, glad of something to take my mind from Finn's poor temper. "Alix often makes Finn angry, and he, her. It is an old thing between them."

"Because he stole her?" Torry smiled as I looked at her sharply. "Aye, Finn told me the story . . . when I asked. He also told me something else." She reached out to smooth my doublet one more time. "He said that did he ever again want a woman the way he had wanted Alix, he would let no man come between them. Not you; not his brother." Her hand was stiff against my chest, her gaze intense. "And I believe him."

I bent down and kissed her forehead. "That is bitterness speaking, Torry. He has never gotten over Alix. I doubt he ever will." I tucked her hand into my arm. "Now come. It is time this wedding was accomplished."

The Great Hall was filled with the aristocracy of Solinde and Homana, and the pride of the Cheysuli. I waited at the hammered silver doors for Electra and regarded the assembled multitude with awe. Somehow I had not thought so many would wish to see the joining of two realms that had warred for so long; perhaps they thought we would slay each other before the priest.

I tired to loosen the knots in jaw and belly. My teeth hurt, but only because I clenched them so hard. I had not thought a wedding would be so frightening. And I, a soldier . . . I smiled wryly. Not this day. Today I was merely a bridegroom, and a nervous one at that.

The Homanan priest waited quietly on the dais by the throne. The guests stood grouped within the hall like a cluster of bees swarming upon the queen. Or Mujhar.

I searched the faces for those I knew: Finn, standing near the forefront. Duncan and Alix; the former solemn, as usual, the latter uncommonly grave. My lady mother sat upon a stool, and beside her stood my sister. My mother still wore a wimple and coif to hide the silver hair, but no longer did she go in penury. Now she was the mother of a king, not the mother of a rebel, and it showed quite clearly in her clothing. As for Tourmaline, she set the hall ablaze with her tawny beauty. And Lachlan, near her, knew it.

I sighed. Poor Lachlan, so lost within his worship of my sister. I had had little time of late to spare him, and with Torry present his torture was harder yet. And yet there was nothing I could do. Nothing *he* could do, save withstand the pain he felt.

"My lord."

I froze at once. The moment had come upon us. *Us*; it was Electra who spoke. I turned toward her after a moment's hesitation.

She was Bellam's daughter to the bone. She wore white, the color of mourning, as if to say quite clearly—without speaking a word—just what she thought of the match. Well, I had expected little else.

She regarded me from her great gray eyes, so heavy-lashed and long-lidded. The mass of white-blonde hair fell past her shoulders to tangle at her knees, unbound as was proper for a maiden. I longed to put my hands into it and pull her against my hips.

"You see?" she said. "I wear your bride-gift."

She did the silver and sapphires justice. Gods, what a woman was this—

Yet in that moment she reminded me not so much of a woman as a predator. Her assurance gave me no room for doubt, and yet I wanted her more than ever. More, even, than I could coherently acknowledge.

I put out an arm. "Lady—you honor me."

She slipped a pale, smooth hand over the green velvet of my sleeve. "My lord . . . that is the *least* I will do to you."

The ceremony was brief, but I heard little of it. Something deep inside me clamored for attention, though I longed to ignore it. Finn's open disapproval kept swimming to the surface of my consciousness, though his face was bland enough when I looked. By each time I looked at Electra I saw a woman, and her beauty, and knew only how much I wanted her.

I spoke the vows that bound us, reciting the Homanan words with their tinge of Cheysuli nuance. It seemed àpropos. Homana and the Cheysuli were inseparable, and now I knew why.

Electra repeated them after me, watching me as she said the words. Her Solindish mouth framed the syllables strangely, making a parody of the vows. I wondered if she did it deliberately. No. She *was* Solindish . . . and undoubtedly knew what she said even as she said it.

The priest put a hand on her head and the other rested on mine. There was a moment of heavy silence as we knelt before the man. And then he smiled and said the words of benediction for the new-made Mujhar and his lady wife.

I had taken the woman; I would keep her. Electra was mine at last.

When the wedding feast was done, we adjourned to a second audience hall, this one somewhat smaller but no less magnificent than the Great Hall with its Lion Throne. A gallery ran along the side walls. Lutes, pipes, tambors, harps and a boys' chorus provided an underscore to the celebration. It was not long before men warmed by wine neglected to speak of politics and waited to lead their ladies onto the red stone floor.

But the dancing could not begin until the Mujhar and his queen began it. And so I took Electra into the center of the shining floor and signaled the dance begun.

She fell easily into the intricate patter of moving feet and swirling skirts. Our hands touched, fell away. The dance was more of a courtship than anything else, filled with the subtle overtures of man to woman and woman to man. I was aware of the eyes on us and the smiling mouths, though few of them belonged to the Solindish guests. There was little happiness there.

"Tell me," I said, as we essayed a pass that brought us close in the center of the floor, "where is Tynstar?"

She stiffened and nearly missed a step. I caught her arm and steadied her, offering a bland smile as she stared at me in shock.

"Did you think I would not ask?" I moved away in the pattern of the dance, but in a moment we were together again.

She drew in a breath that set the sapphires to glowing against the pale flesh of her throat. The girdle chimed in the folds of her skirts. "My lord—you have taken me unaware."

"I do not think you are ever taken unaware, Electra." I smiled. "Where is he?"

The pattern swept us apart yet again. I waited, watching the expressions on her face. She moved effortlessly because she claimed a natural grace, but her mind was not on the dance.

"Carillon—"

"Where is Tynstar?"

Long lids shuttered her eyes a moment, but when she raised them again I saw the hostility plainly. Her mouth was a taut, thin line. "Gone. I cannot say where."

I caught her hand within the pattern of the dance. Her fingers were cool, as ever; I recalled them from before. "You had best content yourself with me, Electra. You are my wife."

"And Queen?" she countered swiftly.

I smiled. "You want a crown, do you?"

The high pride of royalty burst forth at once. "I am worthy of it! Even *you* cannot deny me that."

We closed again within the figure. I held her hand and led her the length of the hall. We turned, came back again, acknowledging the clapping from the guests. The courtship had been settled; the lady had won.

"Perhaps I cannot deny it to you," I agreed. "You will be the mother of my heir."

Her teeth showed briefly. "That is your price? A child?"

"A son. Give me a son, Electra."

For only a moment there was careful consideration in her eyes. And then she smiled. "I am, perhaps, too old to bear your children. Did you never think of that?"

I crushed the flesh and bones of her hand with my own. "Speak not of such nonsense, lady! And I doubt not Tynstar, when he gave you permanent youth, left your childbearing years intact."

Dull color stained her cheeks. The dance was done; no longer did she have to follow my lead. And yet we were watched, and dared not divulge our conversation.

Electra smiled tightly. "As you wish, my lord husband. I will give you the child you want."

I thought, then, the celebration went on too long. And yet I could not take her to bed quite yet. Propriety demanded we wait a little while.

But even a little can be too long.

Electra looked at me sidelong. I saw the tilt of her head and the speculation in her eyes. She judged me even as I judged her. And then I caught her fingers in mine and raised them to my mouth. "Lady—I salute you," I murmured against her hand.

Electra merely smiled.

I thought, later, the world had changed, even if only a little. Perhaps more than just a little. What had begun in lust and gratification had ended in something more. Not love; hardly love, but a better understanding. The recriminations were gone, replaced with comprehension, yet even as we moved toward that comprehension I knew it would not be easy. We had been enemies too long.

Electra's legs were tangled with mine, and much of her hair was caught beneath my shoulder. Her head was upon my arm, using it for a pillow, and we both watched the first pink light of dawn creep through the hangings on the bed.

We had spent the remainder of the night in consummation of our marriage, having escaped the dancing at last, and neither of us had been surprised to find we were so well-matched. That had been between us from the beginning. But now, awake and aware again of what had happened, we lay in silent contemplation of the life that lay before us.

"Do you forget?" she asked. "I was Tynstar's woman."

I smiled grimly at the hangings that kept the chill from our flesh. "You share a bed with *me* now, not Tynstar. It does not matter."

"Does it not?" Like me, she smiled, but, I thought, for a different reason.

I sighed. "Aye, it matters. You know it does, Electra. But it is *me* you have wed, not him; let us leave him out of our marriage."

"I did not think you would admit it." She shifted closer to me. "I thought you would blame me for everything."

I twisted my arm so I could put my fingers in her hair. "*Should* I?"

"No," she said, "lay no blame on me. I had no choice in the matter." She twisted, pulling free of my arm and sitting up to kneel before me in the dawn. "You cannot know what it is to be a woman; to know yourself a prize meant for the winning side. First Tynstar *demanded* me— his price for aiding my father. And then you, *even you*, saying you would wed me when we had lost the war. Do you see? Ever the prize given to the man."

"Tynstar's price?" I frowned as she nodded again. "The cost of Inhlini aid . . ." I shook my head. "I had not thought of that—"

"You thought I *wanted* him?"

I laughed shortly. "You were quite convincing about it. You ever threw it in my face—"

"You are the enemy!" She sounded perplexed I could not understand. "Am I to go so willingly into surrender? Am I to let you think I am yours for the easy taking? Ah Carillon, you are a man, like other men. You think all a woman wants is to be wanted by a man." She laughed. "There are other things than that—things such as power—"

I pulled her down again. "Then the war between us is done?"

The light on her face was gentle. "I want no war in our bed. But do you seek to harm my realm, I will do what I can to gainsay you."

I traced the line of her jaw and settled my fingers at her throat. "Such as seeking to slay me again?"

She stiffened and jerked her head away. "Will you throw *that* in my face?"

I caught a handful of hair so she could not turn away. "Zared *might* have succeeded. Worse yet, he might have slain my sister. Do you expect me to forgive—*or* forget—that?"

"Aye, I wanted you slain!" she cried. "You were the enemy! What else could I do? Were I a *man*, my lord Mujhar, you would not question my intention. Are *you* not a soldier? Do *you* not slay? Why should I be different?" Color stood high in her face. "Tell me I was wrong to try to slay the man who threatened my father. Tell me you would not have done the same thing had you been in *my* place. Tell me I should not have used what weapon I had at hand, be it magic or knife or words." She did not smile, staring intently into my face. "I am not a man and cannot go to war. But I am my father's daughter. And given the chance, I would do it again . . . but he is no longer alive. What good would it do? Solinde is yours and you have made me Queen of Homana. Were you to die, Solinde would be no better off. A woman cannot rule there." A muscle ticked in her jaw. "So I have wed you, my lord, and share your bed, my lord, which is all a woman *can* do."

After a moment I took a deep breath. "There is one more," I said gently. "You can also bear a son."

"A son!" she said bitterly. "A son for Homana, to rule when you are dead. What good does that do *Solinde*?"

"*Two* sons," I said. "Bear me two, Electra . . . and the second shall have Solinde."

Her long-lidded eyes sought out the lie, except I offered none. "Do you mean it?"

"Your son shall have Solinde."

Her chin thrust upward. "*My son*," she whispered, and smiled a smile of triumph.

I was falling. Another oubliette. But this time a woman caught me and took the fear away.

"*Ja'hai*," I murmured. "*Ja'hai, cheysu, Mujhar.*"

Accept this man; this Mujhar. . .

But it was not to the gods I said it.

PART II

ONE

I stared at Finn in anguish. "Why will it not be *born*?"

He did not smile, but I saw faint amusement in his eyes. "Children come in their own time. You cannot rush them, or they hang back—as this one does."

"Two days." It seemed a lifetime. "How does Electra bear it? *I* could not—I could not bear a moment of it."

"Perhaps that is why the gods gave women instead of men the task of bearing children." Finn's tone lacked the dry humor I expected, being more understanding than I had ever heard him. "In the clans, it is no easier. But there we leave it to the gods."

"Gods," I muttered, staring at the heavy wooden door studded with iron nails. "It is not the gods who got this child on her . . . that took *me*."

"And your manhood proven." Finn did smile now. "Carillon—Electra will be well enough. She is a strong woman—"

"Two days," I repeated. "She might be dying of it."

"No," Finn said, "not Electra. She is far stronger than you think—"

I cut him off with a motion of my hand. I could not bear to listen. I had found myself remarkably inattentive of late, being somewhat taken up with the birth of my first child. All I could think of was Electra on the other side of the door; Electra in the bed with her women around her and the midwife in attendance, while I waited in the corridor like a lackey.

"Carillon," Finn said patiently, "she will bear the child when the child is ready to come."

"*Alix* lost one." I recalled the anger I had felt when I had learned it from Duncan. The Ihlini attack on the Keep had caused her to lose the child, and Duncan had said it was unlikely she would ever bear another. And I thought again of Electra, realizing how fragile even a strong woman could be. "She is—not as young as she appears. She could die of this."

Finn shut his mouth and I saw the lowering of his brows. Like most, Finn forgot Electra was twenty years older than she appeared. My reminding him of it served as vivid notice that she was more than merely woman and wife; she was ensorcelled as well, with a definite link to Tynstar. No more his *meijha*, perhaps, but she bore the taint—or blessing—of his magic.

I leaned against the door and let my head thump back upon the wood. "Gods—I would almost rather be in a *war* than live through this—"

Finn grimaced. "It is not the same at all—"

"You cannot say," I accused. "*I* sired this child, not you. You cannot even lay claim to a bastard."

"No," he agreed, "I cannot." For a moment he looked down at Storr sitting so quietly by his side. The wolf's eyes were slitted and sleepy, as if bored by his surroundings. I wished I could be as calm.

I shut my eyes. "Why will they not come and tell me it is born?"

"Because it is not." Finn put a hand on my arm and pulled me away from the door. "Do you wish it so much, I will speak to her. I will use the third gift on her, and tell her to have the child."

I stared at him. "You can do that?"

"It is no different from any other time I used it." Finn shrugged. "Compulsion need not always be used for harm—it can exact an obedience that is not so harsh, such as urging a woman to give birth." He smiled faintly. "I am no midwife, but I think it likely she is afraid. As you say, she is not so young as she looks—she may fear also she will not bear a son."

I swore beneath my breath. "Gods grant it is, but I prefer simply to have her safe. Can you do that? Make her bear the child in safety?"

"I can tell her to do whatever it is women do while giving birth," he said, with excess gravity, "and I think it likely the child will be born."

I frowned. "It sounds barbaric."

"Perhaps it is. But babies are born, and women go on bearing them. I think it will not harm her."

"Then come. Do not waste time out here." I hammered on the door. When the woman opened it I ignored her protests and pushed the door open wider. "Come," I directed Finn, and he came in behind me after a moment's frowning hesitation.

A circle of shocked women formed a barricade around the bed in the birthing chamber. Doubtless *my* presence was bad enough, but Finn was a shapechanger. To their minds we were both anathema.

I thrust myself through them and knelt down beside her bed. Dark circles underlay her eyes and her hair was damp and tangled. Gone was the magnificent beauty I so admired, but in its place was an ever greater sort. The woman was bearing my child.

"Electra?"

Her eyes flew open and another contraction stabbed through the huge belly covered by a silken bedcloth. "Carillon! Oh gods, will you not leave me be? I *cannot*—"

I put my hand on her mouth. "Hush, Electra. I am here to ease your travail. Finn will make the baby come."

Her eyes, half-crazed by pain, looked past me and saw Finn waiting just inside the doorway. For a moment she only stared, as if not understanding, and then suddenly she opened her mouth and cried out in her Solindish tongue.

I gestured him close, knowing it was the only way to ease her. And yet she cried out again and tried to push herself away. She was nearly incoherent, but I could see the fear alive in her face.

"Send him away!" she gasped. A brief grunt escaped her

bitten lips. "Carillon—send him away—" Her face twitched. "Oh gods—*do as I say*—"

The women were muttering among themselves, closing ranks. I had allowed Electra Solindish women to help her through her lying-in because I knew she had been lonely, surrounded by Homanans, but now I wished they were gone. They oppressed me.

"Finn," I appealed, "is there nothing you can do?"

He came forward slowly, not noticing how the women pulled their skirts away from his passage. I saw hand gestures and muttered invocations; did they think him a demon? Aye, likely. And they Solindish, with their Ihlini sorcerers.

I saw a strangeness in Finn's face as he looked on Electra. It was a stricken expression, as if he had suddenly realized the import of the child, or of the woman who bore it, and what it was to sire a child. There was a sudden crackling awareness in him, an awareness of Electra as he had never seen her. I could feel it in him. In nine months I had seen him watching her as she watched him, both with grave, explicit wariness and all defenses raised. But now, as he squatted down beside the bed, I saw an awakening of wonder in his eyes.

Electra's pride was gone. He saw the woman instead; not the Ihlini's *meijha*, not the haughty Solindish princess, not the Queen of Homana who had wed his liege lord. And I knew, looking at him, I had made a deadly mistake.

I thought of sending him away. But he had taken her hand into both of his even as she sought to withdraw, and it was too late to speak a word.

He was endlessly patient with her, and so gentle I hardly knew him. The Finn of old was gone. And yet, as he looked at her, I had the feeling it was not Electra he saw. Someone else, I thought; the change had been too abrupt.

"*Ja'hai*," he said clearly, and then—as if knowing she could not understand the Old Tongue—he translated each word he spoke. "*Ja'hai*—accept. *Cheysuli i'halla shansu.*" He paused. "*Shansu, meijhana*—peace. May there be Cheysuli peace upon you—"

"I spit on your peace!" Electra caught her breath as another contraction wracked her.

Finn had her then. I saw the opaque, detached expression come into his eyes and make them empty, and I knew he sought the magic. I thought again of the vault in the earth and the oubliette that waited, recalling the sensations I had experienced. I nearly shivered with the chill that ran down my spine, raising the hairs on my flesh, for I was more in awe of the magic than ever before. For all the Cheysuli claimed themselves human, I knew now they were not. More; so much, much more.

Finn twitched. His eyes shut, then opened. I saw his head dip forward as if he slept, then he jerked awake. The blankness deepened in his eyes, and then suddenly I knew something had gone wrong. He was—different. His flesh turned hard as stone and the scar stood up from his flesh. All the color ran out of his face.

Electra cried out, and so did Finn.

I heard growling. Storr leaped into the room, threading his way through the women. I heard screaming; I heard crying; I heard Electra's hissing Solindish invectives. I heard the low growl rising; oh gods, *Storr* was in the room—

Finn was white as death with an ashen tinge to his mouth. I put a hand on his arm and felt the rigid, upstanding muscles. He twitched again and began to tremble as if with a seizure; his mouth was slack and open. His tongue was turning dark as it curled back into his throat.

And then I saw it was Electra who held his hand and that he could not break free of her grasp.

I caught their wrists and jerked, trying to wrench their hands apart. At first the grip held; Electra's nails bit into his skin and drew blood, but it welled dark and thick. Then I broke the grip and Finn was freed, but he was hardly the Finn I knew. He fell back, still shaking, his yellow eyes turned up to show the whites. One shoulder scraped against the wall. I thought he was senseless, but he was awake. Too awake, I found.

His eyes closed, then opened, and once more I saw the yellow. Too much yellow; his pupils were merest specks. He stared with the feral gaze of a predator.

He growled. Not Storr. Finn. It came out of a human throat, but there was nothing human about him.

I caught his shoulders as he thrust himself up and slammed him against the wall. There was no doubt of his prey. One of his arms was outstretched in her direction and the fingers were flexing like claws.

"Finn—"

All the muscles stood up from his flesh and I felt the tremendous power, but it was nothing compared to my fear. Somehow I held him, pressing him into the wall. I knew, if I let him go, he would slay her where she lay.

His spine arched, then flattened. One hand fastened on my right arm and tried to pull it free, but I thrust my elbow against his throat. The growl was choked off, but I saw the feral grimace. White teeth, man's teeth, in a bloodless mouth, but the tongue had regained its color.

I gritted my teeth and leaned, pressing my elbow into the fragility of his windpipe, praying I could hold him. "Finn—"

And then, as suddenly as it had come on him, the seizure was past.

Finn sagged. He did not fall, for I held him, but his head lolled forward against my arm and I saw his teeth cut into his bottom lip. I thought he would faint. And yet his control was such that he did not, and as Storr pushed past me to his *lir* I saw sense coming back in Finn's eyes.

He pressed himself up. His head smacked into the wall. He sucked in a belly-deep, rasping breath and held it while the blood ran from his mouth. He frowned as if confused, then caught himself as once more his body sagged. With effort he straightened, scraping his *lir*-bands against the wall. I saw the white teeth bared yet again, this time in a grimace of shock and pain.

"Finn—?"

He said a single word on a rush of breath, but I could not hear it for the exhaustion in his tone. It was just a sound, an expulsion of air, but the color was back in his face. I knew he could stand again, but I did not let him go.

"Tynstar—" It was barely a whisper, hoarse and astonished. "Tynstar—*here*—"

The women were clustered around the bed and I knew I had to get Finn from the room. Electra was crying in exhaustion and fear while the contractions wracked her body. I dragged Finn to the door and pushed him out into the corridor while Storr came growling at my heels, all his hackles raised.

Finn hardly noticed when I set him against the wall. He moved like a drunken man, all slackness, lacking grace. Not Finn, not Finn at all. "Tynstar—" he rasped again. "Tynstar—*here*—"

My hands were in the leather of his jerkin, pushing him into the stone. "By the gods, do you know what you did? Finn—"

If I took my hands away, he could fall. I could see it in his eyes. "Tynstar," he said again. "Carillon—it was *Tynstar*—"

"Not *here*!" I shouted. "How could he be? That was *Electra* you meant to slay!"

He put a hand to his face and I saw how the fingers trembled. He pushed them through his hair, stripping it from his eyes, and the scar stood out like a brand against cheek and jaw. "He—was—here—" Each word was distinct. He spoke with the precise clarity of the drunken man, or the very shaken. A ragged and angry tone, laced with a fear I had never heard. "Tynstar set a trap—"

"Enough of Tynstar!" I shouted, and then I fell silent. From inside the room came the imperative cry of a newborn soul, and the murmur of the women. Suddenly it was there I wanted to be, not here, and yet I knew he needed me. This once, he needed *me*. "Rest," I said shortly. "Take some food—*drink* something! Will you go? *Go* . . . before I have to carry you from this place."

I took my hands away. He leaned against the wall with legs braced, muscles bunching the leather of his leggings. He looked bewildered and angry and completely devoid of comprehension.

"Finn," I said helplessly, "will you go?"

He pushed off the wall, wavered, then knelt upon the floor. For one insane moment I thought he knelt to offer apology; he did not. I thought he prayed, but he did not.

He merely gathered Storr into his arms and hugged him as hard as he could.

His eyes were shut. I knew the moment was too private to be shared, even with me. Perhaps *especially* with me. I left them there, wolf and man, and went in to see my child.

One of the women, as I entered, wrapped the child hastily in linen cloth, wiping its face, then set it into my arms. They were all Solindish, these women, but I was their king—and would be, until I sired a second son.

And then I looked at their faces and knew I lacked a first.

"A girl, my lord Mujhar," came the whisper in accented Homanan.

I looked down on the tiny face. It lacked the spirit of a person, little more than a collection of wrinkled features, but I knew her for mine.

What man cannot know immortality when he holds his child in his arms? Suddenly it did not matter that I had no son; I would in time. For now, I had a daughter, and I thought she would be enough.

I walked slowly to the bed, cradling the child with infinite care and more than a little apprehension. So helpless and so tiny; I so large and equally helpless. It seemed a miracle *I* had sired the girl. I knelt down at the bedside and showed Electra her baby.

"Your heir," she whispered, and I realized she did not know. They had not told her yet.

"Our daughter," I said gently.

Sense was suddenly in her eyes; a glassy look of horror. "Do you say it is a *girl*—?"

"A princess," I told her. "Electra, she is a lovely girl." Or will be, I thought; I hoped. "There will be time for sons. For now, we have a daughter."

"Gods!" she cried out. "All this pain for a *girl*? No son for Homana—no son for Solinde—" The tears spilled down her face, limning her exhaustion. "How will I keep my bargain? *This* birth nearly took me—"

I gestured one of the women to take the baby from me. When I could, I slipped one arm beneath Electra's shoulders and cradled her as if she were the child instead.

"Electra, be at peace. There is no haste in this. We have a daughter and we will have those sons—but not tomorrow. Be at ease. I have no wish to see you grieve because you have borne a girl."

"A girl," she said again. "What use is a girl but to wed? I wanted a *son*—!"

I eased her down against the pillows, pulling the bed-clothes close. "Sleep. I will come back later. There is the news to be told, and I must find Finn—" I stopped. There was no need to speak of Finn, not to her. Not now.

But Electra slept. I brushed the damp hair from her brow, looked again on the sleeping baby, then went from the room to give out the news.

Soon enough the criers were sent out and the bells began to peel. Servants congratulated me and offered good wishes. Someone pressed a cup of wine into my hand as I strode through a corridor on my way to Finn's chambers. Faces were a blur to me; I hardly knew their names. I had a daughter, but I also had a problem.

Finn was not in his chambers. Nor was he in the kitchens, where the spit-boys and cooks fell into bows and curtseys to see their Mujhar in their presence. I asked after Finn, was told he had not come, and went away again.

It was Lachlan who found me at last, very grave and concerned. His arms were empty of his Lady and with him came my sister. I thought first they would give me good wishes when I told them; instead they had news of Finn.

"He took the wolf and left," Lachlan said quietly. "And no horse for riding."

"*Lir*-shape," I said grimly.

"He was—odd." Torry was white-faced. "He was not himself. But he would answer none of our questions." She gestured helplessly. "Lachlan was playing his Lady for me. I saw Finn come in. He looked—ill. He said he had to go away."

"Away!" I felt the lurch in my belly. "Where?"

"To the Keep," Lachlan answered. "He said he required cleansing for something he had done. He said also you were not to send for him, or come after him yourself."

He glanced a moment at Torry. "He said it was a Cheysuli thing, and that clan-ties take precedence, at times, over other links."

I felt vaguely ill. "Aye. But only rarely does he invoke them—" I stopped, recalling the wildness in his eyes and the growling in his throat. "Did he say how long he would stay there?"

Torry's eyes were frightened. "He said the nature of the cleansing depended on the nature of the offense. And that this one was great indeed." One hand crept up to her throat. "Carillon—what did he do?"

"Tried to slay the Queen." It came out of my mouth without emotion, as if someone else were speaking. I saw the shock in their eyes. "Gods!" I said on a rushing breath, "I *must* go after him. You did not see what he was—" I started out the door and nearly ran into Rowan.

"My lord!" He caught my arm. "My lord—wait you—"

"I cannot." I shook loose and tried to move on, but he caught my arm again. "*Rowan—*"

"My lord, I have news from Solinde," he persisted. "From Royce, your regent in Lestra."

"Aye," I said impatiently, "can it not wait? I will be back when I can."

"Finn said you should not follow," Lachlan repeated. "Doubtless he has good reason—"

"*Carillon.*" Rowan forsook my title and all honorifics, which told me how serious he was. "It is Thorne of Atvia. He readies plans to invade."

"*Solinde?*" I stared at him in amazement.

"Homana, my lord." He let go my arm when he saw I was not moving. I could not, now. "The news has come into Lestra, and Royce sent on a courier. There is still time, Royce says, but Thorne is coming. My lord—" He paused. "It is Homana he wants, and you. A grudge for the death of his father, and Atvians slain in Bellam's war. The courier has the news." His young face was haggard with the implications. "Thorne intends to take Hondarth—"

"Hondarth!" I exploded. "He will not set foot in a Homanan city while *I* am alive!"

"He means to raise Solindish aid," Rowan said in a quiet

voice. "To come overland through Solinde, and by ships across the Idrian Ocean, bound for Hondarth."

I thought of the southern city on the shores of the Idrian Ocean. Hondarth was a rich city whose commerce depended on fishing fleets and trading vessels from other lands. But it was a two-week ride to Hondarth, going fast; an even longer march. And the marshes would slow an army.

I shut my eyes a moment, trying to get my senses sorted. First Finn's—seizure; my daughter's birth; now this. It was too much.

I set a hand on Rowan's shoulder. "Where is this courier? And find you what advisors you can. We must send for those who have gone home to their estates. It will take time—ah, gods, are we to go to war again, we must reassemble the army." I rubbed at my gritty eyes. "Finn will have to wait."

When I could, I broke free of planning councils and went at last to the Keep. And, as I rode out across the plains, I came face to face with Finn.

He had left Mujhara without a horse, but now he had one. Borrowed from the Keep, or perhaps it was one of his own. He did not say. He did not say much at all, being so shut up within himself, and when I looked at him I saw how the shadow lay on him, thick and dark. His yellow eyes were strange.

We met under a sky slate-gray with massing clouds. Rain was due in an instant. It was nearly fall, and in four months the snow would be thick upon the ground. For now there was none, but I wore a green woolen cloak pulled close against plain brown hunting leathers. Finn, bare-armed still, and cloakless, pulled in his horse and waited. The wind whipped the hair from his face, exposing the livid scar, and I swore I saw silver in his hair where before it had been raven's-wing black. He looked older, somehow, and more than a trifle harder. Or was it merely that I had not noticed before?

"I wanted to come," I said. "Lachlan said no, but I wanted it. You seemed so distraught." I shrugged, made uncomfortable by his silence. "But the courier had come in from Lestra . . ." I let it trail off, seeing nothing in his face but the severity of stone.

"I have heard." The horse stomped, a dark bay horse with a white slash across his nose and a cast in one eye. Finn hardly noticed the movement save to adjust his weight.

"Is that why you have come back?"

He made a gesture with his head; a thrusting of his chin toward the distances lying behind me. "Mujara is there. I have not come back yet."

The voice was flat, lacking intonation. I tried to search beneath what I saw. But I was poor at reading Cheysuli; they know ways of blanking themselves. "Do you mean to?"

The scar ticked once. "I have no place else to go."

It astonished me, in light of where he had been. "But— the Keep—"

"I am liege man to the Mujhar. My place is not with the clan, but with him. Duncan has said—" He stopped short; something made him turn his head away. "Duncan has not—absolved me of what I tried to do. As the *shar tahl* says: *if one is afraid, one can only become unafraid by facing what causes the fear.*" The wind, shifting, blew the hair back into his face. I could see nothing of his expression. "And so I go to face it again. I could not admit my fear—*i'toshaa-ni* was not completed. I am—unclean."

"*What* do you face again?" I asked, uneasy. "I would rather you did not see Electra."

He looked at me squarely now, and the strangeness was in his eyes. "*I* would rather not see her, also. But you have wed her, and my place is with the Mujhar. There is little choice, my lord."

My lord. No irony; no humor. I felt the fear push into my chest. "Did you truly intend to slay her?"

"Not her," he said softly, "Tynstar."

The anger boiled over. I had not realized how frightened I was that he might have succeeded; how close I had come to losing them both. *Both.* Had Finn slain Electra, there was no choice but execution. "Electra is not Tynstar! Are you blind? She is my wife—"

"She was Tynstar's *meijha*," he said quietly, "and I

doubt not he uses her still. Through her soul, if not her body."

"Finn—"

"It was I who nearly died!" He was alive again, and angry. Also clearly frightened. "Not Electra—she is too strong. It was I, Cheysuli blood and all." He drew in a hissing breath and I saw the instinctive baring of white teeth. "It nearly took me down; it nearly swallowed me whole. It was Tynstar, I tell you—*it was.*"

"Go, then," I said angrily. "Go on to Homana-Mujhar and wait for me there. We will face whatever it is you have to face, and get this finished at once. But there are things I have to discuss with Duncan."

There *was* gray in his hair; I saw it clearly now. And bleakness in his eyes. "Carillon—"

"Go." I said it more quietly. "I have a war to think of again. I will need you at my side."

The wind blew through his hair. The sunlight, so dull and brassy behind the clouds, set his *lir*-gold to shining in the grayness of the day. His face was alien to me; I thought again of the vault and oubliette. Had it changed me so much? Or was it Finn who had been changed?

"Then I will be there," he said, "for as long as I can."

An odd promise. I frowned and opened my mouth to ask him what he meant, but he had set his horse to trotting, leaning forward in the saddle. And then, as I turned to watch, he galloped toward Mujhara. Beside him ran the wolf.

TWO

I rode into the Keep just as the storm broke. The rain fell heavily, quickly soaking through my cloak to the leather doublet and woolens beneath. The hood was no help; I gave up and pushed it back to my shoulders, setting my horse to splashing through the mud toward Duncan's slate-colored pavilion. It was early evening and I could hardly see the other pavilions, only the dim glow of their interior firecairns.

I dropped off my horse into slippery mud and swore, then noticed Cai was not on his perch. No doubt he sought shelter in a thick-leafed tree, or perhaps even inside. Well, so did I.

Someone came and took my horse as I called out for entrance. I thanked him, then turned as the doorflap was pulled open. I looked down; it was Donal. He stared up at me in surprise, and then he grinned. "Do you *see*?"

I saw. His slender arms, still bared for warmer weather, were weighted with *lir* gold, albeit lighter than the heavy bands grown warriors wore. And in his black hair glittered an earring, though I could not see the shape. Young, I thought; so very young.

Duncan's big hand came down on Donal's head and gently moved him aside. "Come in from the rain, Carillon. Forgive my son's poor manners."

I stepped inside. "He has a right to be proud," I demurred. "But is he not too young?"

"There is no *too young* in the clans," Duncan said on a sigh. "Who is to say what the gods prefer? A week ago the craving came upon him, and we let him go. Last night he received his *lir*-gold in his Ceremony of Honors."

I felt the pang of hurt pride. "Could *I* not have witnessed it?"

Duncan did not smile. "You are not Cheysuli."

For four days, once I had been. And yet now he denied me the honor.

I looked past him to Alix. "You must be proud."

She stood on the far side of the firecairn and the light played on her face. In the dimness she was dark, more Cheysuli than ever, and I felt my lack at once. "I am," she said softly. "My son is a warrior now."

He was still small. Seven, I thought. I did not know. But young.

"Sit you down," Duncan invited. "Donal *will* move his wolf."

I saw then what he meant, for sprawled across one of the pelts carpeting the hard-packed earth was a sleeping wolf-cub. Very young, and sleeping the sleep of the dead, or the very tired. He was damp and the pavilion smelled of wet fur; I did not doubt Donal had been out with the wolfling when the rain began.

Donal, understanding his father's suggestion at once, knelt down and hoisted half of the cub into his arms. The wolf was like a bag of bones, so limp and heavy, but Donal dragged him aside. The cub was ruddy, not silver like Storr, and when he opened one eye I saw it was brown.

"He is complaining," Donal said, affronted. "He wanted to stay by the fire."

"He has more hair than you," Alix retorted. "Lorn will be well enough farther back. This is the Mujhar we entertain."

I waved a hand. "Carillon, to him. He is my kin, for all that." I grinned at the boy. "Cousins, of a sort."

"Taj is weary of Cai's company," Donal said forthrightly. "Can *he* not come in, too?"

"Taj is a falcon and will remain outdoors," Duncan said firmly as he sidestepped the flopping wolf-cub. "Cai has stood it all these years; so will Taj."

Donal got Lorn the wolf settled and sat down close beside him, one small hand buried in damp fur. His yellow eyes peered up at me with the bright intentness of unsuppressed youth. "Did you know I have two?"

"Two *lir*?" I looked at Alix and Duncan. "I thought a warrior had only one."

"Ordinarily." Duncan's tone was dry as he waved me down on the nearest pelt. Alix poured a cup of hot honey brew and handed it across. "But Donal, you see, has the Old Blood."

Alix laughed as I took the cup. "Aye. He got it from me. It is the Firstborn in him." She sat back upon her heels, placing herself close to Duncan. "I took *lir*-shape twice while I carried him, as wolf and falcon both. You see the result."

I sipped at the hot, sweet brew. It was warm in the pavilion, though somewhat close; I was accustomed to larger quarters. But it was a homey pavilion, full of pelts and chests and things a clan-leader holds. A heavy tapestry fell from the ridge-pole to divide the tent into two areas; one, no doubt, a bedchamber for Alix and Duncan. As for Donal, he undoubtedly slept by the fire on the other side. And now with his wolf.

"How fares the girl?" Duncan asked.

I smiled. "At two months of age, already she is lovely. We have named her Aislinn to honor my mother's mother."

"May she have all of her *jehan's* wisdom," Duncan offered gravely.

I laughed. "And none of my looks, I trust."

Alix smiled, but her face soon turned pensive. "No doubt you have come to see Finn. He is no longer here."

The honey brew went sour in my mouth. I swallowed with effort. "No. I met him on the road. He is bound for Homana-Mujhar. And no, I did not come to speak to him. I came to speak of Homana."

I told them what I could. They listened in silence, all three of them; Donal's eyes were wide and full of wonder. It was, no doubt, the first he had heard of war from the Mujhar himself, and I knew he would always remember. I recalled the time I had sat with my own father, listening to plots and plans—and how those things had slain him.

But death was not in Donal's mind, that much I could see. He was Cheysuli. He thought of fighting instead.

"I must have allies," I finished. "I need more than just the Cheysuli."

"Then you offer alliances." Duncan nodded thoughtfully. "What else is there to give?"

"My sister," I said flatly, knowing how it sounded. "I have Tourmaline to offer, and I have done it. To Ellas, to Falia, to Caledon. All have marriageable princes."

Alix put a hand to her mouth and looked at Duncan. "Oh Carillon, no. Do not barter your sister away."

"Torry is meant for a prince," I said impatiently. "She will get one anyway; why should I wait? I need men, and Torry needs a husband. A *proper* husband." I could not help but think of Lachlan. "I know—it is not a Cheysuli custom to offer women this way. But it is the way of most. royal Houses. How else to find a man or woman worthy of the rank? Torry is well past marriageable age; the dowry will have to be increased. There will be questions about her virginity." I looked again at Donal, thinking he was too young. But he was Cheysuli, and they seemed always older than I. "Bellam held her for years; he even spoke of wedding her himself. There will be questions asked of that. But she is my sister, and that will count for something. I should get a worthy prince for her."

"And allies for Homana." Duncan's tone lacked inflection, which told me what he thought. "Are the Cheysuli not enough?"

"Not this time," I answered flatly. "Thorne enters in more than one place. Bellam came at us straight away. But Thorne knows better; he has learned. He will creep over my borders in bits and pieces. If I split the Cheysuli, I split my strongest weapon. I need more men than that, to place my armies accordingly."

Duncan studied me, and then he smiled. Only a little. "Did you think we would not come?"

"I cannot *order* you to come, any of you," I said quietly. "I ask, instead."

The smile widened and I saw the merest glint of white teeth. Not bared, as Finn's had been; a reflection of true amusement. "Assemble your armies, Carillon. You will have your Cheysuli aid. Do whatever you must in the way that you must, to win the allies you need. And then we shall send Thorne back to his island realm." He paused. "Provided he survives the encounter."

Alix glanced at him, and then she looked squarely at me. "What did Finn say to you when you met him on the road?"

"Little."

"But you know why he came . . ."

I shifted on the pelt. "I was told it was something to do with cleansing. A ritual of sorts."

"Aye," Duncan agreed. "And now he has had to go back."

The cup grew cool in my hands. "He said he had no other place to go. That you had, in essence, sent him out of the Keep." I meant to keep my tone inflectionless and did not succeed. It was a mark of the bond between Finn and me that I accused even his brother of wrongful behavior.

"Finn is welcome here," Duncan demurred. "No Cheysuli is denied the sanctuary when he requires it, but that time was done. Finn's place is with you."

"Even so unhappy?"

Alix's face was worried. "I *thought* he should not go—"

"He must learn to deal with that himself." Duncan took my cup and warmed it with more liquor, handing it back. It was high honor from a clan-leader; I thought it was simply Duncan. "Finn has ever shut his eyes to many things, going in the backflap." An expressive flick of his fingers indicated the back of the pavilion. "Occasionally, when I can, I remind him there is a front."

"*Something* has set him on edge." I frowned and sipped at the liquor. "He is—different. I cannot precisely say. . . ." I shook my head, recalling the expression in his eyes. "What happened with Electra frightened me. I have never seen him so."

"It is why he came," Duncan agreed, "and why he stayed so long. Eight weeks." His face was grim. "It is rare a liege man will leave his lord for so long unless it has something to do with his clan- and kin-ties. But he could not live with what he had done, and so he came here to renew himself; to touch again the power in the earth through *i'toshaa-ni*." He looked tired suddenly. "It comes upon us all, once or twice; the need to be *cleansed*."

The word, even in Homanan, had a nuance I could not divine. Duncan spoke of things that no Homanan had shared, though once I had shared a fleeting moment of their life. Such stringent codes and honor systems, I thought; could I bind myself so closely?

Duncan sipped at his honey brew. I noticed then that his hair was still black, showing no silver at all. Odd, I thought; Duncan was the elder.

"I am not certain he was cleansed at all," Alix said in a very low voice. "He is—unhappy." Briefly she looked at Duncan. "But that is a private thing."

"Can he say nothing to me?" I could not hide the desperation in my voice. "Be the gods, we have been closer than most. We shared an exile together, and then only because of me. *He* might have stayed behind." I looked at them both, almost pleading to understand. "Why can he say nothing to me?"

"It is private," Duncan repeated. "But no, he can say nothing to you. He knows you too well."

I swore, then glanced in concern to Donal. But boys grow up, and I did not doubt he had heard it before. Finn had taught me the Cheysuli invectives. "He told you what he did, then. To Electra?"

"To Tynstar," Duncan said.

I heard the firecairn crackle in the sudden silence. A hissing mote of sparks flew up. "Tynstar?" I said at last.

"Aye. It was not *Electra* he meant to slay; did you think it was?" He frowned. "Did he tell you nothing?"

I recalled how he had said it over and over, so hoarse and stricken: *Tynstar was here*. And how I had ignored it. "He said—something—"

"Tynstar set a trap," Duncan explained, echoing Finn's own words. "He set it in Electra's mind, so that anyone using the earth magic on her would succumb to the possession."

My body twitched in surprise. "*Possession!*"

The firelight cast an amber glaze across the face before me. Smoke was drawn upward to the vent-flap, but enough remained to shroud the air with a wispy, ocherous haze.

Duncan was gold and bronze and black in the light, and the hawk-earring transfixed my gaze. I smelled smoke and wet fur and honey, sweet honey, with the bittersweet tang of spice.

"The Ihlini have that power," Duncan said quietly. "It is a balance of our own gift, which is why we use it sparingly. We would not have it said we are anything like the Ihlini." Minutely, he frowned, looking downward into his cup. "When we use it, we leave a person his soul. We do little more than *suggest*, borrowing the will for a moment only." Again the faint frown that alarmed me. He was not divulging something. "When it is Ihlini-done, the soul is swallowed whole. *Whole* . . . and not given back at all."

Silence. Duncan put out a hand and touched his son, tousling Donal's hair in a gesture that betrayed his concern as the boy crept closer, between father and *lir*. I thought Duncan knew how avidly the boy listened and meant to calm any fears. The gods knew I had a few of my own.

"Finn reacted the way any Cheysuli would react; perhaps even you." He did not smile. "He tried to slay the trapper through the trap. It is—understandable." His eyes lifted to meet mine squarely. "In that moment she was not Electra to him, not even a woman. To Finn, she was simply Tynstar. Tynstar was—*there*."

I frowned. "Then Tynstar *knew* it was Finn he had—"

"I do not doubt it," Duncan said clearly. "An Ihlini trap will kill. He did not intend to leave Finn alive. But something—*someone*—prevented the death by shattering the trap-link."

"*I* broke it." I recalled how Electra had grasped Finn's hand, leaving blood in the scratches she had made. How he had been unable to break free.

And I recalled, suddenly, how he had slain the Homanan assassin in the Ellasian blizzard, more than a year before. How he had said he *touched* Tynstar, who had set the man a task—

I stood up. Bile surged into my throat. Before they could say a word I bent down and swept up my damp cloak, then went out of the pavilion shouting for my horse.

Alix, running out into the rain, caught my arm as I moved to sling on the cloak. "Carillon—wait you! What are you doing?"

The hood lay on my shoulders and the rain ran into my mouth. "Do you not see?" I was amazed she could be so blind. "Finn thought he slew Tynstar through Electra. Tynstar thought he slew *him*—" I swung up on my horse. *"If one is afraid, one can only become unafraid by facing what causes the fear."*

"Carillon!" she shouted, but I was already gone.

I heard the howling when I ran into Homana-Mujhar. *Howling.* Gods, was Finn a wolf—?

The white faces were a blur, but I heard the frightened voices. *"My lord!" "My lord Carillon!" "The Mujhar!"* I pushed past them all and answered none of them, conscious only of the great beating of fear in my chest.

Howling. Gods, it was Storr. Not Finn. But the screaming was Elecra's.

Weight hung off my shoulders as I pounded up the twisting red stone stairs. I ripped the cloak-brooch from my left shoulder and felt the fabric tear. Weight and gold fell behind me; I heard the clink of brooch on stone and the soft slap of soaked wool falling to the stairs. *"My lord!"* But I ran on.

I burst through the women and into the room. I saw Electra first, white-faced and screaming though Lachlan suggested she be quiet. No need, he said; no need to scream. Safe, he said; unharmed. The wolf was held at bay.

Electra was whole. I saw it at once. She stood in a corner with Lachlan holding her back, his hands upon her arms. Holding her *back*—

—from Finn. From Finn, who was capably cornered by Rowan with his sword, and another man-at-arms. They caged him with steel, bright and deadly, and the wolf in man's shape was held at bay.

He bled. Something had opened the scar so that his face ran with blood. It stained the leather jerkin and splattered down to his thighs, where I saw more blood. His right thigh, where the Atvian spear had pierced. There was a cut in his leggings and blood on Rowan's blade.

He was flat against the wall, head pressed back so that his throat was bared. Blood ran from the opened scar to trickle down his throat, crimson on bronze; I smelled the tang of fear. Gods, it swallowed him whole and left nothing to spit out.

I looked again at Electra and heard the women's frightened conversation. I understood little of it, knowing it to be only Solindish. But I understood the screams.

I went to her and set a hand on Lachlan's shoulder. He saw me, but he did not let her go. I knew why. There was blood on her nails and she wanted more; she would rip the flesh from his bones.

"Electra," I said.

The screaming stopped. *"Carillon—"*

"I know." I could hear the howling still. Storr, locked somewhere within the palace. Locked away by his *lir*.

I turned away again, looking back at Finn. His eyes were wide and wild. Breath rasped in his throat. Even from here, I saw how he shook; how the trembling wracked his bones.

"Out!" I shouted at the women. "This will be better done without your Solindish tongues!"

They protested at once. So did Electra. But I listened to none of it. I waited, and when they saw I meant it they gathered their skirts and scuttled out of the room. I slammed the heavy door shut behind them, and then I went to Finn.

The man-at-arms—Perrin, I knew—stepped out of my way at once. Rowan hesitated, still holding Finn at swordpoint, and I set him aside with one ungentle thrust of my arm. I went through the space where Rowan had stood and caught the jerkin in both hands, pulling Finn from the wall even as he sagged.

"Ku'reshtin!" I used the Cheysuli obscenity, knowing he would answer no Homanan. *"Tu'halla dei!"* Lord to *liege man,* a command he had to acknowledge.

I felt the shaking in the flesh beneath my hands. Fists clenched and unclenched helplessly, clawless and human, but betrayal nonetheless. I had seen the bruises on Electra's throat.

I heard the labored breathing. The howling filled the halls. Human and wolf, both driven to extremes. But at this moment I thought Storr, at least, knew what was going on.

I thrust Finn into the corner, fenced by two walls of stone. I drew back one fist and smashed it into his face, knocking skull against brick. Blood welled up in a broken lip.

"No!" Rowan caught my arm.

"Get you gone!" I thrust him back again. "I am not beating him to death, I am beating him to *sense*—"

A hand closed on my wrist. Finn's hand, but lacking all strength. "Tynstar—"

At least he could speak again. "Finn—you fool! *You fool!* It was a trap—*a trap*—" I shook my head in desperation. "Why did you go in again? Why did you give him the chance?"

"Tynstar—" It hissed out of his bloodied mouth. "Tynstar—*here*—"

"He nearly slew me!" Electra's voice was hoarse and broken. "Your shapechanger tried to slay me!"

"Tynstar was here—"

"No." I felt the futility well into my chest. "Oh Finn, no—not Tynstar. *Electra*. It was a trap—"

"Tynstar." For a moment he frowned in confusion, trying to stand on his own. He knew I held him, and I thought he knew why. "Let go."

"No." I shook my head. "You will try for her again."

It focused him. I saw sense in his eyes again, and the fear came leaping back to swallow him whole once more.

I slammed him against the wall once more as he thrust himself from the stone. Electra shouted again, this time in Solindish, and I heard the rage in her voice. Not only fear, though there was that. Rage. And wild, wild hatred.

"Finn—" I set the elbow against his throat and felt him stiffen at once. We had done it all before.

"My lord." Rowan's voice was horrified. "What will you do?"

"Tynstar's *meijha*," Finn rasped. "Tynstar was *here*—"

I let him go. I let go of the wrist I held, took my arm from his throat and stood back. But this time the sword was in my hand, my sword, and he stopped when I set the point against his throat. "No," I said. "Hold. I will get the truth from you one way or another." I saw the shock in his eyes. "Finn, I *understand*. Duncan has said what it was, and I recall how you were in the Ellasian snowstorm." I paused, looking for comprehension in his eyes. "Do not make it any worse."

He was still white as death. Blood welled in the opened scar. Now, seeing him in extremity, I saw clearly the silver in his hair. Even beneath the blood his face was harder, more gaunt at eyes and beneath his cheeks. He had aged ten years in two months.

"Finn," I said in rising alarm, "are you ill?"

"Tynstar," was all he said, and again: "Tynstar. He put his hand on me."

When I could I looked at Rowan, standing silent and shocked beside me. "How did you come to be here?"

He swallowed twice. "The Queen screamed, my lord. We all came." He gestured at Lachlan and Perrin. "There were more at first, but I sent them away. I thought you would prefer this matter handled in private."

I felt old and tired and used up. I held a sword against my liege man. I had only to look at his face to know why it was necessary. "What did you find when you came?"

"The Queen was—in some disarray. Finn's hands were on her throat." Rowan looked angry and confused. "My lord—there was nothing else I could do. He was trying to slay the Queen."

I knew he meant the leg wound. I wondered how bad it was. Finn stood steadily enough *now*, but I could see the pain in the tautness of his gaunt, bloody face.

Lachlan spoke at last. "Carillon—I have no wish to condemn him. But it is true. He would have taken her life."

"Execute him." Electra's tone was urgent. "He tried to slay me, Carillon."

"It was Tynstar," Finn said clearly. "It was Tynstar I wanted."

"But it was Electra you would have slain." The sword,

for the slightest moment, wavered in my hand. "You fool,"
I whispered, "why have you done this to me? You know
what I must do—"

"No!" It exploded from Rowan's throat. "My lord—you
cannot—"

"No," I said wearily, "I cannot—not that. But there is
something else—"

"Execute him!" Electra again. "There is nothing else to
be done. He sought to slay the Queen!"

"I will *not* have him slain."

It was Lachlan who understood first. "Carillon! It will
bare your back to the enemy!"

"I have no choice." I looked directly at Finn, still caged
by the steel of my sword. "Do you see what you have
done?"

He raised his hands. He closed them both on the blade,
blocking out the runes. The ones his father had made.
"*No.*"

I was nearly shaking myself. "But you would do it again,
would you not?"

The grimace came swiftly; bared teeth and the suggestion of a deep growl in a human throat. "Tynstar—"

"*Electra*," I said. "You would do it again, would you
not?"

"*Aye* . . ." A breathy hiss of sound expelled from a
constricted throat. He was shaking.

"Finn," I said, "it is done. I have no choice. The service
is over." I stopped short, then went on when I could
speak. "The blood-oath is—denied."

His eyes were fixed on mine. After a moment I could
not bear to look at them, but I did. I had given him the
task; it was mine to do as well.

He took his hands from the blade. I saw the lines
pressed into his palms, but no blood. He bled enough
already, inside as well as out.

His voice was a whisper. "*Ja'hai-na*," he said only.
Accepted.

I put the sword away, hearing the hiss of steel on boiled
leather as it slid home. The lion was quiescent; the brilliant ruby black.

Finn took the knife from the sheath at his belt and

offered it to me. My own, once; the royal blade with its golden Homanan crest.

It nearly broke me. "Finn," I said, "I cannot."

"The blood-oath is denied." His face was stark, old, aging. "*Ja'hai*, my lord Mujhar."

I took it from his hand. There was blood upon the gold. "*Ja'hai-na*," I said at last, and Finn walked from the room.

THREE

When I could, I went out into the corridor and moved slowly through the dimness. The torches were unlighted. The hallway was empty of people; my servants, knowing how to serve, left me to myself.

No more howling. Silence. Storr, with Finn was gone. My spirit felt as extinguished as the torches.

I went alone to the Great Hall and stood within its darkness. The firepit was banked. Coals glowed. Here, as well, none of the torches was lighted.

Silence.

I tucked the Homanan blade into my belt beside the Cheysuli knife in its sheath and began shifting the unburned logs in the firepit with my booted feet. The coals I also kicked aside until I bared the iron ring beneath its heavy layer of ash. Then I took a torch, pushed the shaft through the ring, and levered it up until the heavy plate rose and fell back, clanging against the firepit rim. The ash puffed up around it.

I lighted the torch and went down when the staircase lay bare. I counted this time: one hundred and two steps. I stood before the wall and saw how the rain had soaked in from the storm. The walls were slick and shiny with dampness. The runes glowed pale green against the dark stone. I put my fingers to them, tracing their alien shapes, then found the proper keystone. The wall, when I leaned, grated open.

I stood in the doorway. *Lir*-shapes, creamy and veined with gold, loomed at me from the walls. Bear and boar, owl and hawk and falcon. Wolf and fox, raven, cat and more. In the hissing light of the iron torch they moved, silent and supple, against the silken stone.

I went into the vault. I let the silence oppress me.

FoolFoolFool, I thought.

I took the Cheysuli knife from my sheath. The light glittered off the silver. I saw the snarling wolf's-head hilt with its eyes of uncut emerald. Finn's knife, once.

I moved to the edge of the oubliette. As before, the torchlight did not touch the blackness within. So deep, so soft, so black. I recalled my days in there, and how I had become someone other than myself. How, for four days, I had thought myself Cheysuli.

I shut my eyes. The glow of the torchlight burned yellow against my lids. I could see nothing, but I recalled it all. The soft soughing of shifting wings, the pip of a preening falcon. How it was to go trotting through the forest with a pelt upon my back. And freedom, such perfect freedom, bound by nothing more than what the gods had given me.

"*Ja'hai.*" I reached out my hand to drop the knife into the pit.

"Carillon."

I spun around and teetered on the brink while the torch roared softly against the movement.

I might have expected Finn. But never Tourmaline.

She wore a heavy brown traveling cloak, swathed in wool from head to toe. The hood was dropped to her shoulders and I saw how the torchlight gleamed on the gold in her tawny hair. "You have sent him away," she said, "and so you send me as well."

All the protests leaped into my mouth. I had only to say them in a combination of tones; impatience, confusion, irritation, amazement and placation. But none of them were right. I knew, suddenly and horribly; *I knew*. Not Lachlan. Not Lachlan at all, for Torry.

The pieces of the fortune-game, quite suddenly, were thrown across the table from their casket and spread out before me in their intricate, interlocking patterns that double too often as prophets. The bone dice and carven rune-sticks stood before me in the shape of my older sister, and I saw the pattern at last.

"Torry," was all I said. She was too much like me. She let no one turn her from one way when it was the way she wanted to go.

"We did not dare tell you," she said quietly. "We knew what you would do. He says—" already she had fallen into the easy attribution so common to women when they speak of their men "—that in the clans women are never bartered to the warriors. That a man and woman are left to their own decisions, without another to turn them against their will."

"Tourmaline . . ." I felt tired suddenly, and full of aches and pains. "Torry, you know why I had to do it. In our House rank is matched with rank; I wanted a prince for you because you deserve that much, if not more. Torry—I did not wish to make you unhappy. But I need the aid from another realm—"

"Did you think to ask me?" Slowly she shook her head and the torchlight gleamed in her hair. "*No*. Did you think I would mind? No. Did you think I would even protest?" She smiled a little. "Think you upon my place, Carillon, and see how *you* would feel."

The pit was at my back. I thought now another one yawned before me. "Torry," I said finally, "think you I had any choice in whom *I* wed? Princes—and kings—have no more say than their women. There was nothing I could do."

"You might have asked me. But no, you ever *told*. The Mujhar of Homana orders his sister to wed where he will decide." She put up a silencing hand. Her fingers seemed sharp as a blade. "Aye, I know—it has ever been this way. And ever will be. But this once, *this once*, I say no. I say I choose my way."

"Our mother—"

"—is gone home to Joyenne." She saw my frown of surprise. "I told her, Carillon. Like you, she thinks me mad. But she knows better than to protest." The smile came more freely. "She has raised willful children, Carillon—they do what they will do when it comes to whom they marry." She laughed softly. "Think you that I was fooled about Electra? Oh Carillon, I am not blind. I do not deny she was a pathway to Solinde, but she is more than that to you. You wanted her because—like all men who see her—you simply had to have her. That is a measure of her power."

"Tourmaline—"

"I am going," she said calmly, with the cool assurance of a woman who has what she wants in the way of a man. "But I will tell you this much, for both of us: it was not intended." Tourmaline smiled and I saw her as Finn must see her: not a princess, not a gamepiece, not even Carillon's sister. A woman; no more, no less. It was no wonder he wanted her. "You sent him to the Keep to recover from his wounds. You sent *me* there for safety. I tended him when Alix could not, wondering what manner of man he was to so serve my brother's cause, and he gave me the safety I needed. Soon enough—it was more." She shook her head. "We meant to do no harm. But now it comes to this: he is dismissed from his *tahlmorra*, and mine is to go with him."

"*Tahlmorra* is a Cheysuli thing," I told her bleakly. "Torry, no. I do not wish to lose you as well."

"Then take him back into your service."

"I cannot!" The shout echoed in the vault, bouncing off the silent *lir*. "Do you not see? Electra is the Queen, and he a Cheysuli shapechanger. No matter what *I* say in this, they will always suspect Finn of wishing to slay the Queen. And if he stayed, he might. Did he not tell you what he tried to do?"

Her lips were pale. "Aye. But he had no choice—"

"Nor do I have one now." I shook my head. "Do you think I do not want him back? Gods, Torry, you do not know what it was for the two of us in exile. He has been with me for too long to make this parting simple. But it must be done. What else is there to do? I could never trust him with Electra—"

"Perhaps you should not trust *her*."

"I wed her," I said grimly. "I need her. Did I allow Finn to stay and something happened to Electra, do you know what would happen to Homana? Solinde would rise.

No mere army could gainsay an outraged realm. *Murder*, Torry." Slowly I shook my head. "Think you the *qu'mahlin* is ended? No. Be not so foolish. A thing such as that is stopped, perhaps, but never forgotten. For too long the Cheysuli have been hated. It is not done yet." The torch hissed and sputtered, putting shadows on her face. "This time, a race would be destroyed. And with it, no doubt, would also fall Homana."

Tears were on her face, glittering in the light. "Carillon," she whispered, "I carry his child."

When I could speak, albeit a trembling whisper, I said his name. Then, to myself. "How could I not have seen it?"

"You did not look. You did not ask. And now it is too late." She gathered her skirts and cloak with both her hands. "Carillon—he waits. It is time I left you."

"Torry—"

"I will go," she said gently. "It is where I want to be.

We faced each other in the flickering light in a vault full of marble *lir*. I heard the faint cry of hawk and falcon; the howl of a hunting wolf. I remembered what it was to be Cheysuli.

I dropped the torch into the oubliette. "I can see no one in this darkness. A person could stay or she could go—and I would never know it."

Dim light crept down the stairs behind her. Someone held a torch. Somone who waited for Torry.

I saw the tear on the curve of her cheek as she came up to kiss me. And then she was gone, and I was left alone with the silence and the *lir*.

I let the cover fall free of my hands and slam shut against the mouth. The gust of air sent ash flying. It settled on my clothing but I did not care. I kicked coals and pushed wood over the plate again, hiding the ring in ash, and went out of the Great Hall alone.

I meant to go to bed, though I knew I would not sleep. I meant to drown myself in wine, though I knew it would leave me sober. I meant to try and forget, and I knew the task was futile.

Come, lady, and hear of my soul,
for a harper's poor magic
does little to hold
a fine lady's heart
when she keeps it her own.

I stopped walking. The music curled out to wrap me in its magic and I thought at once of Lachlan. Lachlan and his Lady. Lachlan, whose lays were all for Torry.

Come, lady, and listen:
I will make for you music
from out of the world
if you wait with me,
stay with me,
lay with me, too . . .
I will give you myself
and this harp that I hold.

I followed the song to its source and found Lachlan in a small private solar, a nook in the vastness of the palace. Cushions lay on the floor, but Lachlan sat on a three-legged, velvet-covered stool, his Lady caressed by a lover's hands. I paused inside the door and saw the gold of the strings; the gleam of green stone.

His head was bowed over his harp. He was lost within his music. I saw how his supple fingers moved within the strings: plucking here, touching there, ever placating his Lady. He was at peace, eyes shut and face gone smooth, so that I saw the elegance in his features. A harper is touched by the gods, and ever knows it. It accounts for their confidence and quiet pride.

The music died away. Silence. And then he looked up and saw me, rising at once from his stool. "Carillon! I thought you had gone to bed."

"No."

He frowned. "You are all over ash, and still damp. Do you not think you would do better—"

"He is gone." I cut him off. "And so is Tourmaline."

He stared, uncomprehending. "Torry! Torry—?"

"With Finn." I wanted it said so the cut would bleed more quickly, to get rid of the pain at once.

"Lodhi!" Lachlan's face was bone-white. "Ah, Lodhi— *no*—" He came three steps, still clutching his Lady, and then he stopped. "Carillon—say you are mistaken. . . ."

"It would be a lie." I saw how the pain moved into his eyes; how it stiffened the flesh of his face. He was a child suddenly, stricken with some new nightmare and groping for understanding.

"But—you said she was meant to wed. You meant her for a prince."

"A prince," I agreed. "Never a harper. Lachlan—"

"Have I waited too long?" His arms were rigid as he clasped the harp to his chest. "Lodhi, have I waited *too long*?"

"Lachlan, I know you have cared. I saw it from the beginning. But there is no sense in holding onto the hope that it might have been."

"Get her back." He was suddenly intent. "Take her from him. Do not let her go—"

"No." I said it firmly. "I have let her go because, in the end, there was no way I could stop her. I know Finn too well. And he has said, quite clearly, he will allow no one to keep him from the woman he wants."

Lachlan put one hand to his brow. He scraped at the silver circlet as if it bound him too tightly. Then abruptly, as if discovering it himself, he pulled it from his head and held it out in one fist as the other arm clasped his Lady.

"*Harper!*" His pain was out in the open. "*Lodhi*, but I have been a fool!"

"Lachlan—"

He shook his head. "Carillon, can you not get her back? I promise you, you will be glad of it. There is something I would say to her—"

"No." This time I said it gently. "Lachlan—she bears Finn's child."

He lost the rest of his color. Then, all at once, he sat down on the three-legged stool. For a moment he just stared at the wooden floor. Then, stiffly, he set his Lady and the circlet on the floor, as if he renounced them both. "I meant to take her home," was all he said.

"No." I said it again. "Lachlan—I am sorry."

Silently he drew a thong from beneath his doublet. He pulled the leather from around his head and handed the trinket to me.

Trinket? It was a ring. It depended from the thong. I turned it upward into the candlelight and saw the elaborate crest: a harp and the crown of Ellas.

"There are seven of those rings," he said matter-of-factly. "Five rest on the hands of my brothers. The other is on my father's finger." He looked up at me at last. "Oh, aye, I know how things are in royal Houses. I am from one myself."

"*Lachlan*," I said. "Or, is it?"

"Oh, aye. Cuinn Lachlan Llewellyn. My father has a taste for names." He frowned a little, oddly distant and detached. "But then he has eleven children, so it is for the best."

"High Prince Cuinn of Ellas." The ring fell out of my hand and dangled on its thong. "In the names of all the gods of Homana, *why did you keep it secret?*"

A shrug twitched at his shoulders. "It was—a thing between my father and myself. I was not, you see, the sort of heir Rhodri wanted. I preferred harping to governing and healing to courting women." He smiled a little, a mere twisting of his mouth. "I was not ready for responsibility. I wanted no wife to chain me to the castle. I wanted to leave Rheghed behind and see the whole of Ellas, on my own, without a retinue. The heirship is so—binding." This time the smile held more of the Lachlan I knew. "You might know something of that, I think."

"But—all this silence with Torry. And *me!*" I thought he had been a fool. "Had you *said* anything, none of this might have happened!"

"I could not. It was a bond between my father and me." Lachlan rubbed at his brow, staring at his harp. He hunched on the stool, shoulders slumped, and the candlelight was dull on his dyed brown hair.

Dyed brown hair. Not gray, as he had said, pleading vanity, but another color entirely.

I sat down. I set my back against the cold wall and

waited. I thought of Torry and Finn in the darkness and rain, and Lachlan here before me. "Why?"

He sighed and rubbed at his eyes. "Originally, it was a game I wished to play. How better to see your realm than to go its length and breadth unknown? So my father agreed, saying if I wanted to play at such foolishness, I would have to play it absolutely. He forbade me to divulge my name and rank unless I was in danger."

"But to keep it from *me* . . ." I shook my head.

"It was because of you." He nodded as I frowned. "When I met you and learned who you were, I wrote at once to my father. I told him what you meant to do, and how I thought you could not do it. Take Homana back from Bellam? No. You had no men, no army. Only Finn . . . and me." He smiled. "I came with you because I wanted to, to see what you could do. And I came because my father, when he saw what you meant to do, wanted you to win."

I felt a sluggish stirring of anger deep inside. "He sent me no aid—"

"To the pretender-prince of Homana?" Lachlan shook his head. "You forget—Bellam encroached upon Ellas. He offered Electra to Rhodri's heir. It was not in Ellas's interests to support Carillon's bid for the throne." He softened his tone a bit. "For all I would have liked to give you what aid I could, I had my father's realm to think of, too. We have enemies. This had to remain your battle."

"Still, *you* came with me. You risked yourself."

"I risked nothing. If you recall, I did not fight, playing the harper's role." He shook his head. "It was not easy. I have trained as a warrior since I was but a child. But my father forbade me to fight, and it seemed the best thing to do. And he said also I was to go to *watch* and learn what I could. If you won the war and held your realm for a twelve-month and a day, Rhodri would offer alliance."

"It has been longer than that." I did not need to count the days.

"And did you not just send to other realms, offering the hand of your sister in marriage?" The color moved through his face. "It is not my place to offer what I cannot. My father is High King. It was for him to accept your offer, and I had to wait for him." He shut his eyes a moment. "Lodhi, but I thought *she* would wait . . ."

"So did I." The stone was cold against my spine. "Oh Lachlan, had I known—"

"I know. But it was not for me to say." His face was almost ugly. "Such is the lot of princes."

"Could you have said nothing to *her*?"

He stared at the cushion-strewn floor. "I nearly did. More times than I can count. Once I even spoke of Rhodri's heir, but she only bid me to be quiet. She did not wish to think on marriage." He sighed. "She was ever gentle with my feelings, seeking to keep me—a harper—from looking too high, as did her brother, the Mujhar." He did not smile. "And I thought, in all my complacency, she would say differently when she knew. And you. And so I savored the waiting, instead."

I shut my eyes and rested my head against the stone. I recalled the harper in the Ellasian roadhouse, giving me my memories. I recalled his patient understanding when I treated him with contempt, calling him spy when he was merely a friend and nothing more.

And how I had bidden him slay a man to see if he would do it.

So much between us, and now so little. I knew what he would do. "You had no choice," I said at last. "The gods know *I* understand what it is to serve rank and responsibility. But Lachlan, you must not blame yourself. What else could you have done?"

"Spoken, regardless of my father." He stared at the floor, shoulders hunched. So vulnerable, suddenly, when he had always been so strong. "I should have said something to someone."

And yet it would have done no good. We both realized it, saying nothing because the saying would bring more pain. A man may love a woman while the woman loves another, but no man may force her to love where she has no desire to do so.

"By the All-Father himself," Lachlan said wearily, "I think it is not worth it." He gathered up his Lady and rose, hooking one arm through the silver circlet. He had more right to it than most, though it should have had the shine of royal gold.

I stood up stiffly and faced him. I held out the ring on its leather thong. "Lachlan—" I stopped.

He knew. He took the ring, looked at the crest that made him a man—a prince—apart, then slipped the thong over his head once more. "I came a harper," he said quietly. "It is how I will leave in the morning."

"Do *you* leave me, old friend, I will be quite alone." It was all I could say to him; the only plea I would ever make.

I saw the pain in his eyes. "I came, knowing I would have to leave. Not when, but knowing the time would come. I had hoped, for a while, I would not leave alone." The line of his jaw was set; the gentleness of the harper had fled, and in its place I saw the man Lachlan had ever been, but showing it to few. "You are a king, Carillon. Kings are always alone. Someday—I shall know it, too." He reached out and caught my arm in the ritual clasp of friendship. "*Yhana Lodhi, yffennog faer.*"

"Walk humbly, harper," I said softly.

He went out of the room into the shadows of the corridor, and his *Song of Homana* was done.

I went into my chambers and found her waiting. She was in shadow with a single candle lighted. She was wrapped in one of my chamber robes: wine-purple velvet lined with dappled silver fur. On her it was voluminous; I could see little but hands and feet.

I stopped. I could not face her now. To look at her was to recall what Finn had done, and how it had ended in banishment. How it had ended with Torry and Lachlan gone as well. To look at her was to look on the face of aloneness, and that I could not bear.

"*No,*" she said, as I made a movement to go. "Stay you. Do you wish it, *I* will go."

Still in shadow. The wine-colored velvet melted into the shadows. The candlelight played on her hair—unbound, and hanging to her knees.

I sat down because I had no strength to stand. On the edge of my draperied bed. I was all over ash, as Lachlan had said, and still damp from the storm outside. No doubt I smelled of it as well: wet wool and smoke and flame.

She came and stood before me. "Let me lift this grief from you."

I looked at her throat with the bruises on it; the marks of a crazed man's madness.

She knelt and pulled off my heavy boots. I said nothing, watching her, amazed she would do what I, or a servant, could much more easily do.

Her hands were deft and gentle, stripping me of my clothing, and then she knelt before me. "Ah my lord, do not grieve so. You put yourself in pain."

It came to me to wonder whether she had ever knelt for Tynstar.

She put one hand on my thigh. Her fingers were cool. I could feel the pulse-beat in her palm.

I looked again at the bruises on her throat. Slowly I reached out and set my hands there, as Finn had set his, and felt the fragility of her flesh. "Because of you," I said.

"Aye." Her eyes did not waver from mine. "And for you, good my lord, I am sorry he had to go."

My hands tightened. She did not flinch or pull away. "I am not Tynstar, lady."

"No." Neither did she smile.

My hands slid up slowly to cup her skull with its weight of shining hair. The robe, now loosened, slid off her shoulders and fell against the floor: a puddle of wine-dark velvet. She was naked underneath.

I pulled her up from the stone and into my arms, sagging back onto the bed. To be rid of the loneliness, I would lie with the dark god himself.

"I need you," I whispered against her mouth. "By the gods, woman, *how I need you. . . .*"

FOUR

The infirmary tent stank of blood and burning flesh. I watched as the army chirurgeon lifted the hot iron from Rowan's arm, studied the seared edges of the wound and nodded. "Closed. No more blood, captain. You will keep the arm, I think, with the help of the gods."

Rowan sat stiffly on the campstool, white-faced and shaking. The sword had cut into the flesh of his forearm, but had missed muscle and bone. He would keep the arm and its use, though I did not doubt he felt, at the moment, as if it had already been cut off.

He let out his breath slowly. It hissed between his teeth. He put out his right hand and groped for the cup of sour wine Waite had set out on the table. Fingers closed on the cup, gripping so hard the knuckles shone white, and then he lifted it to his mouth. I smiled. Waite had put a powder in it that would ease the pain a bit. Rowan had originally refused any such aid, but he had not seen the powder. And now he drank, unknowing, and the pain would be eased somewhat.

I glanced back over my shoulder through the gap in the entrance flap. Outside it was gray, gray and dark blue, with the weight of clouds and winter fog. My breath, leaving the warmth of the infirmary tent, plumed on the air, white as smoke.

"My thanks, my lord." Rowan's voice still bore the strain, but it lessened as the powder worked its magic.

He began to pull on his fur-lined leathers, though I knew the motion must hurt. I did not move to help because I knew he would not allow it, me being his Mujhar, and because it would hurt his pride. Like all the Cheysuli, he had his pride; a prickly, arrogant pride that some took for condescension. It was not, usually. It was merely a certainty of their place within the boardgame of the gods. And Rowan, though he was less Cheysuli in his habits than Homanan, reflected much of that traditional pride without even knowing it.

I shifted in the entrance, then grimaced in response to the protests of my muscles. My body was battered and sore, but I bore not a single wound from the last encounter earlier in the day. My blood was still my own, unlike Rowan's—unless one counted what I had lost from my nose when struck in the face by my horse's head. The blow had knocked me half-senseless for a moment or two, making me easy prey, but I had managed to stay in the saddle. And it was Rowan, moving to thrust aside the attacker's sword, who had taken the blow meant for me. We were both fortunate the Atvian had missed his target.

"Hungry?" I asked.

Rowan nodded. Like us all, he was too thin, pared down to blood and bone. Because of his Cheysuli features his face was gaunter than mine; because of my beard, no one noticed if I seemed gaunt or not. It had its advantages; Rowan looked ill, I did not, and I hated to be asked how I fared. It made me feel fragile when I was not, but that is the cost of being a king.

Rowan pulled on his gloves, easing into the right one because the movement hurt his arm. He was still pale, lacking the deeper bronze of Cheysuli flesh because of the loss of blood. With his eyes gone black from the drug and the pallor of his face, he looked more Homanan than Cheysuli.

Poor Rowan, I thought: forever caught between the worlds.

He scrubbed his good arm through his heavy hair and glanced at me. He forced a smile. "It does not hurt, my lord."

Waite, putting away his chirurgeon's tools, grunted in

disgust. "In my presence, it hurts. Before the Mujhar, it does not. You have miraculous powers of healing, my lord . . . perhaps we should trade places."

Rowan colored. I grinned and pulled aside the doorflap, waving him outside even as he protested I should go first. The mist came up to chill our faces at once. Rowan hunched his shoulders against the cold and cradled his aching arm. "It *is* better, my lord."

I said nothing about the powder, merely gestured toward the nearest cookfire. "There. Hot wine and roasting boar. You will undoubtedly feel better once your belly is full again."

He walked carefully across the hardpacked, frozen ground, trying not to jar the injured arm. "My lord . . . I am sorry."

"For being injured?" I shook my head. "That was my wound you took. It requires my gratitude, not an apology from you."

"It does." Tension lines marred the youthfulness of his face. He watched the ground where he walked and the thick black hair hid most of his face. Like me, he had not cut it for too long. "You would do better with Finn at your side. I am—not a liege man." He cast me a quick, glinting glance out of drug-blackened eyes. "I have not the skill to keep you safe, my lord."

I stopped at the cookfire and nodded at the soldier who tended the roasting boar. He began to cut with a greasy knife. "You are not Finn, nor ever can be," I said clearly to Rowan. "But I want you by my side."

"My lord—"

I cut him off with a gesture of my hand. "When I sent Finn from my service six months ago, I knew what I was risking. Still, it had to be done, for the good of us all. I do not dismiss the importance his presence held. The bond between Cheysuli liege man and his Mujhar is a sacred thing, but—once broken—there is no going back." I grasped his uninjured arm, knowing there was no *lir*-band underneath the furs and leathers. "I do not seek another Finn. I value *you*. Do not disappoint me by undervaluing yourself." The soldier dropped a slice of meat onto a slab of tough bread and put it into my hands. In turn, I put it into

Rowan's. "Now, eat. You must restore your strength so we can fight again."

The mist put beads of water into his hair. Damp, it tangled against his shoulders. His face was bleak, pale, stretched taut over prominent bones, but I thought the pain came from something other than his arm.

A pot of wine was warming near the firecairn. I knelt, poured a cup and handed it up to Rowan. And then, as I turned to pour my own, I heard someone shout for me.

"Meat, my lord?" asked the soldier with the knife.

"A moment." I rose and turned toward the shout. In the mist it was hard to place such sounds, but then I saw the shapes coming out of the grayness. Three men on horseback: two of them my Homanans, the third a stranger.

They were muffled in furred leathers and woolen wrappings. The mist parted as they rode through and showed them more clearly, then closed behind them again. "My lord!" One of the men dismounted before me and dropped to one knee, then up again. "A courier, my lord."

The gesture indicated the still-mounted stranger. He rode a good horse, as couriers usually do, but I saw no crest to mark him. He wore dark leathers and darker wool; a cap hid most of his head so that only his face showed.

The hot wine warmed my hands, even through my gloves. "Atvian?" I put no inflection in my tone.

The stranger reached up to pull woolen wraps from his face. "No, my lord—Ellasian." Mouth bared, the words took on greater clarity. "Sent from High Prince Cuinn."

Lachlan. I could not help the smile. "Step you down, friend courier. You are well come to my army."

He dismounted, came closer and dropped to one knee in a quick bow of homage. Neatly done. He had a warm, friendly face, but was young, and yet he seemed to know his business. He was red-haired beneath the cap, judging by his brows, and his eyes were green. There were freckles on his face.

"My lord, it pleases me to serve the High Prince. He bids me give you this." He dug into a leather pouch at his belt and withdrew a folded parchment. A daub of blue wax sealed it closed, and pressed into it was the royal crest: a harp and the crown of Ellas. It brought back the vision of Lachlan and his Lady, when he told me who he was.

I broke the seal and unfolded the parchment. It crackled in the misted air; its crispness faded as the paper wilted. But the words were legible.

Upon returning home to Rheghed, I was met with warm welcome from the king my father. So warm, indeed that he showered me with gifts. One of these gifts was a command of my own, did I ever need to use it. I doubt Rhodri ever intended me to be so generous as to loan the gift to you, but the thing is already done. My men are yours for as long as you need them. And does it please you to offer a gift in return, I ask only that you treat kindly with Ellas when we seek to make an alliance.

By the hand of the High Prince,
Cuinn Lachlan Llewellyn

I grinned. And then I laughed, and set my cup of hot wine into the hands of the courier. "Well come, indeed," I said. "How many, and where?"

He grinned back when he had drunk. "Half a league east, my lord. As to the number—five thousand. The Royal Ellasian Guard."

I laughed again, loudly. "Ah Lodhi, I thank you for this courier! But even more I thank you for Lachlan's friendship!" I clapped the courier on his shoulder. "Your name."

"Gryffth, my lord."

"And your captain's?"

"Meredyth. A man close to the High Prince himself." Gryffth grinned. "My lord, forgive me, but we all know what Prince Cuinn intended. And none of us is unwilling. Shall I send to bring them in?"

"Five thousand . . ." I shook my head, smiling at the thought. "Thorne will be finished in a day."

Gryffth brightened. "Then you are near to winning?"

"We *are* winning," I said. "But this will make the ending sweeter. Ah gods, I do thank you for that harper." I took the cup from Gryffth as he went to remount his horse, and watched him ride back into the fog with his Homanan guides.

"Well, my lord," Rowan said, "the thing is done at last."

"A good thing, too." I grinned. "You are not fit to fight with that arm, and now you will not have to."

"My lord—" he protested, but I did not listen as I read Lachlan's note again.

The map was of leather, well-tanned and soft. It was a pale creamy color, and the paint stood out upon it. In the candlelighted pavilion, the lines and rune-signs seemed to glow.

"Here." I put my forefinger on the map. "Mujhara. *We* are here—perhaps forty leagues from the city: northwest." I moved my finger more westerly. "The Cheysuli are here, closer to Lestra, though still within Homana." I lifted the finger and moved it more dramatically, pointing out the Solindish port of Andemir. "Thorne came in here; Atvia is but eight leagues across the Idrian Ocean, directly west of Solinde. He took the shortest sea route to Solinde, and the shortest land route to Homana." I traced the invisible line across the map. "See you here? —he came this way, cutting Solinde in half. It is here our boundary puts its fist into Solinde, and it is where Thorne was bound."

"But you stopped him." The Ellasian captain nodded. "You have cut him off, and he goes no farther."

It seemed odd to hear the husky accent again, though we spoke Homanan between us and all my captains. There were other Ellasians as well, clustered within my tent; I meant Lachlan's gift to know precisely what they were doing.

"Thorne let it be known he was splitting his army," I explained. "He would come overland through Solinde, gaining support from the rebels there. But he also sent a fleet—or so all the reports said. A fleet bound for Hondarth—down here." I set my finger on the mark that represented Hondarth, near the bottom of the map and directly south of Mujhara. "But there was no fleet—no *real* fleet. It was a ruse."

Meredyth nodded. "He meant you to halve your army

and send part of it to Hondarth, so that when he came in
here—full strength—he would face a reduced Homanan
warhost." He smiled. "Clever. But you are more so, my
lord Mujhar."

I shook my head. "Fortunate. My spies are good. I
heard of the ruse and took steps to call back those I had
dispatched to Hondarth; thank the gods, they had not
gotten far. We have Thorne now, but he will not give up.
He will send his men against me until there is no one
left."

"And the Solindish aid he wanted?"

"Less than he desired." Meredyth was older than I by
at least twenty years, but he listened well. At first I had
hesitated to speak so plainly, knowing him more experienced than I, but Lachlan had chosen well. Here was a
man who would listen and weigh my words, then make his
judgment upon them. "He came into Solinde expecting to
find thousands for the taking, but there have been only
hundreds. Since I sent the Cheysuli there, the Solindish
are—hesitant to upset the alliance I made."

Meredyth's expression showed calm politeness. "The
Queen fares well?"

I knew what he asked. It was more than just an inquiry
after Electra's health. The future of Solinde rested upon
the outcome—or issue—of the marriage; Electra would
bear me a second child in three months and, if it were a
boy, Solinde would be one child closer to freedom and
autonomy. It was why Thorne had found his aid so thin.
That, and the Cheysuli.

"The Queen fares well," I said.

Meredyth's smile was slight. "Then what of the Ihlini,
my lord? Have they not joined with Thorne?"

"There has been no word of Ihlini presence within the
Atvian army." Thank the gods, but I did not say it. "What
we face are Atvians with a few hundred Solindish rebels."
I made a quick gesture. "Thorne is clever, aye, and he
knows how to come against me. I am not crushing him as I
might wish, not when he uses my own methods against
me. No pitched battles, merely raids and skirmishes, as I
employed against Bellam. As you see, we have been here

six months; the thing is not easily won. At least—it *was* not, until Lachlan sent his gift."

Meredyth nodded his appreciation. "I think, my lord, you will be home in time to see the birth of your heir."

"Be the gods willing." I tapped the map again. "Thorne has sent some of his army in here, where I have posted the Cheysuli. But the greater part of it remains here, where we are. The last skirmish was two days ago. I doubt he will come against me before another day has passed. Until then, I suggest we make our plans."

Thorne of Atvia came against us two days later with all the strength he had. No more slash and run as he had learned from me; he fought, this time, with the determination of a man who knows he will lose and, in the losing, lose himself. With the Ellasian men we hammered him back, shutting off the road to Homana. Atvian bowmen notwithstanding, we were destroying his thinning offense.

I sought only Thorne in the crush of fighting. I wanted him at the end of my blade, fully aware of his own death and who dealt it. It was he who had taken my sword from me on the battlefield near Mujhara, nearly seven years before. It was he who had put the iron on me and ordered Rowan flogged. It was Thorne who might have slain Alix, given the chance, had not the Cheysuli come. And it was Thorne who offered me insult by thinking he could pull down my House and replace it with his own.

When the arrow lodged itself in the leather-and-mail of my armor, I thought myself unhurt. It set me back in the saddle a moment and I felt the punch of a sharpened fist against my left shoulder, but I did not think it had gone through to touch my flesh. It was only when I reined my horse into an oncoming Atvian that I realized the arm was numb.

I swore. The Atvian approached at full gallop, sword lifted above his head. He rode with his knees, blind to his horse, intent on striking me down. I meant to do the same, but now I could not. I had only the use of one arm.

His horse slammed into mine. The impact sent a wave of pain rolling from shoulder to skull. I bent forward at once, seeking to keep my seat as the Atvian's sword came down. Blade on blade and the screech of stee'—the deflected blow went behind me, barely, and into my saddle. I spun my horse away and the Atvian lost his sword. It remained wedged in my saddle, offering precarious seating, since an ill-timed movement might result in an opened buttock, but at least I had disarmed him. I stood up in my stirrups, avoiding the sword, and saw him coming at me.

He was unarmed. He screamed. And he threw himself from his horse to lock both hands through the rings of my mail.

My own sword was lost. I felt it fall, twisting out of my hand, as the weight came down upon me. He was large, too large, and unwounded. With both hands grasping the ringmail of my armor, he dragged me from my horse.

I twisted in midair, trying to free myself. But the ground came up to meet us and nearly knocked me out of my senses. My left arm was still numb, still useless.

His weight was unbearable. He ground me into the earth. One knee went into my belly as he rose up to reach for his knife and I felt the air rush out. And yet somehow I gritted my teeth and unsheathed my own knife, jabbing upward into his groin.

He screamed. His own weapon dropped as he doubled over, grabbing his groin with both hands. Blood poured out of the wound and splashed against my face. And yet I could not move; could not twist away. His weight was upon my belly and the fire was in my shoulder.

I stabbed again, striking with gauntleted hands. His screams ran on, one into another, until it was a single sound of shock and pain and outrage. I saw the blindness in his eyes and knew he would bleed to death.

He bent forward. Began to topple. The knee shut off my air. And then he fell and the air came back, a little, but all his dead weight was upon me. His right arm was flung across my face, driving ringmail into my mouth, and I felt the coppery taste of blood spring up into my teeth. Blood. Gods, so much blood, and some of it my own. . . .

I twisted. I thrust with my one good arm and tried to topple him off. But his size and the slackness of death undid me, the heaviest weight of all, and I had no strength left to fight it. I went down, down into the oubliette, with no one there to catch me. . . .

Shadows. Darkness. A little light. I thrust myself upward into the light, shouting out a name.

"Be still, my lord," Rowan said. "Be still."

Waite took a swab of bloody linen from me and I realized he tended my shoulder. More blood. Gods, would he turn to cautery? It was no wonder Rowan seemed so calm. He had felt the kiss of hot steel and now expected me to do the same.

I shut my eyes. Sweat broke out and coursed down my face. I had forgotten what pain was, real pain, having escaped such wounds for so long. In Caledon, once or twice, I had been wounded badly, but I had always forgotten the pain and weakness that broke down the soul.

"The arrow was loosed from close by," Waite said conversationally. "Your armor stopped most of the force of it, but not all. Still, it is not a serious wound; I have got the arrowhead out. If you lie still long enough, I think the hole will heal.

I opened one eye a slit. "*No* cautery?"

"Do you prefer it?"

"*No*—" I hissed as the shoulder twinged. "By the gods— can you not give me what you gave Rowan?"

"*I thought* you gave me something," Rowan muttered. "I slept too well that night."

Waite pressed another clout of linen against the wound. It came away less bloody, but the pain was still alive. "I will give you whatever you require, my lord. It is a part of a chirurgeon's service." He smiled as I scowled. "Wait you until I am done with the linens, and you shall have your powder." He gestured to Rowan. "Lift him carefully, captain. Think of him as an egg."

I would have laughed, had I the strength. As it was I could only smile. But when Rowan started to lift me up so Waite could bind the linens around my chest, I nearly groaned aloud. "Gods—are all my bones broken?"

"*No.*" Waite pressed a linen pad against my shoulder and began to bind strips around my chest. "You were found beneath three hundred pounds of mailed Atvian bulk. I would guess you were under it for several hours, while the battle raged on. It is no wonder you feel half-crushed— there, captain, I am done. Let him down again, gently. Do not crack the eggshell."

I shut my eyes again until the sweat dried upon my body. A moment later Waite held a cup to my mouth. "Drink, my lord. Sleep is best for now."

It was sweetened wine. I drank down the cup and lay my head down again, trying to shut out the pain. Rowan, kneeling beside my cot, watched with worried eyes.

I shivered. Waite pulled rugs and pelts up over my body until only my head was free. There were braziers all around my cot. In winter, even a minor wound can kill.

My mouth was sore, no doubt from where the ringmail had broken my lip. I tongued it, feeling the swollen cut, then grimaced. What a foolish way to be taken out of a battle.

"I must assume we won the day," I said. "Otherwise I would doubtless be in an Atvian tent with no chirurgeon and no captain." I paused. "Unless you were taken, too."

"No." Rowan shook his head. "We won, my lord, re-soundingly. The war as well as the day. The Atvians are broken—most of them who could ran back into Solinde. I doubt they will trouble us again."

"Thorne?"

"Dead, my lord."

I sighed. "I wanted him."

"So did I." Rowan's face was grim. "I did not heed you, my lord; I went into battle myself. But I could not find him in the fighting."

The powder was beginning to work. Coupled with the weakness from the wound, it was sucking me into the darkness. It grew more difficult to speak. "See he is buried as befits his rank," I said carefully, "but do not return his body to his people. When my father lay dying of his wounds on the plains near Mujhara, and Thorne had taken me, I asked for a Homanan burial. Thorne denied it to him. And so I deny an Atvian rite to Thorne."

"Aye, my lord." Rowan's voice was low.

I struggled to keep my senses. "He has an heir. Two

sons, I have heard! Send—send word the Mujhar of Homana asks fealty. I will receive Thorne's sons in Homana-Mujhar— far their oaths." I frowned as my lids sealed up my eyes. "Rowan—see it is done—"

"Aye, my lord."

I roused myself once more. "We leave here in the morning. I want to go back to Mujhara."

"You will not be fit to go back in the morning," Waite said flatly. "You will see for yourself, my lord."

"I am not averse to a litter," I murmured. "My pride can withstand it, I think."

Rowan smiled. "Aye, my lord. A litter instead of a horse."

I thought about it. No doubt Electra would hear. I did not wish her to worry. "I will go in a litter until we are but half a league from Mujhara," I told him clearly. "*Then* I will ride the horse."

"Of course, my lord. I will see to it myself."

I gave myself over to darkness.

Waite, unfortunately, had the right of it. Litter or no, I was not fit to go back in the morning. But by the third day I felt much better. I dressed in my warmest clothing, trying to ignore the pain in my shoulder, and went out to speak to Meredyth and his fellow captains.

Their time with me was done. Their aid had helped me accomplish Thorne's defeat, and it was my place now to send them home. I saw to it each captain would have gold to take back to Ellas, as well as coin for the common soldiers. The war with Thorne had not impoverished me, but I had little to spare. All I could promise was a sound alliance for the High King, which seemed to please Meredyth well enough. He then asked a boon of me, which I gave him gladly enough: Gryffth had asked to stay in Homana to serve Ellas in Homana-Mujhar, more an envoy than simple courier. And so the Royal Ellasian Guard went home, lacking a red-haired courier.

I also went home, in a litter after all—too worn to spend time on horseback—and spent most of the journey home sleeping, or contemplating my future. Atvia was mine, did I wish to keep it, although there was a chance Thorne's sons might wish to contest it. I thought they were too young, but could not set an age to them. Yet to try to govern Atvia myself was nearly impossible. The island was too distant. A regent in Solinde was bad enough, and yet I had no choice. I did not want even Solinde; Bellam had, more or less, bequeathed it to me with his death, and the marriage had sealed it. Although I was not averse to claiming two realms my own in place of the single one I wanted, I was not greedy. In the past, far-flung realms had drained the coffers of other kings; I would not fall into the trap. Atvia was Atvian. And did Electra give me an heir this time, I would be happy enough to see Solinde go to my second son.

It was days to Mujhara by litter, and it was well before half a league out that I took to a horse at last. The wound in my shoulder ached, but it was beginning to heal. I thought, so long as I did not push myself too hard, I could ride the rest of the way.

And yet when at last I rode through the main gates of my rose-walled palace, I felt the weariness in my body. My mind was fogged with it. I could hardly think. I wanted only to go to bed, my bed, not to some army cot. And with Electra in my arms.

I acknowledged the welcome of my servants and went at once to the third floor, seeking Electra's chambers. But a Solindish chamberwoman met me at the door and said the Queen was bathing, could I not wait?

No, I said, the *bath* could wait, but she giggled and said the Queen had prepared a special greeting, having received the news of my return. Too weary to think of waving such protestations aside—and wondering what Electra could be planning—I turned back and went away.

If I could not see my wife, I could at least see my daughter. I went to the nursery and found eight-month-old Aislinn sound asleep in an oak-and-ivory cradle, attended by three nursemaids. She was swathed in linens and blankets, but one fist had escaped the covers. She clutched it against her face!

I smiled, bending down to set a hand against her cheek. So soft, so fair . . . I could not believe she was mine. My hand was so large and hard and callused, touching the fragile flesh. Her hair, springing from the pink scalp, was coppery-red, curling around her ears. And her eyes, when they were open, were gray and lashed with gold. She had all of her mother's beauty and none of her father's size.

"Princess of Homana," I whispered to my daughter, "who will be your prince?"

Aislinn did not answer. And I, growing wearier by the moment, thought it better to leave her undisturbed. So I took myself to my chambers and dismissed my body-servant, falling down across my bed to mimic my daughter's rest.

I came up out of the blackness to find I could not breathe. Something had leached the air from my lungs until I could not cry out; could not cry; could not speak. All I could do was gape like a fish taken from the water, flapping on the bank.

There was no pain. Merely helplessness and confusion; pain enough, to a man who knows himself trapped. And does not know why.

A cool hand came down and touched my brow. It floated out of the darkness, unattached to an arm, until I realized the arm was merely covered by a sleeve.

"Carillon. Ah, my poor Carillon. So triumphant in your battles, and now so helpless in your bed."

Electra's voice; Electra's hand. I could smell the scent upon her. A bath, the woman had said; a special greeting prepared.

The cool fingers traced the line of my nose; gently touched my eyelids. "Carillon . . . it ends. This travesty of our marriage. *You* will end, my lord." The hand came down my cheek and caressed my open mouth. "It is time for me to go."

Out of the darkness leaped a rune, a glowing purple rune, and in its reflection I saw my wife. She wore black to swath her body, and yet I saw her belly. The child. The heir of Homana. Did she dare to take it from me?

Electra smiled. A hood covered all her hair, leaving only her face in the light. One hand came up to cradle her belly. "Not yours," she said gently. "Did you really think it was? Ah no, Carillon . . . it is another man's. Think you

I would keep myself to you when I can have my true lord's love?" She turned slightly, and I saw the man beyond her.

I mouthed his name, and he smiled. The sweet, beguiling smile that I had seen before.

He moved forward out of the darkness. It was his rune that set the room afire. In the palm of his right hand it danced.

Tynstar set his hand to the wick of the candle by my bed, and the candle burst into flame. Not the pure yellow fire of the normal candle, but an eerie purple flame that hissed and shed sparks into the room.

The rune in his hand winked out. He smiled. "You have been a good opponent. It has been interesting to watch you grow; watch you come to manhood; watch you learn what it is to rule. You have learned how to manipulate men and make them bend to your will without making them aware what you do. There is more kingcraft in you than I had anticipated, when I set you free to leave this place eight years ago."

I could not move. I felt the helplessness in my body and the futility in my soul. I would die without a protest, unable to summon a sound. At least let me make a sound—

"Blame yourself," Tynstar told me gently. "What I do now was made possible by you, when you sent the Cheysuli from your side. Had you kept him *by* you—" He smiled. "But then you could not, could you, so long as he threatened the Queen. You had Electra to think of instead of yourself. Commendable, my lord Mujhar; it speaks well of your priorities. But it will also be your death." The flame danced upon its wick and sculpted his bearded face into a death's head of unparalleled beauty. "Finn knew the truth. *He* understood. It was Finn who saw me in Electra's bed." His teeth showed briefly as I spasmed against the sheets. One hand went to Electra's belly.

I tried to thrust myself from the bed but my limbs would not obey me. And then Tynstar moved close, into the sphere of light, and put his hand upon me.

"I am done playing with you," he said. "It is time for *me* to rule." He smiled. "Recall you what Bellam was, when you found him on the field?"

I spasmed again and Tynstar laughed. Electra watched

me as a hawk will watch a coney, delaying its stoop until
the perfect moment.

"*Cheysuli i'halla shansu*," Tynstar said. "Give my greetings to the gods."

I felt the change within my body. Even as I fought
them, my muscles tightened and drew up my limbs. Buttocks, feet and knees, cramping so that I nearly screamed,
while my legs folded up to crush themselves against my
chest. My hands curled into fists and a rictus set my
mouth so that my teeth were bared in a feral snarl. I felt
my flesh tightening on my bones, drying into hardness.

What voice there was left to me lost itself in a garbled
wail, and I knew myself a dead man. Tynstar had slain his
quarry.

Cheysuli i'halla shansu, he had said. *May there be
Cheysuli peace upon you*. An odd farewell from an Ihlini
to a Homanan. Neither of us claimed the magic the Cheysuli
held, and yet Tynstar reminded me of it. Reminded me of
the four days I had spent in the oubliette, believing myself
Cheysuli.

Well, why could I not again? Had I not felt the power of
the race while I hung in utter darkness?

My eyes were staring. I shut them. Even as I felt my
muscles wrack themselves against my bones and flesh, I
reached inward to my soul where I could touch what I
touched before: the thing that had made me Cheysuli.

For four days, once, I had known the gods. Could I not
know them again?

I heard the hiss of steel blade against a sheath. And
then I heard nothing more.

FIVE

Silence. The darkness was gone and the daylight pierced my lids. It painted everything orange and yellow and crimson.

I lay quite still. I did not breathe; did not dare to, until at last my lungs were so empty my heart banged against my chest protesting the lack. I took a shallow breath.

I saw the shadow then. A dark blot moved across the sunrise of my vision. It whispered, soughing like a breeze through summer grass. Like spreading wings on a hawk.

Afraid I would see nothing and yet needing to see, I opened my eyes. I saw. The hawk perched on the chair back, hooked beak gleaming in the sunlight and his bright eyes full of wisdom. And patience, endless patience. Cai was nothing if not a patient bird.

I turned my head against the pillow. The draperies of my bed had been pulled back, looped up against the wooden tester posts and tied with ropes of scarlet and gold. Sunlight poured in the nearest casement and glittered off the brilliance. Everywhere gold. On my bed and on Duncan's arms.

I heard the rasp of my breath and the hoarseness of my voice. "Tynstar slew me."

"Tynstar *tried*."

I was aware of the bed beneath my body. It seemed to press in on me, oppressing me, yet cradling my flesh. Everything was emphasized. I heard the tiniest sounds, saw colors as I had never seen them and felt the texture of the bedclothes. But mostly I sensed the tension in Duncan's body.

He sat upright on a stool, very still as he waited. I saw how he watched me, as if he expected something more than what I had given him. I could not think what it was—we had already discussed Finn's dismissal. And yet I knew he was afraid.

Duncan afraid? No. There was nothing for him to fear.

I summoned my voice again. "You know what happened—?"

"I know what Rowan told me."

"Rowan." I frowned. "Rowan was not there when Tynstar came to slay me."

"He was." Duncan's smile was brief. "You had best thank the gods he was, or you would not now be alive. It was Rowan's timely arrival that kept Tynstar's bid to slay you from succeeding." He paused. "That . . . and what power you threw back at him."

I felt a tiny surge within my chest. "Then I *did* reach the magic!"

He nodded. "Briefly, you tapped what we ourselves tap. It was not enough to keep Tynstar in check for long—he would have slain you in a moment—but Rowan's arrival was enough to end the moment. The presence of a Cheysuli—though he lacks a *lir*—was enough to dilute Tynstar's power even more. There was nothing he could do, save die himself when faced with Rowan's steel. So—he left. But not before he touched you." He paused. "You nearly died, Carillon. Do not think you are unscathed."

"He is gone?"

"Tynstar." Duncan nodded. "Electra was left behind."

I shut my eyes. I recalled how she had come out of the darkness to tell me the truth of the child. Gods—*Tynstar's child*—

I looked at Duncan again. My eyes felt gritty. My tongue was heavy in my mouth. "Where is she?"

"In her chambers, with a Cheysuli guard at the doors."

Duncan did not smile. "She has a measure of her own power, Carillon; we do not take chances with her."

"No." I pushed an elbow against the bed and tried to sit up. I discovered no part of my body would move. I was stiff and very sore, far worse than after a battle, as if all the dampness had got into my bones. I touched my shoulder then, recalling the healing wound. There were no bandages. Just a small patch of crinkled flesh. "You healed me . . ."

"We tried." Duncan was very grave. "The arrow wound was easily done. The —other—was not. Carillon—" For a moment he paused, and then I saw his frown. "Do not think Ihlini power is easily overcome. Even the earth magic cannot restore that which has been taken from a soul. Tynstar has power in abundance. What was taken from you will never be regained. You are—as you are."

I stared at him. And then I looked down at myself and saw myself. There seemed to be no difference. I was very stiff and sore and slow, but a sojourn in bed will do that.

Duncan merely waited. I moved again to sit up, found it every bit as difficult as before, but this time I prevailed. I swung my legs over the side of the bed, screwed up my face against the creaking of my joints, and sat there as all my muscles trembled.

It was then I saw my fingers. The knuckles were enlarged hugely, the flesh stretched thin over brittle bones. I saw how the calluses had begun to soften, shedding the toughness I needed against the use of a sword. I saw how the fingers were vaguely twisted away from my thumb. And I ached. Even in the sunlight, I ached with a bone-deep pain.

"How long?" I asked abruptly, knowing I had spent more than days in my bed.

"Two months. We could not raise you from the stupor."

Naked, I wrenched myself from the bed and stumbled across the chamber, to the plate upon the wall. The polished silver gave back my face, and I saw what Tynstar had done.

Carillon was still Carillon, certainly recognizable. But older, so much older, by twenty years at least.

"It is my father," I said in shock, recalling the time-worn face. The tawny-dark hair was frosted with gray with the beard showing equal amounts. Creases fanned out from my eyes and bracketed nose and mouth, though most were hidden by the beard. And set deeply into the still-blue eyes was the knowledge of constant pain.

It was no wonder I ached. I had the same disease as my mother, with her twisted hands and brittle bones, the swollen, painful joints. And with each year, the pain and disability would worsen.

Tynstar had put his hand on me and my youth was spent at once.

I turned slowly and sat down on the nearest chest. I began to shake with more than physical weakness. It was the realization.

Duncan waited, saying nothing, and I saw the compassion in his eyes. "Can you not heal me of this?" I gestured emptily. "The age and gray I can live with, but the illness . . . you have only to see my lady mother—" I stopped. I saw the answer in his face.

After a moment he spoke. "It will improve. You will not be as stiff when some time has passed. You have spent two months in bed and it takes its toll on anyone—you will find it not so bad as it seems now. But as for the disease . . ." He shook his head. "Tynstar did not give you anything you would not have known anyway. He inflicted nothing upon you that time itself would not inflict. He merely stole that time from you, so that a month became ten years. You are older, aye, but not old. There are many years left to you."

I thought of Finn. I recalled the silver in his hair and the hard gauntness of his face. I recalled what he had said of Tynstar: *"He put his hand on me."*

The chest was hard and cold against my naked buttocks. "When my daughter is older, I will be old. She will have a grandsire for a father."

"I doubt she will love you the less for that."

I looked at him in surprise. A Cheysuli speaking of love? —aye, perhaps, when the moment calls for an honesty that can bring me back to myself.

My body protested against the dampness of the chamber. I got up and walked—no, limped—stiffly back to my bed, reaching for the robe a servant had left. "I will have to deal with Electra."

"Aye. And she is still the Queen of Homana."

"As I made her." I shook my head. "I should have listened to you. To Finn. I should have listened to someone."

Duncan smiled, still sitting on his stool. "You know more of kingcraft than I do, Carillon. The marriage brought peace to Homana—at least regarding Solinde—and I cannot fault you for that. But—"

"—but I wed a woman who intended my death from the first moment she ever saw me." The pain curled deeply within my loins. "Gods—I should have known by looking at her. She claims more than forty years—I should have known Tynstar could give those years as well as take them." I rubbed at my age-lined face and felt the twinges in my fingers. "I should have known Tynstar's arts would prevail when I had no Cheysuli by me. No liege man."

"They planned well, Tynstar and Electra," Duncan agreed. "First the trap-link, which might have slain Finn and rid them of him sooner. Then, when that did not work, they used it to draw him into a second trap. Finn, I do not doubt, walked in on Tynstar and Electra when he meant only to confront her. He could not touch Tynstar, but Tynstar touched him, then took his leave and Finn had only Electra. And yet when he told you Tynstar had been present, you thought of the trap-link instead." Duncan shook his head and the earring glittered in the sunlight. "They played with us all, Carillon . . . and nearly won the game."

"They *have* won." I sat huddled in my robe. "I have only a daughter, and Homana has need of an heir."

Duncan rose. He moved to Cai and put out a hand to the hawk, as if he meant to caress him. But he did not touch him after all, and I saw how his fingers trembled. "You are still young, for all you feel old." His back was to me. "Take yourself another *cheysula* and give Homana that heir."

I looked at his back, so rigid and unmoving. "You know Homanan custom. You were at the wedding ceremony; do you not recall the vows? Homanans do not set wives aside.

It is a point of law, as well as being custom. Surely you, with all your adherence to Cheysuli custom, can understand the constraints that places on me. Even a Mujhar."

"Is the custom so important when the wife attempts to slay the husband?"

I heard the irony in his tone. "No. But she did not succeed, and I know what Council will say. Set her aside, perhaps, but do not break the vows. It would be breaking Homanan law. The Council would never permit it."

Duncan swung around and faced me. "Electra is Tynstar's *meijha!* She bears his child in her belly! Would the Homanan Council prefer to have you *dead?*"

"Do you not see?" I threw back. "It has been taken from my hands. Had Tourmaline not gone with Finn, wedding with Lachlan instead, I could have sought my heir from her. Had she wed *any* prince, Homana would have an heir. But she did not. She went with Finn and took that chance from me."

"Set her aside," he said urgently. "You are Mujhar—you can do anything you wish."

Slowly I shook my head. "If I begin to make my own rules, I become a despot. I become Shaine, who desired to destroy the Cheysuli race. No, Duncan. Electra remains my wife, though I doubt I will keep her here. I have no wish to see her *or* the bastard she carries."

He shut his eyes a moment, and then I understood. I knew what he feared at last.

I was tired. The ache had settled deeply in my bones. I felt bruised from the knowledge of what I faced. And yet I could not avoid it. "There is no need to fear me," I said quietly.

"Is there not?" Duncan's eyes were bleak. "I know what you will do."

"I have no other choice."

"He is *my* son—"

"—and Alix's, and Alix is my cousin." I stopped, seeing the pain in the face Alix loved. "How long have you known it would come to this?"

Duncan laughed, but it had a hollow, desperate sound. "All my life, it seems. When I came to know my *tahlmorra*." He shook his head and sat down upon the stool. His shoulders slumped and he stared blankly at the floor. "I have always been afraid. Of you . . . of the past and future . . . of what I knew was held within the prophecy for any son of mine. Did you think I wanted Alix *only* out of desire?" Anguish leached his face of the solemnity I knew. "Alix was a part of my own *tahlmorra*. I knew, if I took her and got a son upon her, I would have to give up that son. *I knew*. And so I hoped, when she conceived again, there would at least be another for us . . . but the Ihlini took even that from us." He sighed. "I had no choice. No choice at all."

"Duncan," I said after a moment, "can a back not be turned upon *tahlmorra*?"

He shook his head immediately. "The warrior who turns his back on his *tahlmorra* may twist the prophecy. In twisting it, he destroys the *tahlmorra* of his race. Homana would fall. Not in a year or ten or twenty—perhaps not even a hundred—but it would fall, and the realm would be given over to the Ihlini and their like." He paused. "There is another thing: the warrior who turns his back on his *tahlmorra* gives up his afterlife. I think none of us would be willing to do that."

I thought of Tynstar, and others like him, ruling in Homana. No. It was no wonder Duncan would never consider trying to alter his *tahlmorra*.

I frowned. "Do you say then that even a *single* warrior turning his back on his *tahlmorra* may change the balance of fate?"

Duncan frowned also. For once, he seemed to grope for the proper words, as if he knew the Homanan tongue could never tell me what I asked. But the Old Tongue would not serve; I knew too little of it. And what I did know I had learned from Finn; he had never spoken of such personal Cheysuli things.

Finally Duncan sighed. "A crofter goes to Mujhara to-day instead of tomorrow. His son falls down a well. The son dies." He made the spread-fingered, palm-up gesture. "*Tahlmorra*. But had the crofter gone tomorrow instead of today, would the son yet live? I cannot say. Does the death serve a greater pattern? Perhaps. Had he lived, would it have destroyed the pattern completely? Perhaps—I cannot say." He shrugged. "I cannot know what the gods intend."

"But you serve them all so blindly—"

"No. My eyes are open." He did not smile. "They have given us the prophecy, so we know what we work toward. We know what we can lose, if we do not continue serving it. My belief is such: that certain events, once changed, can alter other events. Are enough of them altered, no matter how minor, the major one is changed. Perhaps even the prophecy of the Firstborn."

"So you live your life in chains." I could not comprehend the depth of his dedication.

Duncan smiled a little. "You wear a crown, my lord Mujhar. Surely you know its weight."

"That is different—"

"Is it? Even now you face the overwhelming need to find an heir. To put a prince on the throne of Homana you will even take my son."

I stared at him. The emptiness spread out to fill my aching body. "I have no other choice."

"Nor have I, my lord Mujhar." Duncan looked suddenly weary. "But you give my son into hardship."

"He will be the Prince of Homana." The rank seemed, to me, to outweigh the hardship.

He did not smile. "It was your title, once. It nearly got you slain. Do not belittle its danger."

"Donal is Cheysuli." For a moment I was incapable of saying anything more. I realized, in that moment, that even *I* had served the gods. Duncan had said more than once it was a Cheysuli throne, and that one day there would be a Cheysuli Mujhar in place of a Homanan. And now I, with only a few words, made that prediction come true.

Are men always so blind to the gods, even when they serve them?

"Cheysuli," Duncan echoed, "and so the links are forged."

I looked at Cai. I thought of the falcon and wolf Donal claimed, two *lir* instead of one. Things changed. Time moved on, sometimes far too quickly. And events altered events.

I sighed and rubbed at my knees. "The Homanans will

not accept him. Not readily. He is Cheysuli to the bone, despite his Homanan blood."

"Aye," Duncan agreed, "you begin to see the danger."

"I can lessen it. I can take away the choice. I can make certain the Homanans accept him."

Duncan shook his head. "It has been less than eight years since Shaine's *qu'mahlin* ended because of you. It is too soon. Such things are not easily done."

"No. But I can make it easier."

"How?"

"By wedding him to Aislinn."

Duncan stood up at once. "They are children!"

"Now, aye, but children become adults." I did not care to see the startled, angry expression on his face, but I had no choice. "A long betrothal, Duncan, such as royal Houses do. In fifteen years, Donal will be—twenty-three? Aislinn nearly sixteen: old enough to wed. And then I will name him my heir."

Duncan shut his eyes. I saw his right hand make the eloquent sign. *"Tahlmorra lujhalla mei wiccan, cheysu."* All the helplessness was in his voice, and I knew it chafed his soul. Duncan was not a man who suffered helplessness with any degree of decorum.

I sighed and mimicked the gesture, including the Cheysuli phrase for wishing him peace: *Cheysuli i'halla shansu.*

"Peace!" It was bitterly said; from Duncan, a revelation. "My son will know none of that."

I felt the dampness in my bones and pulled the heavy robe more tightly around my shoulders. "I think *I* have known little of it. Have you?"

"Oh, aye," he returned at once, with all the force of his bitterness. "More than you, Carillon. It was to me that Alix came."

The bolt went home. I grimaced, thinking of Electra, and knew I would have to deal with it before more time went by. The gods knew Tynstar had stolen enough.

"I will send for Alix," I said at last, hunching against the chill he did not seem to feel. "And Donal. I will explain things to them both. I would have you send Cai, but there is a task I have for you." I expected a refusal, but Duncan said nothing at all. I saw the weariness in his posture and the knowledge in his eyes. He was ever a step before me. "Duncan—I am sorry. I did not mean to usurp your son."

"Be not sorry for what the gods intend." He gestured the hawk to his arm. How he held him, I cannot say; Cai is a heavy bird. "As for your task, I will do it. It will get me free of these walls." For a moment his shoulders hunched in, mirroring my own, but for a different reason. "They chafe," he said at last. "How they chafe . . . how they bind a Cheysuli soul."

"But the Cheysuli built these walls." I was surprised at the vehemence in his tone.

"We built them and we left them." He shook his head. "*I* leave them. It is my son who will have to learn what it is to know himself well-caged. I am too old, too set in my ways to change."

"As I am," I said bitterly. "Tynstar has made me so."

"Tynstar altered the body, not the mind," Duncan said. "Let not the body affect the heart." He smiled a moment, albeit faintly, and then he left the room.

I went into Electra's chambers and found her seated by a casement. The sunlight set her hair to glowing and made her blind to me. It was only when the door thumped closed that she turned her head and saw me.

She did not rise. She sat upon the bench with the black cloak wrapped around her like a shroud of Tynstar's making. The hood was draped across her shoulders, freeing her hair, and I saw the twin braids bound with silver. It glittered against the cloak.

Tynstar's child swelled her belly. Mine had done it before. It made me angry, but not so angry as to show it. I merely stood in the room and faced her, letting her see what the sorcery had wrought; to know it had been her doing that changed me so.

Her chin lifted a little. She had not lost a whit of her pride and defiance, even knowing she was caught.

"He left you behind," I said. "Was that a measure of his regard?"

I saw the minute twitch of her mouth. I had put salt in

the open wound. "Unless you slay me, he will have me still."

"But you do not think I will slay you."

She smiled. "I am Aislinn's mother and the Queen of Homana. There is nothing you can do."

"And if I said you were a witch?"

"Say it," she countered. "Have me executed, then, and see how Solinde responds."

"As I recall, it was Solinde you wanted freed." I moved a trifle closer. "You wanted no vassal to Homana."

"Tynstar will prevent it." Her eyes did not shift from mine. "You have seen what he could do. You have *felt* it."

"Aye," I said softly, approaching again. "I have felt it and so have you, though the results were somewhat reversed. It seems I have all the years you shed, Electra, and like to keep them, I think. A pity, no doubt, but it does not strip me of my throne. I am still Mujhar of Homana—and Solinde a vassal to me."

"How long will you live?" she retorted. "You are forty-five, now. No more the young Mujhar. In five years, ten, you will be old. *Old.* In war, old men die quickly. And you will know war, Carillon; that I promise you."

"But you will never see it." I bent down and caught one of her wrists, pulling her to her feet. She was heavy with Tynstar's child. Her free arm went down to cradle her belly protectively beneath the heavy cloak. "I exile you, Electra. For the years that remain to you."

Color splotched her face, but she showed no fear. "Where do you send me, then?"

"To the Crystal Isle." I smiled. "I see you know it. Aye, a formidable place when you are the enemy of Homana. It is the birthplace of the Cheysuli and claims the protection of the gods. Tynstar could never touch you there. Not ever, Electra. The island will be your prison." I still held her wrist in one hand. The other I put out to catch one braid and threaded my fingers into it. "You will be treated as befits your rank. You will have servants and fine clothing, good food and wine, proper accoutrements. Everything except freedom. And there—with his child—you will grow old and die." My smile grew wider as I felt the silk of her hair. "For such as you, I think, that will be punishment enough."

"I will bear that child in less than one month." Her lips were pale and flat. "A journey now may make me lose it."

"If the gods will it," I agreed blandly. "I send you in the morning with Duncan and an escort of Cheysuli. Try your arts on them, if you seek to waste your time. They, unlike myself, are invulnerable."

I saw the movement deep in her eyes and felt the touch of her power. Color returned to her face. She smiled faintly, knowing what I knew, and the long-lidded eyes drew me in. As ever. She would always be my bane.

I let go of her wrist, her braid, and cupped her head with both hands. I kissed her as a drowning man clings to wood. Gods, but she could move me still . . . she could still reach into my soul—

—and twist it.

I set her away from me with careful deliberation and saw the shock of realization in her face. "It is done, Electra. You must pay the price of your folly."

The sunlight glittered off the silver cording in her braids. But also off something else: tears. They stood in her great gray eyes, threatening to spill.

But I knew her. Too well. They were tears of anger, not of fear, and I went out of the room with the taste of defeat in my mouth.

SIX

The arms-master stepped back, lowering his sword. "My lord Mujhar, let this stop. It is a travesty."

My breath hissed between my teeth. "It will remain a travesty until I learn to overcome it." I gripped the hilt of my Cheysuli sword and lifted the blade yet again. "Come against me, Cormac."

"My lord—" He stepped away again, shaking his crop-haired head. "There is no sense in it."

I swore at him. I had spent nearly an hour trying to regain a portion of my skill, and now he denied me the chance. I lowered my sword and stood there, clad in breeches and practice tunic while the sweat ran down my arms. I shut my eyes a moment, trying to deal with the pain; when I opened them I saw the pity in Cormac's dark brown eyes.

"*Ku'reshtin!*" I snapped. "Save your pity for someone else! I have no need of such—" I went in against him then, raising the sword yet again, and nearly got through his belated guard.

He danced back, danced again, then ducked my swinging sword. His own came up to parry my blow; I got under it and thrust toward his belly. He sucked it in, leaped aside, then twisted and came toward my side. I blocked, tied up his slash and pushed his blade aside.

The rhythm began to come back. It was fitful and very slow, but I had lost little of my strength. The stamina was blunted, but it might return in time. I had only to learn what it was to deal with the stiffness of my joints and forget about the pain.

Cormac caught his lip between his teeth. I saw the light in his eyes. His soft-booted feet hissed against the floor as he slid and slid again, ducking the blows I lowered. We did not fight for blood, sparring only, but he knew I meant to beat him. He would allow me no quarter, not even if I were to ask it.

It was my hands that failed me finally, my big-knuckled, aching hands. In the weeks that had followed since I had regained my senses, I had learned how weakened they were. My knees hurt all the time, as if some demon chewed upon them from the inside moving toward the outside, but when I was moving I forgot them. Mostly. It was when I stopped that I was reminded of the ache in my bones. But my hands, in swordplay, were the most important, and I had found them the largest barrier to regaining my banished skill.

My wrists held firm, locked against his blow, but the fingers lost their grip. They twisted, shooting pain up through my forearms. The sword went flying from my hands, clanging against the stone, and I cursed myself for being such a fool as to let it go. But when Cormac bent to retrieve it I set my foot upon it. "Let it go. Enough of this. We will continue another time."

He bowed quickly and took his leave, taking his sword with him. My own still lay upon the floor, as if to mock me, while I tried to regain my breath. I set my teeth against the pain in my swollen hands. In a moment I bent down, grimacing against the sudden cramp in my back, and scooped up the blade with one hand.

The sweat ran into my eyes. I scrubbed one forearm across my face and cleared my burning vision. And then, giving it up, I sat down on the nearest bench. I stretched out my legs carefully and gave into the pain for a moment, feeling the fire in my knees. I set back and head against the wall and tried to shut it all out.

"You are better, my lord, since the last time."

When I could, I rolled my head to one side and saw Rowan. "Am I? Or do you merely let me think so?"

"I would not go up against you," he said flatly, coming closer. "But you should not hope for it all, not so soon. It will take time, my lord."

"I have no time. Tynstar has stolen it from me." I scraped my spine against the wall and sat up straight again, suppressing a grimace, and drew in my feet. Even my ankles hurt. "Have you come on business, or merely to tell me what you think I want to hear?"

"There is a visitor." He held out a silver signet ring set with a plain black stone.

I took it and rolled it in my hand. "Who is it, then? Do I know him?"

"He names himself Alaric of Atvia, my lord. Crown Prince, to be precise."

I looked up from the ring sharply. "Thorne is slain. If this boy is his son, he is now Lord of Atvia in Thorne's place. Why does he humble himself?"

"Alaric is not the heir. Osric, his older brother, sits on the Atvian throne." He paused. "In *Atvia*, my lord."

I scowled. "Osric is not come, then."

"No, my lord."

I gritted my teeth a moment, swearing within my mind. I was in no mood for diplomacy, especially not with a child. "Where is this Atvian infant?"

Rowan smiled. "In an antechamber off the Great Hall, where I have put him. Would you prefer him somewhere else?"

"No. I will save the Great Hall for his brother." I stood up, using the wall for a brace. For a moment I waited, allowing the worst of the pain to die, and then I gave Rowan my sword. I shut up the ring in my fist and went out of the practice chamber.

The boy, I discovered, was utterly dwarfed by his surroundings. The Great Hall would have overtaken him completely, and I was in no mood for such ploys. Alaric looked no older than six or seven and would hardly comprehend the politics of the situation.

He rose stiffly as I came into the chamber, having dressed in fresh clothing. He bowed in a brief, exceedingly slight gesture of homage that just missed condescension. The expression in his brown eyes was one of sullen hostility, and his face was coldly set.

I walked to a cushioned mahogany chair and sat down, allowing no hint of the pain to show in my face. I was stiffening after the sparring. "So . . . Atvia comes to Homana."

"No, my lord." Alaric spoke quietly. "My brother, Lord Osric of Atvia, sends me to say Atvia does *not* come to Homana. Nor ever will, except to conquer this land."

I contemplated Alaric in some surprise. He was dressed as befitted his rank, and his dark brown hair was combed smooth. A closer look revealed him older than I had thought. He was perhaps a year or two older than Donal, but the knowledge in his eyes seemed to surpass that of a grown man.

I permitted myself a smile, though it held nothing of amusement. "I have slain your father, my lord Alaric, because he sought to pull down my House and replace it with his own. I could do the same to your own, beginning with you." I paused. "Has your brother a response to that?"

Alaric's slender body was rigid. "He does, my lord. I am to say we do not acknowledge your sovereignty."

I rested my chin in one hand, elbow propped against the arm rest. "Osric sends you into danger with such words in your mouth, my young Atvian eagle. What say you to remaining here a hostage?"

Angry color flared in Alaric's face, but he did not waver a bit. "My brother said I must prepare myself for that."

I frowned. "How old is Osric?"

"Sixteen."

I sighed. "So young—so willing to risk his brother and his realm."

"My father said you had ever been Atvia's enemy, and must be gainsaid." Grief washed through the brown eyes and the mouth wavered a little, but he covered it almost at once. "My brother and I will serve our father's memory by fighting you in his place. In the end, we will win. If nothing else, we will outlive you. You are an old man, my lord . . . Osric and I are young."

I felt a fist clench in my belly. Old, was I? Aye, to his

eyes. "Too young to die," I said grimly. "Shall I have you slain, Alaric?"

Color receded from his face. He was suddenly a small boy again. "Do what you wish, my lord—I am prepared." The voice shook a little.

"No," I said abruptly, "you are not. You only think it. You have yet to look death in the face and know him; had you done it, you would not accept him so blithely." I pushed myself up and bit off the oath I wished to spit out between my teeth. "Serve your lord, boy . . . serve him as well as you may. But do it at home in Atvia; I do not slay or imprison young boys."

Alaric caught the heavy ring as I threw it at him. Shock was manifest in his face. "I may go home?"

"You may go home. Tell your brother I give him back his heir, though I doubt not he will have another one soon enough, when he takes himself a wife."

"He is already wed, my lord."

I studied the boy again. "Tell him also that twice a year Homanan ships shall call at Rondule. Upon those ships Osric shall place tribute to Homana. If you wish continued freedom from Homana, my young lordling, you will pay the tribute." I paused. "You may tell him also that should he ever come against me in the field, I will slay him."

The small face looked pinched. "I will tell him, my lord. But—as to this tribute—"

"You will pay it," I said. "I will send a message for your brother back with you in the morning, and it will include all the details of this tribute. You must pay the cost of the folly in trying to take Homana." I signalled to one of the waiting servants. "See he is fed and lodged as befits his rank. In the morning, he may go home."

"Aye, my lord."

I put a hand on Alaric's shoulder and turned him toward the man. "Go with Breman, my proud young prince. You will not know harm in Homana-Mujhar." I gave him a push from my swollen hand and saw him start toward Breman. In a moment they both were gone.

Rowan cleared his throat. "Is he not a valuable hostage?"

"Aye. But he is a boy."

"I thought it was often done. Are not princes fostered on friendly Houses? What would be the difference?"

"I will not take his childhood from him." I shivered in the cold dampness of the chamber. "Osric is already wed. He will get himself sons soon enough; Alaric will lose his value. Since I doubt Osric has any intention of coming so soon against Homana, I lose nothing by letting Alaric go."

"And when, in manhood, he comes to fight?"

"I will deal with it then."

Rowan sighed. "And what of Osric? Sixteen is neither child nor man."

"Had it been Osric, I would have thrown him into chains." I paused. "To humble that arrogant mouth."

Rowan smiled. "You may yet be able to, my lord."

"Perhaps." I looked at Rowan squarely. "But if he is anything like his father—or even Keough, his grandsire—Osric and I shall meet in battle. And one of us will die."

"My lord." It was a servant in the doorway, bowing with politeness. "My lord Mujhar, there is a boy."

"Breman has taken Alaric," I said. "He is to be treated with all respect."

"No, my lord—another boy. This one is Cheysuli."

I frowned. "Say on."

"He claims himself kin to you, my lord—he has a wolf and a falcon."

I laughed then. "Donal! Aye, he is kin to me. But he should have his mother with him in addition to his *lir*."

"No, my lord." The man looked worried. "He is alone but for the animals, and he appears to have been treated harshly."

I went past him at once and to the entry chamber. There I saw a falcon perched upon a candlerack with all the wicks unlighted. The wolf stood close to Donal, shoring up one leg. Donal's black hair was disheveled and his face was pinched with deprivation. Bruises ringed his throat.

He saw me and stared, his eyes going wide, and I realized what he saw. Not the man he had known. "Donal," I said, and then he knew me, and came running across the floor.

"They have taken my *jehana*—" His voice shook badly.

He shut his eyes a moment, blocking out the tears, and tried to speak apain. "They have taken her . . . and slain Torrin in the croft!"

I swore, though I kept it to myself. Donal pressed himself against me, hanging onto my doublet, and I wanted nothing more than to lift him into my arms. But I did not. I know something of Cheysuli pride, even in the young.

I set one hand to the back of his head as he tucked it under my chin. I thought, suddenly, of Aislinn, wondering what she would think of him when she was old enough to know. This boy would be my heir.

"Come," I said, rising, "we will speak of this elsewhere." I turned to take him from the chamber but he reached up and caught my hand. Instantly I forgot my resolution and bent to pick him up, moving to the nearest bench in a warmer chamber. I sat down and settled him on my lap, wincing against the pain. "You must tell me what happened as clearly as you can. I can do nothing until I know."

Lorn flopped down at my feet with a grunt, but his brown eyes did not leave Donal's face. The falcon flew in and found another perch, piping his agitation.

Donal rubbed at his eyes and I saw how glassy they were. He was exhausted and ready to fall, but I had to know what had happened. As Rowan came in I signalled for him to pour Donal a swallow or two of wine.

"My *jehana* and I were coming here," Donal began. "She said you had sent for us. But there was no urgency to it, and she wanted to stop at the croft." He stopped as Rowan brought the cup of wine. I held it to his mouth and let him drink, then gave it back to Rowan. Donal wiped his mouth and went on. "While we were there, men came. At first they gave my *jehana* honor. They shared their wine and then watched us, and within moments Torrin and my *jehana* were senseless. They—cut Torrin's throat. They *slew* him!"

I held him a little more tightly and saw the stark pity in Rowan's face. Donal had come early to his baptism into adulthood, but Rowan earlier still. "Say on, Donal . . . say on until you have said it all."

His voice took on some life. Perhaps the wine had done

it. "I called for Taj and Lorn, but the men said they would slay my *jehana*. So I told my *lir* to go away." Renewed grief hollowed his face, blackening his eyes. "They put her on a litter and *bound* her . . . they put a chain around my neck. They said we would go to the Northern Wastes. . . ."

I glanced at Rowan and saw his consternation. The Northern Wastes lay across the Bluetooth River. There would be no reason to take Donal or Alix there.

"They said they would take us to *Tynstar*—" Donal's voice was hardly a whisper.

It came clear to me almost instantly. Rowan swore in Homanan even as I said something in the Old Tongue that made Donal's eyes go wide in astonishment. But I could not afford to alarm him. "Was there anything more?"

His face screwed up with concentration and confusion. "I did not understand. They spoke among themselves and I could make no sense of it. They said Tynstar wanted the seed of the prophecy—me!—and my *jehana* for a woman. A woman to use in place of the one he lost to you." Donal stared up at me. "But *why* does he want my *jehana*?"

"Gods—" I shut my eyes, seeing Alix in Tynstar's hands. No doubt he would repay me for sending Electra to the Crystal Isle. No doubt he would use Alix badly. They had opposed each other before.

It was Rowan who drew Donal's attention away from my angry face. "How did *you* win free?"

For a moment the boy smiled. "They thought I was a child, not a warrior, and therefore helpless. They counted my *lir* as little more than pets. And so Taj and Lorn kept themselves to the shadows and followed across the river. One night, when the men thought I slept, I talked to Taj and Lorn, and told them how important it was that I get away. And so they taught me how to take *lir*-shape, though the thing was too early done." His face was pinched again. "*Jehan* had said I must wait, but I could not. I had to do it then."

"You came all the way in *lir*-shape?" I knew how draining it could be, and in a child . . . I had seen Alix, once, when she had shapechanged too often, and Finn as well, after too long a time spent in wolf-shape. It upset the human balance.

"I flew." Donal frowned. "And when I could not fly, I went as a wolf. And when it sickened me, I walked as myself. It was hard—harder than I thought . . . I believed *lir*-shape was easy for a warrior."

I held him a little more tightly. "Nothing is done so easily when it bears the weight of the gods." I rose, lifting him to stand. "Come. I will see you are fed and bathed and given rest in a comfortable bed."

Donal slid down to the floor. "But my *jehan* is here. *Jehana* said he was."

"Your *jehan* has gone to Hondarth and it is too soon for him to be back. Another week, perhaps. You will have to wait with me." I tousled the heavy black hair which had already lost some of its childhood curl. "Donal—I promise we will fetch your *jehana* back. I promise all will be well."

He looked up at me, huge yellow eyes set in a dark Cheysuli face. No Cheysuli trusts easily, but I knew he trusted me. Well, he would have to. I would make him into a king.

Donal braced both elbows against the table top. He rested his chin in his hands. He watched, fascinated as always, as I traced out the battle markings drawn on the map of Caledon. In the past ten days we had spent hours with the maps.

"It was here." I touched the border between Caledon and the Steppes. "Your *su'fali* and I were riding with the Caledonese, and we went into the Steppes at this point."

"How long did the battle take?"

"A day and a night. But it was only one of many battles. The plainsmen fight differently than the Homanans—Finn and I had to learn new methods." Well, *I* had; Finn's methods were highly adaptable and required no reorganization.

Donal frowned in concentration. He put out a finger much smaller than mine and touched the leather map. "My *su'fali* fought with you—so has my *jehan* . . . will *I* fight with you when I am made a prince?"

"I hope I may keep the peace between Homana and other realms," I told him truthfully, "but does it come to war no matter what I do, aye, you will fight with me.

Perhaps against Atvia, does Osric wish to task me . . . perhaps even Solinde, should the regency fail."

"Will it?" He fixed me with intent yellow eyes, black brows drawn down.

"It might. I have sent Electra away, and the Solindish do not like it." I saw no sense in hiding the truth from him. Cheysuli children are more adult than most. Donal was also a clan-leader's son, and I did not doubt he already knew something of politics.

Donal sighed and his attention turned. He pushed away from the table and got off the stool, sitting down on the floor with Lorn. The wolf stretched and yawned and put a paw on Donal's thigh as Donal reached to drag him into his lap. Taj, perched upon a chair back, piped excitedly and then Duncan was in the doorway.

"*Jehan!*" Donal scrambled up, dumping Lorn, and ran across the room. I saw Duncan's smile as he caught his son and the lessening of tension in his face. He scooped up the boy and held him, saying something in the Old Tongue, and I knew he could not know. They had left the telling to me.

"Have you been keeping Carillon from his duties?" Duncan asked as Donal hugged his neck.

"*Jehan*—oh *jehan* . . . why did you not come sooner? I was so afraid—"

"What have you to be afraid of?" Duncan was grinning. "Unless you fear for me, which is unnecessary. You see I am well enough." He glanced at me across the top of his son's dark head. "Carillon, there is—"

"*Jehan*—" Donal would not let him speak. "*Jehan*—will you go now? Will you go up across the river? Will you fetch her back?"

"Go where? Why? Fetch *who* back?" Duncan grinned and moved across the room to the nearest bench. He sat down with Donal in his lap, though the boy was too big to be held. It seemed odd to see Duncan so tolerant of such things; I knew the Cheysuli did not profess to love, and therefore the words were lacking in their language. And yet it was manifest in Doncan's movements and voice as he sat down upon the bench. "Have you lost someone, small one?"

"*Jehana,*" Donal whispered, and I saw Duncan's face go still.

He looked to me at once. "Where is Alix?"

"Alix was—taken." I inhaled a careful breath. "It appears it is Tynstar's doing."

"*Tynstar*—" Duncan's face was ashen.

"You had best let Donal tell you," I said quietly. "It was he who won free and came to me here, to tell me what had happened."

Duncan's arms were slack around the boy. And then suddenly they tightened. "Donal—say what has happened. All of it. Tell me what you saw; tell me what you heard."

Donal, too, was pale. I doubted he had ever seen his father so shaken. He sat hunched in Duncan's lap and told the story as he had told it to me, and I saw the struggle in Duncan's face. It made my own seem a shadow of true feeling.

At last Donal finished, his voice trailing off into silence. He waited for his father to speak even as I did, but Duncan said nothing at all. He merely sat, staring into the distance, as if he had not heard.

"*Jehan*—?" Donal's voice, plaintive and frightened, as he sat on Duncan's lap.

Duncan spoke at last. He said something to Donal in the Old Tongue, something infinitely soothing, and I saw the boy relax. "Did they harm her, small one?"

"No, *jehan*. But she could hardly speak." Donal's face was pinched with the memory and he was frightened all over again.

Duncan's hand on his son's head was gentle in its touch. The tension was everywhere else. "*Shansu, Shansu* . . . I will get your *jehana* back. But you must promise me to wait here until we come home again."

"Here?" Donal sat upright in Ducan's arms. "You will not send me back to the Keep?"

"Not yet. Your *jehana* and I will take you there when we are back." His eyes, staring over Donal's head, were fixed on the distances again. Duncan seemed to be living elsewhere, even as he held his son. And then I realized he spoke to Cai. He was somewhere in the link.

When he came out of it I saw his fear, though he tried

to hide it from Donal. For a moment he shut his eyes, barricading his soul, and then he held Donal more tightly. "*Shansu*, Donal— peace. I will get your *jehana* back."

But I knew, looking at him, he said it for himself and not his son.

"Duncan." I waited until he looked at me, coming out of his haze of shock. "I have spoken to your second-leader at the Keep . . . and the Homanans as well. We are prepared to go with you."

"Go where?" he asked. "Do you know? Do you even know where she is?"

"I assumed the *lir* could find her."

"The *lir* do not need to find her . . . I know where Alix is. I know what he means to do." Duncan set Donal down and told him to take his *lir* and go. The boy protested, clearly frightened as well as offended, but Duncan made him go.

At last I faced him alone. "Where?"

"Valgaard." He saw the blankness in my face. "Tynstar's lair. It is a fortress high in the canyons of Solinde—you have only to cross the Bluetooth and go directly north into the mountains. Cross the Molon Pass into Solinde and you have found it. You cannot help but find it." He rose and paced across the floor, but I saw how his footsteps hesitated. "He would take her there."

"Then we will have to go there and get her."

He swung around. One hand was on the hilt of his longknife; I saw how he wanted to shout, to bring down the walls, and yet he kept himself very quiet. It was eerie. It was the intensity I had seen so often in Finn, knowing to keep my distance. But this time, I could not.

"Valgaard houses the Gate," he said in a clipped, hissing tone. "Do you know what you say you will do?" He shook his head. "No, you do not. You do not know the Gate."

"I admit it. There are many things I do not know."

Duncan prowled the room with a stiff, angry stride. He reminded me of a mountain cat, suddenly, stalking down its prey. "The Gate," he repeated. "Asar-Suti's Gate. The Gate to the Seker's world."

The words were strange. Not the Old Tongue; something far older, something that spoke of foulness. "Demons," I said, before I could stop.

"Asar-Suti is more than a demon. He is the god of the netherworld. The Seker himself—who made and dwells in darkness. He is the font of Ihlini power." He stopped pacing. He stood quite still. "In Valgaard—Tynstar shares that power."

I recalled how easily he had trapped me in my bed, seeking to take my life. I recalled how he had changed the ruby from red to black. I remembered how it was he had stolen Homana from my uncle. I remembered Bellam's body. If he could do all of that while he was *out* of Valgaard, what could he do within?

Duncan was at the door. He turned back, his face set in stark lines of grief and determination. "I would ask no man to risk himself in such a thing as this."

"Alix risked herself for me when I lay shackled in Atvian iron."

"Alix was not the Mujhar of Homana."

"No." I did not smile. "She carried the seed of the prophecy in her belly, and events can change events."

I saw the shock of realization in his face. The risk he spoke of was real, but no greater than what Alix had faced. Had she died in my rescue, or somehow lost the child, the prophecy might have ended before it was begun.

"I will go," I said quietly. "There is nothing left but to do it."

He stood in the doorway. For a long moment he said nothing at all, seemingly incapable of it, and then he nodded a little. "If you meet up with Tynstar, Carillon, you will have a powerful weapon."

I waited.

"Electra miscarried the child."

SEVEN

As one, my Homanan troop pulled horses to a ragged halt. I heard low-voiced comments, oaths made and broken, prayers to the gods. I did not blame them. No one had expected this.

No one, perhaps, except the Cheysuli. They did not seem troubled by the place. They merely waited, mounted and uncloaked, while the sun flashed off their gold.

A chill ran down my spine. I suppressed it and reined in my fidgeting horse. Duncan, some distance away, rode over to ask about the delay.

"Look about you," I said solemnly. "Have you seen its like before?"

He shrugged. "We have come over the Molon Pass. This is Solinde. We encroach upon Tynstar's realm. Did you think it would resemble your own?"

I could not say what I thought it might resemble. Surely not this. I only dreamed of places like this.

We had crossed the Bluetooth River twelve days out of Mujhara: nine Homanans, nine Cheysuli, Rowan and Gryffth, myself and Duncan. Twenty-two men to rescue Alix, to take her back from Tynstar. Now, as I looked around, I doubted we could do it.

The Northern Wastes of Homana lay behind us. Now we faced Solinde, having come down from the Molon Pass, with Valgaard still before us. And yet it was obvious we drew closer. The land reflected the lair.

Icy winds blew down from the pass. Winter was done with in Homana, but across the Bluetooth the chill never quite left the land. It amazed me the Cheysuli could go bare-armed, though I knew they withstood hardship better than Homanans.

Snow still patched the ground beneath the trees, mantling the rocky mountains. Great defiles fell away into canyons, sheer and dark and wet from melting snow. All around us the world was a great, dark, slick wound, bleeding slowly in the sunlight. Someone had riven the earth.

Even the trees reflected the pain of the land. They were wracked and twisted, as if some huge cold hand had swept across them in a monstrous fit of temper. Rocks were split open in perfect halves and quarters; some were no more than powder where once a boulder had stood. But most of them had shapes. Horrible, hideous shapes, as if nightmares had been shaped into stone so all could share the horror.

"We draw close to Valgaard," Duncan said. "This has been the tourney-field of the Ihlini."

I looked at him sharply. "What do you say?"

"Ihlini power is inbred," he explained, "but the control must be taught. An Ihlini child has no more knowledge of his abilities than a Cheysuli child; they know they have magic at their beck, but no knowledge of how to use it. It must be—practiced."

I glanced around incredulously. "You say these—shapes— are what the Ihlini have made?"

Duncan's horse stomped, scraping iron-shod hoof against cold black stone. The sudden sound echoed in the canyon. "You know the three gifts of the Cheysuli," he said quietly. "I thought you knew what the Ihlini claimed."

"I know they can make life out of death," I said sharply. "One Ihlini fashioned a lion out of a knife."

"There is that," Duncan agreed. "They have the power to alter the shapes of things that do not live." His hand swept out to indicate the rocks. "You have felt another of their gifts: the power to quicken age. With the touch of a hand, an Ihlini can make a man old, quickening the infirmities that come with years." I knew it too well, but said nothing. "There is the possession I have spoken of, when they take the mind and soul and keep it. And they can take the healing from a wound. There is also the art of illusion. What is, is not; what is not, seems to be. Those gifts, Carillon, and all shadings in between. That is a facet of Asar-Suti. The Seker, who lends his magic to those who will ask."

"But—all Ihlini have magic. Do they not?"

"All Ihlini have magic. But not all of them are Tynstar." He looked around at the twisted trees and shapechanged rocks. "You see what is Tynstar's power, and how he passes it on. We near the gate of Asar-Suti."

I looked at my men. The Homanans were white-faced and solemn, saying nothing. I did not doubt they were afraid—*I* was afraid—but neither would they give up. As for the Cheysuli, I had no need to ask. Their lives belonged to the gods whose power, I hoped, outweighed that of Tynstar *or* Asar-Suti, the Seker of the netherworld.

Duncan nudged his horse forward. "We must make camp for the night. The sun begins to set."

We rode on in loud silence, necks prickling against the raw sensation of power. It oozed out of the earth like so much seepage from a mudspring.

We camped at last behind the shoulder of a canyon wall that fell down from the darkening sky to shield us against the night wind. The earth's flesh was quite thin. Here and there the skeleton broke through, stone bones that glistened in the sunset with a damp, sweaty sheen. Tree roots coiled against the shallow soil like serpents seeking warmth. One of my Homanans, seeking wood for a fire, meant to hack off a few spindly, wind-wracked limbs with his heavy knife and pulled the whole tree out of the canyon wall. It was a small tree, but it underlined the transience of life near Valgaard.

We made a meal out of what we carried in our packs: dried meat, flat journey-bread loaves, a measure of sweet, dark sugar. And wine. We all had wine. The horses we fed on the grain we carried with us, since grazing was so light, and brought water from melting snow. But once our bellies were full, we had time to think of what we did.

I sat huddled in my heaviest cloak for too long a time. I could not rid myself of the ache in my bones or the

knowledge that we all might die. And so, when I could do
it inconspicuously, I got up and went away from the small
encampment. I left the men to their stilted conversations
and gambling; I went to find Duncan.

I saw him at last when I was ready to give up. He stood
near the canyon wall staring into the dark distances. His
very stillness made him invisible. It was only the shine of
the moon against his earring that gave his presence away.
And so I went near, waited for acknowledgment, and saw
how rigid his body was.

He had pulled on a cloak at last. It was dark, like my
own, blending with the night. The earring glinted in his
hair. "What does he do with her?" he asked. "What does
he do *to* her?"

I had wondered the same myself. But I forced reassurance from my mouth. "She is strong, Duncan. Stronger
than many men. I think Tynstar will meet his match in
her."

"This is Valgaard." His voice was raw.

I swallowed. "She has the Old Blood."

He turned abruptly. His face was shadowed as he leaned
back against the stone canyon wall, setting his spine against
it. "Here, the Old Blood may be as nothing."

"You do not know that. Did Donal not get free? They
were Ihlini, yet he took *lir*-shape before them. It may be
that Alix will overcome them yet."

"*Ru'shalla-tu.*" He said it without much hope. *May it be
so*. He looked at me then, black-eyed in the moonlight,
and I saw the fear in his eyes. But he said nothing more of
Alix. Instead he squatted down, still leaning against the
canyon wall, and pulled his cloak more tightly around his
shoulders. "Do you wonder what has become of Tourmaline?" he asked. "What has become of Finn?"

"Every day," I answered readily. "And each day I regret
what has happened."

"Would you change it, if Finn came to you and asked to
take your *rujholla* as his *cheysula*?"

I found the nearest tree stump and perched upon it.
Duncan waited for my answer, and at last I gave it. "I
needed the alliance Rhodri would have offered, did I wed
my sister to his son."

"He gave it to you anyway."

"*Lachlan* gave me aid. I got no alliance from Rhodri." I shrugged. "I do not doubt we will make one when all this is done, but for now the thing is not formal. What Lachlan did was between a mercenary and a harper, not a Mujhar and High Prince of Ellas. There are distinct differences between the two."

"Differences." His tone was very flat. "Aye. Like the differences between Cheysuli and Homanan."

I kicked away a piece of stone. "Do you regret that Donal must wed Aislinn? Cheysuli wed to Homanan?"

"I regret that Donal will know a life other than what I wish for him." Duncan was little more than a dark blot against the rock wall. "In the clan, he would be merely a warrior—unless they made him a clan-leader. It is—a simpler life than that which faces a prince. I would wish that for him. Not what you will give him."

"I have no choice. The gods—*your* gods—have given me none."

He was silent a moment. "Then we must assume there is a reason for what he will become."

I smiled, though it had only a little humor in it. "But you have an advantage, Duncan. You may see your son become a king. But *I* must die in order to give him the throne."

Duncan was silent a long moment. He merged into the blackness of the wall as the moon was lost to passing clouds. I could no longer see him, but I knew where he was by the sound of a hand scraping against the earth.

"You have changed," Duncan said at last. "I thought, at first, you had not—or very little. I see now I was wrong. Finn wrought well when he tempered the steel . . . but it is kingship that has honed the edge."

I huddled within my cloak. "As you say, kingship changes a man. I seem to have no choice."

"Necessity also changes," Duncan said quietly. "It has changed me. I am nearly forty now, old enough to know my place and recognize my *tahlmorra* without chafing, but each day, of late, I wonder what might have happened had it been otherwise." He shook his head. "We wonder. We ever wonder. The freedom to be without a *tahlmorra*."

The moon was free again and I saw another headshake. "What would happen did I *keep* my son? The prophecy would be twisted. The Firstborn, who gave the words to us, would never live again. We would be the Cheysuli no longer." I saw the rueful smile. "Cheysuli: children of the gods. But we can be fractious children."

"Duncan—" I paused. "We will find her. And we will take her back from him."

Moonlight slanted full across his face. "Women are lost often enough," he said quietly. "In childbirth . . . accident . . . illness. A warrior may grieve in the privacy of his pavilion, but he does not show his feelings to the clan. It is not done. Such things are kept—private." His hand was filled with pebbles. "But were Alix taken from me by this demon, I would not care who knew of my grief." The pebbles poured from his hand in steady, dwindling stream. "I would be without her . . . and empty. . . ."

Near midday we came to the canyon that housed Valgaard. We rode out of a narrow defile into the canyon proper and found ourselves hemmed in by the sheer stone walls that stretched high over our heads. We rode single-file, unable to go abreast, but as we went deeper into the canyon the walls fell away until we were human pebbles in a deep, rock-hard pocket.

"There," Duncan said, "do you see?"

I saw. Valgaard lay before us: an eagle on its aerie. The fortress itself formed the third wall of the canyon, a pendant to the torque. But I thought the fit too snug. I thought the jewel too hard. No, not an eagle. A carrion bird, hovering over its corpse.

We were neatly boxed. Escape lay behind us, Valgaard before. I did not like the feeling.

"*Lodhi*." Gryffth gasped. "I have never seen such a thing."

Nor had I. Valgaard rose up out of the glassy black basalt like a wave of solid ice, black and sharp, faceted like a gemstone. There were towers and turrets, barbicans and ramparts. It glittered, bright as glass, and smoke rose up around it. I could smell the stink from where we stood.

"The Gate," Duncan said. "It lies within the fortress. Valgaard is its sentinel."

"That is what causes the smoke?"

"The breath of the god," Duncan said. "Like fire, it burns. I have heard the stories. There is blood within the stone: hot, white blood. If it should touch you, you will die."

The canyon was clean of snow. Nothing marred its surface. It was smooth, shining basalt, lacking trees and grass. We had come out of winter into summer, and I found I preferred the cold.

"Asar-Suti," Duncan said. "The Seker himself." Very deliberately, he spat onto the ground.

"What are all those shapes?" Rowan asked. He meant the large chunks of stone that lay about like so many dice tossed down. Black dice, uncarved, and scattered across the ground. They were large enough for a man to hide behind.

Or die under, if it landed cocked.

"An Ihlini bestiary," Duncan explained. "Their answer to the *lir*."

We rode closer and I saw what he meant. Each deposit of stone had a form, if a man could call it that. The shapes were monstrous travesties of animals. Faces and limbs bore no resemblence to animals I had seen. It was a mockery of the gods, the *lir* defiled; an echo, perhaps, of their deity. Asar-Suti in stone. A god of many shapes. A god of grotesquerie.

I suppressed a shiver of intense distaste. This place was foulness incarnate. "We should beware an obvious approach."

Duncan, falling back to ride abreast, merely nodded. "It would be unexpected did we simply ride in like so many martyrs, but also foolish. I do not choose to die a fool. So we will find cover and wait, until we have a plan for getting in."

"Getting in *there*?" Rowan shook his head. "I do not see how."

"There is a way," Duncan told him. "There is always a way to get in. It is getting out that is difficult."

Uneasily, I agreed.

It was, at last, Gryffth who found the way in. I was astonished when he offered himself, for he might well be boiled alive in the blood of the god, but it seemed the only way. And so I agreed, but only after I heard his explanation.

We knelt, all of us, behind the black-frozen shapes, too distant for watchers to see us from the ramparts. The white, stinking smoke veiled us even more, so that we felt secure in our place of hiding. The stones were large enough to offer shade in sunlight as well. In the shadows it was cool.

Gryffth, kneeling beside me, pulled a ring from his belt-pouch. "My lord, this should do it. It marks me a royal courier. It will give me safe entrance."

"*Should*," I said sharply. "It may not."

Gryffth grinned a little. His red hair was bright in the sunlight. "I think I will have no trouble. The High Prince has said, often enough, that I have the gift of a supple tongue. I will wind Tynstar around this finger." He made a rude gesture with his hand, and all the Homanans laughed. In the months since the Ellasian had joined my service, he had made many friends. He had wit and purpose, and a charming way as well.

Rowan's face was pensive. "When you face Tynstar, what will you say? The ring cannot speak for you."

"No, but it gets me inside. Once there, I will tell Tynstar the High King of Ellas has sent me. That he wishes to make an alliance."

"Rhodri would never do it." Rowan exclaimed. "Do you think *Tynstar* will believe you?"

"He may, he may not. It does not matter." Gryffth's freckled face was solemn, echoing Duncan's gravity. "I will tell him High Prince Cuinn, in sending men to the Mujhiar, has badly angered his father. That Rhodri wishes no alliance with Homana, but desires Ihlini aid. If nothing else, it will gain Tynstar's attention. He will likely host me the night, at least. And it is at night I will open the gate to let you in." His smile came, quick and warm. "Once in, you will either live or die. By then, it will not matter what Tynstar thinks of my tale."

"*You* may die." Rowan sounded angry.

Gryffth shrugged. "A man lives, a man dies. He does not choose his life. Lodhi will protect me."

Duncan smiled. "You could almost be Cheysuli."

I saw Gryffth thinking it over. Ellasian-bred, he hardly knew the Cheysuli. But he did not think them demons. And so I saw him decide the comment was a compliment. "My thanks, Duncan . . . though Lodhi might see it differently."

"You call him the All-Wise," Duncan returned. "He must be wise enough to know when I mean you well."

Gryffth, grinning, reached out and touched his arm. "For that, clan-leader, I will gladly do what I can to help you get her back."

Duncan clasped his arm. "Ellasian—*Cheysuli i'halla shansu.*" He smiled at Gryffth's frown of incomprehension. "May there be Cheysuli peace upon you."

Gryffth nodded. "Aye, my friend. And may you know the wisdom of Lodhi." He turned to me. "Does it please you, my lord, I will go in. And tonight, when I can, I will find a gate to open."

"How will we know?" Rowan asked. "We cannot go up so close . . . and you can hardly light a fire."

"I will send Cai to him," Duncan said. "My *lir* can see when Gryffth comes out and tell me which gate he unlocks."

Rowan sighed, rubbing wearily at his brow. "It all seems such a risk . . ."

"Risk, aye," I agreed, "but more than worth the trying."

Gryffth stood up. "I will go in, my lord. I will do what I can do."

I rose as he did and clasped his arm. "Good fortune, Gryffth. May Lodhi guard you well."

He untethered his horse and mounted, reining it around. He glanced down at Rowan, who had become a boon companion, and grinned. "Do not fret, *alvi*. This is what I choose."

I watched Gryffth ride away, heading toward the fortress. The smoke hung over it like a miasma, cloaking the stone in haze. The breath of the god was foul.

EIGHT

The moon, hanging over our heads against the blackness of the sky, lent an eerie ambience to the canyon. The smoke clogged our noses. It rose up in stinking clouds, warming our flesh against our will. Shadows crept out from the huge stone shapes and swallowed us all, clutching with mouths and claws. My Homanans muttered of demons and Ihlini sorcerers; I thought they were one and the same.

Duncan, seated near me, shed his cloak and rose. "Cai says Gryffth has come out of the hall. He is in the inner bailey. We should go."

We left the horses tethered and went on by foot. Cloaks hid our swords and knives from the moonlight. Our boots scraped against the glossy basalt, scattering ash and powdered stone. As we drew nearer, using the shapechanged stones to hide us, the ground warmed beneath our feet. The smoke hissed and whistled as it came out of the earth, rising toward the moon.

We worked our way up to the walls that glistened in the moonlight. They were higher even than the walls of Homana-Mujhar, as if Tynstar meant to mock me. At each of the corners and midway along the walls stood a tower, a huge round tower bulging out of the dense basalt, spiked with crenelations and crockets and manned, no doubt, by Ihlini minions. The place stank of sorcery.

The nearest gate was small. I thought it likely it opened

into a smaller bailey. We had slipped around the front of the fortress walls and came in from the side, eschewing the main barbican gate that would swallow us up like so many helpless children. But the side gate opened, only a crack, and I saw Gryffth's face in the slit between wall and dark wood.

One hand gestured us forward. We moved silently, saying nothing, holding scabbards to keep them quiet. Gryffth, as I reached him in the gate, pushed it open wider. "Tynstar is not here," he whispered, knowing what it would mean to me. "Come you in now, and you may avoid the worst of it."

One by one we crept in through the gate. I saw the shadows of winged *lir* pass overhead. We had also wolves and foxes and mountain cats, slipping through the gate, but I wondered if they would fight. Finn had said the gods' own law kept the *lir* from attacking Ihlini.

Gryffth shut the gate behind us, and I saw the two bodies lying against the wall. I looked at him; he said nothing. But I was thankful nonetheless. Like Lachlan, he served me as if born to it, willing, even to slay others.

We were in a smaller bailey, away from the main one, and Valgaard lay before us. The halls and side rooms bulged out from a central mass of stone. But we seemed to be through the worst of it.

We started across the bailey, across the open spaces, though we tried to stay to the shadows. Swords were drawn now, glinting in the moonlight, and I heard the soughing of feet against stone. Out of the bailey toward an inner ward while the walls reared up around us; how long would our safety last?

Not long. Even as Gryffth led us through to the inner ward I heard the hissing and saw a streamer of flame as it shot up into the air from one of the towers. It broke over our heads, showering us with a violet glare, and I knew it would blast the shadows into the white-hot glare of the sun. No more hiding in the darkness.

"Scatter!" I shouted, heading for the hall.

My sword was in my hand. I heard the step beside me and swung around, seeing foe, not friend, with his hand raised to draw a rune. Quickly I leveled my blade and took him in the throat. He fell in a geyser of blood.

Rowan was at my back, Gryffth at his. We went into the hall in a triangular formation, swords raised and ready. The Cheysuli had gone, slipping into the myriad corridors, but I could hear the Homanans fighting. Without Tynstar's presence we stood our greatest chance, but the battle would still be difficult. I had no more time left to lose.

"Hold them!" I shouted as four men advanced with swords and knives. I expected sorcery and they came at us with steel.

Even as I brought up my sword I felt the twinge shoot through both hands. In all my practice with Cormac I had not been able to shed the pain of my swollen fingers. As yet they could still hold a hilt, but the strength I had taken for granted was gone. I had to rely more on quickness of body than my skill in elaborate parries. I was little more than a man of average skill now, because of Tynstar.

Gryffth caught a knife from a hidden sheath and sent it flying across the hall. It took one Ihlini flush in the chest and removed him from the fight. Three to three now, but even as I marked their places I saw Rowan take another with his sword. Myself, for the moment, they ignored. And so, knowing my sword skill was diminished, I decided to go on without it. Did the Ihlini want me, they could come for me. Otherwise I would avoid them altogether.

"Hold them," I said briefly, and ran into the nearest corridor. The stone floor was irregular, all of a slant, this way and that, as if to make it difficult for anyone to run through it. There were few torches in brackets along the walls; I sensed this portion of the fortress was only rarely used. Or else the Ihlini took the light with them when they walked.

The sounds of fighting fell away behind me, echoing dimly in the tunnel-like corridor. I went on, hearing the scrape of sole against stone, and waited for the attack that would surely come.

I went deeper into the fortress, surrounded by black basalt that glistened in the torchlight. The walls seemed to swallow the light, so that my sword blade turned black to match the ruby, and I felt my eyes strain to see where I was going. The few torches guttered and hissed in the shadows, offering little illumination; all it wanted was Tynstar to come drifting out of the darkness, and my courage would be undone.

I heard the grate of stone on stone and swung around, anticipating my nightmare. But the man who stepped out of the recess in the wall was a stranger to me. His eyes were blank, haunted things. He seemed to be missing his soul.

Silently, he came at me. His sword was a blur of steel, flashing in the torchlight, and I jumped back to avoid the slash that hissed beside my head. My own blade went up to strike his down. They caught briefly, then disengaged as we jerked away. I could feel the strain in my hands, and yet I dared not lose my grip.

Again he came at me. I skipped back, then leaped aside, and the sword tip grated on stone. And yet even as I moved to intercept, the Ihlini's blade flashed sideways to stop my lunge and twist my sword from my hands. It was not a difficult feat. And so my weapon clanged against the black stone floor and I felt the hot pain in my knuckles flare up to pierce my soul.

The blade came at me again, thrusting for my belly. I sucked back, avoiding the tip, and felt the edge slice through leather and linen to cut along my ribs. Not deeply, scraping against one bone, but it was enough to make me think.

I jumped then, straight upward from the floor, grabbing the nearest torch and dragging it from its brackets. Even as the Ihlini came at me again I had it, whirling to thrust it into his face. The flame roared.

The sorcerer screamed and dropped his sword, hands clawing at his face. He invoked Asar-Suti over and over again, gibbering in his pain, until he slumped down onto his knees. I stepped back as I saw one hand come up to make an intricate motion.

"Seker, Seker. . . ." He chanted, rocking on his knees while his burned face glistened in the torchlight. "Seker, Seker. . . ."

The torch was still in my right hand. As the Ihlini

invoked his god and drew his rune in the air, the flame flowed down over the iron to caress my hand with pain.

I dropped the torch at once, tossing it toward the wall while my knuckles screamed with pain. The flame splashed against the stone and ran down, flooding the floor of the corridor. As the Ihlini continued to chant, his hands still clasped to his face, the fire crept toward my boots.

I stepped back at once, retreating with little aplomb. My sword, still lying on the stone, was in imminent danger of being swallowed. The flame poured across the floor like water, heading for my boots.

"Seker, Seker—make him *burn!*"

But he had made a deadly mistake. No doubt he intended only his enemy to burn, but he had not been clearly distinct. He himself still knelt on the floor, and as the stone caught fire from the river of ensorcelled flame so did he. It ran up his legs and enveloped his body in fire. I kicked out swiftly and shoved the sword aside with one boot, then ran after it even as the river of fire followed me. I left the living pyre in the corridor, scooped up my sword and ran.

It was then I heard the shout. Alix's voice. The tone was one of fear and desperation, but it held a note of rage as well. And then I heard the scuffle and the cry.

I ran. I rounded the corner and brought up my sword, prepared to spit someone upon it, but I saw there was no need. The Ihlini lay on the ground, face down, as the blood ran from his body, and Alix was kneeling to take his knife. She already had his sword.

She spun around, rising at once into a crouch. The knife dropped from her hand at once as she took a two-handed grip on the sword. And then she saw me clearly and the sword fell out of her hand.

I grinned. "Well met, Alix."

She was so pale I thought she might faint where she stood, but she did not. Her eyes were huge in a bruised and too-thin face. Her hair hung in a single tangled braid and she wore a bedrobe stained with blood. It was not her own, I knew, but from the man she had slain.

I had forgotten the gray in my hair and the lines in my face; the altered way I had of standing and moving. I had forgotten what Tynstar had done. But when I saw the horror in Alix's eyes I recalled it all too well. It brought home the pain again.

I put out one hand, ignoring the swollen knuckles. "Do you come?"

Briefly, she looked down at the dead Ihlini. Then she bent and scooped up the knife, moving to my side. Her free hand was cool in my own, and I felt the trembling in it. For a moment we stood there, soiled with blood and grime and in the stink of our own fear, and then we forgot our weapons and set arms around each other for a desperate moment.

"Duncan?" she asked at last, when I let her free of my arms.

"He is here—do not fret. But how did you trick the Ihlini?"

She glanced back briefly at the dead man. "He was foolish enough to unlock my door. To take me somewhere, he said. He did not expect me to protest, but I did. I took up a torch and burned his knife-hand with it."

I put out my own knife-hand and touched her hollowed cheek. "How do you fare, Alix?"

Briefly there was withdrawal in her eyes. "I will tell you another time. Come this way with me." She caught up the hem of her bedrobe and went on, still gripping the knife in one hand.

We hastened through the corridors and into a spiral stair. Alix went first and I followed, falling behind as we climbed. We went up and up and I grimaced, feeling the strain in my knees. My thighs burned with the effort, and my breath ran short. But at last she pushed open a narrow door that I had to duck to get under, and we stepped out onto the ramparts of the fortress.

Alix pointed. "That tower is a part of Tynstar's private chambers. There is a stairway down. If we get there, we can go down unaccosted, then slip into the wards."

I caught her hand and we ran, heading for the tower. I heard the sounds of fighting elsewhere, but I knew we were badly outnumbered. And then we rounded the tower, looking for the door, and I stopped dead. Out on the wall walkway stood a familiar figure— *"Duncan!"*

He spun around like an animal at bay. His eyes were startled and fearful. "No!" he shouted.

Alix jerked free of my hand and started to run toward him, calling out his name, but something in Ducan's face made me reach out and catch her arm. "Alix—wait you—"

The moonlight was full on Duncan's face. I could see the heaving of his chest as sweat ran down his bare arms. His hair was wet with it. "Go from here—*now* . . . Alix—do not tarry!"

Alix tried again to free herself from my hand but I held her tightly. "Duncan—what are you saying? Do you think I will listen to that—?" Briefly she twisted her head to glare at me. "Let me *go*—"

Duncan took a step toward us, then stopped. His face turned up toward the black night sky. Then he glanced back at me, briefly, and put out a hand toward Alix. "Take her, Carillon. Get her free of this place—" He sucked in a deep, wavering breath and seemed almost to fall on his feet. I saw then, in the moonlight, the blood running down his left arm. "Do you hear me? Go now, before—"

What he intended to say was never heard in the thunderclap that broke over our heads. I recoiled, flattening against the tower, and dragged Alix with me. With the explosion of sound came a burst of light so blinding it painted everything stark white and stole our vision away.

"Do I have you all, now?" came Tynstar's beguiling voice.

I saw him then, moving along the wall from another tower. Duncan was between the Ihlini and us. He put out a hand in my direction and cast a final glance at Alix. "Get her *free*, Carillon! Was it not what we came to do?"

I ran then, dragging her with me, and took her into the tower. I ignored her protests. For once, I would do what Duncan wanted without asking foolish questions.

I did not dare take a horse for Alix from our mounts for fear of leaving another man afoot. So I swung up onto my own, dragged her up behind me and wheeled the horse about in the shadow of shapechanged stone.

Alix's arms locked around my waist. "Carillon—wait you. You cannot leave him behind."

I clapped spurs to my horse and urged him away, sending him from the smokey, stinking haze that clung to black-clad Valgaard. *Away* I sent him, toward the defile and freedom.

"Carillon—"

"I trust to his wits and his will." I shouted over the clattering hooves. "Do *you* not?"

She pressed herself against me as the horse slipped and slid on basalt. "I would rather stay and help—"

"There." I interrupted. "Do you see? *That* is why we run—"

The nearest stone shape reared up just then, shaking itself free of the ground. It lurched toward our mount, reaching out its hands. No, not hands: paws. And claws of glassy basalt.

Alix cried out and pressed herself against me. I reined in my horse with a single hand and jerked our mount aside, shouting for Alix to duck. We threw ourselves flat, avoiding the slashing claws, and the sword I held outthrust scraped against the beast. Sparks flew from the blade on stone: steel against a whetstone, screeching as it spun.

We rode past at a scrambling run as the horse tried to keep his balance. Chips of stone flew up to cut our faces as iron-shod hooves dug deeply into basalt. I saw then that all the stone shapes were moving, grating across the ground. They had none of the speed or supple grace of fleshborn animals, but they were ghastly in their promise. Most were hardly recognizable, being rough-cut and sharply faceted, but I saw the gaping mouths and knew they could crush us easily.

Yet another lurched into our path. I reined in the horse at once and sat him on his haunches, knowing he scraped his hocks against the cruel stone. Alix cried out and snatched at my doublet, holding herself on with effort. I spurred relentlessly, driving the horse to his feet, and saw the lowering paws.

A bear; not a bear. Its shape was indistinct. It lumbered after us, hackles rising on its huge spinal hump, ungainly on glassy legs, and yet I knew it might prevail. The horse was failing under us.

Smoke shot up beside us: the breath of the god himself. It splattered me full in the face and I felt the blood of the god. It burned, how it burned, as it ate into my beard. But I dared not put a hand to my face or I would lose control of the horse. And I refused to lose my sword.

The smoke shot up with a screeching hiss, venting its wrath against us. It stank with the foul odor of corruption. The horse leaped aside, nearly shedding us both; I heard Alix's gasp of surprise. She slid to one side and caught at my arm, dragging herself back on the slippery rump. I heard again the scream of the smoke as it vomited out of the earth.

The canyon grew narrow and clogged with stone. The defile beckoned us on. We had only to get through it and we would be free of the beasts. But getting to it would be next to impossible with the failing horse beneath us.

Another vent opened before us. The horse ran directly into it and screamed as the heat bit into his belly. He twisted and humped, throwing head between knees, and then shed us easily enough. But I did not complain, even as I crashed against the stone, for the horse was caught by the bear.

I pushed myself up to my feet, aware of the pain in my bones. I still had my sword and two feet and I did not intend to remain. I went to Alix as she sat up from her fall, grabbed her arm and dragged her up from the stone.

"Run," I said, and we did.

We dodged the stone beasts and jumped over the smoke, threading our way as we ran. We gasped and choked, coughing against the stench. But we reached the defile and ran through, knowing it too narrow to give exit to the beasts. We left behind the smoke and heat and went into the world again.

The ground was laced with snow. Twisted trees hung off the walls and sent roots across the earth, seeking what strength they could find in the meager soil. Behind us reared the canyon with its cache of beasts and smoke.

Alix limped beside me, still clinging to my hand. She was barefoot; I did not doubt it hurt. Her bedrobe was torn and burned away in places. But she went on, uncomplaining, and I put away my sword.

I took her to a screen of wind-wracked trees that huddled by a rib of canyon wall. There we could hide and catch our breath, waiting for the others. I found a broken stump and sat down upon it stiffly, hissing against the pain. My aching joints had been badly used and I felt at least a hundred. No more was I able to perform the deeds of a younger man, for all I was twenty-five. The body was twenty years older.

Alix stood next to me. Her hand was on my head, smoothing my graying hair. "I am so sorry, Carillon. But Tynstar has touched us all."

I looked up at her in the moonlight. "Did he harm you?"

She shrugged. "What Tynstar did is done. I will not speak about it."

"Alix—" But she placed one hand across my mouth and bid me to be silent. After a moment she squatted down and linked both hands around my arm.

"My thanks," she said softly. "*Leijhana tu'sai*. What you have done for me—and what you have *lost* for me—is more than I deserve."

I summoned a weary smile. "Your son will be Prince of Homana. Surely his *jehana* has meaning to us both."

"You did not do this for Donal."

I sighed. "No. I did it for you, for myself . . . and for Duncan. Perhaps especially for Duncan." I set my swollen hand to her head and tousled her tangled hair. "He needs you, Alix. More than I ever thought possible."

She did not answer. We sat silently, close together, and waited for the others.

One by one the warriors returned, on foot and mounted on horseback. Some came in *lir*-shape, loping or flying as they came through the trees; we were not so close that the magic could be thwarted. But I saw, when they had gathered, that at least four had been left behind. A high toll, for the Cheysuli. It made it all seem worse.

Rowan came finally at dawn. He and Gryffth were mounted on a single horse, riding double from the defile. Blood had spilled from a head wound to stain Rowan's leathers dark, but he seemed well enough, if weary. He prodded Gryffth with an elbow and I saw how the Ellasian drooped against Rowan's back. I got up, feeling the pop in both knees, and reached out to steady Gryffth's dismount. He had a wound in one shoulder and a slice along one forearm, but both had been bound.

Rowan got down unsteadily, shutting his eyes as he put one hand to his head. Alix knelt beside him as he sat and parted his hair to see the wound. He swallowed and winced as her fingers found the swelling.

"This is not from a sword," she said in consternation.

"No. His sword broke. So he grabbed down to torch and came at me. I ducked the flame but not the iron." He winced again. "Let it be. It will heal of its own."

Alix moved away from him. For a moment she looked at the others, all wounded in her rescue, and I saw how it weighted her down. Of us all, I was the only Homanan. The others, save Gryffth, were all Cheysuli.

The Ellasian leaned against a boulder, one arm pressed against his ribs. His freckled face, in the pale sunlight of dawn, was ashen, streaked with blood and grime, but life remained in his bright green eyes. He pushed a hand through his hair and made it stand up in spikes. "My thanks to the All-Father," he said wearily. "Most of us got free, and the lady brought out as we meant."

"And for that, *my* thanks," said Duncan from the ridge, and Alix spun around.

He stepped down and caught her in his arms, crushing her against his chest. His cheek pressed into her tangled hair and I saw the pallor of his face. Blood still ran from the wound in his left arm. I saw how it stained his leathers and now her robe. But neither seemed to care.

I pushed myself up from my tree stump. I moved stiffly, cursing myself for my slowness, and then stood still, giving them their reunion. It was the least I could do.

"I am well," Duncan answered her whispered question. "I am not much hurt. Do not fear for me." One hand wove itself into her loosened braid. "What of you? What has he done to you?"

Alix, still pressed against his body, shook her head. I could not see her face, but I could see his. His exhaustion was manifest. Like us all, he was bloodstained and filthy and stinking of the breath of the netherworld. Like us all, he was hardly capable of standing.

But there was something more in his eyes. The knowledge of terrible loss.

And I knew.

Duncan put Alix out of his arms and sat her down on the nearest stump, the one I had vacated. And then, without a word, he stripped the gold from his arms and set it into her lap. With deft fingers he unhooked the earring and pulled it from his lobe. He was naked without his gold. Still clothed in leather, he was naked without the gold.

And a dead man without his *lir*.

He set the earring into her hand. *"Tahlmorra lujhalla mei wiccan, cheysu."*

She stood up with a cry and the gold tumbled from lap and hands. "Duncan—*no*—"

"Aye," he said gently, "Tynstar has slain my *lir*."

Slowly, tentatively, trembling, she put out her hands to touch him. Gently at first, and then with possessive demand. I saw how dark her fingers were against the flesh of his arms that had never known the sun, kept from it by the *lir*-bands for nearly all of his life. I saw how she shut her hands upon that flesh as if it would make him stay.

"I am empty," he said. "Soulless and unwhole. I cannot live this way."

The fingers tightened on his arms. "Do you go," she said intently, "do you leave me, Duncan . . . I will be as empty. I will be unwhole."

"Shansu," he said, "I have no choice. It is the price of the *lir*-bond."

"Do you think I will let you go?" she demanded. "Do you think I will stand meekly by while you turn your back on me? Do you think I will do *nothing?*"

"No. And that is why I will do *this*—" He caught her before she could move and cradled her head in his hands.

"*Cheysula*, I have loved you well. And for that I will lessen your grief—"

"No!" She tried to pull out of his arms, but he held her too well. "Duncan—" she said, "—do not—"

As she sagged he caught her and lifted her up. For a moment he held her close, eyes shut in a pale, gaunt face, and then he looked at me. "You must take her to safety. Take her to Homana-Mujhar." He tried to steady his voice and failed. "She will sleep for a long time. Do not worry if, when she wakes, she seems to have forgotten. It will come back. She will recall it all, and I do not doubt she will grieve deeply then. But for now . . . for us both . . . this ending is the best."

I tried to swallow the cramp in my throat. "What of Tynstar?"

"Alive," Duncan said bleakly. "Once he had struck down Cai—I had nothing left but pain and helplessness." He looked at Alix's face again as she slept in his naked arms. And then he brought her to me and set her into mine. "Love her well, my lord Mujhar. Spare her what pain you can."

I saw the tears in his eyes and he moved back. Then one foot struck an armband on the ground, sending it clinking against the other, and he stopped short. He touched one naked arm as if he could not believe its loss, and then he walked away.

NINE

Donal's young face was pinched and pale. He sat quietly on a stool, listening to what I said, but I doubt he really heard me. His mind had gone elsewhere, choosing its own path; I did not blame him. I had told him his father was dead.

He stared hard at the floor. His hands were in his lap. They gripped one another as if they could not bear to be apart. The skin of his knuckles was white.

"*Jehana*," he said. That only.

"Your mother is well. She—sleeps. Your father gave her that."

He nodded once. No more. He seemed to understand. And then his right hand rose to touch his left arm, to finger the heavy gold. I could see it in his mind: Cheysuli, and bound by the *lir*. As much as his father had been.

Donal looked up at me. His face was starkly remote. He said one word: "*Tahlmorra*."

He was an eight-year-old boy. At eight, I could not have withstood the pain. I would have wept, cried out, even screamed with the grief. Donal did not. He was Cheysuli, and he knew the price of the *lir*-bond.

I had thought, perhaps, to hold him. To ease what pain I could. To tell him how Duncan had gotten his mother free, to illustrate the worth of the risk undertaken. I had thought also to assuage his guilt and grief by sharing my own with him. But, looking at him, I saw there was no need. His maturity mocked my own.

Alien, I thought, *so alien. Will Homana accept you?*

I lifted Alix down from her horse. She was light in my arms, too light; her face was ashen-colored. She had come home at last to Duncan's pavilion—six weeks after his death—and I knew she could not face it.

I said nothing, I simply held her. She stared at the slate-colored pavilion with its gold-painted hawk and recalled the life they had shared. She forgot even Donal, who slid slowly off his horse and looked to me for reassurance.

"Go in," I told him. "It is yours as much as his."

Donal put out a hand and touched the doorflap. And then he went inside.

"Carillon," she said. No more. There was no need. All the grief was in her voice.

I put out my arms and pulled her against my chest. With one hand I smoothed the heavy hair. "Now do you see? This is not the place for you. I would have spoken earlier, but I knew it would do no good. You had to see for yourself."

Her arms were locked around me. Her shoulders shook with the tears.

"Come back with me," I said. "Come back to Homana-Mujhar. Your place is there now, with me." I rocked her gently in my arms. "Alix—I want you to stay with me."

Her face turned up to mine. "I cannot."

"Do not fret because of Electra. She will not live forever—when she is dead I will wed you. I will make you Queen of Homana. Until then . . . you will have to content yourself with being merely a princess." I smiled. "You are. You are my cousin. There is a rank that comes with that."

Slowly she shook her head. "I cannot."

I smoothed back the hair from her face. "All those years ago—seven? eight?—I was a fool, I lived in arrogance. I saw what I was told to see by an uncle I abhorred. But now I am somewhat older—older, even than *that*—" I smiled a little, thinking of my graying beard and aching bones—"somewhat wiser, and certainly less inclined to heed such things as rank and custom. I wanted you then, I want you now—say you will come with me."

"I owe Duncan more than that."

"You do not owe him personal solitude. Alix—wait you—" I tightened my arms as she tried to pull away. "I know how badly you hurt. I know how badly it bleeds. I know how deeply the pain has cut you. But I think he would not be surprised did we make a match of it." I recalled his final words to me and knew he expected it. "Alix—I will not press you. I will give you what time you need. But do not deny me this. Not after all these years."

"Time does not matter." She stood stiffly in my arms. "As for the years—they have passed. It is done, Carillon. I cannot be your *meijha* and I cannot be your wife."

"Alix—"

"By the gods!" she cried. "I carry Tynstar's child!"

I let go of her at once and saw the horror in her eyes. "Tynstar did *that* to you—"

"He did not beat me." Her voice was steady. "He did not harm me. He did not *force* me." Her eyes shut for a moment. "He simply took my will away and got a child upon me."

I thought of Electra, banished to the Crystal Isle. Electra, who had lost the sorcerer's child. An heir. Not to me or to my title, but to all of Tynstar's might. He had lost it, and now he had another.

I could not move. I wanted to put out my hands and touch her, to tell her I did not care, but she knew me better than that. I could not move. I could only think of the Ihlini and his bastard in her belly.

Alix turned from me. She walked slowly to the pavilion. She put out one hand and drew back the doorflap, though she did not look inside. "Do you come in? Or do you go back?"

I shut my eyes a moment, still aching with the knowledge. Again, I lost her. But this time not to Duncan. Not even to Duncan's memory. That I might expect.

But not this. Not losing her to *Tynstar*. To a bastard Ihlini child!

By all the gods, it hurt. It hurt like a knife in my loins. I wanted to vomit the pain.

And then I thought of hers.

I let out my breath. Looking at her, I could see it hurt her worse. And I would not increase the pain by swearing useless vows of vengeance. There was already that between Tynstar and me; one day, we would end it.

I went to her. I took the doorflap out of her hands and motioned her inside. And then we both turned to go in and I saw Finn beside the fire.

The light was stark on his face. I saw again the livid scar that marred cheek and jaw; the silver in his hair. Then he rose and I saw he had grown thin. The gold seemed heavier on his arms.

"*Meijha,*" he said, "I am sorry. But a *tahlmorra* cannot be refused. Not by an honorable man. And my *rujho* was ever that."

Alix stood very still but her breath was loud in the tent. "You *knew*—?"

"I knew he would die. So did he. Not how. Not when. Not the name of the man who would cause it. Merely that it would happen." He paused. "*Meijhana,* I am sorry. I would give him back to you, could I do it."

She moved to him. I saw the hesitation in her steps. I saw how he put his arms around her and set his scarred cheek against her hair. I saw her grief reflected in his face.

"When a *lir* is lost," he said, "the others know at once. Storr told me . . . but I could come no sooner. There was a thing I had to do."

I was wrung out with all the emotions. I needed to sit down. But I did not. I stood there, waiting, and saw Donal in the shadows. He sat between two wolves: one a ruddy young male, the other older, wiser, amber-eyed Storr.

Alix pulled out of Finn's arms but she did not move away. I saw how one of his hands lingered in her hair, as if he could not let it go. An odd possessiveness, in view of his actions with Torry. But then I could not blame him; Alix needed comfort. From Finn, it would undoubtedly be best. He was her brother, but also Duncan's. The bloodlink was closer than that which cousins shared.

I sighed. "Electra has been banished. She lives on the Crystal Isle. There is no question about her complicity in Tynstar's attempt to slay me. Did you wish it—you could take up your place again."

He did not smile. "That time is done. A blood-oath, once broken, is never healed. I come home, aye, to live in the Keep again—but nothing more than that. My place is here, now. They have named me Cheysuli clan-leader."

Alix looked at him sharply. "You? In Duncan's place?" She caught her breath, then went on. "I thought such things were not for you."

"Such things were for my *rujho*," he agreed, his gravity an ironic measure of Duncan's, "but things change. People change. Torry has made me different." He shrugged. "I have—learned a little peace." He used the Homanan word. I liked *shansu* better.

"I am sorry," I said, "for the time you lost. I should never have sent you away."

He shook his head. "You had no choice. I saw that, when Torry made me. I do not blame you for it. You let her go with me. You might have made her stay."

"So you could take her from me?" I shook my head. "No. I knew the folly in trying to stop you."

"You should have tried," he said. "You should have kept her by you. You should have wed her to the Ellasian prince . . . because then she would still be alive."

I felt the air go out of my chest. The pavilion spun around me. The firecairn was merely a blot of light inside my skull. "Torry is—*dead*?"

"Aye. Two days before Duncan lost his *lir*. It was why I could come no sooner."

"Finn," Alix said, "oh, Finn—*no*—"

"Aye," he said roughly, and I saw the new pain in his eyes. It mirrored that in my own.

I turned to go out. I could not stay. I could not bear to see him, knowing how she had loved him. I could not bear the grief. I had to deal with it alone.

And then I heard the baby cry, and the sound cut through me like a knife.

Finn let go of Alix. He turned and pulled the tapestry aside. I saw him kneel down and gather a bundle from the pallet. He was gentle. More gentle than I had ever seen him. Incongruous, in him. But it seemed to fit him well, once I got over the shock.

He brought the bundle to us and pulled away the wrappings from a face. "Her name is Meghan," he said. "She is four months old . . . and hungry. Torry—could not feed her, so I became a thief." Briefly he smiled. "The cows were not always willing to be milked."

Meghan continued to cry. Finn frowned and shifted her in his arms, trying to settle her more comfortably, but it was Alix who intervened. She took the baby from his arms and sent Donal to find a woman with an infant. She cast a glance back at Finn before she followed Donal out. "No more the milk-thief, *rujho*. I will save your pride by finding her a wetnurse."

I saw a shadow of his familiar grin as she slipped outside the pavilion. It took the hardness from his face and lessened the pain in his eyes. I saw it now, where I had not before. He had lost more than a brother.

And I had lost a sister. "Gods," I said, "what happened? How did Torry die? Why . . . *why?*"

The smile dropped away. Finn sat down slowly and motioned me down as well. After ten months, too long a time, we shared company again. "She was not bred for privation," he said. "She had pride and strength and determination, but she was not bred for privation. And carrying a child—" He shook his head. "I saw she was ill some three months after we left Homana-Mujhar. She claimed it was nothing; a fever breeding women sometimes get. I thought perhaps it was; how was I to know differently? I did not expect her to lie." He threaded one hand through his hair and stripped it from his face. He was gaunt, too thin; privation agreed with him no more than it had with her.

"Say on," I said hollowly.

"When I saw she got no better, I took her to a village. I thought she needed the companionship of women as well as a shelter better than the rude pavilion I provided. But—they would not have me. They called me shapechanger. They called me demon. They called her whore and the child demon's-spawn. Sorcerer's get." The anger was in his eyes and I saw the beast again, if only for a moment. But I also saw the guilt he had placed upon himself. "Shaine is dead and the *qu'mahlin* ended . . . but many prefer to observe it. And so she bore Meghan in what shelter I could provide, and weakened each day thereafter." He shut his eyes. "The gods would not hear my petition, even when I offered myself. So I gave her Cheysuli passing when she was dead, and brought her daughter home."

I thought of Torry, weak and ill. I thought of Torry bearing the child. I thought of the Homanans who had cursed her because of Finn. Because of Shaine's *qu'mahlin*. And I thought how helpless a king I was to stop my uncle's purge.

"I am sorry, Carillon," Finn said. "I did not mean you to lose her twice."

"Blame Shaine," I said wearily. "My uncle slew my sister." I looked at him across the fire. "Do you mean to keep Meghan here?"

"This is her home," he repeated. "Where else would Meghan live?"

"At Homana-Mujhar," I said. "She is a princess of Homana."

He stared at me. "Have you learned nothing? Are you still chained by such things as *rank*? By the gods, Carillon, I thought by now you might have learned—"

"I have," I said. "I have. I do not mean to take her. I merely wanted you to think. You have admitted Torry died because the privation was too hard. Do you give the same life to your daughter?"

"I give her a Keep," he said softly. "I give her what her blood demands: the heritage of a Cheysuli."

I smiled. "Who speaks now of rank? You have ever believed yourself better than a Homanan."

He shrugged. "We are as the gods have made us."

I laughed. I pushed to my feet and popped my knees, trying to ease my joints. The ride had tried my strength. Finn rose as well, saying nothing. He merely waited. "Privation has rendered you less than what you should be," I said gruffly. "Have Alix put flesh on your bones. You look older the way you are."

His black brows rose. "Who speaks of age should look in the silver plate."

"I have," I said, "and turned it to the wall." I grinned and put out my arm, clasping his again. "Tend Meghan well, and bring her to me often. She has other blood besides the shapechanger taint, and I would have her know it."

Finn's grip was firm. "I doubt not *your* daughter will need a companion. As for the Mujhar of Homana, he requires no single liege man. He has all the Cheysuh clans to render him aid when he needs it."

"Nonetheless," I said, "I would have you take the knife back." I slipped it from the sheath. The gold hilt gleamed softly in the light from the firecairn: rampant Homanan lion and a blade of purest steel.

I thought he would not take it. Another was in his sheath, one of Cheysuli craftsmanship. But he put out his hand and accepted it, though there was no blood-oath to accompany the acceptance.

"*Ja'hai-na*," he said quietly.

I went silently out of the tent.

My horse still waited. I took up the reins but did not mount at once. I thought of Alix, tending to Meghan, and the child within her belly. She would need Finn. She would need Meghan. She would need all the strength of the Cheysuli when Tynstar's child was born. And I knew she would have it in abundance.

I waited a moment, aware of something familiar. I could not put name to what it was, and then suddenly I knew. It was a flute, a sweet-toned Cheysuli pipe. The melody was quite simple, and yet I knew it well. The last time I had heard it, it had been upon a harp, with a master's hands upon the strings. Lachlan's hands, and the song *The Song of Homana*. And now it had come to the Keep.

I grinned. Then I laughed. I mounted my horse and turned him, ready to go at last, but Donal was in my way. He put up his hand and touched the stallion's nose as I reined him to a halt. Lorn sat at his left side.

"Cousin," Donal said, "may I come?"

"I go back to Homana-Mujhar."

"*Jehana* has said I may go." He grinned a grin I had seen before."

I leaned down and stretched out my hand, swinging him up as he jumped. He settled behind the saddle. "Hold on," I said, "the royal mount may throw us."

Donal leaned forward against my back. "Make him *try*."

I laughed. "Would you like to see me tumble?"

"You would not. You are the Mujhar of Homana."

"The horse does not know titles. He knows only your substantial weight." I kneed the stallion out and felt the arching of his back. But after a moment he settled.

"Do you see?" Donal asked, as the wolf trotted beside the horse. I looked for Taj and found him, a dot against the sky.

"I see," I admitted. "Shall we gallop?"

"*Aye!*" he agreed, and we did.